THE TRUTH ABOUT EVE

An Eve Sumptor Novel

JOURDYN KELLY

The Truth About *Eve*

An Eve Sumptor Novel

by Jourdyn Kelly

Other books by Jourdyn Kelly

Eve Sumptor Novels:
Something About Eve
Flawed Perfection
The Truth About Eve

The Destined Series:

Destined to Kill
Destined to Love
Destined to Meet

The LA Lovers Series:

Coming Home
Fifty Shades of Pink
Coming Out
Becoming

Copyright © 2019 by Jourdyn Kelly
Published by Jourdyn Kelly
All Rights Reserved.

No part of this book may be used or reproduced, scanned, or distributed in any printed or electronic form without permission. Please do not participate in or encourage piracy of copyrighted materials in violation of the author's rights. Purchase only authorized editions.

ISBN Number - 978-0-9982725-4-2

This is a work of fiction. Names, characters, places, and incidents either are the product of the author's imagination or are used fictitiously, and any resemblance to actual persons, living or dead, businesses, companies, events, or locales is entirely coincidental.

Cover Art by: Jourdyn Kelly
Interior Design by: Buoni Amici Press

A Note from the Author

I heard you. Eve and Lainey are the two characters that I get the most feedback for. Perhaps it's because people feel the story isn't done. Perhaps they thought I took the "easy" way out. It was never easy, and maybe you'll find out why decisions were made when reading this book. I've had discussions about this on my author page on Facebook, and while I disagree with the "easy" way, I can see how the story isn't done. It's why I have written Eve's therapy sessions and write the ladies into the LA Lovers series. Eve is hard to let go. She was my first character, and she will always be special to me. As will Lainey. I won't write a book unless I have a good story in my head and know where I want to go with it. But I do get inspired by your (my readers) enthusiasm for my characters. Because of your encouragement and passion, a story developed. I hope you enjoy it.

Chapter One
Therapy

The sins of the father.

"How are you today, Eve?" Dr. Willamena Woodrow sat quietly after the question and allowed her patient to evaluate her. It was natural for patients to scrutinize her before pouring their souls out to her. She did the same while the silence lingered. When offered during the initial evaluation of those closest to Eve, she had refused any personal anecdotes from Eve's husband and best friend. She preferred to make her own first-impression opinions. However, she couldn't resist the draw of local celebrity, Eve Sumptor. Willamena's niece, coincidentally, was friends with Eve, yet the doctor and the art gallery owner had never met before. Imagine her surprise when the request for a therapist came in with the familiar name attached.

Eve studied the woman in front of her. Following a thorough background check, Eve was impressed to find that Dr. Woodrow had been a psychiatrist for more than twenty-five years with a degree from the prestigious Johns Hopkins University. The woman was poised, in her mid-fifties, and well-groomed with warm chestnut hair that sparkled with a touch of gray. Everything about the woman — and the office — was soothing, yet Eve was aggravated, nonetheless. It wasn't the doctor's fault. Therapy just wasn't where Eve wanted to be.

"I'm fine."

Willamena smiled, hoping Eve saw it as an understanding smile. She was no stranger to problematic patients. Though she had a feeling Eve would be one of her most difficult to date.

"You realize we have an hour together? It might be helpful if you were more elaborate with your answers."

Eve felt the corners of her mouth twitch for the first time since walking into the office. She found herself actually liking the doctor a bit more.

"I'm not sure what to say," Eve confessed.

"Why don't you start with why you're here."

Eve laughed. "Because my husband and best friend thought I needed to talk to someone."

"You don't think you do?" Dr. Woodrow twirled her pen in her hand. With her trusty notebook in her lap, she was ready to take notes when Eve spoke more than a few words. Some called the practice archaic, preferring to record sessions. Willamena, however, thought that method was too invasive and a potential security risk. Handwritten notes that only she could decipher was more Willamena's style.

"I've done well enough on my own so far," Eve answered.

"Hmm." Willamena opened her notebook and made her first entry. **Not used to others caring.** Once done, she picked up a stack of files to her right. As heartbreaking as they were, the police reports, news articles, and medical reports had been studied, then studied again. "I've read your story, Eve. Anyone would have a difficult time in your situation. It isn't uncommon to seek someone to talk to."

"I'm not used to seeking anyone out."

"Maybe it's time you do."

Whether it was time or not, Eve didn't feel she had much choice. Adam and Lainey bombarded her with this request, practically giving her no alternative but to agree. Eve's only stipulation was that *she* got to pick the doctor. When her friend and business consultant

Rebecca Cuinn recommended Dr. Woodrow, Eve conceded. The fact that the doctor was Rebecca's aunt doubled Eve's trust in the recommendation.

Now, the doctor watched Eve silently, patiently. When Eve said nothing more, Willamena sighed.

"Have you started painting again?" she asked softly.

Eve winced. Stupidly, she had disclosed that tidbit of information in the preliminary interview. Yeah, she knew it was important, but it was a difficult subject to talk about.

"No."

"Why do you think that is?"

It was Eve's turn to sigh. If she knew that, she wouldn't have to be here. To the outside world, Eve Sumptor-Riley's life was perfect. Her relationship with her husband Adam was healthy again. Her friendship with her best friend Lainey was wonderful. And even Adam and Lainey's relationship was on the mend. At least that's what it seemed like on the surface. Still, she couldn't pick up a paintbrush and create.

"I don't know." Eve's voice sounded smaller than she would have liked, but not being able to paint was killing her.

"Then, let me help you find that out."

The quiet offer agitated Eve. Not that she didn't think the doc was sincere. But she had been on her own since she was fourteen. Why the hell couldn't she get over whatever this block was?

"I've survived a lot in my life. I don't understand why I can't get past this."

"You may have survived, but are you certain that you've gotten over your past, Eve?"

Eve took a moment to think about the question. She could admit that she had moments when the past caught up with her. That's normal, right? Most days, she was fine. At least she used to think so.

"No." Eve's answer surprised even her. She had opened her mouth to say yes.

"Then we should start there. In fact, why don't we start with your childhood."

Eve snickered at the clichéd psychobabble, then cleared her throat when she caught Dr. Woodrow's expression. There was the tiniest bit of disapproval much to Eve's astonishment. She didn't think psychiatrists were allowed to show emotion. Oddly enough, the slight reaction made Eve trust Woodrow a little more.

"Where should I start?"

"What's the first thing that comes to your mind?"

Eve closed her eyes and thought back to things she wanted to forget. The first image that popped into her head was of her mother, bloodied and crying, huddled in the closet with Eve when she was a little girl. Her mother would rock Eve, whispering that everything would be okay. Eve believed her until it continued to happen repeatedly. Eventually, Eve stopped believing her and began resenting her more each time they huddled in that closet.

"Help me forgive my mother." Eve's voice was barely a whisper, and the words brought tears to her eyes. She had no idea she still harbored feelings of blame for her mother. The love between mother and daughter had always overshadowed everything else.

Well, hell. Apparently, there was something to this shrink business after all. Eve was glad she was rich. With as many things as she had gone through, it was going to take many, many hours to get through them all.

Chapter Two

"Hey, beautiful." Adam greeted Eve at the door, leaning in for a kiss. He was disappointed when Eve turned her head, offering her cheek instead.

"Where is Bella?"

"It's late. She's sleeping."

"Right. I'm going to check in on her, then take a shower."

Eve tried moving past Adam, but he blocked her way. "Hang on. Your first therapy session was tonight. I thought we could talk about it."

"That's not how this works." Eve raised a brow when Adam looked as though he was about to argue. "The thing about therapy is it's private, Adam. Besides, I've talked enough tonight. I'm exhausted." *Mentally and physically*, she thought silently.

"You're mad at me," he called after her as she walked away. "For making you go to therapy."

Eve glanced back. "No one makes me do anything anymore. I agreed to this because I'm not painting, and I want to know why. I'm not angry with you. But I also don't feel the need to share with you."

"Are you going to share with her?"

Eve shook her head wearily. Not as an answer to his absurd question, but with disbelief that he had the audacity to ask it.

"Goodnight, Adam."

She left him standing in the foyer, staring after her. What more did he want from her? A recording of everything she had said? Did he think she went there to confess all her sins and he's entitled to those confessions? Eve sighed as she climbed the stairs and headed towards Bella's room.

Eve stood at the door watching Bella breathe. Her little chest raised and lowered so peacefully that it was mesmerizing. No matter what happened in Eve's life, *this* was one thing she had done right. No matter what she felt, what she went through, or if she ever painted again, Eve would never regret having Bella. She crept to the side of the bed and knelt, taking Bella's tiny hand in hers.

"*I love you, baby girl. I'm doing the best I can. I want to be a mother you can be proud of. I don't want you to go to therapy one day and realize you resent me. I can't tell you that I won't make mistakes. I will. But I will always protect you. I will always be here.*" She kissed Bella's hand softly and swept the fringe of bangs off the sleeping girl's face. With one last look, Eve stood to leave.

"Momma?"

Eve chuckled lightly. "You little faker. Have you been awake this whole time?"

Bella shook her head with a yawn. "No, momma."

Eve smiled. She loved hearing Bella's little voice. Rs were particularly hard for her, but Eve thought it was adorable.

She squinted at Bella. "Hmm." She walked back over. "Should I believe you?"

Bella giggled and nodded enthusiastically. Then she raised her little arms and wiggled her fingers wanting a hug from her momma.

Eve pulled Bella to her and smothered her with kisses until she squealed with delight. She tickled Bella before the little girl threw her off balance by wrapping her arms around Eve's neck. They both tumbled onto the small bed with Eve doing her best not to hurt the young girl.

"Oof! When did you get so strong?"

The two-year-old giggled and flexed her tiny muscles. She

bounced up to her knees with the energy only a child possessed and took Eve's face in her little hands. "Miss you, momma."

"I missed you, too, Bug."

"Eww! No bug!"

"You're *my* bug! C'mere." She pulled Bella onto her lap. "Are you listening?"

"Yes, momma."

The seriousness on Bella's face nearly made Eve laugh and cry at the same time.

"I know I missed having dinner with you tonight. And bathtime, and cuddles, and kisses goodnight. I'm sorry. There will be times when momma has to do things that keep her away for a little while. But never for long. And even when I'm not here, I'm *always* here." Eve placed her hand over Bella's heart. "Do you understand, baby girl?"

"Yes, momma," Bella answered unconvincingly. "Always home?"

"Always." Eve stood with the little girl still in her arms and slid her back under the sheets.

Bella nodded — obviously approving of her momma's answer — and yawned again. She had tried staying awake earlier to see her momma and give cuddles but didn't quite make it.

"Stay, momma?"

Eve gave a fleeting thought to her shower and Adam. Bella's toddler bed was *not* made for someone Eve's size. But such a request could not be ignored. It didn't matter to Eve that she would be hanging half off the bed. Not if it made her daughter happy. "Scooch. Make some room for me."

"Yay!"

"Lainey?"

Lainey jumped at the sound of Jack's voice. She had been standing out on the back porch wondering how Eve's first therapy session went. Worry had plagued her all night, and when Eve didn't call her after the session, concern turned to fear. What if the doctor told Eve that what she needed was to stay away from Lainey? Lainey shook her head in an attempt to get rid of that thought.

She glanced back at her husband. Despite more graying in his hair and the wrinkles around his brown eyes, he was still attractive. "Yes?"

"You've been out here for a while." He craned his neck to look over at their neighbors' house. "Can you see them in a compromising position through a window or something?" He chuckled at himself, but Lainey didn't find it funny. "Come in and let's go to bed."

The wind whipped Lainey's dark blonde hair into her eyes, and she pushed at it to look at her watch. "It's only nine o'clock, Jack."

"Yeah. The boys are asleep, and I could use some relaxation."

Take a bath. Normally, Lainey would be open to some "relaxation." But the way Jack said it made her think things wouldn't be mutual. He had been getting better at not being selfish during their lovemaking, but lately, it was hit or miss for Lainey. Sure, she loved him and loved being with him, but there were times he made sex feel like a chore. Besides, her mind was preoccupied with Eve now, and that wasn't fair to Jack or herself.

"I'm just not in the mood, Jack."

"Come on, Lainey. It's been over a week. You spend too much time at your work, and I'm feeling neglected."

Translation: I'm falling behind on my wifely duties, Lainey thought with frustration. "I'm sorry you feel that way."

"You can make it up to me." He held his hand out to her. "Let's go."

Lainey frowned. "Still not in the mood, Jack. You can go on up. I'm going to stay out here for a while."

"I'm getting a little tired of this, Lainey. You come home exhausted, dinner is often late, I had to hire someone to come in and clean the house, and your sons . . ."

"My sons know where I am at all times, and they're fine with it. I go to all their activities, I'm home early more times than not, and you're just as capable of cooking dinner as I am. And, as I recall, you offered to hire someone to clean the house to be helpful. Now you're going to throw it in my face?"

Jack's scowl was met with equally angry green eyes. She knew that he *still* didn't like her having a career. He was old-fashioned that way. He believed the wife had her place inside the home. And Lainey adhered to that for many years. Until she just couldn't anymore. She had a master's degree in Art History that was collecting dust as much as she was. That's when she decided to get out of the house and do something for herself. It would have been impossible to predict what would happen after that. What did it say about her that she wouldn't change it for the world?

"Do what you want, Lainey. Stay out here all night for all I care." Jack spat angrily.

He slammed the sliding glass door hard enough to make Lainey wince. *He's going to be pissed if he breaks that thing. And it'll probably be my fault.* She shook her head at his childishness. She was so used to this behavior by now that she let it go pretty quickly.

Lainey turned back to the railing and leaned her elbows on it. It didn't take long for her mind to focus again on Eve. It took all her strength not to take out her phone and call. As concerned as she was about Eve's mental state, she couldn't justify potentially interrupting something. And that was something she did *not* want to think about.

"Mom?"

Why are people sneaking up on me tonight? Lainey turned to see her oldest son standing behind her.

"Hey, sweetie. Your dad told me you were sleeping."

"Dad forgets I'm not a little kid anymore and don't go to bed at eight."

Kevin was right. He wasn't a little kid anymore. *When the hell did that happen?* The brat was now taller than she was. And his voice was way too deep for Lainey's liking. She could remember when he would look up at her and tell her he loved her in his little squeaky voice.

"You can stop that now," Lainey said wistfully.

"Huh?"

"Growing up. I don't like it."

A deep chuckle coming from her little boy made Lainey shake her head.

"You'll probably have a better chance at getting Darren to stop growing. I think he has already."

Lainey smacked his arm playfully. "Leave your brother alone. He'll have his growth spurt just as you did."

"Mom," Kevin whined. "Do you have to say that?"

"What?" Lainey asked innocently. "Growth? Spurt?"

"You're evil."

Lainey laughed. She was well aware of Kevin's dislike of talking about puberty. But how would he know she loved him if she didn't tease him?

"Sorry, not sorry."

Kevin rolled his eyes. There were times his mom could be cool, but he'd never let her know that. He nodded in the direction of Eve's house.

"She okay?"

Lainey looked over in surprise. She had never discussed Eve's problems with Jack or the boys. It wasn't her place to disclose such personal things. "What do you mean?"

"I'm not stupid, mom. Eve has been pretty stressed out lately. That's not normal for someone like her."

"Someone like her?" Lainey repeated stupidly. She was still trying to wrap her head around her son's observance. If he saw Eve's distress when she was so good at hiding it, what else did he see? Did he know about her and Eve?

"Eve is the coolest person I know," Kevin said. "And I'm not just talking about being awesome. But lately, she's seemed a little, um, off."

"You think she's awesome?" Lainey shook her head and waved her hands. *That* was not the point here. Kevin has had a crush on Eve since the two met, but "awesome" was high praise from the teenager. "Eve has," she cleared her throat, "been through a lot. Things have happened recently that have been quite upsetting, but she's dealing with it."

"You know, mom, you can talk to me. I'm old enough . . ."

"I know," Lainey interrupted. At least she knew he thought he was old enough to know everything that was going on. But how would he feel if he knew what had happened between Eve and her? How much would he hate her? "I can't talk about it, sweetie. I can't betray Eve's trust like that."

Kevin studied her for a second, then looked over at Eve's house again. "Yeah, okay. I get that. Keep it in mind, though? I know dad isn't exactly easy to talk to and he doesn't really like Eve. So, if you need to talk, you know, I'm here."

She stared at her eldest son. His tawny hair was a little too long, and it fell in his hazel eyes. God, he was growing into an intelligent, caring, observant, good-looking young man. It was enough to break Lainey's heart as much as it made her proud. If she ever lost his love, she didn't know what she would do. She wrapped her arms around his neck, having to stand on her tip-toes to do so.

"Thank you."

He shrugged sheepishly like the fifteen-year-old teenager he was. "Sure."

Lainey looked up at him, sensing there was more he wanted to say. "Did you need something, sweetie?"

"Uh. N-no. I just wanted to, you know, see how you were doing. I heard dad slam the door, so I figured things were, um, tense."

"You're checking on me?" Kevin nodded. "It's my job to take care of you and your brother." She smiled at him and patted his cheek. "I'm fine. Everything's fine. Your dad gets a little frustrated when I don't conform to his antiquated ideas. He'll get over it."

Kevin laughed. "He better. Women aren't taking any crap anymore."

"Watch it," Lainey warned with a grin.

"That's why he doesn't like Eve, isn't it?" He asked, moving on quickly. "She's too strong for him."

Lainey couldn't help but wonder if Kevin saw her as weak for putting up with Jack's "crap."

"Your father likes Eve well enough, honey."

Kevin snorted. "Right. Anyway, I should go finish my homework."

Lainey raised a brow. "You didn't finish before coming out here?"

Kevin smirked at his mom. "I was going to the kitchen for some fuel when I heard the commotion."

"Fuel." Lainey shook her head. They had eaten no more than two hours ago.

"I'm a growing boy, mom. I need food."

Maybe I should stop feeding him, Lainey thought with a smile. In no hurry to go back inside, Lainey took a seat on one of the lounge chairs they kept on their deck and took advantage of the beautiful, clear night. She decided it was fruitless to worry about not hearing from Eve. So, instead, Lainey focused on the stars and allowed her mind to wander.

"You didn't come to bed."

Eve looked up from her phone. Adam looked handsome as usual in a dark suit paired with a pale pink shirt. She always loved how he didn't shy away from colors. Or how he could go from business to casual seamlessly.

"Sorry. Queen Bella demanded my presence, and I fell asleep in there." She made a show of stretching her aching back. "There's no saying no to Queen B."

Adam's lips twitched. "Ah, yes. It is hard to say no to little Miss Thing. She takes after her momma in that way."

Eve chuckled lightly. "I think she's completely surpassed my authority. And it only took her two years." She smiled proudly. "She's a genius."

Adam laughed. "I'll agree with that." He took a seat next to Eve at the kitchen table. They had moved into this house a little more than three years ago after getting married. He knew Eve loved living in the city, but she was more than willing to move to the suburbs when they had found out she was pregnant. When the house next door to Eve's best friend became available, they jumped at the perfect opportunity. Of course, Adam hadn't known then what he knew now about Eve and Lainey's relationship.

He cleared his throat hoping it would clear his mind from that thought. "I was hoping to show you how sorry I was about the way I acted when you got home."

Eve set her phone to the side, giving her attention to Adam. "Sex doesn't solve everything, Adam."

He reached over and took her hand. "I know. I shouldn't have pushed you to talk last night. And I shouldn't have brought Lainey up."

Eve squeezed his hand slightly. "I wasn't in the greatest of moods, and I could have handled things in a nicer way." She sighed. "You know, things are bound to get worse before they get better. I hope you're ready for that."

"Of course, I am. I want you to work everything out, Eve. I want you to be happy again."

You may not like the outcome. The thought popped into Eve's head so quickly that it stunned her. *Where the hell did that come from?*

"Momma! Look showts!"

Eve pulled her hand from Adam's and turned towards Bella who was trailed by her nanny, Lexie. The toddler did a pirouette, modeling her new shorts that had cute little flowers all over them. She paired them with her favorite Wonder Woman shirt that she had worn so much it was beginning to fade.

"You look absolutely perfect, Bug!"

Bella giggled. "I momma's bug," she explained to a smiling Lexie. "No gwoss kind!"

"Well, *obviously* you're the cutest kind of bug ever!" Lexie exclaimed exuberantly. She looked up at Eve and Adam. "I thought I'd take her to the park today. Is that okay?"

"Yes, by all means." Eve understood Lexie's concerns. It wasn't that long ago Eve's family was being threatened — once again — by Eve's past. Though that threat was now gone, Eve remained diligent in her efforts to keep those she loved safe. She never told Adam that the security detail she had on him, Bella, and Lainey continued. This was *her* burden to bear, not his. Not Lainey's. And most certainly not Bella's. This was not the legacy she wanted to leave her daughter. So, she would protect them no matter the cost to her.

Eve bent in her chair, getting face to face with her daughter. She placed her palms on Bella's small face. "Have fun, baby girl."

Bella put her palms on Eve's face. "Be good, momma."

Eve laughed. "I will if you will." She kissed Bella's entire face making the little girl squeal with delight. "I love you."

"Wuv you, momma! We go now. Bye, daddy! Wuv you!"

With that, the small, yet demanding young girl took Lexie's hand and nearly dragged her towards the front door.

"Just like her momma," Adam reiterated with a laugh. "Always ready to conquer the world."

"Hmm. Speaking of, I do have to get going," Eve smiled.

"Will you be late tonight?"

Eve got up and gathered her things. "No, I don't think so. I have a few meetings regarding the new gallery, but nothing that should keep me too late."

"Good." Adam rose as well. "I could pick up some food on the way home. Since you'll already have it on your mind, there are a couple of things I want to go over with you concerning the LA gallery."

She had hired Adam's firm as architects for her gallery knowing full well that working with a spouse wasn't always the best idea. *Yet, you have no problems working with Lainey.* For the second time that morning, Eve was bewildered by her involuntary thoughts. "Problems?"

Adam wrapped his arms around his wife. "No, not at all. Just some design stuff I wanted to run by you."

"Sounds good, but no take out. I'll cook something." She straightened Adam's tie.

"Even better. Then, maybe when Bella's asleep, I can be the one who demands your time tonight. All night."

Eve smiled. She couldn't tell him that she just wasn't in the mood. Not after everything she had put him through. Besides, sex was a big part of their relationship. Who would she be if she couldn't give him that? *Fuck. I'm going to need a lot of therapy.* "I look forward to it."

The honk of a horn startled Lainey, nearly causing her to drop everything in her hands. She glanced over her shoulder and saw Eve's white Lexus at the end of her driveway and defiantly ignored the small jump in her pulse.

"Need a ride?" Eve called out.

Lainey bumped the door of her car closed with her hip and made her way down to Eve. "I didn't hear from you last night, so I wasn't sure if you'd be here," she said as she got in and tossed her stuff in the backseat.

"I'll *always* be here, Lainey."

Lainey opened her mouth to say something but changed her mind.

"What?" Eve asked gently.

"Nothing." At least nothing that she felt she could talk about now. Eve had enough to deal with without having to deal with Lainey's feelings. "You look tired. That's all."

Eve snorted, somehow having the ability to make even that sound sexy. "Thanks. You look beautiful."

Lainey rolled her eyes and hoped Eve didn't notice the blush she could feel creeping up her neck. Their physical relationship might have ended a while ago, but she still felt that rush in her veins when Eve looked at her a certain way or said things like that to her.

"You always look beautiful, Eve," Lainey stated matter-of-factly. "Even when you look tired."

Eve smiled and winked at Lainey. "Yes, well, it's not easy to sleep on a toddler bed with a two-year-old who, despite her small stature, is a bed hog."

Lainey chuckled lightly, refusing to admit — even to herself — that she was happy it wasn't Adam that kept Eve up last night.

"I can't believe you slept on that bed all night. I know how big you like your beds . . ." Lainey's mouth snapped shut.

"Hmm," Eve hummed softly, then cleared her throat. "There's no saying no to Bella. Besides, I wanted to be there with her. I missed our time we spend together before she goes to sleep because of . . ."

Because of the therapy session, Lainey finished for Eve silently. As much as Lainey wanted to know how that session went, she wouldn't ask. If Eve wanted to talk, she would.

"You're a good mother, honey."

Eve glanced over at Lainey and smiled. There was an uncertainty in that smile that concerned Lainey, and she hoped Eve would come to her soon with what was on her mind. But for now, she would give Eve the space she needed.

Eve leaned on the railing overlooking her gallery. After a flurry of meetings all morning long, she was finally getting a free moment to herself. She immediately spotted Lainey who was busy with a client. Even so, those beautiful green eyes lifted to Eve's, locking with gray for a split second that felt like an eternity. The connection was broken when the customers directed Lainey to another part of the gallery. Eve's eyes followed until a specific display came into her view.

Lainey's display. Seeing it never failed to bring back memories for Eve. From her first meeting with Lainey who initially applied to be an accountant at Sumptor, Inc. to the night this display was revealed during the re-opening of Sumptor Gallery, NY. Eve could never have predicted how much each of those events would change her life. She stared at the display that had had only minor changes in the years that had passed. It remained joyful, sexy, and seductive, yet held a hint of mystery — an unknowing of what's to come.

The night of the re-opening came flooding back to Eve's mind. And heart. She could smell Lainey's scent, taste Lainey's essence, and feel every inch of Lainey's body as though she were right back there. That fateful night when Lainey showed up at her door, and they made love for the first time. Despite knowing the loss she would face, she would make the same decision she made that night — every single time.

"Eve?"

Eve blinked, then frowned. "I thought you were downstairs with a client."

"I was," Lainey responded carefully. "Mikey is finalizing everything with them. You've been standing here for so long that I thought I'd come to check on you." She glanced out over the railing to where Eve had been staring. "Are you . . ."

"Did you mean it?" Eve interrupted abruptly. She certainly couldn't tell Lainey what she had just been thinking about.

Lainey's brows furrowed in confusion. "Mean what?"

"When you said I was a good mother."

Lainey's heart ached to hear that same uncertainty she witnessed in Eve's smile earlier that morning. "Of course, I did, honey. Your relationship with Bella is so beautiful to watch. Why would you doubt yourself?"

Eve laughed mirthlessly. "Therapy. I spent the night talking about how I resented my mother for lying to me. And then realizing that it wasn't her I needed to forgive, but myself. There are days when I doubt myself and my ability to be who Bella needs me to be, and this therapy shit is going to make that so much worse before it makes it better."

The vulnerability in Eve had Lainey moving closer and laying a hand on Eve's arm. Her thumb involuntarily began making soothing strokes. "Being a mother is both the hardest and the most rewarding thing we will ever do, honey. We'll never be perfect at it, but even in our flaws we're at least trying. You're *already* everything Bella needs just by being her mother. She knows you love her. She feels that."

"Is love enough?" Eve asked quietly.

"It is when it's true," Lainey answered with the same quietness.

Eve risked a quick look at the display again and nodded. "I need to get back to these meetings. I'll need you to sit in on a few if you're not busy."

"Sure. Just let me know when you need me."

Their eyes locked. Both experienced the deep connection they had to each other. One they thought would eventually fade. After all this time, it only grew stronger.

Eve cleared her throat. "Right, well, I'm going to . . ." She gestured to her office. "Maybe we can grab lunch after this next call?"

"Deli? Turkey club on wheat with the cheddar cheese melted?" Lainey smiled. "I'll bring it up around noon, and you can fill me in on what I need to know."

Eve grinned. "Sounds perfect. Oh, and thank you. For not asking me about therapy but waiting for me to come to you. You knew I would, didn't you?" Lainey shrugged making Eve chuckle. Then, she winked her signature wink and disappeared into her office.

"*I hoped*," Lainey whispered to the closed door. She looked at the display again, thinking of the expression on Eve's face. "*I think of that night, too. Every day.*"

Chapter Three
Therapy

The sins of the daughter.

"Eve," Dr. Woodrow set her leather-bound writing pad aside and slipped off her glasses. "If you expect these sessions to work, you have to be honest with me. With yourself."

"What would you like me to say, Doctor?"

Eve refused to fidget. She had spent many years training herself to remain calm and strong. It had always proven to be extremely helpful in her line of work. After everything Eve had been through, it was essential. Here with Dr. Woodrow, she couldn't stop twisting her wedding ring around her finger.

"It isn't my job to tell you what to say, Eve. It's my job to listen to what you need to let go." Dr. Woodrow noticed the small gesture and made a mental note. Eve was composed and poised, but when she was faced with her past, she became insecure. Of course, Willamena knew that if she said that out loud, this session would be over in an instant. So, she faced Eve the way she knew the woman would appreciate.

Eve observed as the doc sat back in her chair, her elbows on the arms of the chair and steepled her fingers. It was a show of confidence that Eve knew well. She was waiting, patiently, for Eve to open up. It had taken Eve years to open up to someone. In her thirty plus years, she had only trusted two people with her sordid past. And had slept with both. Sitting in front of someone who wanted her to divulge every secret, without any other pretense, somehow made Eve feel more exposed.

"You asked me to help you forgive your mother," Dr. Woodrow said over Eve's silence. "Are you sure that's what you feel?"

"Obviously you're not," Eve answered dryly. The doc said nothing, just kept waiting. *Damn. She's good.* "I don't know what I feel, to be honest with you. I wanted her to be honest with me, but she wasn't."

"She's your mother, Eve. You're a mother now. What would you do with Bella in this situation?"

"Adam would never hurt me," Eve seethed. How could the two situations possibly be compared?

"I know that," she said softly at Eve's outburst. "I'm not saying Adam would hurt you. I merely want you to think about how you would have reacted if the tables were turned."

Eve sighed. Of course, she would have done the same thing her mother did. She thought she was protecting Eve, and she did the best she could have in her situation. Blaming her was blaming the victim, and Eve knew better than most not to do that. The truth was, Eve was not blaming her mother. She wasn't even mad at her mother. However, it was much easier to blame someone else than it was to blame yourself.

"Eve? Many emotions just crossed over your face. Do you want to tell me what you were just thinking?"

"It's a bit overwhelming for me that you can read me so well after a short amount of time."

"It's my . . . You know, that's not true. I was going to go with the line of it being my job. While it is, and I'm damn good at my job, it's more than that with you." Willamena's eyes flickered with amusement when she sensed Eve's uneasiness with her admission. Even so, she continued. "You remind me of my niece. I feel particularly protective of you. It may be unprofessional to some, but I think it will give me a better insight into you."

Eve and Rebecca had grown close over the years. The similarities between them were unmistakable, and Eve could understand why Dr. Woodrow felt a familiarity. Still, the admission shook her.

"You barely know me." Eve's voice was a mere whisper. She hadn't had a mother figure since she was fourteen and didn't know how to react to the feelings Dr. Woodrow brought out in her. Should she feel guilty about her desire to feel the love and caring of a mother figure? She nearly laughed at the idea. *Just one more thing to add to my arsenal of guilt.*

"I believe you of all people know that feelings can occur quite instantly and without warning."

It was true. Eve had felt something instantaneously with both Adam and Lainey. It had been — and in Lainey's case, still is — intense, scary, and immensely satisfying. She felt another brick fall out of her wall of protection and wondered when the hell she started trusting people she hardly knew. She also wondered if she could get away with blaming Lainey for that.

"Now, are you ready to tell me what the emotions were all about?" Dr. Woodrow asked, unwittingly interrupting Eve's inner musings.

"I realized it wasn't my mother that I need to forgive," Eve answered honestly. She hesitated on elaborating further even when she noticed the doc's questioning look. It wasn't out of spite, but a real defense mechanism for Eve to be evasive. "I should have been able to help her."

"Eve — "

"I know," Eve interjected quickly. "I was a kid, what could I have done? But there had to have been something. Something that would have kept her alive. Kept her with me."

To Eve's utter horror and shock, she felt tears flood her eyes. She was determined to blame that on Lainey as well. The woman had indeed done a number on Eve. Opening her heart had made Eve susceptible to . . . feelings.

"Do you think that's why you would do anything to keep those you love safe? Even go as far as stepping in front of a gun — twice?"

The doctor's tone was even, though Eve still heard a hint of disapproval.

Eve thought back to that night her father showed up at her gallery. She could still feel the paralyzing fear when he held a gun to Lainey's head. She could still feel the rage and humiliation of Lainey seeing her practically seducing her father to keep his attention off Lainey. And she knew she would do it all again, including pulling that trigger, if it meant Lainey was safe.

"My life means nothing without the people I love," Eve stated simply.

"Can you not see they feel the same about you?"

"That's not what I think about. I wasn't able to save my mother. I'll be damned if I don't save those closest to me when it's because of me they were in danger in the first place."

Willamena shook her head slightly and picked up her writing pad again, jotting down notes. When she finally looked at Eve again, she smiled kindly.

"Before we get deeper into that, we need to spend more time on this guilt you feel towards your mother, Eve. If you can't forgive yourself for something that isn't your fault in the first place, I'm afraid you won't be able to get rid of this block you have."

Eve couldn't recall the last time she picked up a paintbrush. The desire was there, but the creativity wasn't. The blank canvas continued to be blank. Even in Eve's head, when there used to be idea after idea, it remained blank. The threat of not being able to paint or create art again caused her to shudder.

Art was an essential outlet for Eve. It had gotten her through some of the most devastating times in her life. Without it, Eve was frightened by what the impact would be. Would she actually go crazy? *Probably*, she thought miserably. She needed it as much as she needed her family. As much as she needed Lainey.

Without art, Eve didn't feel like Eve. If Adam or Lainey couldn't see the woman they fell for, how long would she be able to keep them? Even worse, how would she be able to raise her daughter with confidence and potential she didn't feel herself?

"How? How do I forgive fourteen-year-old me for not being able to save my mother?"

"We go back. You'll have to relive it all in order to give yourself a different outcome."

"It will never be different, Doctor," Eve told her grimly. "She will still be dead. I will still have been brutalized. Innocent people will still have been killed or threatened because of me. Reliving it means going through that pain all over."

"It is not the outcome *outside* I am talking about, Eve. It is what happened *inside*. Starting with the first time you knew something was wrong in your household."

As much as Eve wanted to walk away, to never relive this through words since she relived it in her dreams often enough, she eventually agreed. She had no other choice.

Chapter Four

"I'll be going to LA soon," Eve announced over breakfast. Adam looked up from the papers he was going over and just stared. It didn't faze her one bit. She handed Bella her glass of juice with a wink.

"I go, momma?" Bella picked up her napkin and wiped her mouth as her momma taught her.

"Do you want to go?" Eve leaned over and bopped Bella's nose with her finger.

"Yeah! I go LA, daddy!" Bella jumped up from her seat and started for the stairs.

"Where are you going, bug?" Eve called out.

"Get toys!"

Eve laughed as Bella raced into her playroom as fast as her little legs would carry her. She eyed Adam who was still staring. Yeah, she should have discussed it with him first. But after what she did for him in bed the night before, she was hoping he was happy enough to agree to anything.

"Next week would be better for me. If you had talked to me about this, I could have given you my schedule," Adam responded, trying to remain calm.

Eve heard the edge in his voice, and her hackles went up. So much for last night helping her. "I am not asking for your permission, nor do I work around your schedule."

"And were you going to ask if you could take my daughter?"

Eve's nostrils flared. "*Our* daughter. I'd rather have her with me than with a nanny all day and night while you're at the office. She enjoys being at the gallery with me."

Adam raised a brow. "And is . . ."

"If your next question is if Lainey is going, the answer is yes. She is my assistant. This is her job."

Adam sighed. He was getting nowhere with Eve by letting jealousy rear its ugly head again. All he was doing was screwing up big time with his wife which is the last thing he needed right now. It was time to try a different tactic. "I did it again, didn't I? Sorry, beautiful. You've been standoffish since your, um, sessions."

It was Eve's turn to raise an eyebrow. "You didn't think I was standoffish last night."

Adam's lip twitched. Last night had been amazing as usual. Even so, he could tell that Eve wasn't entirely present. He had a feeling it had something to do with the mood she had been in since her last therapy session. He was beginning to wonder if this was such a good idea.

"Last night was fantastic. I guess that's why I was surprised by your announcement this morning. I know we didn't do much talking, but you could have mentioned it."

"I'm mentioning it now."

Adam knew better than to push her too far. "How long will you be gone?"

"A few days." Eve could tell that Adam was doing his best to be understanding and supportive. "I told you it would get worse before it got better, Adam." She stood. "I'm doing my best considering. Now, I better get in there and make sure Bella isn't packing every single toy she owns."

Lainey pushed her eggs around on her plate. Her stomach was in knots, and the thought of actually putting food in there made her nauseous. Ever since Eve told her they would be traveling to LA, Lainey could practically feel the ulcer forming. She loved traveling with Eve. What she hated was having to tell Jack she wouldn't be home for a few days. Time to rip off the band-aid.

"Hey, Darren, guess what." She figured that by getting the boys on her side first, it would help her with Jack.

The eight-year-old looked up, mouth full of pancakes that were doused with syrup. "Wha?"

"I'll be flying to LA next week!" Lainey went for full-out enthusiasm. She knew Kevin would be supportive, but Darren was a little more bothered when it came to Lainey leaving home for a bit.

Darren chewed his food thoughtfully. "With Eve?" he asked finally.

"Yes. We have to set up a new gallery there." She glanced at Jack whose eyes were boring into her. It was as though he thought she would change her mind just by the sheer disappointment in his look.

"Will you get to fly in the private plane?"

"Only way to fly," Lainey answered with a grin.

"Can I come?"

"Not this time, sweetheart. You have school. But I will absolutely take you when school is out. Sound good?" She knew she was practically bribing him, but she had learned as a mother that sometimes you had to do what you had to do.

Darren grinned back. "Sounds good!"

"Sounds good to me, too, as long as I get to go," Kevin laughed. "It's cool that you get to travel, mom."

"I forbid it." Jack pushed his plate away and sat back, crossing his arms.

"Excuse me?"

"Your obligations are here with this family, Lainey. Not gallivanting around."

"*This isn't the 50s*," Kevin muttered under his breath.

"What did you say, young man?"

Lainey patted Kevin's hand. "Why don't you boys finish getting ready for school. Your ride will be here soon."

"Yeah, okay." Kevin leaned over and kissed his mom on the cheek. "*Good luck.* C'mon, squirt."

"I'm not a squirt!" Darren argued as he ran after his big brother.

"Jack . . ."

"The answer is no, Lainey. If Eve wants to leave her family, that's Adam's problem. But she doesn't need her secretary with her."

"Is that what you think I am?" Lainey sat up straight in her chair. She had spent most of their marriage backing down to keep the peace. Since meeting Eve, she had grown stronger, no longer willing to back down. "I have a master's degree, Jack, or did you forget that? I'm not a secretary. I am the assistant curator for one of the most prestigious galleries in the world. The fact that you can't appreciate that tells me we haven't solved anything in our marriage."

"We do fine when you're . . ."

"Compliant?" Lainey finished for him. She had thought after her 'near-death' experience Jack would appreciate her more. And for a while, he did. Obviously, things had gone full circle, and Lainey was right back where she was when she applied for the accounting job at Sumptor, Inc.

"A good mother," Jack countered.

Oh, yeah. He knew exactly which buttons to push to turn that guilt on fully. At this point, at least when it came to her sons, Lainey was ready for it.

"The boys have a quiet week next week. I won't be missing any big games or concerts, I checked. And Eve was gracious enough to put off this trip until next week so that I wouldn't miss Darren's concert."

Jack scoffed. "Gracious. She's still taking you away from your family, and I'm tired of it. No more, Lainey."

Lainey stared down a defiant Jack and wondered if Eve ever had this problem with Adam. The difference was, Adam knew about

Eve and Lainey's past. Jack was merely an ass. If Eve *did* have this problem, how would she deal with it?

Lainey smiled, confusing Jack. She knew *precisely* how Eve would deal with it. "I wasn't asking for your permission, Jack. I have a job, and I'm going to do it. The boys are fine with it, so it would be wise for you to get on board."

"Is that a threat?" Jack asked as Lainey stood.

"Not at all. I'm telling you that I won't go through this again, Jack. I'm not your mother or your slave. I'm a woman in my forties with a mind of her own. Someone you can't bully anymore." *Oh, Eve would be so proud*, Lainey thought with a secret smile.

"I wish you wouldn't provoke him like that, Lainey." Eve checked the temperature of Bella's french fries before placing them in front of her on the highchair. "Try to keep the ketchup wearing at a minimum, yeah, bug?"

"'Kay, momma."

Despite the cuteness of the scene before her, Lainey was annoyed with Eve's lack of appreciation. "I thought you'd be proud of how I stood up for myself."

Eve heard the disappointment in Lainey's voice and looked up at her. If they hadn't been in a diner, surrounded by people, she would have taken Lainey's hand. For now, she had to work with what she had. So, she smiled softly at her companion.

"I am. I just fear for your safety sometimes."

Lainey's eyebrows shot up. "You think Jack would," she glanced at Bella. At two years old, little ears could also be a big mouth, "*hurt me?*"

It was completely ridiculous. Right? Yes, Jack was old-fashioned and a bit controlling, but he wouldn't hurt her.

Eve shrugged slightly. "I think when people's buttons are pushed they are capable of anything. I specifically remember how he was that time you told him you were taking the boys to spend the weekend with me. He grabbed your arm, and he *hurt* you."

Lainey remembered that weekend, too. Very well. She remembered *everything* about that weekend, except that. It had been so out of character for Jack to touch her in such a manner. Perhaps that's why she forgot about it. Or, maybe she had better things to reminisce about.

"I can take care of myself," she said finally, albeit not as strong as she would have preferred. "Besides, the boys were there. Kevin would never let Jack get away with anything."

Eve sighed softly, thinking about her therapy sessions. She had believed she could protect her mother, too. Eve accepted a fry from her daughter that had been drowned in ketchup. As disgusting as it looked, she popped that fry in her mouth as though it was the most exquisite delicacy she had ever had.

"I was a year younger than Kevin when my mother was . . ."

She didn't finish her sentence, but Lainey knew what Eve meant. "That's different, Eve," she said delicately.

"Why? Because Kevin is a boy?"

"Because Kevin is bigger than Jack now. And he works out, plays football, and thinks his dad's views are outdated."

Eve nodded thoughtfully. It was true. Kevin did have more of an advantage than she did all those years ago. The biggest one being that Jack, while old-fashioned, was not the murdering psycho that Tony was. "I'm sorry. This therapy sh – stuff has been tough. Woodrow seems to think that reliving everything from my past will somehow help me. I think it's making me paranoid."

Lainey hated the fact that Eve had to recall those horrible times in her past. God, she wished she could comfort Eve in some way. "Maybe she's right," Lainey said finally. "I've read that talking about . . . things helps lessen their power."

"You've read?" Eve asked with a tilt of the head.

Lainey lifted a shoulder. "I wanted to be able to help if you needed me."

I always need you. Eve cleared her throat. "Well, I'm glad that you will be with me in Los Angeles, then."

Bella clapped her messy hands together. "Wainey coming, too?" She handed Lainey two fries. "I go, too!"

"You are, huh?" Lainey took the proffered food without hesitation and ate them with enthusiasm. She had two sons. Extra ketchup on fries wasn't the worst thing she'd ever had to pretend to like. "Thank you! And since you're coming with us, we can make it a fun girls' trip!"

"Yay!" Bella did a little boogie in her chair.

"Bug, you're getting food everywhere," Eve said with a chuckle.

"Sawwy, momma." Bella took the napkin from her mother and sloppily wiped her hands and mouth. Once she was satisfied, she threw it to the side and dug into her food again.

Eve shook her head with amusement. No one could ever accuse Bella of not being thorough. She looked back up at Lainey who was watching her affectionately. A moment passed between them before Eve forced herself to break the contact. There were too many damned feelings that she didn't know how to process right now.

"I, um, haven't been the greatest wife lately," she said softly, hoping Bella was too engrossed in her food to pay attention.

"I doubt that," Lainey responded with the same softness.

Eve smiled sadly. "It's true. I've been distant and moody. I blame it on the therapy, and maybe it is that to some extent. But I can't help feeling that there's something else." She leaned in a little closer, satisfied when Lainey did the same. "I didn't even think to ask him to go to LA with me. I also didn't discuss taking Bella with me. Nor did I consider how he'd feel knowing you would be going with me."

Lainey lowered her head. "I'm sorry."

"It's not your fault."

"Isn't it?"

This time Eve didn't hold back. She took Lainey's hand in hers. "No. We can't change what *we* did. All we — including Adam — can do is move on."

Move on. Those two words caused an ache in Lainey that she couldn't explain. This is the life they both chose, right? So, why did she still have these feelings? And was it healthy to read into Eve's "something else" statement? She pulled her hand back.

"If it's going to cause problems with your marriage, I could stay here."

Eve immediately sensed the change in Lainey's demeanor and regretted whatever she said that caused it. Unfortunately, these days when Eve was feeling blameworthy, she quickly reverted to her defense mechanism. Authority. "No, Lainey. I need you with me in LA."

"Eve, you've opened many galleries without me . . ."

Eve raised a brow. "You are my assistant." Realizing what she was doing, and to whom, she stopped and shook her head. That's not how she ever wanted to treat Lainey. She was *not* just another employee. Trying to use her authority on Lainey like that made her no better than Jack or Adam. "I apologize for that. I will honor whatever decision you make, Lainey. But please don't make it by thinking it would help me if you didn't go. It would not."

Lainey couldn't help but smile. Eve had grown so much in the few years they had known each other. She would like to think that she had some influence on that change. "Well, I can't waste my awesomeness this morning and let Jack believe he won, now can I?"

Eve let out a relieved laugh. "Absolutely, not. Now finish up. We have a lot to do before we leave next week."

"You'll never be rid of me, Little Eve." The pale man laughed, spraying blood in Eve's shocked face. "You really thought killing me would work? I'm in your head, girl."

"Fuck you, Tony."

"Yeah, a whore like you would enjoy that." Tony leered at Eve, causing her skin to crawl.

"You're the one who made me a whore, Daddy.*" She could feel the weight of the gun in her hands. Oh, how she longed to lift it and empty what was left of the bullets into Tony's head.*

Tony laughed. "You're still pretending you hated it. Admit it, girl, you loved every minute. You think I don't know how you let that man of yours treat you? How you beg him to hurt you? I did you a favor. Fucker knows I did him a favor, too."

Blood dripped from the side of Tony's mouth. His teeth were stained red, creating a gory contrast with the pastiness of his skin.

"You're not real." Though Eve's heart nearly pounded through her chest, she managed to remain calm.

"Oh, I'm real, little Eve. You blame me for your mother's death. But you know, deep down, she killed herself. She was a crazy bitch. You're just like her. Therapy won't help you, girl. Your mother passed it down to you, and you'll pass it down to your daughter." He laughed again. *"You will both end up in the same place as your mother."*

Eve jerked awake. She sat up, panting, as she tried to escape the images of her dead father. Her head pounded with every beat of her racing heart. "*Damn it!*" she whispered vehemently.

"Eve? You okay, beautiful?" Adam asked sleepily.

"Yeah, just a headache. I'm going to get some aspirin. Go back to sleep." She patted him gently on the shoulder and slipped out of bed. As she reached the door of the bathroom, she turned back to Adam. Her husband was already snoring softly again, and an unbidden thought came to her aching head. *Lainey would never have let me get away with that.*

She closed the door behind her and stared at herself in the mirror. "What is wrong with you?" she asked her reflection. Eve turned on the water, inviting the shock of cold when she splashed her face. Reliving all the shit she had been through was proving to be just as hard the second time around. Bruises, cuts, and bullet holes tended to heal. It was the emotional bit that hurt the most. That was exactly why Eve closed that part off years ago. Whose bright idea was it to open *that* up?

It wasn't just her past, though. It was here and now. It was the future. Nothing felt settled for Eve. She was stuck in this odd limbo where she couldn't grasp who she truly was. For a woman like Eve, that was a dangerous place to be.

With one last look in the mirror, she blotted her face dry and quietly made her way to Bella's room. The most relaxing thing for Eve these days was watching Bella sleep peacefully. If she couldn't have painting, at least she had this. The love and bond between mother and daughter were strong, and Eve had no doubts that she would do whatever it took to keep Bella safe. Just as Eve's mother did for her. Her resentment towards her mother was misplaced, to say the least. After her last therapy session, Eve could no longer ignore her own guilt of not being able to save her mom.

She sat down in the chair next to Bella's bed with a heavy heart. *"I'm not crazy, bug,"* she whispered to her sleeping daughter. *"Just lost."*

Bella giggled quietly in her sleep and Eve wondered what she was dreaming about. Whatever it was, Eve made a vow to ensure that little giggle never disappeared.

Lainey walked into the gallery and looked up towards Eve's office. Eve hadn't shown up that morning to drive into work together, and there had been a sick feeling in the pit of Lainey's stomach ever since. There were no calls, no messages. More importantly, there was no Eve.

There had been no indication that they weren't driving in together. In fact, Eve had explicitly said she would be there. Usually prompt, when Eve was an hour late, Lainey waited until Adam left for work before walking next door to make sure everything was okay. Once there, she was greeted by Lexie and Bella who told her Eve had left very early that morning.

"Good morning, Mrs. Stanton."

Lainey made an effort to snap out of her melancholy mood and smiled at Mikey. The young man had kept busy the past few years going to night school and majoring in Art History as well as working for Eve. Having been incredibly impressed with his knowledge at such a young age, Eve had been very generous in giving Mikey the prestigious job of assistant curator even before he finished his degree. Technically, Lainey thought pleasantly, he was the assistant to the associate curator. But well on his way to managing a gallery himself.

"Good morning, Mikey. Is Eve in?"

Mikey frowned and glanced up towards the offices. "Oh. I haven't seen her, yet. I thought she was coming in with you."

So did I. "She had a few meetings this morning," Lainey lied. "I guess they're taking a little longer than she expected." She patted Mikey on the shoulder. "I'll be upstairs if you need me."

"Yes, ma'am."

Lainey hurried up the stairs, grateful for the time she had spent recently on the elliptical machine. She paused at Eve's door before continuing to her own. If she didn't know Eve so well, she wouldn't be worried about something as simple as having to drive into work alone. But she did know Eve. She knew Eve had enemies. She knew Eve tended to shut down when she thought others would get hurt. Lainey put a hand on her aching stomach.

"Oh, God. Please tell me someone's not trying to kill her. Again." She took her phone out of her purse and dialed Eve's number. She sighed heavily when it went straight to voicemail.

"*Eve?*" Lainey sighed again and hung up. What the hell could she say anyway? If this were related to Eve's therapy, she would have to wait until Eve was ready to talk. Lainey certainly wouldn't force her. And what if this was something like it was with Tony or Laurence? Or Detective Carter? Or Agent Donovan? God, what if Madame Bussiere was after Eve now? *Jesus*! Lainey could feel the bile rising in her throat. Could she handle watching Eve go through that again?

"Don't even go there, Lainey. It's probably nothing. Most likely. Hopefully." She shook her head. All she was succeeding in doing was stressing herself out more. *Work,* she told herself. *Just work and don't think the worst.* Though that was easier said than done, that's exactly what Lainey did. What did it matter if she checked her phone every other minute?

Eve knelt in the grass and whispered a small prayer before reaching out and touching a simple headstone. She had chosen something simple because that's how the woman buried here was. Simple, yet strong. Kind and far too good for the hand she had been dealt in life. Eve long wondered how someone like her mother ended up with a man like Tony Sumptor.

Marie Bailey
1966-2001
Beloved Mother

"Hi, momma. I'm sorry it's been so long since I've visited. Life has been . . . complicated to say the least. I know that's not an excuse, but it's all I have." Not caring about dirtying her black slacks, she sat down. "I've been going to therapy." She chuckled. "Bet you never thought that would happen. I didn't either. However, people I care about thought it would be a good idea. After last night, I'm not so sure. Tony came to visit me."

Eve told her mother as much of her dream as she could remember. Unfortunately, that was quite a lot. As much as she wished she could forget it *and* him, Tony was stuck in her head.

"Intellectually, I know he's most likely being manifested by talking about him in my sessions." *Oh, God. I'm starting to sound like a shrink. Fantastic.* "But his message . . . I know you weren't crazy, momma. I know that with every fiber of my being. But I must be harboring some fear that perhaps *I* am. I refuse to believe that I'm feeling this way because I have any remorse for killing him."

Eve sighed. This was the first place she thought to come to when she woke up still sitting in the chair in Bella's room. As she confessed before, she hadn't been here in a while. Even after all this time, it still hurt that this was the only way to speak to her mother. But it was her mother she needed right now more than anything else.

"The world is much safer for Bella with him gone," she continued. Then smiled when she thought of her daughter. "God, momma, I wish you could have met Bella. You would be so proud of her. She's headstrong and sassy. And she's only *two*! I'm in a lot of trouble, and I wouldn't have it any other way," she chuckled lightly, then sighed. "She's the reason I can't lose my mind, momma. The problem is, I don't know who I am right now. For so many years, I've prided myself on being strong and fighting every challenge head-on and winning. I don't know how to win this."

Her phone buzzed, and she automatically ignored the call without looking at the display. Adam had been frustrated with her this morning. Not only for not coming back to bed but for not talking to him about what was truly wrong and leaving the house early without explanation. She didn't have it in her to listen to more grievance from him right now. Then she caught the name displayed from the corner of her eye.

"*Lainey*," she whispered and listened to the message. The simple murmur of Eve's name touched her deeply. Lainey hadn't needed to say anything else. She said it all with that one quiet word. "She's worried about me. God, momma, what am I going to do? She's one of the reasons I'm so lost. Maybe *the* reason. My feelings for her are completely inappropriate and, yet, I can't stop them. I try so hard to convince myself that letting her go was the right thing to do." She stared up at the sky. The sun was rising, coloring the morning in vibrant oranges and blues, waking up the city. "I saved her. I did what I couldn't do for you. I saved her from Tony. After that incident, I was so sure that letting her go was what was best for her. For everyone. But . . . what if she's the answer, momma? Can I live with the person I am without her? Can I be the person Adam needs me to be without compromising who I truly need to be in Bella's eyes? Is my sanity worth hurting so many?"

So many questions without answers. Eve thought of the people who would be affected by her selfishness. And the thought of hurting the children troubled her the most. *I made the right decision*, she told herself. One day, she would believe it without question. She hoped.

Lainey stared at the invoice in front of her until the words blurred from her vision. She had been in the office for over an hour and still no word from Eve. Hell, she didn't even know if Eve had received her message.

"Message," she scoffed, interrupting the silence in her office. "You said her name. What is she supposed to respond with?"

Talking to herself wasn't going to make things any better; that's for sure. She had already gone through every possible scenario of where Eve could be. Unfortunately, knowing Eve's life, those scenarios weren't great. So, instead of working herself up into a frenzy, she had organized orders alphabetically, caught up on emails, checked their hotel reservations for their trip to L.A., wondered briefly why Eve didn't have a home in California when it seemed like she had a house everywhere else, and drank three cups of coffee. In hindsight, the coffee probably wasn't such a good idea. The energy boost allowed her to finish the tasks meant to occupy her mind in record time. And it made her jittery.

"Hey."

Lainey blinked and looked up into Eve's beautiful gray eyes. *Well, she's alive.* As happy as she was about that, she was pissed that Eve appeared quite composed while Lainey felt undone.

"Good morning."

She is not happy. "I'm sorry."

Lainey raised a brow. "For?"

"I told you I would always be there, and I wasn't today. I'm sorry."

It took Eve saying it out loud for Lainey to realize that's exactly what she had been the most upset about. She gestured to the chair in front of her desk for Eve to sit.

"The day you said that I nearly said you couldn't promise that. It's one of the things that scares me the most about you," Lainey said carefully.

Eve frowned. "Scares you?"

"Yes," Lainey nodded. "You think it's easier to shut down when emotions get to be too much. I'm always afraid that one day you'll decide . . ."

Lainey trailed off and Eve leaned forward. "Decide what, Lainey?"

Yes, Lainey. Decide what? That she doesn't love you anymore? That you're not worth the drama you cause between her and Adam? That your mood swings are too much to handle? She shook her head. "It doesn't matter."

"It matters to me. Please?"

"I have no right to be upset that you didn't tell me where you were or didn't answer my call. Still, there's this battle inside me that I never seem to be able to win. I can sit here and tell you I worry about you. And as true as that is, it's the thought of you shutting me out that scares the shit out of me. I'm sorry, Eve."

Eve knew how difficult it was for Lainey to profess that to her. It had been more than apparent to her that Lainey had struggled with her feelings from the moment she felt something more than she should have for Eve. It was the lethal combination of guilt, love, and jealousy that caused Lainey's occasional outbursts. Eve understood that as much as she wished it didn't happen. Those outbursts hurt them both, and the one thing Eve wanted to avoid was hurting Lainey.

"I went to visit my mother," Eve said softly, noting the confusion and surprise in Lainey's expression.

"I — I didn't know she was buried close by." In the years they'd known each other, Eve had never mentioned her mother's burial place. As well as she thought she knew Eve, there would always be something new to learn. Was that a blessing? Or a curse?

"No one does," Eve revealed with a small shrug. "One of the first things I did when I got back to New York was have her remains moved out of the place where Tony had buried her. He had her in some crowded cemetery with a gaudy tombstone touting only the Sumptor name. I bought the plots surrounding her at the new place, had it fenced in, and used her maiden name on the headstone. It was my way of giving mom her own identity back."

"That's beautiful, honey."

"Least I could do," Eve muttered, then cleared her throat. "I had a nightmare last night."

Lainey's expression softened even further. "Another night terror?"

Eve shook her head. "Just a nightmare. It wasn't about what happened to me. It was Tony. I could see the blood, feel the weight of the gun, but he was laughing at me. Telling me my mother was crazy, passed it down to me, and I will pass it down to Bella."

During Eve's explanation, Lainey had gotten up and walked

around her desk to sit closer. "Honey, you're not crazy," she said, taking Eve's hand.

Eve raised a brow. "No? Wasn't it you who wanted me to go to therapy?"

"Not because I think you're crazy. Eve, with what you've been through in your life? A weaker person would have crumbled years ago. You flourished despite the odds. But even the strongest of women need a helping hand occasionally. Honestly, it amazes me that you were able to cope by yourself for so long."

"I was getting by, Lainey. I didn't want to see what it had done to me. So, I kept it at bay."

"Until I came along." It was half an apology from Lainey and half gratefulness that she was able to open Eve's heart.

"Yes, well, you're quite persuasive when you want something," Eve jested. "What if he's right, Lainey? Obviously, it was my subconscious that made 'Tony' say those things. I think the thing that I fear the most is not being Eve. If I can't do the things or be the person that defines me . . ." *then how will you love me?* Eve shook her head. Those spontaneous thoughts were coming more often.

"Eve, honey, *you* are you. Everything you do, whether it was how you were before or who you become, *that's* what defines you. We live and learn. Adapt to the changes in our lives. We grow. And we hope that the people around us grow with us. But how long can we stunt our own growth to protect others without losing ourselves in the process?"

Eve instinctively knew that Lainey was asking herself the same question. It created an equal amount of hope and fear inside her. And a ton more questions.

"I think Dr. Woodrow broke us," she chuckled in an attempt to lighten the mood.

Lainey smiled. "I haven't had a session with her, so I'll blame psychology 101." She laughed at Eve's surprised expression. "I told you I've been reading. I'm nowhere near having Dr. Woodrow's caliber of expertise, but I'm learning enough to see my own mistakes."

"You don't make mistakes."

Lainey scoffed with mirth. "I make a ton of them, and you know it."

"I know no such thing," Eve winked. She slipped her hand from Lainey's after a gentle squeeze. "I should do some actual work before we leave next week." She rose. "Thank you for listening."

"Always. Eve," Lainey called as Eve reached the door. When Eve turned back, giving Lainey her full attention, Lainey continued. "Why don't you have a house in LA?"

Eve laughed and shook her head. "You certainly keep me on my toes, Mrs. Stanton. Is that one of your three questions?"

Lainey nearly blushed at the question. In and of itself, it was an innocent question. However, pair it with what happened after the first time Eve asked her that question on her private plane and all kinds of erotic memories came to life.

"I think I've earned more than three questions, don't you?"

Eve grinned. "Indeed."

Chapter Five
Therapy

The power of the past.

Crash!
    The sound woke me up from a deep sleep, and I felt my lips start to tremble. I wanted to call out for my mommy, but something kept my mouth shut. Then, I heard the yelling.
    Daddy was loud. I had never heard him sound like that before, and I wondered if it was really him, or if someone else was here. But mommy called him by name, pleading with him to calm down.
    Smack! Crash!
    I didn't even bother trying to stop the tears. I'm only nine years old, but I know something is terribly wrong. I know daddy is hurting mommy, and I need to help her. But he's scary. I hear mommy crying, I can hear the pain in her voice, and my little legs scurried to the door, flinging it open.
    "Daddy! Stop!"
    He had his hands around mommy's neck, and I could tell she was having trouble breathing. She looked at me then, her eyes widening with shock. She tried to shake her head. She tried to speak but couldn't because of the hold daddy had on her. Daddy looked back at me, his face contorted with anger.
    "Get back to your room! Now!"
    "Daddy, you're hurting mommy!" I ran to him and jumped on his arm,

putting all my weight on it. He didn't budge his hand from mommy, but he used his free hand to push me away. When I tried pulling him away again, he finally released mommy. That was the last thing I remember before seeing his fist come flying to my face.

"Damn it."

Eve was back in Dr. Woodrow's office, safe and sound. Her mother was still dead, but then again, so was Tony now. The latter was, of course, Eve's doing. She still couldn't conjure up the feeling of remorse. She wondered if that was normal. Should she feel sorry for stealing the life of the man who took her mother and her innocence away from her?

"Are you okay, Eve?" Dr. Woodrow observed Eve. She had heard many things in her years of being a psychiatrist. It didn't save her from empathizing with Eve's tragic past.

Eve nodded, not trusting her voice.

"That was a pretty powerful memory. Is that the first time you recall knowing your father was abusive to your mother?"

"Yes," Eve responded quietly.

"And the first time he hit you?"

"That hard, yes."

"He had hit you before that?"

"He's always been abusive — in one way or another." She knew she was evasive, but she wasn't ready for that conversation, yet.

Dr. Woodrow merely nodded and wrote a note in her leather-bound notebook. **Father possibly sexually abusive. Will wait for the patient to disclose when comfortable doing so.**

"And is that the last time you tried helping your mother?" the doctor asked at last.

Eve couldn't help the stab of guilt that shot through her. A lump formed in her throat, and she struggled to swallow it down.

Willamena saw the wave of emotions flash across Eve's face. She saw Eve literally try to swallow down the guilt. "Eve, you were so young, and he hurt you so badly. It is only natural for you to have been afraid to stand up to him again."

"I should have risked it for my mother."

"Do you think she wanted that?"

Eve hesitated, hearing her mother's voice in her head. *'Don't ever do that again, baby girl. I can handle him. Please don't make him hurt you like that again. Stay away from him as much as you can.'*

"Eve?"

"No. She didn't want that."

"Can you begin to tell yourself that you did what you had to do to keep from being hurt? Can you forgive yourself for doing what you know your mother wanted you to do?"

After taking a deep breath and letting it out slowly, Eve answered. "I can try."

Chapter Six

"I would move here just for this pie," Lainey said with a full mouth of cherry pie. She looked up and saw Eve and Bella staring at her. "What?"

"Wainey, you siwwy!"

"You have some right," Eve gestured to her own chin and laughed at the slight blush on Lainey's beautiful face.

"Shut up," Lainey muttered good-naturedly. "You just don't know how to enjoy such delicacies."

"Oh, believe me, I do."

Lainey's blush deepened when Eve winked at her. It was such a slippery slope they were playing on. Was the flirting fair to either one of them? At this moment, Lainey didn't want to think about that. She simply wanted to enjoy her company, the hint of how it used to be between them, and her pie.

"Good, bug?" Eve let Lainey — and herself — off the hook. She always felt bolder when they traveled together. Of course, flirting was as far as she would dare take it these days. No matter how hard Lainey was to resist, Eve reminded herself constantly of the decision she made. If that didn't work, she would call Adam.

Bella nodded enthusiastically. It was the toddler's first-time visiting Ellie's Diner. Eve was quite sure it wouldn't be her last. In fact, she was afraid Bella would demand an Ellie's Diner be opened in New York. Lainey would back her up one-hundred percent. *I wonder if Ellie would consider franchising*, Eve thought with amusement.

"It looks like everyone is enjoying their dessert." Ellie Montgomery, the owner of Ellie's Diner, smiled at Bella. By the looks of it, there was as much pie on the little girl's face as there was in her tummy. Ellie loved it. She remembered when her daughter Jessie was that young. She missed those days sometimes.

"I think we're going to need a couple of pieces to take back to the hotel," Eve laughed, giving their new friend a wink. Having such a wonderful establishment so close to her gallery would undoubtedly be a draw. Once her patrons had a taste of Ellie's cooking, the diner would be an instant favorite. That's why, even though Ellie didn't specialize in catering, Eve was confident she made the right choice. *At least I can do that in one area of my life.*

"You got it," Ellie chuckled, and held up a full pot of coffee. "Would you like more coffee?"

Desperate to ignore this newfound voice in her head, Eve nodded. Besides, the coffee was as good as the food in this place. "Please. Lainey?"

Lainey smiled cheekily as she took the last bite of her pie. "I'll never get to sleep tonight, but it's too good to pass up. Hit me."

Eve sat back and watched Lainey chat amicably with Ellie as she filled their cups. God, she loved this playful, easygoing side of Lainey. It was as if a switch was flipped when Jack wasn't around, and Lainey could let go and be her happy-go-lucky self. With her husband, Lainey was more reserved and quieter. Almost like a different person. This relaxed side of her best friend? This was the side Eve loved to see.

Across the table, Lainey was having similar thoughts. Though hers ran towards how Eve seemed rather tense since picking her up that morning. The five-hour plane ride had been unusually quiet other than Bella's occasional ramblings when she was awake. Eve barely said a word. Something was bothering her best friend, and Lainey didn't know what to do about it. Eve had made it clear that asking her how a therapy session went was the wrong thing to do. So, Lainey would wait. And worry.

The thoughts of both women, along with Ellie's important conversation with Bella about cartoon characters, were interrupted when the bells above the diner door jingled. Like a wildfire, Blaise — the florist making the arrangements for Eve's gallery opening — stormed in. The fiery woman was muttering something about an infuriating man, laced with expletives that Eve wasn't sure were appropriate for her young daughter's ears. The only thing that made it acceptable was Eve was sure Bella didn't understand most of Blaise's insults that were most likely some New Zealand slang.

"Blaise, dear, there are children present."

Eve chuckled at the sweet, yet bluntly disapproving way Ellie scolded her friend.

"Sorry. But that man . . . ugh! I need my tea. And red velvet." Blaise finally realized who she was standing next to. "Oh! I'm sorry." She gave Eve and Lainey an apologetic smile and tweaked Bella's little nose. It was possibly the only part of her face that didn't have pie on it.

"Sure, *now* you're sorry," Ellie muttered with a laugh.

"It's quite alright." Eve tried handing Bella a napkin, but it was refused. Eve shook her head and shrugged her shoulders. Bath time was going to be an event. "How are you, Blaise?"

"I'm good. Though, I'd feel much better with a cup of tea and some red velvet," Blaise responded with a pointed look at Ellie.

"You know where the kitchen is. *I'm* actually working."

Blaise huffed. "Fine. But I also require my best friend's ear so that I can bit, er, *complain* about a certain someone." She turned back to Eve, struck as always by the sheer beauty of the woman. "I hope to see you again when I'm in a better frame of mind."

"We'll stop in your shop tomorrow to show Bella some of your flowers. Maybe she can pick some of her favorites for the opening."

"Perfect!" Blaise smiled at the three of them and took off towards the kitchen.

"Sorry about that," Ellie laughed. "There are only two things that make her tolerable when she's in a mood. Especially when Greyson Steele is the cause."

"Tea and cake?" Lainey asked with a smile.

"More so the whiskey that goes in the tea and then the cake," Ellie explained with an eye roll. "I'll get a couple of pieces of pie ready for you ladies to take with you. If you need anything else, please let Charity know." Ellie took a deep breath. "*Three, two, one.*"

"Ellie!" Blaise called from the kitchen.

Eve laughed when Ellie cocked an eyebrow at her. As the diner owner walked away, Eve looked at her daughter. Bella watched the blonde woman until she disappeared behind the kitchen door. Then, Eve *swore* she saw her two-year-old shake her head, shrug, and turn her attention back to her pie.

Lainey laughed out loud. "Oh my God, she is *definitely* your daughter!"

"You saw that, too!"

Lainey, still laughing, nodded. "You are in so much trouble."

In true Eve Sumptor fashion, the penthouse suite they were staying in was beyond luxurious. Lainey had never seen such a beautiful hotel room before. Room, however, was sorely understating the place. At more than 5,000 square feet, the "room" was bigger than Lainey's entire house. It was considerably larger than what they needed, or what they usually stayed in when they were there. But Lainey was sure Eve was giving Bella the star treatment.

They had watched a movie in the media room, Bella got her bath in an enormous deep-soaking tub, and they played games until Bella could no longer keep her eyes open. Lainey became concerned at one point when, during a particularly competitive game of hide and seek, they were unable to find the toddler. As it turned out, Bella had fallen asleep under the colossal bed.

Despite having enough room to spread out and have sections to themselves, the three decided to sleep in the same bedroom. *That* had been Bella's idea. However, neither Lainey nor Eve refused. And that's where Lainey was now. Though a sprawled-out Bella separated her and Eve, Lainey still felt a bit flustered being in bed with Eve. She didn't think Eve was having the same problem since she was fast asleep.

Then she heard a sound coming from Eve. With the instinct of a mother, Lainey knew immediately Eve was in the throes of a nightmare. Wary of waking Bella during such a time, Lainey quietly rolled out of bed and went to Eve's side. She knelt and took Eve's hand just as she began to move.

"*Eve? Eve, honey, you're having a nightmare. You need to wake up.*" Lainey rubbed her thumb across the back of Eve's hand. She had read that abruptly waking someone from a nightmare could cause them to lash out. With Bella so close, Lainey tried calmly bringing Eve out of her restless sleep. Eve mumbled something Lainey had heard before. With a gentle touch, she pushed Eve's bangs from her clammy forehead. "*Eve, you have to wake up, honey, please. It's a dream. Only a dream. I'm right here.*"

Eve woke suddenly, her eyes staring straight into Lainey's. "*Lainey.*" She sat up, scrubbing her face with trembling hands. "I'm sorry."

"Please, don't be. Was it Tony, again?" Lainey asked softly, glancing in Bella's direction.

"How did you know?"

"You said 'don't hurt her.' I've heard that from you before."

Eve didn't respond so Lainey motioned towards the door with her head. She was still holding Eve's hand and wasn't ready to let it go, yet. They quietly made their way out of the room and Lainey guided them towards the kitchen.

"Do you want some tea?" Lainey asked after Eve settled herself at the kitchen island.

"Does it come with whiskey?" Eve asked, causing Lainey to chuckle.

"I'll have to see what's in the mini bar."

"With how much this room costs, that mini bar better be super huge and stocked with all of the finest liquors ever made," Eve joked.

"That may be the first time I've ever heard you complain about the price of something." Lainey gave Eve a crooked grin.

"I wasn't complaining. I was merely making an observation," Eve winked. "And just so you know, I didn't pick this place. Bella did. We were looking at hotels on the computer together, and she clicked a link. Apparently, she liked the way this room looked." Eve shrugged.

"So much trouble," Lainey mumbled with a laugh and placed a steaming cup of tea in front of Eve. "No whiskey, but it is chamomile."

"Practically the same thing." Eve smiled and thanked Lainey. She took a drink, burning her tongue slightly. She didn't mind. The pain reminded her she was awake. They sat in silence for a while. Eve could tell Lainey had questions, yet she said nothing. "You want to ask," Eve said finally.

"I won't," Lainey responded evenly.

Silence lingered a bit longer this time before Eve began to talk. She told Lainey about her last therapy session, about having to relive the day Tony struck her so hard she lost the courage to help her mother, about the nightmares she's having now. Once she opened up, she couldn't stop.

"My mother was in this one," Eve said of the nightmare she just awoke from. "But it was different than the others. I wasn't a little girl. I was me. Tony was still dead by my hand, and I still held the gun. But none of that mattered. He kills her, and there was nothing I could do. I couldn't save her." She shook her head. "I don't know if I can do this, Lainey. I don't know if I can handle going through this over and over again."

"Then take a break from therapy," Lainey suggested cautiously.

Eve raised a perfectly sculpted brow. "You're the one who thought it was a good idea to do this."

"And I stand by that. But I know you, Eve. You don't like feeling out of control, and that's what therapy is doing to you. I think that by taking a break and making your own schedule of when you go, you can take back some of your power."

Eve blinked at Lainey. It wasn't often that people surprised her, but Lainey did it quite often. "How many psychology books have you read?"

Lainey took a sip of her tea before responding. "Enough to know that rejecting therapy because you feel out of control won't help you."

Eve almost smiled. Lainey was beginning to sound like Dr. Woodrow. The only reason she didn't smile was because . . . well, she was beginning to sound like Dr. Woodrow. Eve could only handle one therapist in her life at a time.

"Why am I spending a ton of money on Woodrow when I can just talk to you?" It was meant to be a joke. Mostly.

Lainey shook her head. "Oh, no. I don't have the heart to see you hurting. Woodrow can keep her day job. I'll keep mine."

"As my BFF?"

Another look passed between them before Lainey responded with a simple, uncomplicated "mmhmm."

There was more to that "mmhmm" than being an innocent BFF, and it caught Eve off-guard. Being flustered was rare for Eve. It was just one more thing that made her feel out of control. "You should get some sleep."

"I can keep you company if you don't want to drink alone," Lainey suggested.

"It's tea. Without whiskey," Eve laughed. "But I do enjoy your company, so thank you."

This time, the silence was comfortable. Each woman was lost in their thoughts. Eve wondered how she was going to get rid of these dreams again. It had taken her years the first time around. She didn't have the patience for years this time around. Taking a break was probably a good idea presently. But if she wanted to beat this, for good, Eve had a feeling she would have to face *everything*.

Lainey had her own demons to deal with. She positively could *not* tell Eve that she was reading the psychology books for herself as much as for Eve. Jack would never allow Lainey to go to therapy. He would think of it as a blemish on the Stanton name. Besides, what did Lainey have to be depressed enough about to see a therapist? Didn't *he* give her everything she needed?

Eve carefully watched the emotions on Lainey's face and read her perfectly. *Like an open book.* "What is it?"

"Hmm? Oh, nothing. I guess I'm just a little tired."

Eve, of course, didn't believe her, but she wouldn't push. Instead, she stood and held her hand out. "Come on. Let's go to bed."

Eve and Lainey stood in the middle of the gallery and took in the progress. Despite having a few art pieces, the place was in disarray with construction. It was, however, coming together quite well. Once the interior was done, it would be just as much a part of the exhibits as the actual art.

"Adam is doing a great job," Lainey said, ending the silence between them. After her inappropriate dream last night, she wasn't sure what she could or should say. Adam seemed like a safe subject.

Eve glanced over at Lainey. "Yes, he is." Of course, she had noticed Lainey's quietness this morning. Now, she was sure she knew why. Especially if Lainey's dreams were anything like Eve's after their talk over tea.

"How is his company doing?"

When he was asked to be a partner at his former company, Adam had decided that starting his own firm was what he really wanted to do. And, with Eve's backing — financially and supportively — his firm was flourishing.

"Very well. Having a client such as Sumptor, Inc. or Sumptor Galleries has opened the door to many other valuable contracts."

Lainey heard a tone, but before she could address it her attention was pulled elsewhere.

"Wait! Not there!" She touched Eve gently on the forearm. "Sorry. I'll be right back."

"Go get 'em, tiger," Eve laughed, grateful for the distraction. She knew she had let her annoyance seep through. Unfortunately, she didn't know how to explain it. To herself or Lainey. Having dodged it, for now, didn't mean Lainey wouldn't remember later. She heaved a resigned sigh and looked over at her daughter. They had set up a little art station for her, gave her a smock, some art media, and let her go to town. "What are you drawing, bug?"

Bella looked up, a determined look on her face, then smiled at her momma. "You, me, and Wainey, momma! See?" She picked up the colorful sheet of paper. "In da big woom!"

Eve's eyebrows shot up. The drawing was, indeed, a child's rendering of the three of them in the same bed. Adam was going to *love* that. *Hmm. Perhaps that's one for the office.*

"It's beautiful, bug! I bet Lainey will love it, too!"

Bella grinned proudly, then went back to her work. Eve watched for a while as Bella picked colors, talked to herself, hummed, and ignored everything else around her. It was precisely how Eve used to be when she painted. *Used to be*, Eve thought sadly.

"I heard you were in town."

Eve turned from Bella and her own dismal thoughts and saw Rebecca Cuinn standing in front of her. Judging by looks alone, one would never guess that the petite, beautiful woman with flowing blonde hair was a dominatrix. However, once you got to know Rebecca, you saw how power didn't always come in big packages.

"Mistress." Eve dipped her head in greeting.

Rebecca clicked her tongue. "The only time you get to call me that is if you're in my room." She gave Eve a small hug. "It's serendipity that you're here."

"Oh? Are you here socially or for business?"

Rebecca tilted her head. "A bit of both, I suppose."

Eve gestured to a more private area where she could talk freely with Rebecca yet keep a watchful eye on Bella. "You have piqued my interest."

"I think I've found the perfect artist for you."

Eve raised a brow. "Since when did you start procuring artists?"

"Since I started fucking her." Rebecca had the good grace to wince at her own words. She quickly glanced at Bella, satisfied that her little slip up wasn't heard by the toddler.

Eve took a wild guess. "Cass?"

Not too long ago, Rebecca had shown up in New York desperate to escape feelings she was having for Cass Giles. For two months,

Eve watched as Rebecca worked tirelessly on business proposals for both Sumptor, Inc. and Sumptor Galleries. The picture of Rebecca as a brilliant businesswoman was easier to believe. However, regardless of how brilliant she was, Eve couldn't stand to see Rebecca so miserable personally. She eventually convinced Rebecca to go back home to LA and try to work things out. Apparently, it worked.

"Yes," Rebecca confessed. "We ran into each other a couple of weeks after I got back. I guess that was serendipity as well."

"And she's an artist?"

"An amazing one. I was going to call you to discuss looking at Cassidy's work as a favor to me. Then I found out you were here."

"Wow. She must be amazing if you're coming to me for a favor." In the years they'd known each other, Rebecca had never struck Eve as someone who paid much attention to art. Eve supposed that would be changing.

"I've never been so moved by the stroke of paint," Rebecca said. Then she remembered who she was talking to. "Present company's work excluded."

Eve chuckled. "Good save. But my ego is healthy enough to realize that art is subjective." She thought for a moment. "Alright, I'll take a look. Have her bring in her portfolio before I leave."

"Therein lies the problem." Rebecca continued when Eve merely looked at her. Eve Sumptor wasn't one with copious amounts of patience when it came to her galleries. "She's not what you would call a 'conventional' artist."

"Meaning?"

"Meaning she never thought she was canvas or gallery material. If you want to see her work, you'll have to drive around and look at the walls."

Both of Eve's eyebrows shot up. "Graffiti?"

It wasn't something Eve was opposed to. In fact, she thought graffiti artists were remarkably talented. It would quite possibly be perfectly accepted here at the LA gallery.

"Not graffiti. Murals. Beautiful, powerful murals." Rebecca saw skepticism on Eve's face. "Look at them. Please? If you don't agree with me, then we move on. No hard feelings. If you do agree, maybe you can convince her to put her work on canvas."

Eve pursed her lips. "Very well. Expect a very critical eye."

"I wouldn't ask for anything less from you. Thank you." Rebecca pulled a piece of paper out of her back pocket. "Here are the addresses of some of her work." She craned her head and looked around the gallery. There was still a lot of work to do, but she could tell it was going to be incredible. What a break it would be for Cassidy if Eve showed her work. "Is Lainey here?"

Eve glanced up from the paper she had been looking at. "Yes. She's around here somewhere giving someone hell for doing something wrong."

The thought of sweet Lainey Stanton with a whip caused Rebecca to laugh. "She would make quite the dominatrix," she teased. She knew of Eve and Lainey's past. She also knew Eve was very sensitive about it. However, she couldn't resist a joke or a chance to give her opinion now and then.

Eve laughed. She would never have agreed if Lainey had not changed since their first meeting. But now? Oh, yeah. Lainey's confidence was becoming a force to be reckoned with. "You may be right."

"How long will you be here? Perhaps we can have dinner or lunch?"

"With your new girlfriend?"

Rebecca nearly choked at the thought. "We — we're not there, yet."

"Fair enough," Eve allowed with a sly smile. Since Rebecca always gave her hell about Lainey, it was going to be fun being able to return the favor. "We're here for a couple more days. I'll text you if we have some time for lunch or dinner."

"Perfect. Give Lainey my love."

Eve cocked a brow at the mischievous wink. "Goodbye, Mistress." She could hear Rebecca's laugh even as the door closed behind her. *I need to rethink some of my friendships*, Eve thought with mirth before going back to Bella and kneeling next to her. "How are you doing, bug?"

Bella muttered a somewhat enthusiastic good, but never looked up from her work-in-progress. Eve couldn't blame her. She was the same way when she was absorbed in her work.

"Was that Rebecca?"

Eve looked up at a slightly flustered Lainey. "Yes. She gives her love."

"Well, if that's why she was here, she could have waited. Maybe I should go visit her place of business," Lainey joked.

"Everyone is a comedienne," Eve muttered and stood. She smiled wickedly at Lainey. "Rebecca said you'd make a great dominatrix. Do you think she's right?"

"On a serious note," Lainey chuckled nervously, purposefully ignoring Eve's question. "Did she get her head out of her *ass* regarding that woman she was pining over?"

Eve laughed heartily. "Oh my god, I wish you had been here to say that to her face."

"Uh, that woman has a whip and knows how to use it. I'm perfectly fine just saying it to you."

With a shake of her head, Eve draped an arm around Lainey's shoulders. She dipped her head close to Lainey's ear. *"I'll never tell,"* she whispered.

Lainey managed to control the shiver that made a leisurely journey through her body. "So," she cleared her throat, "What are you working on Bella?"

Bella distractedly slid one of her finished "works" towards the edge of the table.

Reluctantly, Eve removed her arm and picked up the drawing. "It's the three of us in the huge bed," she explained. "Isn't it beautiful?"

Lainey's eyes widened. "It's — it's wonderful!" Bella looked up at her and beamed. "I think it would look perfect in your momma's office!"

"Yeah, momma! Put in oppice?"

"I wouldn't dream of putting it anywhere else, bug." She eyed Lainey who was failing abysmally at hiding her laughter. "Is everything back to specifications?" she asked, nodding towards the construction workers.

Lainey rolled her eyes. "Yes. You know, you're much more intimidating than I am. If you had been there, it wouldn't have taken as long as it did."

"I doubt that. Besides, I was allowing you to spread your wings and give more input." Eve bumped her shoulder to Lainey's. "Now that you've taken care of everything want to go for a ride?"

"You're ready to leave? We have so much work to do."

"We *will* be working." She handed Lainey the paper with addresses. "It turns out that Cass is an artist. A muralist."

"Interesting! Rebecca either *really* likes this girl to come to you for a favor. Or, Cass is good at what she does." Lainey pursed her lips. "That didn't come out right."

Eve laughed. "I know what you meant. Let's go find out which one it is. Bug, you ready to go?"

"No!"

"Okay. We'll be back in a while. We're going to look at huge paintings on the walls of buildings. Maybe get ice cream. Ready, Lainey?"

"Let's go!"

The two women began walking towards the door.

"Wait!" Bella ran after them as fast as she could. "I wanna see walls!"

Lainey looked at Eve. "Art over ice cream? Definitely yours."

Chapter Seven
Therapy

No remorse.

"You've missed a few sessions, Eve." Dr. Woodrow glanced up at Eve with slight disapproval. When her assistant relayed to her that Eve had rescheduled multiple sessions, Willamena became concerned. She knew memories of Eve's past would be painful to relive, but as a therapist, Willamena knew it was what was best for Eve. Trying to forget it was one thing. Fighting through it could mean never having to remember to forget.

"Sorry about that. I am a busy woman." It was rare for Eve to feel guilty about working. Of course, that wasn't her only reason for not coming to sessions. She was trying to do as Lainey said and take back some of her control. Unfortunately, Adam didn't quite see it the same way. He wanted whatever this was that Eve was going through to be over. According to him, that couldn't happen if she wasn't "putting in the effort."

"Have you been able to paint?" Woodrow asked pointedly. She was confident she already knew the answer.

Eve grimaced sheepishly. "No." She sighed. "I'm not avoiding this. I want to paint. But I do have galleries to fill and run."

"Hmm."

Dr. Woodrow scribbled a few notes in her leather-bound notebook — **_Patient is exhibiting the need to control the situation. By making her own schedule, she wants me to know that she has command of her situation._** — then focused on Eve once again. Her face gentled when she thought about where she would ask Eve to go next. This wasn't going to be an easy session.

"Would you like to talk about the day you found your mother?"

Eve fought back the bile that was her automatic reaction when she thought about that day. Her head screamed NO. But what if this was it? What if Dr. Woodrow truly was her way to get past whatever it was blocking her creativity? *Shit.*

"What about it?"

Though Eve tried sounding strong, Willamena heard the fear. "What do you remember about that day?"

"Coming home and finding my mother dead," Eve answered flatly. *Turn off the emotions, and it won't hurt. As much.*

Dr. Woodrow sighed quietly. "Eve, in order for this to work, you're going to have to let go of the attitude. I realize you use it as a defense mechanism, but it has no place here." In an unusual display of affection, Dr. Woodrow leaned forward and touched Eve's hand briefly. It was unprofessional, but there were times when a patient needed to know they weren't alone. "There's nothing to be afraid of in here."

Eve took a deep breath, closed her eyes and felt completely raw as she thought back to that day.

"What do I remember about that day?" Eve repeated. "I remember my life coming to an abrupt end. I remember losing the one person in this world that loved me." Tears brimmed, but just like that day, they never fell.

Dr. Woodrow looked at Eve sympathetically and wrote a couple of notes before she continued. "You knew right away that it wasn't suicide, didn't you?"

"Yes." There had been no doubts, even in Eve's fourteen-year-old mind, that her father killed her mother. No doubts that the "suicide note" was forced. Marie would have never left Eve with Tony if she had a choice. Never.

"You were the one that brought your father to justice?" Willamena had done her homework when it came to Eve. She knew the answers to questions such as this. However, if she could get Eve to give her account of things, it would help Willamena assess the situation.

Though Eve knew it wasn't what the doctor was asking, she could feel the gun in her hands, the struggle to gain control, the squeeze of the trigger, and the warmth of blood flowing through her fingers. His and mine. Yes, Eve would agree that she brought Tony to justice.

"I turned him in, yes," she answered finally.

"How did you feel about that?"

"Like I was too late."

Dr. Woodrow looked up sharply. It wasn't the answer she had been expecting. "You didn't feel as though you got revenge?"

"My mother was dead. Tony was alive. Even in jail, he was able to make my life hell. He killed my soul that day. So, no, I didn't feel vengeful. I just felt . . . late."

"Did that change after Tony died?" Willamena needed to tread lightly here. From what she had read, Tony's death was self-defense. Perhaps even accidental. Even so, taking a life had to be challenging to live with.

"From my hands, you mean?" Eve asked. The huskiness of her voice made it nearly unrecognizable even to herself.

"Well, since you brought that up, did you feel remorse for Tony's death?"

"No."

Willamena felt no surprise at the answer. She understood where Eve was coming from, especially after having just spoken about her mother's death. She nodded slightly and made a note. **Patient expected me to be disappointed in her lack of remorse. She may feel "broken" because of that lack.**

"Okay." Dr. Woodrow glanced at Eve's hands, noticing they trembled despite how tightly Eve held them together. "I think that's enough for today. Next session, we'll talk about what happened after you ran away from the authorities."

Fantastic, Eve thought sarcastically. That was something she wasn't looking forward to. Her only hope for getting through tonight's and the next session was knowing that her baby girl was at home waiting for her. That, and the fact that Lainey was picking her up. That thought alone allowed her to stand, albeit on shaky legs. She smoothed her black skirt free of wrinkles.

"You should have wine for these sessions, Doctor." Eve gave Dr. Woodrow a wry grin. "Or perhaps some brandy."

Willamena chuckled. "I'll keep that in mind. Eve?" she called out as Eve's hand reached for the door. As a doctor, she normally would keep personal thoughts to herself and allow her patients to come to terms with their feelings. However, because she thought Eve needed it, she broke her rules. "For what it's worth, I think your lack of remorse for your father's death is natural. You were defending yourself and someone you love dearly. You did for Lainey what you felt you couldn't do for your mother. You weren't too late."

Eve felt a faint flush creep up her neck. A lightness settled over her in a way she hadn't felt in years. If ever.

"Thank you."

Chapter Eight

"*Excusez-Moi?*"

Lainey turned from inspecting the changes she made on her display to find a sharply dressed, slick man standing behind her. Slick was the perfect way to describe him with his overly gelled hair, expensive, designer suit, and shoes that were so shiny she could use them to put her make-up on.

"May I help you?" she asked with a polite smile.

"Ouí, er, yes. I am looking for . . ." The tall man checked the paper he held in his hand. "Ms. Eve Sumptor."

For reasons unbeknownst to her then, his heavy French accent raised the hairs on the back of her neck. "Do you have an appointment?"

"No. It is, how you say, important that I speak to her immediately."

"What is the nature of your business?" Lainey asked. She may be over-stepping her boundaries, but she had a gut feeling she needed to.

"It is private. Now, you will tell her I am here, yes?"

"No. I am Ms. Sumptor's assistant. I'll need to know what this is regarding before I interrupt her important meeting." There was no meeting, of course. In actuality, Eve was going through heaps of new artists' works to make up for a sudden vacancy they had at the LA Gallery.

As it turned out during that drive in LA weeks back, they found Cass's work to be as awe-inspiring as Rebecca had suggested. As a result, Eve immediately wanted Cass as her featured artist during the opening of the gallery. That news did not sit so well with one of the artists they had already procured. He had been livid when a "no-talent, lesbian graffiti thug" was chosen over him as the highlighted artist. Lainey had decided to get rid of him altogether with no complaints from Eve.

The man huffed. "Very well. I am Guillaume Cortet. I am the attorney for Madame Bussiere . . ."

"No," Lainey interrupted immediately when she heard the name. She pointed towards the elevators. "Out."

"*S'il vous plait,* there is a matter that I must speak to Ms. Sumptor about privately."

"Nope. Whatever that woman wants, she can go to hell."

"Madame . . ."

"Don't call me that. Look, I'm sorry, but I don't care what Bussiere wants. Tell her never to try to contact Ms. Sumptor again."

"*Elle est morte,*" he said with an air of displeasure directed at Lainey's blatant disrespect.

Lainey knew only a couple of French words because of Eve, but even she could translate something like *morte*. Dead. Madame Bussiere was dead. Should she feel sorry for being relieved by that news? If she was dead, that meant she could no longer hurt Eve. Right? But then, why was this man here on Bussiere's behalf?

"Be that as it may, Ms. Sumptor has no interest in anything having to do with that woman. Now, please, I'm asking you to leave without making a scene."

The man looked down his nose at Lainey. She was sure he thought her to be quite uncivilized. If that's how she had to be perceived to protect Eve, so be it.

"Very well. You will see to it that she gets these papers, ouí?"

Out of pure instinct, Lainey reached for the envelope that was rudely thrust at her. *Sure. I'll see that she gets them,* she thought sourly.

She bit her cheek to keep from laughing when the shiny man slipped slightly on the polished floor as he pivoted away from her.

"*Au revoir,*" she muttered as she tested the weight of the package she held and struggled with what to do. If her mood was anything to judge by, Eve had had a difficult therapy session the night before. Lainey couldn't bring herself to make it worse by delivering this. At least, not yet. She would give Eve a little time before having to deal with whatever Bussiere cooked up before dying.

"Everything okay?"

Lainey jumped a little at the sound of Eve's voice. From the balcony, that sensuous timbre reverberated throughout the gallery, weaving in and out of statues and sculptures, hitting Lainey from every angle. She turned, hiding the envelope behind her back. She felt terrible about what she was doing but had to believe it was the right thing for now.

"Yes, everything is fine. How long have you been standing there?"

Eve stretched, the hem of her shirt lifting enough to give Lainey a glimpse of the smooth skin beneath. "Not long," she answered, oblivious to the chaos she was creating in Lainey's mind. "I thought I heard someone come in, so I thought I'd take a break and see if you needed any help."

I definitely need help, Lainey thought with a blush. "Um, no. Just a solicitor." That was the truth, right? Partial? Wasn't that what they were called in France? Lainey had no clue, but she was going with it anyway. "All is good."

Eve eyed Lainey. Something was off. Then again, Eve had just spent the last two hours sifting through portfolios of hundreds of artists from all media. For all she knew, *she* could be the one that was off.

"Okay. Well, I'm starving. Food?"

Lainey looked at her watch and laughed. "You're the boss. If you want to have lunch at ten a.m., who am I refuse?"

"Brunch," Eve corrected with faux haughtiness. "Lunch comes later."

Lainey shook her head. "I'll have something sent up."

"Will you eat with me? Or at least keep me company?"

The heft of the envelope in her hands only increased as the minutes ticked by. Or perhaps that was the heft of her conscience.

"Sure!" It was a tad overly exuberant, but luckily Eve didn't seem to notice. "I'll be up when the food gets here. Anything, in particular, you'd like?"

Eve shrugged as she turned back towards her office. "You know what I like."

"Mom?" Kevin frowned when his mom continued to stare off at whatever the heck she was staring at. She sat at the kitchen table, a thick envelope trapped under her fidgeting hands. "Mom?" he tried again.

Lainey blinked and looked up at her oldest son in confusion. "What are you doing up?"

"I could ask you the same thing. It's like three in the morning. Have you even been to bed, yet?" She'd been in a mood since she returned home from work. Kevin didn't think much about it at the time because things were still done. Dinner was still on the table, she still spoke to him about his day, and his dad was still pissy about trivial things. All in all, it was a typical night. But his mom sitting here alone in the dark was not normal.

"Can't sleep," Lainey murmured. "How about you? You're usually dead to the world at this time. Something on your mind?"

He knew she was deflecting the conversation away from her. That was okay with Kevin for now since he did have something he wanted to talk to her about. But eventually, he wanted to know what was in the envelope and if it was going to affect him and Darren.

"Kinda. I'm hungry." He went to the fridge and grabbed a few things to make a sandwich.

Lainey shook her head. "I know you and Darren are growing boys, but I seriously wonder where the heck you put all that food."

"In mah belly!" Kevin patted his flat belly for emphasis, then shrugged. "Football takes a lot of energy." He eyed his mom, gauging her mood. She was distracted, but not necessarily upset. "Hey, ma. Could I run something by you?"

There was something in Kevin's voice that caught Lainey's attention. For the first time since she received that stupid envelope, she pushed it to the side and stopped thinking about it.

"Of course."

"Cool." He didn't dare look at her. Instead, he busied himself with making a fat sandwich. He wasn't even that hungry, but it gave him something to do to counteract his nervousness. "So, um, what would you say if I told you I didn't want to play football anymore?"

Lainey's eyebrows shot up. Kevin had been playing football since he was five years old. As far as she could tell he loved it. And it had been the one thing Jack actually helped him with, though Lainey didn't always agree with his teaching techniques. He would continuously tell Kevin that football would teach him to be a man instead of the importance of team building skills. Jack was *not* going to like this news.

"Is this something you've thought long and hard about?"

"Yeah. It wasn't an easy decision, mom. But it's just not fun anymore."

"Can you talk me through why that is?"

Kevin sighed deeply and took a big bite of his sandwich. This was why he loved talking to his mom. She listened, discussed, and advised. Unlike his dad who simply demanded whatever *he* wanted.

"Some of the guys on the team are like straight up bullies." He started to use the back of his hand to wipe his mouth, then remembered his mom hated that. So, he picked up a napkin. "They pick on kids smaller or different than them, and I can't stand it. And the way they treat girls?" He just shook his head.

Lainey felt an overwhelming sense of pride in her son. Darren, her younger son, had always been the sensitive one. Kevin, on the other hand, was more analytical. It's what made him a good leader as the quarterback on the football team. To hear he was not willing to tolerate bullying made her heart soar.

"Have you told your coach about it?" She knew it was

unpopular to be a "snitch," but mean kids were so much more dangerous these days.

"Yeah, I did. He shrugged it off. Said they were just messing around. This isn't messing around, ma. They're *harassing* these kids. I don't want to be associated with that anymore."

"Would you like me to talk to him? Or the principal?"

"No!" He cleared his throat. "Sorry. I didn't mean to yell at you. But I can't have my mommy fighting my battles for me. I'll talk to my principal when I get in tomorrow. Hopefully, he does something, or I'm going to have to quit, mom."

Lainey opened her mouth, then closed it again. She didn't like being called his "mommy" in such a derogatory way. But he was right. He was a young man now and needed to figure things out himself. If things got bad, however, he better be ready to have his *mommy* fighting for him.

"Very well," she said reluctantly. "I'll leave it to you."

"Thanks. Now the hard part. What do you think dad will say?"

Oh. Jack. "I'm sure he'll understand." *Yeah, right.*

Kevin snorted. "Yeah, right. I don't know why he cares, though. He never goes to the games. I think he likes telling people his son is the quarterback on a varsity team."

"I'm sure that's not true, Kevin." The problem was, she *wasn't* sure about that. Kevin was right. Jack never did go to the games. He didn't like his schedule being disrupted. However, he never missed an opportunity to brag to anyone who would listen that his oldest son was the "leader of the football team." His words. He's already prepping Darren to follow in Kevin's footsteps even though their youngest son would rather be in a band uniform than a football uniform.

"You're constantly taking up for him, mom." He lifted his chin towards the envelope his mom was failing miserably at hiding from him. "I take it those aren't divorce papers."

Lainey nearly choked on her spit. "N—no. Do you . . .?" She shook her head. She definitely wasn't ready for *that* discussion right now. Lainey tapped the envelope with her fingertips. "No, but I'm pretty sure I screwed up."

If those aren't divorce papers, then I agree, Kevin thought sourly but kept that thought to himself. "Wanna talk about it?"

Lainey debated for less than a minute. "I lied to Eve. Well, technically I kept something from her, but still. It wasn't like I wanted to lie to her, but she's been through so much lately. I didn't want to put her through more . . ."

"Mom. *Mom!*" Kevin took Lainey's hand in his. "Did you do it to protect her?"

"Yes."

"Then you did the right thing."

"That's not how this works, Kevin. Lying is lying. And Eve is *not* the type of person who tolerates . . ." She couldn't help but think of their affair. Both had been lying for years. Why was it that lying *to* Eve instead of *about* her is what felt wrong? "She doesn't like being thought of as weak. I'm afraid she'll see this as me thinking she was too weak."

"Mom, if I've learned anything from you it's that sometimes we have to do things that others won't like to save them from themselves. Keeping something harmful from Eve doesn't make her weak. It just means you care enough to help her. I think she'll see that."

"When did you get so smart?" Lainey sniffled. Her son was undeniably becoming a young man. *Damn it.*

"I was born that way," he laughed and squeezed her hand. "If it bothers you this much, mom, you're going to have to tell her. I don't think I've ever seen you this weird."

Lainey snatched her hand back with feigned indignation. "I am not weird."

"Of course, you're not," Kevin chuckled. "I should get to bed."

"Clean up your mess first. And if you want, I can tell your father about football."

"Nah. Thanks, but this is my deal, remember?" Kevin picked up his trash. "It'll all work out. I've also learned from you that you have to either live for yourself or lose yourself." He kissed her on top of the head. "Good night."

As he walked out of the room, his words sunk in. Did he think she had lost herself? Or was he proud of her for getting a job and living for herself? She shook her head. One problem at a time. Right now, she had to figure out how to break it to Eve that Bussiere was dead.

Eve stood back and assessed the board in front of her. After poring over hundreds of submissions for a new artist for Sumptor Gallery, LA, she finally narrowed the list down to twenty. Since the artist she was replacing turned out to be homophobic, Eve had decided only to include artists from the LGBTQ community to show her support.

"Ahem."

The quiet clearing of the throat caught Eve's attention, and she looked over her shoulder.

"Hey," she smiled at Lainey. "Come on in."

"This is, um, organized." Lainey's hands were shaking. All morning she had been going over and over what she would say to Eve about the visitor she had yesterday. After stalling for as long as she could, she realized that the sooner she did this, the sooner her stomach would stop hurting. Yet, she found herself stalling even longer by examining everything Eve had set up. "I see you've narrowed it down to dozens instead of hundreds."

Eve chuckled. "With no help from you, thank you very much."

"Someone has to run the gallery," Lainey teased back. Thank goodness her voice was steady and didn't betray her nervousness.

"That's what I have Mikey for, silly. This," she gestured to the board, "is all your fault."

"Ha! Like you would've let him get away with his hatefulness. Do you have a favorite?"

Eve glanced over at Lainey. When the word "yes" sprang to mind, it had nothing to do with what was on the board.

"One stands out more than the others, yes. Which one speaks to you?"

"Oh! Um . . ."

"You had no problem dismissing the other guy. Don't be shy now."

Lainey rolled her eyes at Eve. Not many people could get away with that, so Lainey tried to sneak an eye roll in as often as she could.

"Fine," she bumped Eve's hip to push her out of the way. As soon as she cleared her mind of her dilemma, there was one style that stood out to her. She pointed. "This one."

There was something about the red, yellow, and orange hues that stood out. Not just because they were vibrant, but because of the way they were used. If you looked at the painting with a critical eye, you could see the silhouette of a woman that the colors form. The violent strokes spoke of heartbreak and anger. Still, there was a softness around the woman. Lainey interpreted it as the woman in the painting caused pain but was also the subject of incredible love. It was tragically honest and beautiful.

"That's the one I chose as well," Eve said softly. "It looks like we'll be going to Italy soon."

"Italy?"

"Mmhmm. It seems H. Agosti is somewhat of a recluse. A representative submitted her work. We'll need to make sure H. agrees to have her work shown and without such demands that her rep is making." Eve turned to Lainey. "You will be able to go with me, yes?"

Lainey hesitated. After her conversation with Kevin, she knew Jack wasn't going to be in the most agreeable moods once he discovered Kevin's plans. She almost laughed out loud. That was nothing new. When it came to Lainey's job, he was *never* in an agreeable mood.

Eve felt a tad deflated. She had traveled many times by herself. It wasn't a big deal. However, she had gotten used to having Lainey as a companion. "If you can't . . ."

"No, I can," Lainey said quickly.

Eve studied Lainey for a moment. "What's wrong, Lainey? You've been quiet all morning. Are you and Jack doing all right?" She *hoped* that sounded like genuine concern. This therapy shit was messing with Eve's head, and she had to warn herself that Jack was not Tony.

Lainey sighed. "I don't know. I mean, he's Jack," she said as if that explained everything. Somehow, she thought Eve knew exactly what she meant. "Kevin told me last night that he wants to quit football." Okay, it wasn't *the* problem, but it was indeed *a* problem that they were going to have to deal with if Italy was in the cards. She nearly sighed at the thought of exploring Italy with Eve. They may travel for work, but Eve always seemed to carve out time to show Lainey the world.

Eve's perfectly arched brows shot up. "Seriously? But he's so good at it." She put a hand over her heart and feigned utter despair. "What will we do with our Friday nights now?"

Lainey laughed. Even though she wasn't a big football fan, Eve would sometimes accompany Lainey to the Kevin's games. She said it was to show support. Lainey believed it also had something to do with eating terrible hotdogs and giving Bella a different experience than what Eve had growing up.

"I'm sure Adam will enjoy having you back."

This time Eve rolled her eyes playfully. "He works late even when he's home. Big clients mean hours at the drafting table. He likes the peace and quiet when Bella and I have our girl time." She gestured to the couch that adorned her office. "Why is Kevin quitting football?"

Lainey sat, making room for Eve next to her, and explained about the bullying Kevin had spoken about. "He said it just wasn't fun for him anymore."

"You've raised some great kids, honey. I bet you're proud of him for taking a stand."

"I am beyond proud. I'm just afraid Jack won't be. Which always makes life *so* great," Lainey said sarcastically.

"So, that was the hesitation when I asked about Italy?"

"Part of it." Lainey got up and walked to the table near the door. She had discreetly deposited the envelope there when Eve had invited her in. With a deep breath, she took the envelope and sat back down. "This is the other part."

Eve frowned. "What is that?"

Another breath. "I lied to you yesterday. But *only* because you've been through a lot lately. And I care so much about you. I just wanted to protect you . . ."

"Lainey," Eve interrupted softly. "Tell me."

Breathe, Lainey. "The visitor we had yesterday, who I told you was a solicitor?" Eve nodded. "Technically, I didn't lie about that." Eve raised a brow and Lainey lowered her head. "He was a lawyer, Eve. For Madame Bussiere."

Eve blinked, and her heart skipped a couple of beats when she heard the name. "What did he want?"

"To give you this." Lainey lifted the envelope but didn't relinquish it. "Eve, she's dead." Lainey waited, but Eve said nothing. "Eve?"

"I heard you, Lainey."

"Are you okay?"

"I — I don't know. I thought I'd feel something. Relief? Vindicated. But I don't feel anything." Eve looked up at Lainey whose face was filled with compassion. "They're all dead, Lainey. Everyone who hurt me. Tony, Laurence, the other men that night, Billy. And now Bussiere. They're all gone."

"And you are the one left standing," Lainey reminded her gently. "You won, honey."

"Why doesn't it feel like it?"

"I think you're in shock. Maybe you'll feel different once this sinks in."

"Maybe," Eve said absently. "What's in it?" she asked, nodding towards the envelope.

"I don't know. I couldn't betray your privacy by opening it." It seemed like a silly thing to say since Lainey *did* keep this from Eve. But she had her limits.

"Will you?" Eve asked softly.

"Oh!" That was something Lainey hadn't prepared for. Did she even *want* to know what was inside? The thought took her back to the last time Eve received an envelope from Madame Bussiere. It had been devastating to Eve and Lainey had not been there for her.

This time, she could be. With that in mind, she opened the envelope with steady hands.

Eve's hands, however, trembled slightly and she clenched them together. She hoped to hell there weren't more photos of her in compromising positions. Just because she had to be in therapy and think about those times didn't mean Lainey needed a reminder.

"It's a bunch of legal papers," Lainey said interrupting Eve's inner musings. "And a letter that's in French." She looked up at Eve. "I can't read it, honey."

Eve held her hand out, grateful that it seemed steady enough. "Is that all?"

"Um, no. There's a check for . . . wow. $387,972." Lainey observed Eve as she scanned the letter. The woman was infuriatingly impossible to read. Eve's face never revealed a single emotion, yet Lainey felt as though she, herself, would pass out at any given moment.

"It's her share," Eve said finally. "That money is what she made off of my body." She smiled when Lainey dropped the check as though it were on fire. "The documents are deeds. She left me the café. Apparently, she wanted to atone for her mistakes before she died. The letter states that she wanted to contact me months ago but didn't feel she deserved forgiveness."

Eve had said it with such a lack of emotion that it took Lainey a moment to process what she had just heard before she shook her head. "That's one thing I agree with her about. She doesn't deserve it." She hesitated, realizing that wasn't her decision. "Do you?"

Eve remained quiet as she thought about how she felt. The truth was, she had no idea how to feel. It was apparent, as Eve reread the letter, that the old woman who brutalized her, sold her, and betrayed her had found some modicum of shame for her role in Eve's traumatic past. Did that — along with these inconsequential tokens — make up for *any* of that? Did it obligate Eve to accepting the written apology of a dead woman?

"I don't know what I feel right now," she said finally. "Perhaps I will when everything sinks in."

Lainey nodded, freely accepting Eve's answer. She couldn't

imagine the emotions all of this, plus therapy, has brought up. "What are you going to do?" Lainey asked softly. "If you burn the place down, can I watch?"

Eve smiled sadly. "That would be quite satisfying, wouldn't it?"

"But?" Lainey asked, hearing the uncertainty in Eve's tone.

"But it's housed in a historical, pre-war building. I can't destroy something like that."

"Understandable." Lainey tried to imagine the place, but her mind kept showing her Eve's past. She quickly shook her head to get rid of that image. "So, ahem, back to the question of what to do."

Eve had a feeling she knew what Lainey had been thinking of. That place held the demons of terrible memories. If she couldn't burn it down, she'd have to scrub the place clean of those past monsters. The only way to get rid of the negative was to do something positive. "We'll turn it into a home for girls who need a safe place. A place where they can learn and grow. To be the women this world needs."

Tears welled up in Lainey's eyes. "That's perfect, honey." She toed the check. "And this?"

Eve thought about everything Lainey had told her earlier and Kevin's stand against bullies. "Have Kevin and Darren each choose a charity and divide it among them."

Lainey gasped. "Eve, this is a lot . . ."

"Lainey," Eve interrupted. "There isn't one cent of that money that I want or need. If I had any doubt that it could do good for someone else, I would destroy it. But it can. So, if I need one speck of good to come out of what I went through, it would be this." She brought her eyes to Lainey's. "Thank you for shielding me. Protecting me. And being the one who broke the news to me."

Lainey leaned forward and took Eve's hand. "So, you forgive me?"

Eve smiled. "There's nothing to forgive. I wouldn't have wanted to hear this from some strange French lawyer. Especially yesterday after a particularly hard session. What you did, you did out of love." She let that linger in the air for a whisper before continuing. "I'm not weak, Lainey, but there are times when it gets too hard to be strong. You were strong for me. Thank you."

A tremendous weight lifted off Lainey's shoulders, and she felt a sense of peace wash over her. It was more than she could have hoped for when she spent the night worrying about the consequences of her actions. At that moment, she knew she would always follow her heart when it came to Eve. What that meant for her future, she hadn't a clue.

Chapter Nine
Therapy

Being resourceful.

"Why did you feel you needed to run after your father was arrested, Eve?" Dr. Woodrow placed a cup of hot tea on the table next to Eve before returning to her seat. She had spent the first ten minutes of the session trying — and failing — to assess Eve's peculiar demeanor. There was *something* different, but Willamena would have to wait until Eve was more forthcoming to know the reason.

Eve knew Dr. Woodrow was frustrated with her. She knew her attitude was off. But she had decided before this session not to talk about the death of Bussiere until she had a better grasp on her feelings. Eve picked up the delicate cup and brought it to her lips as she pondered her answer. Jasmine tea, light and calming, touched her taste buds. Knowing the course this conversation would go, something hard and mind-numbing would have been preferred, but it didn't look like she was going to get that.

"Decided against the brandy?" Eve asked teasingly. She was procrastinating. God, she hated this part. The first time she spoke of her past to *anyone* was when she finally opened up to Lainey. She thought then that it was the hardest thing she had ever had to do. Until she had to tell Adam. One would think it would be easier by now, especially with a sympathetic, yet unbiased professional. However, just thinking of that time in her life depressed her immensely.

"Do you need alcohol to get through this?" Dr. Woodrow asked, her pen poised to write her opinions on Eve's anticipated response. She caught Eve's look, knowing that her notepad was a sore spot for the elegant woman. Willamena had her thoughts about that, as well, which she wrote a simple *"Self-conscious"* in her notebook. "Are you worried about what I'm writing?" She asked, raising her brows in question.

Eve *was* worried about those notes. She wasn't typically one who cared much about what others thought of her. At least not the general public. Why did this cause her such anxiety? "Reading my mind? That is true dedication for a head shrink."

Though she appreciated Eve's attempt at humor, Dr. Woodrow couldn't allow the constant avoidance when things got uncomfortable for Eve. "You're not answering any of my questions, Eve."

"Because I don't want to," Eve sighed. "I've never made it a secret that I didn't want to do this, Doctor. This isn't easy for me to talk about."

"I can't imagine it is," Dr. Woodrow readily agreed. "But you need to let this go. Let me help you, Eve." She paused to write a couple of notes. ***There's an obligation to her loved ones to be here. I find it hinders some of the true feelings within. For this to work, the patient must come to realize that this will only work if she* wants *it to. For herself.*** She placed the pen in the crease of the notebook and looked up at Eve again, holding her gaze. "You should be doing this for you, not because you feel it would make Adam and Lainey happy."

As much as she hated this, she knew it was a vital part of bringing back her creativity. "I am. Believe me, if I didn't feel like I needed this, I wouldn't be here. Needing this and wanting it are two different things."

Dr. Woodrow nodded, satisfied with the truth of Eve's answer.

"Alright. Then back to my original question. Why did you feel you needed to run?"

Eve sat up straighter in her chair, setting her tea aside. "My father threatened me. He told me that no matter where he was, he would be able to get to me. I knew he had people within the authorities. I just didn't know how far up they went. I ran because I didn't know if I was safe."

"You were so young, how did you know where to go? How did you even get past customs?"

"I am a very resourceful person," Eve answered vaguely. "I just didn't know he would be that cruel." She snorted derisively. Of course, she knew he could be cruel. She had, unfortunately, been too naïve to believe he would hurt her any more than he already had.

Eve's last statement about her father was said so quietly, Dr. Woodrow nearly missed it. It struck such a cord she had to ask her next question.

"Why would you say that?"

"I found out that Tony orchestrated everything that happened to me in Paris. Just one more way for him to hurt me. He did the same to my mother."

"Did the same?"

Eve swallowed down the bile. "Whored her out as he did me. Used us and our bodies to pay off his debts."

Dr. Woodrow cursed softly, then couldn't help but chuckle — an odd sound given the conversation — when she saw Eve's eyebrows raise in surprise.

"Sorry. I try not to let myself get emotionally involved with my patients. But when I hear how a father put his daughter through so much pain, it . . . well, it pisses me off."

"My my, Doctor. Don't hold back." Eve gave Dr. Woodrow her most charming smile and a quick wink. Truth be told, Eve appreciated the doctor's anger towards what Eve went through. Anger directed at her father was much better than pity or even disgust directed towards Eve.

Dr. Woodrow chuckled again. It wasn't often she lost her professional composure. But friends of her niece, especially ones who had similar traumatic backgrounds, tugged her heartstrings. "I'll try to refrain from personal dialogue while we're in this room."

"Fair enough," Eve said, even though she didn't mind the occasional outbursts. They let her know that the rage she felt inside was natural.

"Have you ever felt safe, Eve?" Dr. Woodrow asked suddenly. It was a question she asked a lot of the abuse victims she counseled. The answer was usually the same which made her particularly interested in Eve's.

Eve paused. She hadn't been prepared for the question. Talk about her past? Sure. It was hard as hell, but she could force herself to do it. She could probably talk about feelings as well if she had to. But feeling safe? Did she? She still had security following those she loved, but how did that translate to her own safety?

"I do now." *I think*, she thought silently. "After Tony died, I started feeling safe and letting myself feel happiness. Lainey helped me with that. And when I decided to let Adam in, I found my safe haven in his love."

Willamena wondered if Eve knew she had a "tell" when she said something she didn't believe 100%. "And when the latest problems occurred, you regressed?"

Eve shrugged slightly.

Noting Eve's discomfort, Dr. Woodrow changed tactics. "We're getting ahead of ourselves. I want to go back to your time in Paris before we get into everything else."

Eve picked up her now tepid tea and sipped. She closed her eyes, trying to get past the heartache she still felt when she thought of what Adam went through because of her. She almost welcomed the pain of talking about Paris.

"I was a whore. What more do we need to discuss? It's over."

"Eve," Willamena gave Eve a look that was normally reserved for mothers who are disciplining their child. *So much for keeping my professional composure*, she chastised herself. "You know very well you were not a whore. You were forced to do things no woman, and especially a child should have to do."

Eve had heard it all before. And she could tell herself again and again that it was over. Yet, there was no letting it go. It was a cancer that would eat at her daily if she allowed it. And it would if she kept fighting the good doctor.

"Very well," she said, reluctantly. "What would you like to hear about it?"

"I don't want details unless you feel you need to discuss them. I want to know how you felt."

Eve's hands trembled as she set the teacup back on the table. Dr. Woodrow surprised her when she laid a gentle hand over hers.

Once again, Willamena let her professional composure slip. At least this time she could say her expert opinion guided her personal feelings. "Let's continue this in the next session. I don't want to push you too hard."

"Afraid I'll close up?"

"Honestly? Yes. It's your defense. So, we'll take this slow. I can't offer you alcohol, but I can offer you my expertise and understanding. I can offer a sympathetic and non-judgmental ear. Will that be enough for you?"

Will it, Eve wondered? She hoped so. "As long as you don't put me on any medication, we'll be fine, Doctor," she smiled and silently thanked Dr. Woodrow for making her feel safe within these walls.

Chapter Ten

Eve sat in bed, propped up by three plush pillows. A book laid open in her lap, but the words swam on the page. It was always like this after an especially harsh session. She couldn't sleep, couldn't concentrate. Spending time with Bella helped, but her daughter had gone to bed hours ago. Sex had also been a great mood-lifter. Unfortunately, given the nature of her recent session, Eve wasn't in the mood. Of course, Adam tried to be understanding. She just wasn't sure he *did* understand.

"Will you be up late?"

Eve looked up. Usually, her heart would skip a beat at the sight of his chiseled body. The way his black silk pajama pants hung low on his hips never failed to turn her on. Until now. She blamed it on the abundance of emotions and memories flooding her mind.

"Um," Eve frowned, confused by her lack of a sex drive. "I can go to the sitting room if I'm bothering you."

"Not bothering me, beautiful. It's just that I have an early meeting and . . ."

"And you need sleep," Eve finished for him. She didn't remind him that not ten minutes before he had been propositioning her for sex. She closed her book and gathered a pillow. "I'll try not to stay up too late."

"Mmm." Adam had already tucked himself into bed, his back to

Eve. He was trying desperately not to feel rejected by his wife. It was proving to be harder than he expected. *This was your doing*, he told himself. *You wanted her to go to therapy.* Too bad it felt like "finding herself" meant losing sight of him.

"Goodnight."

Adam sighed and sat up. "Eve?" He waited until she turned back to him. "Is there anything you need to talk to me about?"

She knew what he wanted. He was going to be disappointed in her answer. "I have to go to Italy soon."

Adam frowned. Whatever he thought she was going to say, that was not it. "Italy?"

"Yes. I haven't made arrangements for the trip, yet. So, this is me talking to you about it first."

Well, it's a start, Adam thought. "Why Italy?"

"There's an artist there that I want to talk to about showing her work in the LA gallery opening."

"You know, they've invented this crazy thing called the telephone. I hear it even works when calling other countries."

Eve smiled when Adam grinned. "I tried that. Turns out, the artist is a bit of a hermit, and I can only get through to her representative. I need to bypass that representative to see if the crazy demands are actually hers. Telephones don't do that, *amant*."

His blood warmed at the endearment. "Understood. When will you be going?"

"We'll most likely leave in a week or so. Depending on Lainey's schedule with the boys."

Adam averted his eyes, reminding himself that Lainey was Eve's assistant. It was normal for her to go on business trips with Eve.

"Keep me updated on the date? I'll make sure I'm home for Bella. Unless you're taking her?"

"Not this time. It'll be a quick trip, hopefully." She faltered a bit. She hadn't told him about Bussiere, yet, so this next part would be a little harder. "I, um, will have to go to Paris soon, as well."

"Another artist?"

"No. This is personal. Bussiere is dead."

Adam flinched. It was a name he knew well. One that haunted his dreams. One he hated with his entire soul.

"I'm not sure I understand why that requires you going to Paris, beautiful. She's gone. You're rid of her now."

"Except I'm not." *And may never be.* "She left me the café. Apparently, she wanted to make amends for what she did."

Adam scoffed. "And you believe her? You're so naïve as to take that shit hole and say 'yeah, sure, I forgive you'?"

Eve's nostrils flared, and she counted to ten before she said anything. "If you believe I'm naïve enough to forgive such atrocities blindly, you don't know me at all. I am, however, a businesswoman who recognizes a good opportunity when she sees one."

"Going to turn it into another gallery? More business trips to Paris?" Adam scrubbed his stubbled face. His temper had flared when he heard the awful name which wasn't ideal with his already frustrated state. Regrettably, he was taking it out on the wrong person. His mouth spewed out the words before he could stop them.

"Goodnight, Adam."

"Eve, wait. I — I'm sorry. You sprang this on me, and I wasn't prepared to hear that name."

"Right. Next time, I'll try to ease you into the news that someone who used to torture *me* has died."

"I didn't mean it that way. Am I not allowed to be angry about the things that happened to you? It affects me, too, you know."

"Ah, yes. A night where I'm not in the mood to fuck you. How devastating that must be for you." She held up a hand when he opened his mouth to speak. "I'm turning the place into a safe harbor for young girls to go to, by the way." She pivoted furiously, tossing her pillow and book on a nearby chair. When she felt this angry, being near the cause wasn't healthy for her. Eve decided that she would be sleeping in *her* safe harbor tonight. In Bella's room.

"I'm sorry!" Adam called out. "Eve!" He threw back the covers and scrambled after her.

"I'd stay away from me right now if I were you," she warned.

Adam pulled his hands back. She hated being grabbed, and that was precisely what he had been about to do.

"Listen, beautiful, I'm sorry. We're both frustrated."

"Frustrated?" Eve was perilously close to losing her composure. It took a great amount of effort to keep from yelling loud enough to wake Bella. "You think that reliving everything I've gone through *frustrates* me?! It *hurts*, Adam." She stepped away when he lifted his hand to touch her. "What do you feel when you think about what you went through. Because of me."

The question surprised him. "I — they never should have gotten to me. I should have been more careful so that they couldn't use me against you."

"That's your answer?" Eve was painfully aware that Adam didn't dispute that it was her fault. "You had security. They got through them, drugged you, beat you, and electrocuted you." *When I was too much of a coward to answer to my* sins. "None of that upsets you?"

Adam blew out a breath. "What answer do you want from me, Eve?"

"I want you to tell me how you *really* feel, Adam. I want you to tell me you blame me for what Laurence and Billy did to you. Instead of snippets of petty jealousy for Lainey, have it out with me. Do *something*, Adam!"

Adam rubbed the back of his neck, roughly. "I thought you'd be happy that I'm being understanding." He grunted, then sighed wearily. "I'm not sure how things ended up like this tonight. It's my fault, I know." He brought his hand up and scrubbed it through his hair. "What I should have said from the very beginning is, I'll be there for you. I'll clear my schedule and go to Paris with you. I support you in whatever you decide."

They were beautiful words. Everything she could want to hear in this situation. Perhaps that's why she didn't believe they were genuine. Not after the truth of what Adam thought had already been on display. And especially not after he refused to respond to her pleas.

"Don't bother. I have all the support I need."

Lainey knocked softly on Eve's door, poking her head in when Eve responded.

"Hey. I've been going over the boys' schedule."

Eve looked up. "Are you going to come in or have I scared you away with my dour attitude this morning."

Lainey smiled, closing the door behind her as she walked in. She took her usual seat, sat back, and crossed her legs. "I've known you for a few years now. Your dour attitude doesn't scare me. Anymore."

Eve laughed, and it felt good after a night like last night. It didn't help her mood that Adam had left the house before she even woke up. There was also the headache, stiff neck, and fatigue from a restless sleep.

"Good to know. You were saying about the schedule?"

"Well, Kevin said he was quitting football today, so you can cross off those home games I put on your calendar." Lainey winked at Eve. "Darren's schedule seems to be pretty light for the next couple of weeks."

Eve flipped through her calendar unnecessarily. She had already discussed Bella's care with Lexie. She also had a conversation with her daughter about having to miss out on a couple of cuddle nights. Those weren't easy. Eve would almost rather deal with demanding customers than an upset little girl. Even though Bella wasn't happy about it, she still cuddled with Eve and made her momma promise to not stay away for too long.

"Make the arrangements for whenever is most convenient for you," Eve said, yawning.

Lainey leaned back in her seat, poised to ask Eve what was going on despite vowing not to. However, before she could even form her question, her cell phone rang, startling her. The boys were in school, and she was with Eve. Who the hell was left to call her? Lainey dug the phone out of her back pocket and frowned when she saw the number of Kevin's school.

"Hello. . . This is she. . . What. . . Is he okay? . . . Yes, yes, of course. I'll be right there."

Eve had sat up, listening intently when Lainey's tone turned concerned. "What's wrong?"

"It's Kevin," Lainey answered, gathering her things in a hurry. "Apparently, he's been in a fight."

Eve stood immediately. "I'll drive."

Lainey looked over her shoulder with a wobbly grin. Concern for her son had her adrenaline pumping, although the school assured her he was fine. That small bit of relief allowed her to find Eve's declaration funny.

"You have to drive, honey. You drove us into work this morning."

"Oh, right." Eve yawned again. "On second thought, you drive." She tossed her keys to Lainey before they descended the stairs. "Mikey! The gallery is yours!"

"It's about time!" Mikey called back with a grin. He caught the lilt of Eve's laughter as the elevator doors closed.

"Go." Eve urged Lainey ahead of her. "I'm right behind you."

Lainey didn't hesitate. She walked briskly to the principal's office, bypassing the receptionist. "Kevin!"

"Mom." Kevin waved his free hand while the other held a bloodied rag to his nose. "I'm fine."

"You're not fine. You're bleeding."

"Mrs. Stanton," Principal Kordecki stood from behind his large desk. He was a big man, but that's where the intimidation ended. All Lainey ever thought when she looked at the red-headed man was how he would kiss your feet if you gave him enough money. "Mrs. Stanton!"

Lainey raised her eyebrow at Kordecki's tone. *She* wasn't one of the wealthy parents, so the man never afforded her the respect he had for dollar signs.

"I'm making sure my son is okay, Mr. Kordecki. You are not my priority."

"I should be. Your son is in a lot of trouble."

"I didn't start it, mom. I was just . . ."

"You were not asked to speak, young man," Mr. Kordecki boomed.

Lainey straightened, looking at the man square in the eye. "You will not speak to my son in that way. I want to know what happened."

"Your son . . ."

"Were you there when it happened, Mr. Kordecki?"

"Well, no, but . . ."

"Then, I don't need to hear from you." Lainey turned to Kevin. "What happened?"

"A couple of the guys from the team were harassing my friend. I usually walk her to her classes because they've done it before, but Coach kept me in his office. He was still yelling at me for quitting the team. When I finally made it back up here, I saw what they were doing. Mom, she kept telling them to stop touching her, but they wouldn't leave her alone. So, I stepped in."

"You started a fight, young man. And, under our zero-tolerance policy, you are to be expelled."

Lainey's head whipped around, and she looked at the man incredulously. "Did you hear what he said? They were harassing the girl, and Kevin stepped up. Why aren't they in here? Why isn't she?"

"Because there's no need. According to the boys, your son started it."

"The boys? You mean the ones who were harassing . . ."

"That's speculation."

"Kevin just *told* you what happened. And if you bothered to bring . . ." she looked to Kevin for a name.

"Mia."

Lainey turned back to Kordecki. "Did you speak to Mia?"

"As I said, there's no need to disrupt classes any more than they already have been, Mrs. Stanton. The boys were just . . ."

"*Oh my God, if you say, 'just being boys,'*" Lainey muttered eliciting a chuckle from Kevin. She gave him a stern look because of the situation they were both in, but inside, she was proud of her son. Not everyone would risk getting in trouble by stepping up to help someone in need.

"That's exactly what they were doing, Mrs. Stanton. I'm sure Mia would tell you the same thing."

"No, she wouldn't," Kevin mumbled.

"Who were the boys?" Lainey asked, effectively cutting off Mr. Kordecki's pending reprimand.

"Wyatt and Landon," Kevin answered when Kordecki refused.

"Now I get it," Lainey drawled. "Their daddies give the football program a lot of money. That's why they're not in here and being punished."

Mr. Kordecki sighed heavily. "I should have called Mr. Stanton. He would understand the importance of these donations to the football program and these boys. I won't ruin their chances at scholarships because they were joking around."

"But you'll ruin my son's?"

"He quit the team, Mrs. Stanton," he stated as if that were reason enough to punish him.

"Another source of contention for you, I'm sure. He was your best quarterback. Yet, didn't he come to you complaining about some of the boys on the team? What did you do? Anything? Kevin quit because no one did anything when he reported this. You tout this zero-tolerance, but I guess that doesn't apply to people whose daddies give you tons of money."

"I don't expect you to understand the influence these parents have, Mrs. Stanton."

Lainey laughed and opened her mouth to let out some sarcastic retort when she was interrupted.

"Mr. Kordecki?" The elderly receptionist called out. "Dr. Yeong is on line one."

"Tell her I'm in a meeting," he barked back.

"Sir, she's adamantly requesting that you answer now."

Lainey could almost feel the indignant reluctance from the man. She knew Dr. Yeong was the superintendent. AKA, Mr. Kordecki's boss. Perfect timing. She wondered if she could get an audience with Dr. Yeong to appeal this ridiculous expulsion.

"Dr. Yeong, I'm in a meeting with a parent . . . Yes, that's correct . . . Of course, I know who she is . . . But the young man started . . .

No, they're not in here at the moment . . . No, she isn't either . . . I didn't think it was necessary . . . Excuse me? Are you firing me? On what grounds? But . . . Yes, ma'am." He slammed down the phone, face ruddied by either embarrassment or anger. Perhaps both. He looked at Lainey with disdain. "How?"

Lainey shook her head. The man had just been fired, and he's blaming it on her? How could she have had anything . . .

"Are you done here, Lainey?"

Mr. Kordecki sprang up, his hands immediately reaching for his tie to straighten it. "Mrs. Sumptor!" He looked from one woman to another, realization dawning on him as he slumped back down. Sumptor, Inc. was a chief benefactor of the private school he was no longer employed at. If he had known Mrs. Stanton was connected with Mrs. Sumptor, he would still have a job. As it stood now, he knew he had no chance to appeal his termination.

"And you thought I didn't know influential people." Lainey shook her head. "Come on, Kevin."

Kevin stood but didn't make a move towards the door. "What about the guys? They shouldn't be able to get away with what they did."

"They won't," Eve answered. "Mei will be starting a full investigation of the things going on here."

"Dr. Yeong," Lainey explained to a confused Kevin. "The superintendent is looking into this." She turned back to Eve. "How did you know?"

"Thin walls and Kordecki's voice carries."

Kevin looked over at Eve. He didn't know how she did it, but he was grateful. "I don't know how you did that, but thanks."

Eve shrugged. "It was just a phone call. Come on. Let's get out of here."

"I didn't need ice cream, mom. I'm not a kid."

Lainey watched with amusement as he took a big bite of his favorite pistachio ice cream. "I didn't drive here," she laughed.

"Maybe *I* wanted ice cream," Eve retorted playfully. She had her own cone filled with banana ice cream.

Lainey averted her eyes when Eve's pink tongue snuck out to catch the drip of melting ice cream. Lainey had read enough psychology books to understand that as hard as she tried to hide her attraction to Eve from everyone else, she couldn't hide it from herself.

"So, like, how'd you do that?" Kevin asked. "I mean, you just walk into some school, and the principal begins to stutter and knows your name. And you, like, got him fired. I didn't realize gallery owners were so powerful."

Lainey snorted, and Eve laughed. She knew Kevin wasn't trying to be rude. It was a legitimate question. In New York City, there was a multitude of galleries. Eve was reasonably confident that not all of them could pull off what she did.

"I'm not just a gallery owner," she began to explain.

"You're Wonder Woman?"

Eve shook her head, chuckling when Lainey curtsied and saluted with her ice cream. "Stop. I'm merely a businesswoman who tries to help the community as much as I can. Sumptor, Inc. is a big contributor to your school, and I am acquaintances with Dr. Yeong."

"Most people wouldn't fire someone because an *acquaintance* asked them to, Eve," Lainey pointed out.

Eve shrugged. "She was returning a favor. And, technically, I didn't ask her to fire Mr. Kordecki. That was all her idea after she heard what was going on." She grinned at Lainey. "I was sad that she interrupted your meeting, actually."

Lainey's brows furrowed. "I wasn't. I was dangerously close to throat punching that man."

Eve's laugh rang out, accompanied by Kevin's. "That's why I was sad! I would have paid to have another wing built on that school to see that!"

Lainey rolled her eyes. "You are a bad influence on my son."

"Nah," Kevin spoke up despite the mouthful of ice cream cone.

"I like seeing you stand up for yourself, mom. Maybe Eve is a *good* influence on *you*."

"Smart kid," Eve muttered playfully.

"Hush, you. I was capable of standing up for myself before we met."

"(Cough) sure you were (cough)."

"I don't care if you are my son, I will throw this ice cream at you," Lainey warned with mirth. Kevin was right. She had been a push-over for most of her marriage with Jack. After she started working with Eve, that began to change. She couldn't be more thankful for that.

"You wouldn't," Kevin chuckled. "You like rocky road too much to waste it." He ran when Lainey cocked her arm.

"Amateur," Lainey said, then took a big bite of her cherished rocky road. "Thank you, by the way," she said to Eve quietly. "I'm glad you were there with me."

"As am I."

Chapter Eleven
Therapy

A portrait of the past.

As she had a habit of doing in every session, Willamena handed Eve a cup of hot tea.

"Thank you." Eve sipped gingerly, testing the temperature, and almost choked when the burn of brandy hit the back of her throat. Her eyes popped open wide as she stared at Dr. Woodrow incredulously.

"You asked for it." She chuckled softly at Eve's mock scowl. This was yet another example of how she treated Eve differently than her other patients. "Are you relaxed?"

"You could have warned me," Eve teased before taking another sip. Interesting mix of jasmine and brandy. Not something she would think of herself, but not necessarily displeasing.

"Ah, true, I could have. But what fun would that be?" Willamena smirked.

It seemed to Eve as though Dr. Woodrow was in a feisty mood. Perhaps she was trying to make today easier for Eve. Unfortunately, it was going to take much more than a splash of liquor in a calming cup of tea to accomplish that.

"Tell me how your week has been going," Willamena continued.

"Are you procrastinating for me, Dr. Woodrow?"

"Not procrastinating, Eve. However, no ethics law says we cannot have a normal conversation." She smiled kindly, pleased when Eve returned the gesture.

"Very well. My week has been busy. I'm getting the gallery ready for a show for a local artist. I believe it will be successful. Which reminds me, I will have to miss next week."

"The showing is next week during your session time?" Dr. Woodrow asked skeptically.

"No." Eve grinned at the doctor's disapproval. "I'm not avoiding my session, Dr. Woodrow. I won't be in the country. Lainey and I have to travel to Italy for a couple of days to procure a few items for the Los Angeles gallery and hopefully a new artist."

"Italy? How exciting. Would you like to discuss how Adam feels about Lainey traveling with you?"

Eve's eyebrow raised at the question. They had yet to get fully into the whole "Lainey relationship" portion of Eve's life. It was only eluded to when they did the preliminary interview.

"You don't think I can see the depth of your feelings for Lainey when you speak of her?" Dr. Woodrow asked gently.

Eve closed her eyes briefly before locking gazes with Dr. Woodrow. "Adam trusts me," she said a bit too harshly. "We've discussed everything, and he knows Lainey and I are just friends. Now."

"Eve, I did not mean to upset you or imply that . . . "

"I know," Eve interrupted. "I apologize for my attitude." She lowered her gaze. It's not the doctor's fault that Eve still felt guilty about Lainey. Guilty for their affair. Guilty that she still thought of her in that way. She forced herself to think about something else. Even going back through her past would be easier than dealing with the shame of her feelings.

"Eve . . . "

"I'm here to talk about when I ran away to Paris and what happened to me, correct? That is where we are now?"

Dr. Woodrow sighed softly and nodded. She picked up her notebook and rolled her pen between her fingers. And waited.

"My father took my mother and me to Paris once when I was small. He had had a particularly good week gambling and was feeling generous, I suppose. Of course, he went there to gamble more or do whatever else he did, but mother and I had fun. We stayed there for a few weeks in a small café that had rooms for rent. It wasn't the greatest place, in fact, it was quite filthy, but I didn't mind it. Momma was with me, and that's all that mattered to me. Tony spent most of the nights down in the bar or somewhere else, sometimes never coming back to the room. After Tony was arrested for my mother's murder, I fled to the only place I remembered. Madame Bussiere's."

Eve was aware of how fast she was speaking. She hoped she was at least making sense. Thinking of Bussiere reminded Eve that the old woman was dead. A tidbit she still had yet to tell the doctor. She didn't think tonight would be the night, either. She took another drink of tea to stall and scrunched up her nose. The brandy was no longer pleasant as the tea had become cold.

"Would you like more?"

Eve nodded, handing the doctor her cup.

"Brandy?"

"No, thank you. I can do this sober." She hoped.

Dr. Woodrow refilled her cup, handing it back over to Eve, before settling back into her seat. "Was this Madame Bussiere kind to you and your mother when you had visited before?"

Eve detected a hint of distaste when the doctor mentioned Bussiere's name and smiled to herself. She knew instinctively that the good doctor disliked Bussiere explicitly for her part in what happened to Eve. Eve was fortunate to have found a therapist who cared. If Eve *had* to go through therapy, she might as well be comfortable.

"She was pleasant enough, I suppose. I didn't give it much thought, though. I didn't feel I had any other options. I was young. Money would have eventually run out. I was hoping that Bussiere would agree to let me live there if I helped out around the place."

Eve never imagined just how Bussiere would make her help.

"When did things change for you?" Dr. Woodrow asked gently.

"When I was sixteen," Eve murmured. She remembered it as clearly as if it had happened yesterday. "I had once believed it was because my body had begun to change, and the men in the bar began noticing. I only learned recently that Bussiere had betrayed me and told Tony where I was. He began paying off his debts with my body." Eve paused, taking another sip of her tea. She wished now that she had accepted the offer of brandy.

"Would you like to stop?"

"No. I want to get past this part."

"Alright then. Take your time, Eve."

"We only have an hour session," Eve joked lamely.

Dr. Woodrow smiled. "You're my last session for the day. It's okay if we go over."

Again, Eve found herself lucky to have found such a caring shrink. Though, she was quite certain Dr. Woodrow would disapprove of Eve calling her a shrink. Even mentally.

"When Bussiere came to me one night she noticed one of my drawings," Eve continued finally. Her thoughts were jumbled, which was reflected in the randomness of her story. The hope was, Dr. Woodrow would be able to decipher Eve's chaotic recollections. "She thought it was good and demanded I paint for her. She figured she could make a lot of money off my paintings. I thought I'd be able to get what I needed if I agreed, so I asked her for supplies and agreed to paint for her. Huge mistake."

"You must know that whether you had asked her for supplies or not, she would have demanded the things she demanded from you," Dr. Woodrow said when Eve became silent.

"Logically I understand that, Doctor. But for years I believed that that was the thing that made Bussiere ask those things of me. It was a catch 22 for me. My art helped me survive, but the way I got the supplies was slowly killing me." She took a deep breath, closing her eyes. "When Bussiere asked me to go up to the room with a man, I didn't know what to expect. She told me it was to paint a portrait. I became hopeful that I had misunderstood what I had originally thought she wanted from me. That hope grew when the man really did just want a portrait painted. When he returned a few more times for portraits, I should've been warier and less hopeful."

"You were still a child, Eve."

"But I had already seen evil, Dr. Woodrow. I shouldn't have been that naïve. I should have prepared myself for what I *knew* in my heart was coming."

"You hold so much guilt inside of you."

Oh, if you only knew, Eve thought silently. The guilt never seemed to go away. "If I had just prepared myself for that night," she said out loud.

"Then what, Eve?" Dr. Woodrow asked. "Do you think you would have felt different about it? You were a virgin, and someone was taking advantage of you. Raping you. How could you have possibly prepared yourself for that."

"I agreed to it," Eve protested weakly.

"Did you feel you had any other choice? Did you want it?"

"No." The answer was barely a whisper.

"It was rape, my dear Eve. You should hold no guilt for that. That woman, Tony, and those men are the ones to blame. *They* are the ones that should hold guilt. Not you, Eve."

Trying to grasp logic about that time in her life was just as hard as the emotions she was feeling.

Dr. Woodrow reached over and squeezed Eve's hand briefly. "Do you know how many there were?"

The question was asked hesitantly, as though Dr. Woodrow hadn't wanted to have to ask. Eve almost wished she hadn't, yet she shook her head. "I lost count." Her voice sounded so small and childlike to her own ears, and it shocked her. *A chink in my armor. Damn it.*

Willamena set her notebook aside. She didn't have to write down Eve's reaction to remember it. She had seen that sadness before in her niece. As a psychiatrist, it was essential to be able to let go of vicarious trauma. Seeing women as strong and successful as Eve and Rebecca tremble with fear from a past of horrors was unforgettable. "It's okay. Let's stop here. We don't have to talk about this anymore if you don't want. Next time, we can begin with how you got away."

"Okay." Eve forced her voice to be stronger. A lot stronger than she felt at the moment, at least.

"May I ask you something?"

Eve nodded, still not trusting her confidence.

"When you leave here, do you find comfort with Adam or Lainey?"

The question had Eve expelling a shocked gasp. Even though there was no hint of judgment, she wasn't prepared for her defensive response. "I'm in love with Adam. He is the one who comforts me," she retorted hotly. *Liar.* Eve rubbed her temple as though the action would erase the unwanted thoughts.

"Eve, please." Dr. Woodrow lifted her hands in a placating gesture. "I meant nothing by that. I wasn't judging you. I'm merely trying to get to know all there is to know. It's not uncommon to feel strongly about two people."

"I love my husband," Eve stated again. At this point, she wasn't sure who she was trying to convince more.

"I have no doubts about that. But you also love Lainey, correct?"

"Why are you doing this?" Eve whispered. It was too much. She had been trying to bury her feelings for Lainey since Adam found out about them. *Unsuccessfully.* She had promised Adam that nothing would ever happen between her and Lainey ever again. She wouldn't hurt him like that again. She couldn't. Not after everything he went through because of her. *Yet, you still want her.*

"Eve, the whole point of therapy is to be completely open and honest. Not only with me, but with yourself. If you don't, how do you expect to let it all go?" Willamena could practically see the internal struggle within Eve. She picked up her notebook — much to Eve's dismay, she was sure — and jotted down a quick note. **The patient says the words but doesn't necessarily believe them. Or, she's trying her hardest to convince herself that what she says is the whole truth.**

"I'm not ready for this. Please."

"Okay. It's alright. I'll stop." Dr. Woodrow once again closed her notebook and set it on the table next to her. She carefully laid her pen on top as though she were disarming herself. "I'm sorry I upset you, or if you feel I've pressured you."

Eve merely nodded slightly and stood.

"Eve?"

Though it took a truckload of willpower, Eve paused with her hand on the doorknob. She turned to face the doctor.

"I am sorry."

Eve recognized the distress in Woodrow's eyes and wondered if she believed she had lost Eve's trust. "I know. And I understand why you asked. I'm just not ready to face those questions right now." She offered the doctor a slight smile. "I'll see you in a couple of weeks, doc. We'll get through my past, and then we'll tackle my feelings. I can only handle one at a time."

"I promise, I'll let you set the pace." Willamena smiled back and stood to approach Eve. "Have a safe trip." Dr. Woodrow squeezed her forearm gently.

"Thank you. Good night."

Eve closed the door gently behind her and stood there for a moment. Questions ran through her head like a marathon. Lainey was picking her up tonight on her way home from the gallery while Adam was home with Bella. Would she confide in Lainey, again, while leaving Adam in the dark? Normally there would be no hesitation. But now . . . now Eve had to wonder if it was because she was seeking comfort from Lainey or just friendship.

"*Why can't it be both?*" She whispered to herself. It didn't have to mean she wanted more. Right? *Wrong.*

Chapter Twelve

"That's right, Eve. Fight back. Do you know how hard it makes my cock when you fight back?"

Eve looked into the golden-brown eyes and found nothing but evil. Her heart pounded in her chest so hard she thought it would explode. He was on top of her, holding her down, and there was nothing she could do about it. Her strength had dissipated leaving nothing but fear.

"Get off me, Laurence," she demanded weakly.

He laughed. "You were always my favorite. Did you know I couldn't be with my wife for months after I had you? Such a young, sweet pussy."

"Fuck you!" Eve bucked with all her might, but the man didn't budge.

"I knew you liked it," he sneered. "You can't even choose between that man of yours and that beautiful woman. Can't say I blame you. A nice, juicy pussy is hard to resist. Isn't it, Eve?"

"I will kill you!" Eve spat.

"You're too late, Eve. I'm already dead." He grinned wickedly. "Now I'm in your head." Laurence laughed, sending chills down Eve's spine. "I can get to you any time."

Eve struggled as Laurence's weight confined her. His fingers dug into her arms, and his pelvis pushed painfully into hers.

"Get off!" She kicked her legs, but when he didn't budge, the panic she felt as a seventeen-year-old girl being brutalized by older men who should have known better bubbled up to the surface in the form of a scream.

"Eve! Wake up, beautiful, please." Adam pressed his body to Eve's to control her thrashing. "You're dreaming, Eve. Come back to me, beautiful."

"Get off!" Eve's eyes popped open. Golden brown turned to brilliant blue. "Get off me!" She was beginning to hyperventilate, and Adam wasn't moving.

"Momma?"

Bella's small voice pierced through Eve's frantic haze. She immediately stopped struggling yet continued to push at Adam. "*Get off me*," she whispered harshly, giving one more hard push.

Adam rolled away, confusion clouding his brain. Was she mad at him? All he was trying to do was help.

"Momma? Daddy hurt you?"

Eve threw back the covers, dropping off the bed to her knees. She held her arms out. She never even noticed the shocked and hurt look on Adam's face. "Come here, bug."

Bella ran to her mom and threw herself into her arms. The little girl had tear streaks down her pink cheeks.

"Look at me, baby girl." Bella obeyed. She sniffled as she held her mother's eyes. Eve was taken aback by the strength she found hidden behind the tears. "You know your daddy would never hurt me, right?"

"Momma yell. Daddy no nice." Bella's bottom lip trembled.

"Oh, my sweet girl." Eve kissed Bella's entire face before explaining. "Momma was having a nightmare, sweetie. Daddy was just trying to help."

Bella's eyes slid to her dad, and so did Eve's. She now saw what she had missed before. It broke her heart. He couldn't have known that trying to help was causing more panic. Or that Bella would hear and make the assumptions of a two-year-old who couldn't process what she was seeing.

"You hewp momma, daddy?"

"Yeah, baby girl." Adam cleared the emotion from his throat. "I would never hurt you or your momma."

Bella stepped away from Eve and walked to the side of the bed. It was too tall for her to get up herself, so Eve gave her a boost. Once she was up there, she crawled onto her daddy's lap.

"Wuv you."

A tear ran down Adam's cheek. "I love you, too, baby."

"Can I get in on this lovefest," Eve asked with a smile. She was still feeling the effects of the nightmare. Probably would for a while. But right now, there was something more important to take care of. Her night terrors had never touched Bella before. Eve had hoped she would be rid of them by the time Bella was old enough to understand what was happening. She wasn't so lucky tonight. Pair that with Adam's obvious pain and Eve obtained a new thing to be guilty about. However, as Bella raised her arms, Eve filed that away for another day.

Adam peered at Eve over Bella's head. "*I'm sorry*," he mouthed.

Eve shook her head and leaned over to kiss him gently on the lips. "*Thank you*."

"Kevin!"

Lainey rushed into the kitchen. "Jack! It is six o'clock in the morning. What on earth are you yelling for?"

Jack tossed his newspaper aside. "Where is my son?"

Lainey rolled her eyes as she turned and made her way to the fridge. "Kevin is most likely trying to pry his eyes open at this time of day. Then, he'll take a shower, get dressed, come downstairs, eat a ton of food, and go to school. We all have our routines, Jack."

Jack scowled. "I don't appreciate your flippancy, Lainey. I received an email this morning telling me my son has quit the football team."

Shit. She and Kevin had yet to tell Jack about Kevin's decision. Jack had been in a particularly pissy mood the night before, and Lainey thought it would be better if they waited. Of course, she would have waited longer than a few hours. Maybe a couple of days. Or never. This wasn't something she was looking forward to.

"Mmhmm." She heard a loud thump as Jack slammed his coffee

cup down.

"You knew? And you didn't think it was important enough to tell me? Your son is ruining his life."

Now he's my son. "We were going to tell you, Jack." She faced him. "Honestly, though, why do you care? You never go to the games."

"It's not about the games, Lainey! It's about life-lessons and learning how to be a man."

Ah, yes. Why would you need to be there for that? Damn it! She wished she had the courage to say these things out loud. Eve wouldn't hold back. However, Lainey wasn't Eve. Years of being compliant will take some time to get over.

"Kevin has no problems with being a gentleman, Jack. If you knew why . . ."

Jack scoffed loud enough to interrupt Lainey. "I'm not talking about a pansy, Lainey. Without football, Kevin won't get the training he needs for the military."

"Military?! Jack, have you lost your ever-loving mind? Kevin has never once mentioned joining the military."

"It's something he needs, Lainey. He's too soft. Too much of a momma's boy."

Lainey laughed mirthlessly. "You call your mother every other day at precisely the same time. Or is that why you think he needs to join the military? So he doesn't end up like you?"

The chair scraped the floor and nearly tumbled over as Jack rose suddenly. Lainey had never been afraid of her husband in all the years they'd been together. The look in his eye now changed that.

"What's going on?" The sleepiness eroded when Kevin walked into the kitchen. He didn't like the look his father had. Nor did he like the fear in his mother's eyes. It normally took him a good hour and a bunch of calories to get to the "fully functioning" part of his day. However, Kevin was more alert at this moment than he could ever remember being. Nervous energy flowed through him, trying to burst from the seams. He bounced on the balls of his feet when Jack turned his anger towards him.

"You will not quit football."

Controlled anger permeated the air around them. Kevin's nervous energy became animosity. He couldn't believe his father was treating his mom like this over a silly game. And a done deal.

"Too late. I quit yesterday," he said defiantly.

"I remedied that situation. Your coach expects you at practice."

Kevin shook his head. "Do you ever get tired of trying to control people's lives? I'm not going back, dad. I don't like coach's tactics. On or off the field."

"This is not a discussion, Kevin. You will do as you're told."

"I told him he could quit," Lainey said, grateful that her voice didn't betray the uneasiness she felt.

"You don't have the authority to do that," Jack spat.

"Are you kidding me? *I'm* his mother! *All* authority is mine." She risked taking a step closer. "He chose to do this for a damn good reason. I support him and so should you. But even if you don't, Jack, Kevin does not have to play."

Jack ignored Lainey, focusing on Kevin. "You don't play, you don't do anything else," he warned. "You're grounded. No more phone, TV, or going out. And unless you get your scholarship through football, you will pay for your college."

"Jack, that's enough."

"Shut up, Lainey! This is between my son and me."

"*Our* son. And I'm not allowing this. You don't know the whole story."

"I don't care about whatever idiotic reason he gave you!" Jack took a menacing step towards Kevin, coming up short when Lainey stepped between them.

"Mom, I got this," Kevin said hurriedly. He tried to push his mother behind him. There was no way he was going to let his dad do anything to hurt his mom.

"No, you don't. Get your brother and go to school."

"No way! I'm not leaving you alone with him!"

Lainey looked up at her son. "Kevin, please. Take your brother and go to school." Kevin sighed and glared at his father before pivoting angrily. Lainey watched as he stomped his way upstairs, then turned back. "How dare you?"

"Me? I am the man of this family. It is my job to turn these boys into men. You are not helping. What with you getting a job instead of taking care of them, letting them do whatever the hell they want. It's time for you to get back to your job of being a real mother."

"Good morning, beautiful." Adam kissed Eve on top of her head.

Eve finished the email she was writing and set her phone to the side, smiling at Adam. "Good morning, *amant*."

"I take it Bella is up and about since she wasn't in our bed this morning."

Eve chuckled. "Yes. She woke up pretty early. We had a nice time playing boss and assistant."

"Let me guess; you were the assistant for the first time in your life?" Adam smiled.

Eve shrugged with a grin. "I'm happy to let her express her enthusiasm for being assertive. She's now expressing herself with Lexie."

Adam laughed softly. He was glad that Bella had someone like Eve teaching her how to be independent. There was no better role model in Adam's mind. He tapped his phone on the table and cleared his throat.

"Do you want to discuss what happened last night?"

Eve's brow furrowed. "As I explained to Bella, I had a nightmare. Nothing more, nothing less."

"Eve, they've been more frequent lately. Maybe, I don't know, but maybe therapy wasn't such a good idea."

"Seriously?" Eve shook her head. "You begged me to go, Adam."

"I know. But I guess I didn't realize what it would do to you. Before therapy, things were fine. You couldn't paint, but I think you could get over that yourself. At least you weren't having these awful dreams all the time. My god, Eve, my daughter thought I was hurting you!"

She stared at Adam for a full ten seconds. "Do you know why I never let you stay the night?"

Adam blinked, his brain trying to comprehend what he thought was a change in subject. "Because you didn't want to get too close."

"And because I had night terrors almost every night of my life. I never wanted you to see me that way. So out of control." Knowing he wouldn't appreciate it as much as she did, Eve refrained from telling him that Lainey made her see that she had nothing to be ashamed of. "Therapy may be bringing them back, but I have to think that this is a step towards stopping them altogether."

"What it's doing is coming between us, Eve."

Another full ten seconds. "I never took you as a selfish man, Adam. Not when you whined about me cooking for Lainey's boys. Not even when you flaunted that woman in my restaurant in an attempt to make me jealous, but this? I asked you if you could handle this. You said you could."

"I —"

Whatever Adam was about to say was interrupted by a pounding on the front door.

"I'll get it." Eve didn't wait for Adam's response. Her stomach began to hurt as she neared the door. The pounding was persistent, and it caused nervousness in Eve that she didn't understand. She opened the door to a frantic Kevin.

"She made me leave!"

"What?" That ache in her stomach worsened. "Calm down and tell me what's going on."

"Mom! She and dad are fighting because of me! Because I wanted to quit stupid football. She should have let me stay. I can protect her!"

Eve was on the move. "Go inside!"

"Eve?" Adam called out.

"Stay with the boys and Bella. I'll be right back."

Adam caught up to her, taking the chance by grabbing her arm to stop her. "What's going on?"

"Let go of me." Eve took a deep breath. "Lainey and Jack are fighting. I'm going to go over and get Lainey. I'll be right back."

"I'll do it."

"No. You won't. Please, Adam, go back inside with Kevin and Darren. Tell them everything is fine."

"And if it isn't?"

"It will be."

"What happened to you?" Lainey asked Jack. She was genuinely curious. Had he always been this way? He couldn't have been. She wouldn't have married him. Would she have?

"I'm not the one who changed, Lainey. *You* are. I want my old wife back."

"We were doing so well. After the shooting, you were more attentive. I thought we had turned a corner."

Jack scoffed. "Another reason you should stay home and away from Eve. Don't pretend you haven't changed since then, as well. What happened to all the sex, Lainey? You rarely take the time to pleasure me these days."

Lainey vibrated with anger. "Is that why you're being such a Neanderthal? Because you're not *getting* any?"

Jack gripped Lainey's upper arm, pulling her closer. "I am being the man of the house. I'm *trying* to keep my family together and my boys from being weak. I work all day, so my family can live in this house. It is not too much to ask that you are here, taking care of your family. That includes taking care of me."

"How about *you* stay home, Jack." Lainey was aware that what she was about to say would make the situation worse. He was already hurting her arm. Yet, she was going to say it anyway. She would have to examine why she was provoking him later. "I make more money than you."

Jack's face turned red, and his hand squeezed harder on her arm. "You ungrateful bitch. I have had enough of this. You're quitting your job."

"No, I'm not." Lainey pushed against his chest. "In fact, I'm going to Italy next week."

"Like hell you are. I'm putting my foot down, Lainey. No more of this bullshit. Telling Kevin he can quit football, traveling, not being here for the kids or me. It's done."

"You can't make me quit, Jack. Any more than you can make my son do something he doesn't want to do."

Jack's lips curled into an ugly smile. "I can."

"What you can do is let go of Lainey."

Both Jack's and Lainey's heads whipped around at Eve's voice. This time when Lainey shook, it was with apprehension. She had seen that look on Eve's face before. It scared her then as much as it did now. Lainey knew that each time she witnessed it, it was in defense of her. She wasn't scared for herself, but Jack.

"Get out of my house," Jack snarled.

Eve ignored him and looked at Lainey. "Do you want me to leave?" Lainey could only shake her head. Eve's cold eyes found Jack again. "I won't tell you again. Let go of her."

"This isn't any of your business."

"I'm *making* it my business, Jack." Eve stepped closer. "If you're not afraid of me, I can call in Lainey's security detail."

Lainey's eyes snapped to Eve's, but Eve wasn't looking at her. What a time to find out that Eve still had security following her. Why? Was there another threat? Didn't Eve herself say that everyone from her past was dead and gone? The questions in her head faded when she felt Jack's grip loosen.

"Lainey is quitting," he said suddenly. "Tell her, Lainey."

Lainey rubbed her arm and shook her head. "No, I'm not." She turned to Eve. "Can we get out of here?"

"Of course."

"Lainey!" Jack bellowed.

Lainey made a show of looking at her watch. "You're late for work, Jack." He hated being late. She nearly laughed when he hmphed, picked up his briefcase, and practically ran out the door.

"Are you okay?" Eve asked softly.

"Yes. How did you know to come over here?"

"Kevin and Darren are at my house." Eve carefully replaced

Lainey's hand with hers, gently rubbing Lainey's arm. "Kevin was worried."

Lainey closed her eyes in shame. It was unfortunate that Kevin thought things were bad enough to get Eve. It was even worse knowing Eve witnessed the scene between Lainey and Jack. How could Lainey go on feigning a perfect marriage now?

She pulled away from Eve and grabbed her purse. "Let's go. On the way to the gallery, perhaps you can tell me about this security detail."

Eve grimaced. "Would I be able to get away with saying I was bluffing?"

"Nope." Lainey stopped at the door. "Are you in trouble again?"

"No, honey." Eve sighed. "What Tony did to you and what happened to Adam scared the hell out of me. I guess I haven't gotten over it, yet. Your security is just a precaution, nothing more."

"You would tell me if you were in danger, right? Or if I was?"

"I learned my lesson the last time, Lainey. I promise. There's no threat. Except maybe from your husband."

Lainey shook her head. "Jack is just angry that I didn't tell him about Kevin."

"Don't do that, Lainey. Don't make excuses for him. Nothing about how he treated you was acceptable."

"Fine. It wasn't. But it's nothing you should be concerned about."

Lainey's words cut Eve to the core. Did Lainey think she wouldn't be concerned? Didn't she know how Eve felt about her?

"I didn't mean that the way it sounded, Eve." The pain in Eve's eyes caused Lainey's heart to ache. "I only meant that you have enough going on."

"Stop. Whatever is going on in my life, Lainey, it stops for those who matter the most. That includes you." Eve cupped Lainey's face in her palms. *Don't make me go through this again,* she whispered.

Lainey stepped into Eve and wrapped her arms around her. "I'll be okay. I promise I'll come to you if I feel I can't handle Jack. Deal?"

"Deal."

Chapter Thirteen

"It's so beautiful here." Lainey took in a deep breath of the crisp Italian air. The afternoon couldn't have been more beautiful for Lainey's first time here.

Eve watched with a mixture of amusement and admiration. She had been to Italy several times. However, seeing it through Lainey's eyes was like seeing it for the first time. They had landed a little more than two hours ago, but Lainey insisted they walk around before going to the hotel. Since Eve couldn't say no to Lainey, she sent their luggage ahead and took Lainey sightseeing. Of course, that meant eating as well. Eve was sure by the time this trip was over she would be ten pounds heavier.

"Would you like some pastries?" Eve asked. She could smell the undeniable aroma of Italian pastries in the air and wondered if that's what Lainey thought was "so beautiful."

"Oh, God. Yes, I do! But I don't think I could eat another bite. I don't even want to think about what I've already eaten. We haven't even been here that long. I'm going to have to pace myself."

Eve laughed. "How about we get some to take back to the hotel?"

Lainey groaned. She wanted whatever was creating that heavenly scent but debated whether it was worth it. "My metabolism doesn't work nearly as hard as yours does. All of this food is going to go to my ass."

Involuntarily, Eve's eyes traveled down. *Such a great ass.* "Ahem, we'll be doing a lot of walking, so I think we can afford a few indulgences." Her phone chimed. *Saved by the bell.* "My sources tell me that Ms. Agosti lives not far from here," she said as she checked her messages.

"I take it her assistant didn't want to give up the location?" Lainey asked, threading her arm through Eve's. Despite being stuffed and worried about her waistline, she guided them to a nearby pastry shop. She justified it by acknowledging that she had been working out more lately. If she happened to gain a few pounds, hopefully, she wouldn't have too many problems getting it back off.

"She insists on having her outrageous demands met before seeing her *client.*"

"She knows exactly who you are. Odds are, she's trying to extort whatever she can from you. Too bad for her you're not stupid."

Eve smiled. "Always looking out for me, hmm?"

"Always." Lainey opened the door to a nearby pastry shop. The aromas that hit them were mouthwatering. Whatever they ended up getting probably wouldn't make it back to the hotel. "Oh boy. Don't judge me if I choose one of everything in this place."

Eve feigned shock and disappointment. "Uh, I'm totally going to judge you! Who brought you here? You're going to diss me by only getting *one* each?!"

Lainey started laughing the moment Eve gasped and clutched her non-existent pearls. God, she loved playful Eve. "Sorry! Two. I'll get two of everything."

"Better," Eve muttered playfully. "Macchiato?"

"Please. Grab us a seat?"

Eve chuckled. "Decided you can't wait after all?"

Lainey lifted a brow. "Be nice to the woman ordering pastries for you."

Eve raised her hands in concession. "Apologies, *mia cara.*" She bowed slightly, then went to order their coffees.

Lainey sighed softly. She didn't know much Italian, but she

knew that. And she knew how it made her feel when Eve said it to her. *Married. We're both married.* Unfortunately, thinking of Jack depressed Lainey. And it made her wonder if leaving the boys alone with him was such a good idea. Kevin assured her they would be fine. To be on the safe side, Lainey asked Eve to transfer her security to her boys while she was gone. Eve was happy to do so.

Her sigh now was somber. E*nough of that. We're here to work and enjoy our time together.* Lainey made her order, not quite buying everything in the store, but close.

"Did you get the struffolis?" Eve asked when Lainey joined her.

"Of course. *More* than two." Lainey slid into her chair opposite of Eve. The younger woman was sipping her cappuccino, the foam sticking to her top lip. "I should, um, text Jack and let him know I made it."

Does he care? Eve kept the question to herself. "Go ahead. I promise not to eat everything while you're ignoring me."

Lainey scoffed and rolled her eyes. "Like I could ignore you. I need to make sure you keep your promise." She took her phone out and shot off a quick text to Jack. Then another one to Kevin telling him to let her know if anything happens and she loved him and Darren. "I —" She burst out laughing when she looked up and saw Eve.

Eve cocked her head to the side. "Wha?"

"How many of those struffolis do you have in your mouth?"

"One."

"One, huh?" Lainey was used to things like this with her boys. Seeing a beautiful, sophisticated woman such as Eve stuffing her mouth with pastries and lying about it, tickled Lainey. "You're a nut; you know that, right?"

Eve shook her head, giving Lainey her best innocent look. She may have bitten off more than she can chew, literally. But it was worth it to see the stress drain away from Lainey's face. She swallowed just as Lainey received a text.

"Everything okay?"

Lainey flipped her phone over. "Yep. That was Kevin. Darren

asked if they could order pizza for dinner tonight, so he can feel like they're here with me."

"He's sweet. I bet Bella would love it if they went over and shared with her."

"Adam wouldn't mind?"

"Of course, not. He'll be happy he doesn't have to cook." Eve handed Lainey a cannoli. "How are things with Jack since that day?"

"Oh, Eve. I don't want to talk about that. Not now." They weren't great, but that was her problem, not Eve's.

"Fair enough." Eve was disappointed. However, she knew better than anyone else that there were times when talking about problems became tedious.

"I'm not saying I won't tell you, honey. I just don't want to think about it here."

"Hey, I get it, okay? I just wanted to make sure you were all right."

"Right now, I'm great. You made sure I didn't have to worry about the boys, I'm in Italy, I'm eating *a lot*, and I'm with you." Lainey gave Eve a smile. "I miss my boys already, but I'm sure you know how that feels with Bella."

"I do. She had Lexie text me the minute she got there." Eve took out her phone and opened her text app. Eve turned it so Lainey could see. "Bella selfie."

Lainey laughed. "Oh, she's adorable! I'm glad she likes the pajamas I got her."

"They're her favorite." Eve zoomed in on the pic, getting a good look at the unicorn pajamas. "She tells me she can't sleep without them, which means Lexie gets extra to do a small batch of laundry every other day," she chuckled.

"Kids. Gotta love them." Lainey took a bite of the cannoli. "Why are these so damn good? I didn't think I liked cannolis, but I may need to find some anonymous group to kick these things now."

"They're different here," Eve explained with a smile. "Authentic."

"If I were H. Agosti, all I would demand are these things."

"Good to know," Eve winked. "But, since cannolis aren't likely to help us, what do you think will?"

Lainey nearly choked on her pastry. It wasn't a terrible way to go, eating delicious desserts, but she'd rather not. "I thought you had a plan!"

"I do," Eve grinned. "I just wanted to see you squirm."

"You're rotten! I should throw this thing at you!" Lainey threatened. Instead of tossing the cannoli at Eve, she popped the rest in her mouth. "You're lucky it's so good."

Eve wondered how long it had been since she had laughed so much. She was lucky. Having Lainey in her life made everything slightly more bearable. Her companion licked the creamy filling from her lips and Eve almost moaned.

"We should go to the hotel and go to bed." Eve's eyes widened at the way that sounded. "What I mean is, it's been a long day of travel and eating. We should rest up for tomorrow."

It was Lainey's turn to grin. She cherished the moments when Eve would lose her composure with her. To her, it was a testament to the fact that Eve could drop the façade Lainey knew she often hid behind.

"We just had coffee," Lainey pointed out with delight. She could probably sleep if they went back to the hotel. Then again, she was staying in the same suite — different rooms this time — as Eve, so perhaps she was being a bit delusional. Besides, teasing Eve was too fun. "I could probably go all night."

Eve spent years learning how to compose herself. It took every single technique she ever mastered not to spew coffee all over the table in front of her. She caught that mischievous twinkle in Lainey's eye. *The little minx is teasing me!*

Eve's lips spread into a slow, sensual smile. "Is that right?" She leaned forward, dropping her voice an octave. "If jetlag is ailing you, I know a surefire cure."

Lainey swallowed hard. She started this. She was pretty sure Eve was trying to finish it. "And, ahem, what is that?"

"That is a long, hot, steamy . . . bath."

Lainey knew she was blushing. Still, she couldn't give up this easily. She mirrored Eve's position. "I hope it's a big tub," she said seductively. "I like to spread out."

Eve couldn't stop the groan this time. She acknowledged that they were walking a thin line. But flirting didn't hurt anyone. Did it? "Okay, okay. You win." She playfully wiped her brow with a napkin. "Let's get out of here so you can take your bath. I'll stick to a shower." *A cold one.* There was a sudden urge to call Adam. With the way she was feeling at the moment, it was probably best that she didn't ignore it.

"How did you find out where she lived?" Lainey peered out the window taking in the delightful scenery.

"I have my resources." Eve glanced over at her companion and smiled. Lainey was like a kid in a candy store. Despite her halfhearted complaints of having too much food, Lainey insisted on eating pasta for dinner. Eve obliged by ordering a few different dishes from places she knew Lainey would love and having them delivered to their room. Of course, now they had enough leftovers to last much longer than they would be there. To Eve, it was worth it to watch Lainey enjoying herself.

Lainey shifted in her seat. "Just how many "resources" do you have?"

Eve laughed. "I do a lot of business here in Italy, honey. To be successful, you need a good rapport with the well-established patrons in the community. People who have had an ear to the ground for longer than you or I have been alive."

"And these patrons know our artist?"

"Seems she's been peddling her stuff since before she was a teen."

"Why are you just hearing about her now?"

Eve frowned. That was a good question. She's owned a gallery here for years and not once had H. Agosti pinged her radar. Granted, she had left most of the gallery business here up to her local curator. She would have to ask him this very question.

"I don't know," Eve answered finally.

Lainey patted Eve's leg right above her knee. "It's okay. I'm sure you'll find out that answer before we leave."

Lainey's maternal instincts and obvious knowledge of her made Eve smile. It also reminded Eve of her conversation with Adam and Bella last night. Bella had spent her entire portion of the conversation telling Eve about every second of her day. Once that was over, Eve had to return the favor. Adam, however, wouldn't be as enthusiastic to hear she was having fun with Lainey. With that in mind, Eve kept the conversation on him and the business. As a silent partner, she knew the ins and outs of Adam's architect firm probably more than he wished.

"Here, honey," Lainey said abruptly.

Eve blinked. "Hmm?"

"You missed the turn. Are you okay?"

"Yes, sorry." She shook her head. "My mind was wandering." She slowed down to look for a place to turn around. Typically, she would have a chauffeur, but she wanted this alone time with Lainey. Besides, she didn't want to seem too pretentious to her, hopefully, new client. Though when she saw the house, Eve didn't think having a red carpet rolled out for her to walk on would be pretentious at all.

"Wow," Lainey murmured, echoing Eve's thoughts. "I guess she's doing well for herself."

"I guess so."

The unique architecture was something Adam would appreciate. The home was built around a cluster of trulli giving the villa a quirky character. Through the opened windows, she could smell the jasmine gardens that surrounded the large stone courtyard. Large olive trees were blooming around the property giving it the aura of a perfect Italian home.

"I have to say, if I lived here I probably wouldn't leave either," Lainey joked.

"Would you like to?" Eve asked as she rolled to a stop and cut the engine.

"What?" Surely Eve wasn't going to offer to buy this gorgeous house. Lainey thought back to her first auction with Eve. She mentioned she liked a little jade Buddha with rubies and diamonds encrusted in the golden necklace around its neck. Before Lainey realized what was happening, Eve had bought it for her for sixty-thousand dollars.

"Would you ever consider leaving New York? Or living in a different country?"

"Oh, um, I don't know. I mean, I briefly thought about leaving New York when I was pregnant with Kevin." Lainey shrugged. Her recent situation with Jack wasn't ideal. Perhaps that's why the idea intrigued her more than it should have. "I grew up in New York, but change can be good, right?"

Eve smiled. "Mmhmm. Ready?"

"As long as you're doing all the talking, let's go."

"Scared?" Eve laughed.

"I've seen the demands. Eccentric may be a nice word for this woman. So, yeah. A little scared."

"I honestly don't think those came from her, but we'll see. Come on. I'll protect you."

Lainey chuckled, but it was a promise she knew Eve was good for. Hadn't she already taken a bullet for her? "Right behind you."

Eve stepped up to the massive door. The narcissist in her was impressed as she pressed the high-tech doorbell. Oddly enough, the technology only enhanced the properties uniqueness. The door opened revealing a short woman in a maid's uniform.

"*Sì?*"

"*Buon giorno. Sono qui per verdere* H. Agosti."

The woman looked surprised by the request. Obviously, Agosti didn't get many visitors. The maid looked from Eve to Lainey and back again, tongue-tied. She hesitated long enough to make Eve doubt her Italian.

"*Signora?*" she tried again.

"*Mi dispiace. Scusimi.*" And just like that, the door was closed in their faces.

"Well. I have no idea what was said, but that seemed a bit rude."

Eve nudged Lainey playfully with her shoulder. "I think she was shocked to see people showing up here."

"*Che diavolo vuoi?*" A voice barked through the intercom. It most certainly wasn't the voice of the woman who had answered the door. This one was deeper. Raspier.

"*Now that was rude,*" Eve whispered in Lainey's ear. Eve repeated her greeting and was met with silence. She realized then that she had not introduced herself or said what her intentions were. "I apologize," she continued in Italian. "My name is Eve Sumptor . . ."

There was a distinct click, interrupting Eve's explanation. The door opened.

"Hmm. It seems like everyone just opens up when they hear your name," Lainey muttered, then blushed when Eve looked at her with a smirk and a raised brow. "T-that is not . . . I didn't . . . never mind." She pushed a laughing Eve through the door.

"How do you find me?"

Eve turned toward the voice, finally putting a face to the gruff sound. She wasn't expecting to see such a beautiful, young woman. The brunette hair was long, cascading down the woman's back. She was perhaps five or six years older than Eve, and taller than her by a few inches. Strong. Not thin, not broad. Just strong as though she spent a good amount of time taking care of herself. Her dark brown eyes watched Eve, full lips pursed as she waited for an answer.

"She has resources," Lainey answered, surprising herself. She had also been taken aback by this woman's appearance. She didn't know what she expected. Maybe someone a bit undone? Stained pajamas, mussed hair, not-so-fresh smell. Lainey knew that was a horrible stereotype, and she was undoubtedly proved wrong by the glamorous woman in front of them.

"H. Agosti?" Eve asked, ignoring Lainey's little quip.

"*Sí.* Why are you here?"

Oh, good. English, Lainey thought with relief. She seriously needed to learn some languages if she wanted to keep up with Eve.

"I'm Eve. This is my business partner, Lainey," Eve explained evenly. She didn't let the woman's bad attitude deter her. She imagined that being a hermit for so long would depreciate communication skills. "We've seen your work and want to represent you in our newest gallery."

"Los Angeles," H. said. After Eve's confirmation, she continued. "I don't go anywhere. I don't talk to people. You should have gone through my manager."

Though her accent was strong, Agosti's English was perfect. Eve was once again impressed. "I talked to your manager. Frankly, I didn't like what she had to say. I'm not one to play games, Ms. Agosti. That's all your manager wanted to do."

"Henley."

"Pardon?"

"You can call me Henley."

She gestured for Eve and Lainey to follow her. Both women took in their surroundings as they walked through the expansive house. Beautifully decorated, but sparse. Eve knew that method very well. Henley Agosti had been hurt. She hid from the world, only showing bits and pieces through her art. That, however, was not what they were here for.

"What did she ask for?" Henley asked suddenly.

Eve rattled off a list of demands that she had memorized. From daily stipends in the thousands to a home, studio, and an expensive vehicle. Not to mention a twenty-four seven chef, executive assistant, and personal assistant. As much as Eve agreed that Henley's work was worth millions, she wasn't about to accede to such demands.

"Jesus," Henley shook her head. "She knows who you are." She handed both Eve and Lainey a bottle of sparkling water. "Everyone knows who you are. Your gallery here is the most sought after for artists. She probably figured if you sought me out, you could pay for what you've done." She paused. "Why not here in my country? In my city? Why should I come to the states?"

"I just recently came across your work as I was researching to find another established artist. I don't know how you slipped under my radar for so long."

"Excuse me," Lainey interrupted. "What did you mean by 'pay for what you've done'?"

Henley sighed. "Camilla, my manager, believes you've hurt my reputation. She's not easy to deal with as you've seen. As a result, my work has been banned from your gallery here. But now, here you are offering me a spot in Los Angeles, and she's taking advantage of it."

"She or you?" Lainey asked with a bit of heat.

Eve hid her proud smile. It seemed Lainey didn't need her protection after all. Not when she was busy protecting Eve.

"No, no. Not me," Henley said genuinely. "Camilla, she is very protective of me and my work. There are times she goes too far, but she's harmless."

Eve looked around the villa. "Harmless," she repeated. "You're renting this place instead of owning it. You're secluded. You just said you were banned from my gallery here. How harmless is she, Henley?"

Henley scoffed. "You don't understand anything."

Lainey stepped forward. "If anyone understands, Henley, it's Eve," she said gently. "Your work is incredible. So much so it has made it to Eve in New York despite your rep here. Having someone like Camilla speak for you when you know you wouldn't make these demands for yourself, is what's damaging your reputation."

"She's all I have. I can't — I don't like dealing with the world. All I want to do is paint."

"Me, too," Eve said. Unfortunately, she couldn't even do that anymore. "Here's my proposal. Be a featured artist for Sumptor Galleries, LA. Exclusively. Which means, no other galleries can have access to any new work. Come to Los Angeles for a minimum of six months, and I will give you the apartment with a studio, and a stipend for the duration of our contract."

"What is the catch?" Henley asked skeptically.

"Camilla is not invited."

"But!"

Eve held up her hand to silence Henley. To her surprise, it worked. "If she shows up, I will consider our arrangement to be null and void."

"Because she asked for a few things that are nothing to someone like you?"

"No. because I don't believe she has your best interest in mind. Henley, she asks for all these things in her name. This place," she gestured widely, "is under her name. She's listed on your bank account."

"She does that so I don't have to deal with it. How do you know all this?"

"I make it my job to know who I'm bringing in-house, Henley. I truly hope you're right about her. But ask yourself this; what would happen if you couldn't paint anymore? Would she still be there?"

"That would never happen," Henley answered with indignance.

"Art is never a guarantee. Make sure that the people in your life are." Eve let that sink in. "Do we have a deal?"

Henley took a deep breath, letting it out slowly. "*Sí.*"

"How did you know about the place and the bank account?" Lainey asked. They had left Henley more than thirty minutes ago after having taken care of the paperwork. Eve had insisted that Henley have a lawyer, not her manager, look it over before signing it. Henley signed it anyway stating she trusted Eve. As trustworthy as Eve was, Lainey was sure Henley merely didn't want to have to talk to anyone else. "Don't tell me you own the place. And the bank."

Eve laughed. "No. Though I may look into buying that villa when Henley is ready to leave." She glanced over at Lainey and winked. As she turned her attention back to the road, she continued. "I couldn't find much on Agosti. So, I did a background check on Camilla. Once I saw she was listed on Agosti's bank account, I assumed they would live together. A search for an address popped up with that house and Camilla as the renter."

"Resources, huh? When did you become Sherlock?" Lainey was impressed.

"Background checks are as simple as a few clicks on the computer, silly." Eve checked the GPS. They were about an hour from their hotel. And two hours from a quaint village she knew. This was their last night in Italy together and Eve wanted to make it special for Lainey. Unfortunately, they had an early flight in the morning. "Are you hungry?"

"I think it's an unwritten rule that when you're in a beautiful place with amazing food, you have to eat every couple of hours."

Eve laughed. "Well, we wouldn't want to break the rules, now would we?"

Lainey settled into her seat and sighed. She loved this car. Eve had called it some kind of insect. Lainey glanced at the car's emblem on the steering wheel. Alfa Romeo. Now she remembered. Eve had called it a Spider. Though she hated spiders, Lainey could certainly get used to this one.

The leather bucket seats practically hugged her in a soft embrace. The two-seater sports car was white, of course, but the interior was an intense red that called to Lainey's soul. It was an impractical car for a mother of two. But here in Italy, with Eve, it was perfect.

"I wish we had more time here," she said absently.

Eve glanced over. Lainey had her head back on the headrest, eyes closed. She wasn't even sure if Lainey knew she had said the words out loud.

"Do you want to stay?"

Lainey opened one eye. "What?"

"Do you want to stay?" Eve repeated. "Just one more day. I can take you for a tour around Rome. We can play tourist."

Silence filled the space between them as Lainey thought about it. Part of her, the part that was being hugged by the buttery leather seats of this car, wanted to be reckless and stay. The other part, the mother part, knew she couldn't. Jack wouldn't understand, and she didn't want him taking it out on the boys.

"I can't," she said finally and opened both eyes to look at Eve. "I'm sorry. I . . ."

"Lainey," Eve reached over and put her hand on Lainey's knee. "It's okay. It was just a suggestion."

Lainey felt the heat of Eve's hand burning through her jeans. God, she wished just once she wouldn't have such a visceral reaction to simple gestures. She could blame her problems with Jack. Or, she could be honest with herself. She placed her hand on top of Eve's and squeezed, then slowly withdrew. Apparently, she wasn't ready for honesty. It felt terrible when Eve removed her hand. It was for the best. Right?

"So, food." Eve cleared her throat. She hadn't meant anything by touching Lainey. It was second nature to her, and she rarely held back with Lainey. Okay, that wasn't exactly true. Since they had made the decision not to be together again, Eve held back quite a bit. She had to. But that was different. "I know of this little village not too far from here. They have the most incredible olive oil. A strapping young man named Antonio will teach you how it's made and flirt shamelessly with you. Would you like to go?"

"Two questions. Will it be served with some of that amazing Italian bread? And can I take some home?"

"Yes, and yes."

"Then, yes. Though I could do without the flirting from Antonio."

The two laughed heartily. Tension may be a part of their relationship. But it was the respect and love that got them through it all. Eve was getting extremely tired of feeling guilty about that.

Chapter Fourteen
Therapy

Matters of the heart.

"Welcome back, Eve."

Eve smiled at Dr. Woodrow but didn't say anything. For some reason, she was nervous about being back here in her office. After coming back from Italy with Lainey, seeing Dr. Woodrow was effectively making her feel . . . well, like she needed a shrink.

"You are very pensive today. Would you like to tell me what's going on in your head?" Willamena kept her tone without judgment, yet she felt a shift in Eve.

"Not really." The words came out sharper than Eve intended, and she cringed inwardly. *Damn it get in control, Eve!*

Dr. Woodrow studied her patient until she saw Eve shift uncomfortably in her seat. Something was clearly bothering the elegant woman.

"Very well. How about you tell me about your trip?"

"What about it?"

Willamena let out a small sigh as she sat back and crossed her legs. She placed her ever-present notebook on her knee and silently wrote notes. ***Patient is feeling a lot of emotions today including extreme irritability. Unwilling to talk about*** *what is making her feel this way. To help, I must break through the wall.*

"What do you write?" Eve asked, curiosity getting the best of her.

Willamena looked up from her notebook. "Pardon?"

"In your notebook. Do you write about how crazy you think I am?" Eve was aware the question was completely childish. She could have kicked herself for asking. But it was out now. Not much to do except wait for an answer.

"Do you believe I think you're crazy?"

Eve's nostrils flared with frustration. The psychiatrist standard 'answer a question with a question' was irritating!

"Are you going to answer my question, Doc, or just continue jotting whatever it is you're jotting?" Whew. Her annoyance was off the charts today. She could blame jetlag, but she had been back for a few days.

"Does this bother you?" Dr. Woodrow asked instead of answering, lifting her notebook. She then lifted her hands in a placating gesture when she noticed Eve getting angrier. "Alright, Eve. If you're truly curious, I'm writing notes about you. I don't record the sessions for security reasons. When I take notes, I'm basically noting what your reaction to something is. The animation of your face, whether you laugh or cry, whether you cringe or smile. Your eyes hold many answers that you don't say out loud. If you would like to read them, you're welcome to. But I do not believe you're crazy. In fact, I believe you're one of the strongest people I've ever met."

"Right," Eve snorted.

"Why do you doubt that?"

"Because I'm here. Obviously, I'm not strong enough to get over whatever it is that's keeping me from painting."

"Eve, what you have been through would make a lot of people give up living altogether. You not only lived, but you thrived. That, my dear, is strength. Needing help doesn't diminish that strength. I think it makes you stronger that you have the courage to seek guidance."

Eve took a moment to let the doctor's words sink in. Did she believe her? She wasn't sure, but she was trying.

"I apologize for my attitude," she said quietly.

"It's alright. Would you like to tell me why you were so irritated?"

"I don't know." Of course, Eve wasn't exactly truthful, and she had a feeling Dr. Woodrow knew it when she said nothing. It was as though she was waiting on Eve to get to the truth. *Sigh.* "Fine. I'm afraid to learn how you feel about my trip with Lainey."

Dr. Woodrow's eyebrows furrowed. "Why would you care what I think about that? Eve," she continued before Eve could answer, "that wasn't meant to be a negative question. I honestly would like to know why my opinion on that matters to you."

"I don't want you to judge me," Eve confessed softly.

"Did you do something with Lainey?"

"No! Of course not!"

"So, you believe I would judge you merely for going out of town on business with your associate?"

"Lainey is more than an associate. You know that."

"You're right, I do. So that's why you think I would judge you? Because I know there's more there?"

"Yes."

"Eve?" She waited for Eve to meet her gaze. "Did you want something to happen while you were in Italy?"

Eve felt the blush creep up her neck, and abruptly stood to pace. She had tried so hard to keep her mind on business while in Italy. Even staying in the same room, Eve made sure they were never in any situation that could become intimate. When she and Lainey weren't working or eating, she was on the phone with Adam and Bella. Despite all that, Eve still felt those familiar feelings when she was with Lainey. And she hated herself for it. Lainey was having problems with Jack again, and all Eve could think about was solving those problems. By taking Jack's place.

"I can see you beating yourself up for whatever you were feeling, Eve. I believe that's a large part of the reason you cannot paint. You are trying to close a part of you because it scares you."

"I won't hurt my husband like that." Eve heard the words come out of her mouth and couldn't help but wonder if she would hurt him no matter what she did.

"Eve, I'm certainly not telling you to continue your affair with Lainey . . . "

Eve's head whipped around, and she stared at Dr. Woodrow with a scowl. "I was *not* married when Lainey and I were together!"

"You're right. But she was," Willamena reminded Eve gently.

Eve blew out an exasperated breath and unceremoniously slumped back into her chair.

"I know, okay. I *knew*! And I *still* pursued her! What kind of person does that?"

"From what I can understand, you didn't force Lainey to be with you. It takes two, Eve. To be honest with you, I think your relationship was extremely beneficial to both of you."

"It was wrong!" Eve exclaimed, quite loudly.

"I'm not advocating cheating, Eve," she explains calmly. "However, both of you needed something that no one else was successful in giving either of you. Can you deny that it helped you open your heart to Adam?"

"It almost destroyed us, and now I can't paint."

"You're afraid. Do you feel if you open your heart fully again, you'll fall back into bed with Lainey?"

Eve was stunned by the doctor's frankness. "My answer to your first question is yes. When we were in Italy together, I thought about it."

Patient deflects when asked about feelings for ex-lover. Dr. Woodrow made the note before looking at Eve, waiting for her to continue once again.

"I can't help how I feel about Lainey. She was the first person that made me feel safe. Someone I knew would never hurt me. I didn't have to be in constant control with her."

"You didn't feel that with Adam?"

"I felt more with Adam than with anyone before. But I was always hesitant."

"Can you tell me why?"

"Adam is a wonderful man. He's intelligent, funny, attentive, extremely sexy. Everything a woman could possibly want in a man."

"But?"

"I was afraid of losing him if he found out that I was a whore." There was more to that, but Eve couldn't bring herself to vocalize it. At least not yet.

"Eve. I find that description you use for yourself offensive."

"It's the truth, Doc." Eve shrugged, trying for nonchalance. She didn't think the doctor was buying it. "You can try prettying it up by calling it something else, but if it looks like a duck and walks like a duck . . ."

"Eve, you were forced! It was completely beyond your control, and I do not want you to belittle yourself like that!"

Eve was startled speechless by Dr. Woodrow's outburst. She knew the doctor cared about her. She had said as much before. But to hear her so exasperated threw Eve.

"You're right," Eve conceded. "I've always used that description as a way to keep myself closed off."

"I apologize for my little outburst there, Eve."

Eve waved away her apology. "It's fine. I was just trying to explain why I felt so different with Adam. He was an extremely jealous person. If someone looked at me for too long, he didn't like it. He was never mean about it, but I thought if he found out about my past, he would never forgive me."

"And Lainey seemed more accepting? Was it easier because she is a woman?"

"Yes. To both questions." Eve's eyes closed as she thought of the differences between Adam and Lainey. "My fears about Adam were unfounded. He's the most understanding and loving man. If only I had trusted him before I let my emotions get away from me with Lainey." Even as she said the words, her heart ached. She didn't want to think about never having had the experiences she had with Lainey. The ever-present — frustrating — guilt made its presence known. But which love did she feel guilty about?

"Playing 'what if' never works, Eve. We're not here to talk about what you should have or shouldn't have done."

"I know," Eve sighed. "I am afraid."

"Of letting go again?"

"*Yes,*" Eve whispered.

The look on Eve's face at that moment had Willamena scribbling in her notebook. ***The subject of the patient's past relationship and the feelings that invokes scares the patient so much I am afraid she will shut down even more. Take care during this subject. Also note: By suppressing these feelings, she is either lying to herself or trying to convince herself that she is wrong about how she feels. I have yet to determine which love she feels is wrong.***

"I don't think you're ready for this yet, Eve."

"What did you just write?"

Willamena tilted her head and regarded Eve for a moment before handing her the notebook. She watched carefully as Eve read her latest notes.

Eve handed the notebook back to Dr. Woodrow. "You saw all of that on my face?"

"In your eyes, yes."

Eve sighed deeply. The note was completely correct. When she talked about Lainey, she felt as though her life was unraveling. Or incomplete. But she couldn't lose Adam. She loved him too much. Why else would she have decided to marry him? But God, the thought of losing Lainey caused her heart to pound faster, and she couldn't catch her breath.

"Eve?"

"What do I do?" Eve gasped.

Dr. Woodrow leaned towards Eve and placed a gentle hand on her knee. "Relax. We don't have to figure everything out right now. In fact, when we last spoke, we were supposed to talk about the time you turned yourself in and left Paris."

Hard subject, but not nearly as difficult as talking about Lainey. So, Eve nodded.

"Good. I think this is a good time to call it a night. I'm sorry we got into a subject you weren't ready for."

"We have to do it sometime," Eve said amicably.

"You're right. And we will go into it more when the timing is right. For now, go home to your husband and little girl and try to relax."

"Thanks, Doc. Next week?"

"I'll be here," she smiled. "Goodnight, Eve."

Chapter Fifteen

"Momma, momma, momma!"

Eve turned from the refrigerator and bent to catch her running daughter in her arms.

"Where's the fire, bug?"

Bella giggled. "No fire, siwwy."

"No fire, huh? Then why all the mommas?" Eve looked around comically. "Are there more of me?" She gasped. "Did you find more mommas while I was in Italy?"

By this time Bella was squealing with laughter, only getting louder when Eve started tickling. "No, momma! Pease!"

"Are you a monkey's uncle?"

"Yes!"

"Good answer!" Eve kissed Bella's whole face, then set her cute little butt down on the counter. "Now, how about you *calmly* tell me what you ran in here about."

Bella took a deep breath. She was still panting from all the laughing. "I go work with you," she said matter-of-factly.

Eve raised a brow. "Oh? Are you telling or asking?"

Bella lowered her eyes. "Asking, momma."

"Good girl. Momma has a few meetings, but if you want to come with me, we'll bring you some crayons. Sound good?"

"Yeah!" Bella threw her arms in the air, beckoning her mom.

She hugged Eve tightly around the neck, kissing her noisily on the cheek.

"Momma loves you," Eve said softly.

"Wuv you, momma."

"Good. Now, let Lexie help you get ready, okay?"

"'Kay!" Bella let out a big "weeee" when Eve picked her up, spinning her once before setting her down.

"I guess I missed the love fest." Adam received a quick hug from Bella before she took off. "What was that all about?"

"She was buttering me up so I'd take her to work with me," Eve smiled. She walked to her husband and straightened his tie. "You look nice."

"Thanks, beautiful. I have an important meeting with that up and coming tech company today."

Eve reached up and kissed Adam softly on the lips. "For luck," she said with a smile.

"I'll definitely get the contract now," Adam grinned. "I don't know what time I'll be home tonight."

Eve patted him on the chest. "It's okay. Bella, Lainey, and I are going to have a little girls' night. We're going to go see that new cartoon movie Bella has been bugging us about."

Adam nodded. "When did you make these plans?"

Eve sighed. "Please don't start. I talked to Lainey this morning, and the boys are going to a different movie. We thought it was a good opportunity to take Bella."

"I see."

"Adam, I knew about your meeting. I also know that when something big like this comes up, you tend to stay late. It's just a movie. One you didn't care about seeing."

"I get it, Eve. You don't ask permission." He walked past her and filled his travel mug with coffee. "Just once, I wish you would remember she's *my* daughter, too."

Eve took a cleansing breath. "I do remember, Adam." She turned to him. "Is it because I didn't discuss it with you first or because Lainey is going with us?"

She was seriously getting tired of this argument. No matter what she did, how much sex she had with him, how much she told him she loved him, he would always have this issue. Even when he tried to be understanding, Eve could see the doubt in his eyes. It was her fault. She was adult enough to acknowledge that. But what more could she do? *Try not having feelings for Lainey.*

"Does it matter?" Adam answered. "I have to go. I guess I'll see you later tonight."

"Adam," Eve called out. "We can't keep doing this. I'm not trying to hurt you. I'm just trying to live as normally as I can despite all the shit."

Adam exhaled. "You're right. I'm sorry." He put his things down and went to his wife. Lately, he had been so blinded by jealousy and the feeling of rejection that he lost sight of the real issue. He pulled Eve into a hug and could feel the tension. "I've been stressing out over this bid and taking it out on you."

"That's not what this is, Adam, and you know that."

"Can we agree that it's part of it?" Adam asked sincerely. "I'm not going through what you are, Eve, but I have stuff, too. Sometimes I forget to check my jealousy. Can you blame me?"

"I haven't been with Lainey for a long time, Adam. Since before I agreed to marry you. I'll admit that what we did was wrong because *she* was married. But you need to stop pretending that I betrayed you with her."

That was *not* what she meant to say, but her irritation had hit its threshold.

"You're right." Adam let his arms drop. "You didn't fuck me over. Just Jack. Have fun at the movies."

Eve kept quiet. She knew that if she took the bait, they'd be fighting for days. She didn't have the energy for that.

I apologize for this morning.

Eve sent the text to Adam then put her phone in the top drawer of her desk without waiting for an answer. She couldn't shake the regret for what she said to him. *Her* feelings were not his fault.

Lainey, of course, could sense something was wrong. But, being her best friend, she didn't push the issue.

She shook her head. Eve Sumptor did not build her empire by worrying about other people's feelings. She didn't survive all these years by letting her feelings consume her. And she certainly wouldn't let the launch of Sumptor Galleries, LA suffer because she was a fucking mess right now. A knock at her office door startled Eve. It wasn't her daughter's knock. Nor was it Lainey's.

"Come in." Her heart sank to her stomach when she saw the familiar sandy blonde hair and beard. "Captain Harris. What's wrong?"

Charlie Harris's golden-brown eyes crinkled in a smile. "I should be used to that. No one likes seeing a homicide cop show up at their door."

"I'm sorry." Eve stood and walked to Charlie. She gave him a small kiss on the cheek and invited him to sit. "If you could just settle my heart?"

"No one is hurt or dead, Eve," he said gently. "I'm not here on business." He shrugged a little. "Well, not really."

"All right. Now instead of being nervous, I'm intrigued. You haven't visited me in months."

"My turn to apologize," Charlie said, patting his heart as a gesture that he meant what he said. "I don't want to make excuses."

"But?"

He sighed. "I wanted you to hear this from me, not through your connections at the precinct. I'm retiring."

Eve's eyebrows shot up. "Come on, Charlie. So your hair is getting a little gray. That doesn't mean you're old enough to retire." She winked at him to soften the blow of her joke.

Charlie gave her a small smile. When he didn't immediately defend his gray hair, Eve's instinctive alarms went off.

"What is it that you're not telling me, Charlie?"

"I'm being pushed out, Eve."

Eve leaned forward, her elbows resting on her desk. "Pushed out? They're forcing you to retire?" Charlie nodded. "Why?"

"Reasons," he said vaguely. He should have known Eve wouldn't accept that answer. Besides, he came here for a reason. It was best not to get on her bad side by not being straight with her. "It's been brewing for a while, Eve."

"Since Maurice?" Eve guessed. When Charlie confirmed her suspicions, she continued. "Why give you the captain's position only to force you out a couple of years later?"

"For show, I'm guessing. I've heard whispers behind my back since I took Maurice down. How I turned on my partner. Didn't matter that he was dirty or a murderer. They thought I chose the pretty girl over brotherhood." He shook his head. "It just so happened that that "pretty girl" was friends with the Commissioner. Now that he's stepped down, they found their path to me."

"That's bullshit." Eve stood and began to pace. "I'll talk to this new commissioner. And if he doesn't listen, I'll go straight to the mayor."

"Eve, no." Charlie got up as well. "That's not why I'm here. I can't trust my back with these guys."

Eve nodded. "You're a good cop, Charlie. What if I can get you into another . . ."

"I'd have to move to another state, Eve. The blue blood runs deep and far. I betrayed it when I turned on my partner."

"A murderer. He killed innocent people, Charlie. Because of me."

"No, because of Tony," Charlie corrected vehemently. "And his own greed. This isn't on you any more than it's on me."

"How can I help you?" Eve asked, skipping over the debate on whether she was responsible or not.

Charlie shifted uncomfortably. As much as he hated asking for favors, he was about to ask a big one from Eve.

"I am a good cop, Eve. And I'm not ready to sit on the beach and sip piña coladas."

Eve chuckled. "Weird. That sounds good to me."

He smiled. "Maybe someday. I'm in my forties. I'm still in my prime. I don't know. Maybe it's a good thing that they're forcing me out. The job is dangerous enough without having to worry about the guys you're working with."

"You're stalling, Charlie," Eve smiled. "But I think I've gotten to know you well enough to know what you're trying to ask."

"You do?"

"Mmm." Eve went to her desk. She grabbed a pen out of the holder and a post-it. After scribbling a few things down, she handed it over to Charlie. "Call James. He handles all my security. If you want a job, Charlie, it's yours."

He took the piece of paper. It may not have been a promotion at the NYPD, but to Charlie, it was better. He respected Eve. And he knew she trusted him to do a good job. Otherwise, she would never offer. "I don't know how to thank you, Eve. I —"

"No thanks necessary. You'll be an asset to the team, Charlie. Private security can be very lucrative. And since everyone who tried to kill me is now dead, it'll be like getting paid to sit on a beach and drink piña coladas."

"That's not funny, Eve."

She laughed. "It kinda is." She punched his shoulder playfully. "Thank you for coming to me."

"To be honest, I wasn't sure I would. But, if I'm going to work for anyone besides the city, I'd like it to be you. Protecting you has been an honor."

Eve cleared her throat. *More emotions. Damn it.* "Thank you."

She walked Charlie out, stopping by the railing as he continued down the stairs. Lainey looked up at her questioningly and Eve smiled. *I'll tell you later,* she mouthed.

"See ya later, boss!" Charlie called out, waving at Lainey as he passed by.

Another look passed between the two women, and this time Eve shrugged. She knew Lainey would be up as soon as she was finished with the customers she was currently dealing with. Until then, Eve felt the need to visit her daughter in the playroom.

"I still can't believe they forced Charlie out." Lainey reached into the popcorn bucket and grabbed a handful.

"I know. He didn't want me to talk to the mayor, but I'm not sure I can let this go."

"What go, momma?" Bella asked with a mouthful of popcorn.

Eve looked down at her little girl. "My popcorn! You little thief!" Bella giggled, filling Eve's heart. She had been bemoaning having emotions all day. But at this moment, they were overflowing, and she wouldn't have it any other way. God, she loved this little girl.

Lainey smiled at the two. It made her miss the times when her boys were young enough to want to be around her. They were here at the theater with them but didn't want to watch some "kid movie." She allowed them to see a PG movie when Kevin promised her there wasn't anything too bad in it.

"What can you do?" Lainey asked, going back to their original conversation.

Eve lifted a shoulder. "If they're willing to defend a . . . person like Maurice, there's a chance they're like him. The least I can do for Jackie, Meredith, and everyone else this has hurt, is request an investigation."

Lainey chuckled, then covered her mouth when Eve gave her a look. "I'm sorry. *Why* you're doing it is not funny. But this is the second investigation you're going to initiate. Is this going to be your new hobby?"

Eve laughed. "No. But if I see a problem that I may be able to fix, I'll do what I can to fix it."

The two women held each other's eyes for a moment. Was what they felt for each other a problem? Was it fixable? Did they want to fix it? And what did that mean? They both jumped a little when Bella squealed.

"On, momma!" Bella wiggled around in her seat, getting comfortable. This wasn't her first movie in a big theater. Her momma had taken her a few times before. It was one of Bella's favorite things to do. She got to eat junk food, sit in a comfy chair, and be with two of her favorite people. She snuck another handful of popcorn and smiled.

Lainey unlocked the front door and let the boys go in ahead of her. They all enjoyed their time at the movies, discussing the differences on the way home. Of course, Bella took center stage, talking animatedly about her film. The boys humored her by energetically oohing and ahhing at every detail. Lainey found it to be hysterical. Eve found it to be charming. They were all still laughing when Eve dropped them off at their house.

"You guys go up and get ready for bed." She kissed them both. "I'll be up in a bit to tuck you in." Lainey laughed when the boys groaned. They never knew if she was serious or not. There were times when she did tuck them in even though they both thought they were too old for it. But she used her "mother's prerogative" to overrule them.

"Uh," Kevin began, trying to think of a way to get her to forget about babying them. "We were kinda hungry. Right, squirt?"

"Yeah!" Darren readily agreed. "Thirsty, too." He ran past them towards the kitchen.

"You two had a ton to eat at the theater. How on earth can you still be hungry?" Lainey asked as she trailed after her sons.

She stopped cold when she saw the state of her kitchen. It was a mess. Dirty pans crusted with — she wasn't sure what it was — were still on the stove. Plates were piled up in the sink. She couldn't believe it. Jack was the only one here. Why would he need so many dishes? And why in the hell didn't he clean up after himself?

Unfortunately, she knew the answer to that question. He had made it clear lately that she was not living up to her duties as a wife. He also knew that she couldn't stand having a mess in her kitchen. By leaving this mess, he was forcing her to do her "job." Lainey blew out a breath.

"Get a snack, a *light* snack, and take it upstairs with you," she ordered softly and started gathering the pots off the stove.

"Hey, squirt," Kevin whispered, knowing his younger brother hated seeing his mom upset. He nodded towards the stairs and Darren took off without question or comment about being called squirt. Again. "Let me get that, mom."

"No, no. You need to get to bed. You have school tomorrow."

"And you have work." He took the pans from her. "Why do you let him treat you like this?"

"Kevin."

"Mom. I'm serious. He's a jerk because we're not doing what *he* wants us to do. I can handle the cold shoulder he's giving me, but this is bullshit."

"Kevin! Language!"

"I'm sorry, mom, but this is ridiculous. And you're just going to clean it up without saying anything. Look at this." He went to the sink and flipped some plates angrily. "Half of this stuff isn't even dirty. But he put a plate for all of us in here trying to prove some stupid point."

"Kevin, enough, please. Just go upstairs."

"Nope." Kevin turned on the water and picked up a sponge. "I'm going to rinse these pans out, put the plates in the dishwasher, and put salt in the sugar."

"You don't — wait, what? What was that about salt?"

"It'll be perfect for dad's coffee in the morning."

"Kevin!" Lainey couldn't help but laugh. "You are not going to put salt in the sugar. *I* use that! Look," she turned him to her. "I appreciate what you're doing. I do. But this is my mess," she looked around. "Literally. *My* mess. I know you don't understand why I put up with it, but maybe one day you will."

"If you're doing it for me, I don't want you to. I can handle him, mom."

"You shouldn't have to handle him, Kevin. You're fifteen." She hugged him. "I am so proud of the young man you've become, but you need to be a kid."

Kevin pulled back. "I'm *your* kid. Every day it's something. Your job, me quitting football, you not *giving* him enough. Yeah," he grimaced. "I hear him sometimes. It's always about him, mom. I'm not even sure he gives a crap about anyone else."

"Oh, honey. Your father loves you." Kevin scoffed, but she continued anyway. "He does. And he wants the best for you."

"And you?"

"Well, that's . . . that's between your father and me. Listen, honey, I'm not perfect either. We all have our flaws. Sometimes it's easier to clean the mess and move on."

"Is that what Eve would tell you to do?"

Lainey blinked at him. "What does Eve have to do with this?" she asked carefully. Had he seen something between them earlier that night?

"She's your best friend. Maybe you should talk to her about what's going on here."

"No. I told you before that Eve has a lot on her plate right now. There's no need to bother her with this."

"Did you know Wyatt and Landon were suspended? Coach was fired, too. It seems to me, if you have a problem, all you have to do is talk to Eve Sumptor-Riley about it."

Unless she's part of the issue, Lainey thought grudgingly. Of course, Lainey didn't think of Eve as a problem. The problem was her *own* feelings. That certainly wasn't Eve's fault.

"I agree that Eve is very good at fixing other people's problems. But right now, she must focus on herself. Your father leaving a few dishes in the sink is nothing compared to what she's been through."

Kevin shook his head. "Don't do that, mom. Don't make your problems less important. I bet Eve would tell you the same thing."

"Enough." Lainey took a calming breath. Kevin was merely trying to help. He didn't deserve her irritability. "I'm sorry. I don't mean to snap at you, sweetie. But you need to let me handle this my way. I need *you* to worry about school work and your next adventure."

Kevin put his hands on his mom's shoulders. "I worry about you. But," he continued before she could argue with him, "I'll do as you ask."

"For once," Lainey mutter playfully. "Now, will you go check on your brother and make sure he brushed his teeth, please?"

"Yes, ma'am," Kevin sighed dramatically. "Will you at least think about what I've said?"

Lainey nodded, then gave Kevin a small push. "Go." The truth was, there was nothing she wanted more than to talk to Eve about everything. She felt guilty enough about that. No matter how much of an ass Jack was being, she was still married to him. She made vows. And, now, so had Eve. Is that why Lainey tolerated Jack's attitude? Was it betraying Jack that made her feel guilty about her feelings for Eve? Or was it breaking Adam's trust again? She sighed to herself. At least her confusion gave her an excellent excuse to seclude herself in the guest bedroom to read.

Chapter Sixteen
Therapy

Fight or flight?

"Let's discuss the night you decided to turn yourself in, Eve." Willamena instinctively knew this session would be particularly hard for Eve. Although she had brandy on hand, she thought it was best for Eve to be clear headed. Dulling the senses wouldn't dull the pain.

Eve flinched as she thought about that night. Not only because of what happened to her but because it made her think of the two people who nearly destroyed her. Her father was a terrible man. That was a given. However, what Laurence did to her, and ultimately what Billy did, came close to breaking her. Hell, maybe it had broken her, and that was why she was here now.

"Okay," Eve said softly but didn't continue. She didn't know how, or if she wanted to.

Dr. Woodrow sat quietly, waiting Eve out. It was a risky move with someone like Eve Sumptor who was difficult to intimidate. And, honestly, she didn't want to intimidate her. Willamena merely wanted to give Eve the space she needed, the time she needed, to open up about something so devastating.

"Laurence and his buddies finished with me, and I knew I

couldn't take anymore. I decided to take my chances with the authorities. I thought it couldn't get much worse than what happened to me. Even if they threw me in jail, it would have been better than what happened to me." Eve paused, then whispered, "*Death would have been better.*"

"Let's go over what happened to you," Dr. Woodrow prodded gently, her notebook poised on her knee.

"Do we have to?"

"Of course not. But I think it would help you."

"How?"

"Call it a cleansing of the soul. A purging of all of the horrible things that happened to you."

"I've already told Adam and Lainey. Shouldn't my soul be cleansed by now?" Eve smirked. It was more of a defense mechanism than a desire to be an asshole.

Dr. Woodrow cocked her head to one side and regarded Eve until the younger woman shifted in her seat. "When was the last time you had a nightmare about that night?" she asked.

Damn it. Eve's night terrors had all but stopped after she had told Lainey and Adam what had happened to her. Though, after what happened with Laurence and Billy, they had made a sporadic comeback. Then, of course, there were the recent dreams starring Tony and Laurence that still gave Eve chills. Her soul still needed cleansing.

"Two nights ago," Eve admitted grudgingly. This time Tony and Laurence took turns taunting her. She had been relieved that Adam slept through this one.

"Same one as usual?"

"Yes." It wasn't quite a lie. Some elements were the same. However, Eve hadn't been ready to delve into the specifics of what Tony and Laurence say to her in recent dreams.

"And it's about that night?" Willamena asked, continuing when Eve nodded. "Is it a memory?" Another nod. "So, not a nightmare necessarily. You are defenseless when you are sleeping. You cannot keep your brain from recalling those events. What we're trying to do is make your brain believe that it is over, and those men cannot hurt you anymore."

"I already know that," Eve said defensively.

"Yes, you do. But your defenseless brain has not made that connection yet," Dr. Woodrow countered kindly. "You're still holding on to it, holding on to everything. By doing that, you are keeping a part of yourself closed off to everyone. Including your daughter."

Eve wanted to argue. She wanted to yell that she loved her daughter with all her heart. And while that was true, something about what the doctor said clicked. Eve held back. From Bella, from Adam. From Lainey. The realization of that caused a tear to roll down Eve's cheek. She accepted the tissue that Dr. Woodrow handed her, wincing a little when the doctor wrote something in her notebook. She couldn't help but wonder what the sight of her crying meant to Willamena.

"It was my seventeenth birthday," Eve began quietly. "All I wanted to do was paint. I had already decided by then that I wanted out of that life, but I didn't know how. I was going to take that night to come up with a plan. But then Laurence showed up." She shuddered going back to that night. "He had three men with him and had paid Bussiere to disappear. He watched as the other men . . ."

"Take your time, Eve. And remember, you're safe here. No one can hurt you."

Eve took a deep breath. "Two of them held me down. They didn't need to. I didn't struggle. I knew from before that if I struggled, it would be worse. But it didn't matter to them. They wanted it rough. They wanted to hurt me. They wanted me to struggle. If I just laid there, I would get slapped. Still, I didn't fight back. They'd hit me again and again until I finally tried to block them. When I did that, they laughed. I heard Laurence say 'finally,' but I didn't understand what it meant at that time. He walked over to me, grabbed my hair and pulled me towards him. He told me that he bought me, and I will give him what he wants. I tried to tell him I wasn't fighting, but he just hit me again and yelled at me. '*Fight back, bitch! If I wanted a wet noodle, I'd be fucking my wife!*'."

God. I don't know if I can do this. Eve struggled to keep her composure. It occurred to her then that she had never gone into detail with either Lainey or Adam. They know she was brutalized, but they had no idea what *actually* happened.

"I fought back. I hit, kicked, bucked with all my might. It only seemed to spur them on, make them more brutal. I was so torn. A part of me wanted to stop fighting because I knew it's what they wanted. And another part of me wished that I had been stronger. I wanted to hurt them. But they were too strong for me. They would rotate. Two would hold me down, while the other did what they wanted to me. It didn't matter to them if I was bleeding, if . . . if I had never been *taken* a certain way, or if I was trembling with pain, they just kept going. Then, Laurence decided it was his turn. He waited until I was barely conscious and did things to me that . . ."

"Okay, Eve. That's enough," Dr. Woodrow said, barely able to control her feelings. "No one should ever have to go through what you went through. Especially a child."

Eve noted that the doctor's knuckles were white as she clutched her pen. She wondered if listening to her tale made Willamena think about Rebecca.

"How did you get away?" the doctor asked after a quiet moment between the two of them.

"Bussiere came in to check on me after they . . . finished. It was the only time she looked even mildly ashamed. She helped me clean up, promising that I would have the next day off. Not that I believed her since I should have been alone that night, but perhaps she thought no one would want me since I was bruised and battered."

Eve took another offered tissue from Dr. Woodrow and dabbed her eyes that kept leaking with tears for her teenaged self.

"Thank you," she murmured. "Anyway, Bussiere left my door unlocked that night. Maybe she didn't think I was in any shape to try and escape. Or perhaps she was disturbed enough to forget," she said knowing her voice was tinged with disbelief. Bussiere had kept pictures from that night. She couldn't have been *that* disturbed. "When I didn't hear the lock click, I waited until I knew Bussiere would be asleep and I left. I didn't take anything with me, I just ran.

I honestly don't know how I made it miles away with the way I was feeling. Adrenaline can be a life-saver, I suppose. When I was finally far enough away to feel marginally safe, I called . . . Agent Donovan."

"How did he act with you back then?" Woodrow asked cautiously.

"At first he was annoyed with me because I had made him look like a fool letting a fourteen-year-old get away from him. Then we became friends. I knew at one point that he was becoming infatuated, but I never encouraged him. I liked him. However, with the way I was feeling about the opposite sex at that time, I decided it was better for him if I didn't get involved with him."

"Did he become belligerent at any time because of your decision?"

"By that time, I had begun drinking heavily, taking pills, smoking, and doing my own kind of revenge. I don't think I paid much attention to him. Maybe he resented me for that. I don't know. He was always kind to me, helping me. That's why when he did what he did, I was shocked. Completely stunned. He hurt me so much by what he did. I thought he was my friend."

Willamena had a strong recollection of the case. She had read every detail of the police report involving the kidnapping of Adam. Agent William Donovan of the FBI had coordinated the abduction with Laurence. That alone would have been enough to cut Eve to the core. Plotting to kill her husband only *after* she confessed to an affair with Lainey was twisting the knife.

"I certainly don't know Agent Donovan's psyche at the time he did this to you, Eve, so I can only speculate." Willamena crossed her legs and sat back.

"Anything is better than nothing, I suppose."

"Well, I believe he thought of himself as your protector."

"*Protector!*" Eve shouted with disbelief. "Some protector! He nearly got me killed! He would have killed Adam!"

"Eve, please." Dr. Woodrow lifted her hands in a calming gesture. "First, I wasn't finished. Second, I told you this is only an opinion based on what I know of the case and what you've told me."

Eve hung her head sheepishly. "Sorry."

"It's understandable for you to find anything positive said about this man to be offensive to you. Just let me finish the thought, and if you want to discuss, we will."

Eve agreed with a nod.

"You were young when he met you. He was an FBI agent assigned to keep you safe. When you ran away, it affected him. When you called him to turn yourself in, he became your protector again. He watched you become a woman. It's no secret that you're a beautiful woman, Eve. You have admirers everywhere. I can only imagine Agent Donovan became one himself, then became dismayed by your continued disinterest."

"He was married," Eve argued. "He moved on."

"Do you believe that? You called him when you were in trouble, correct?" As soon as she asked the question, she saw the dismay in Eve's face. Willamena didn't need to write down how guilty Eve still felt.

"Yes," Eve muttered. This was all her fault. If she hadn't called Donovan when her father was after her, Adam would never have been put in danger.

"I can see you beginning to blame yourself for Agent Donovan's actions."

Eve's eyes widened. "How?"

"You have a very expressive face, Eve. What Agent Donovan did was *not* your fault. I only mentioned you calling him because I imagine it brought him back to being your protector. Even after he became married and had children, he never let you go. He may have continued with his life had you not contacted him, but I honestly believe he would have reached out to you at some point. Especially if he had read about your marriage to Adam."

"Why? Why couldn't he just move on with his life? We were never intimate. I told him I wasn't interested. He was a part of a time in my life I didn't want to remember."

"Obsession," Willamena answered matter-of-factly. "Most people, I believe, have the mindset to move on. Others let it consume them. Agent Donovan let it consume him until he believed he was the only one that could keep you safe and make you happy."

Eve considered Dr. Woodrow's explanation. Still, she found no remorse inside for the man. "I can't be sorry he's dead. I've tried. But Adam was hurt, and my marriage was almost destroyed. If Laurence hadn't deviated from the plan, Donovan would have let Adam be killed. I can't forgive him for that."

While Willamena understood the reluctance to forgive, she knew firsthand how that could stunt personal growth. "By not forgiving him, you are keeping him close."

"Then tell me how I let go," Eve pleaded.

"Only you can do that. When you are ready," she answered softly. "You don't have to feel bad that he is gone, but you need to let go, Eve. Let him go. Let Laurence go. Let Tony go." Willamena placed a gentle hand on Eve's. "Let the past go. I know that is easier said than done, but it's something that we will continue to work on. Okay?"

Eve nodded.

Dr. Woodrow leaned back in her chair and studied Eve. "I would like to ask you something before we finish for the night."

"Okay."

"How would you feel about having Lainey and Adam join you for a session? Separately of course," Willamena said quickly when she saw the sheer panic on Eve's face. She had a feeling her query would be faced with resistance. But Eve must be aware that her dueling feelings for two of the most important people in her life were holding her back as well.

"I - I don't know," Eve stammered which pissed her off. It was a matter of survival and pride to maintain her composure. One simple suggestion knocked her off her axis.

"That's alright. I know it would be difficult for you, and possibly for Adam and Lainey, but I think it would be beneficial for all of you." Willamena waited for a response that never came. She sighed softly then said, "Will you at least think about it? If you feel you might be able to do it, then talk to both Adam and Lainey and see how they would feel. Is that okay?"

"Yes. I will think about it. I promise."

"Good. Now I know tonight was extremely difficult for you, so my advice is to go home, take a relaxing bath and let Adam hold you."

Eve smiled slightly. Having anyone hold her now didn't sound appealing. But she would give it a try. "That sounds like something I can do. I'll see you next week, Doc."

"Next week. Goodnight, Eve."

Chapter Seventeen

Adam stood silently for a moment, watching Eve move around the kitchen. Her beauty never failed to take his breath away. God, he loved her. He wished he knew how to get back to who they were before. Before Lainey. Before Tony. Before Laurence and Billy. Before therapy. They weren't perfect then, but the distance he felt now seemed insurmountable. Even after the night they had last night, there was a difference. Eve was different.

He could blame marriage if he were naïve enough. But he knew what kind of woman Eve was. He knew firsthand the incredible passion that was in her. The only hope Adam had was that after the therapy he practically pushed her into, Eve would remember what they were to each other. Or was he romanticizing a relationship he knew was flawed from the beginning? She had always held him at arm's length. Was he naïve? Truly naïve enough to believe that would have changed when they exchanged vows or had a child together?

"Coffee?"

Adam blinked, and Eve's face came into clear view. She held his travel mug up. It was a sweet gesture, yet her smile fell short of reaching her eyes.

"Thanks. So, last night was . . ."

"Great," Eve finished quickly. "Unless you'd rather I apologize for waking you up?"

Adam gave her his best boyish grin. "You think I mind waking up to you f . . ."

Eve put her hand over Adam's mouth. "Little ears are around. Not to mention Lexie."

"She's here early."

"Yes," Eve nodded. "I have an early day today. In fact, I have to get going now. Bug!" she called out, giving Adam a quick peck on the lips. "See you tonight?"

"Yeah, I shouldn't be too late." Adam felt that distance again. Maybe he could surprise her later with flowers or something to help his cause. Then, perhaps, they could pick up where they left off last night.

Eve stared out the window of her office. She did this often when her mind was racing faster than she could keep up. The people milling about below would make her wonder. Were they happy? In love? Stressed? Scared? Alone? If they looked back up at her, what would they see? Would they see the broken woman behind the façade?

"Eve?"

Lainey's soft voice penetrated Eve's morose thoughts.

"Yes?"

"May I come in?"

Eve turned, a frown on her face. "You know you're always welcome in here."

"I didn't want to assume," Lainey said as she shut the door behind her. "You've been a bit distant today. I thought maybe you needed some space."

Not from you. Eve inhaled deeply. "I'm sorry. It's not you." Eve turned back to the window as Lainey stepped up beside her. "How many of those people down there do you think are in therapy?" she asked suddenly.

"Hard session?" Lainey asked gently.

"They're all hard," Eve answered evenly. "Why can't I forget everything? Just pretend everything that happened to me wasn't real?"

"Because it was, honey." It hurt Lainey's heart even to say the words. But she wouldn't be helping Eve by saying empty words. "And to answer your question, I'm sure many are seeking help. I would hope they — and you — know that there's no shame in that."

Eve leaned on the windowsill. "Oh, Lainey. I'm not ashamed of being in therapy. I'm ashamed of my response to it. I'm ashamed that I can't control how it makes me feel."

"I think that's the point, honey. *Not* controlling your emotions but letting them go in a safe environment."

"I did that with you," Eve said quietly.

"You confided in me, yes. But you still controlled your feelings. Don't you remember when I cried for you, you asked why you couldn't cry for yourself?"

"I remember." It seemed like Eve could cry at the drop of a hat these days. Not that she would let anyone see that. Not even Lainey. Some things were meant to stay hidden. It was for the best.

"There's something else." Lainey knew Eve well enough to know when she wasn't being entirely forthcoming.

"It's nothing you want to know," Eve said. *Please don't pursue this. What I did was terrible enough. Telling you would be even worse.*

"When it comes to you, Eve, there's nothing I don't want to know. Especially if there's a possibility I can help." She put her hand on Eve's arm. "All I want is for you to be happy."

A familiar pain constricted Eve's heart. *You made your decision, Eve.* "Lainey."

She saw Lainey's determination. Eve knew Lainey well enough to know she wasn't going to give up. She wouldn't push, of course. She would silently worry. That was Lainey's heart.

"I fucked Adam last night."

It took a hell of a lot of willpower, but Lainey's hand stayed on Eve's arm. *You asked.* "Oh. Well, that's . . . normal. You're married. Why wouldn't you two, um, make love?"

"That's just it, Lainey. We didn't "make love." I used him. My session was about the night Laurence . . ." She shivered slightly and felt Lainey's hand squeeze her arm gently. "Anyway, sleep was difficult. The dreams were killing me. I — I didn't *want* to be with Adam." *I needed you.* "But I did it to try and get rid of the images in my head. The worst part about it is, I don't even believe I was fully present."

Lainey, unfortunately, knew that feeling very well. She never expected Eve to feel that way with Adam, though.

"That's understandable, Eve."

"How? Hmm?" Eve turned to look at Lainey. "How is it understandable to *anyone* how I treated my husband last night? Or this morning when I could barely look him in the eye? If it had been you I used, would you have understood that?"

"Yes." Lainey ignored the jump in her pulse and Eve's scoff. "I would because that's what one does for someone they love. They help them when they need it. Even if that means being used."

Eve stared at her best friend. Was she saying what she thought Eve wanted to hear? Or was she saying even more than what Eve was ready to accept? The night before, when she needed Lainey, it wasn't sex Eve thought about. It was just Lainey. Her presence. Her companionship. Her friendship. Her love. Why didn't she want that from Adam?

"Will you come to a session with me?" Eve blurted out.

"W-what?" That was *not* even close to what she expected Eve to say.

"Dr. Woodrow thought it would be a good idea for me to have you with me during one of my sessions."

"I, um, I . . ."

"If you don't want to, I understand. I don't particularly like going myself. But I promised the doctor I would ask."

"It's not that I don't want to, Eve." *I'm just afraid the doctor will see right through me. She'll see how I really feel about you.* "Sessions are personal. You said Dr. Woodrow thought it was a good idea for me to be there, but do you?"

"Actually, she asked that both you and Adam be there," Eve corrected. "It scares the shit out of me. However, I'm willing to try whatever she suggests if it will help."

Lainey understood the reasoning. Still, the thought of being in the same room discussing personal feelings with both Eve and Adam didn't sound appealing. However, she would do anything for Eve.

"When do you want me there?" she asked softly.

Eve watched her companion for a moment. She saw apprehension. "Just you, Lainey," she soothed. "Even I don't want you and Adam to be there with me together. It's too much. We can do it separately. Whenever you are available, I'll make the arrangements."

Lainey let out a breath. That made her feel marginally better about going. "Anytime, Eve. I'll make myself available for you anytime."

Eve stood and smiled. "Thank you. I know it's a big ask, and I adore you for agreeing even though it causes you to feel dread."

Lainey chuckled. "Not dread." She paused. "Okay, a little dread. Or a lot. Not being there for you, of course, just . . ."

Eve pulled Lainey in for a hug, effectively shutting her up. "I understand, Lainey."

Just then, the door of her office opened. "Hey, beautiful. I —"

Adam stopped in his tracks when he saw Lainey in his wife's arms. He was beginning to believe that she would always hold a place between him and Eve.

God, Eve wished she didn't feel guilty for merely hugging her best friend. It was an innocent gesture, yet the way Adam was looking at her made it feel dirty. Even if Eve had an overwhelming urge to kiss Lainey, she hadn't gone through with it. It was *that* feeling that had her gently, but firmly, pushing Lainey away. A move that hurt them both.

"Adam, what are you doing here?"

"Interrupting, apparently," he answered with a frown.

"It wasn't what it looked like," Lainey interjected, annoyed with Adam's insinuation.

"No? You weren't just in my wife's arms?"

"Adam," Eve warned. "It was a hug. An innocent hug between two best friends."

"There's nothing innocent when it comes to Lainey, Eve."

"Excuse me?" Eve did *not* like what Adam was implying. Whatever her feelings were for Lainey, neither of them deserved this treatment for such a simple gesture.

"Your past . . ."

"Is the past, Adam," Eve said coldly. "I will not have you come into *my* office unannounced and make accusations. Lainey agreed to go to therapy with me, and I was thanking her. It's as simple as that."

That wasn't the right thing to say, either. Adam raised a dark brow. "So, *she's* allowed to know what goes on in your sessions, but your husband is not?"

"You're being childish, Adam."

Lainey, feeling more uncomfortable than ever, cut in. "I should leave you two alone."

"Yes, you should," Adam snarled.

"You don't have to go anywhere," Eve said gently. She ignored Adam's mutterings and kept her attention on Lainey. None of this was her fault.

"No, it's fine, Eve." Lainey pleaded silently with Eve to let her go. "I need to get back downstairs anyway."

"I'll be down in a bit." Neither Eve nor Adam said anything else until Lainey shut the door behind her. As soon as Eve heard the click, she turned on her husband. "How dare you?"

"How dare I? I'm not the one hanging all over some woman I used to fuck!"

Eve moved towards him. "Watch yourself, Adam."

Adam scoffed. "Me? I've been asking you about your damned sessions for months now. But it's not me you're asking . . ."

"Dr. Woodrow asked that you *both* be there," Eve interrupted coolly.

Adam was speechless. "Oh. I — you must understand what it's like for me to see you two together," he said, trying desperately to justify his outburst. "It almost feels like you're flaunting this thing between you on purpose. Are you trying to make me jealous?"

Eve's brow lifted, and her nostrils flared. Her husband was dangerously close to pissing her off beyond her limits.

"First, I'm not you." She remembered perfectly the time Adam brought another woman to Eve's place of business for the sole purpose of making her jealous. "Second, I had no idea you'd be here. Speaking of, you still have yet to tell me *why* you're here."

"I thought I'd surprise you by taking you out to lunch." Adam felt their relationship slipping even further into the abyss. Of course, his attitude wasn't helping anything. Then again, neither was Lainey always being in the picture. "If the doctor wanted us both there, why didn't you ask me this morning to go to therapy with you?"

"Because I was in a hurry."

"Then why not last night?" He was fishing for *something* to make himself feel better about the scene he walked in on. About his marriage.

"Because I wasn't sure I wanted to ask either one of you," Eve answered honestly. "Now, I'm not sure I want *you* there."

"Look, Eve." Adam took a step towards her, stopping when he saw the look in her eyes. "We keep having this fight, and it's killing me."

"Not *we*, Adam. *You.* Lainey is my best friend. There will always be a special bond between us. I can't change that. I won't."

"She's a wedge between us."

"No, she's not. She has not done one thing to undermine our marriage, Adam."

"Your past . . ."

"Is just that!" Eve thundered. "Stop bringing it up every time Lainey is around!"

"Answer me one thing, Eve. Would you be as understanding if I were still friends with someone I'd been intimate with?"

Eve tilted her head. "Like the woman you poached from your old company?" she asked.

Adam frowned. "She was before us. How did you know about her?"

"I may be a silent partner of your firm, but that doesn't mean I haven't done my due diligence on *all* employees, Adam."

"It's not the same. We're colleagues," Adam argued. It made him nervous that she knew such private details. Not that he was trying to hide anything from his wife. It's just that that relationship had ended the moment he had met Eve.

"So are Lainey and I." Eve held up her hand. "I've had enough of this. Perhaps it's a good thing for you to come to a session with me. It seems we have a lot of issues to work out."

"In front of Lainey?"

Eve laughed mirthlessly. "No." *I won't put her through that.* "You'll be attending separate sessions."

Adam wasn't sure he liked the thought of that, either. But at this point, he'd take what he could get. So, he nodded.

"Let me know when and I'll clear my schedule. About lunch?"

"Go without me." Eve turned away from him and walked to her desk. "Next time you want to surprise me, don't."

He wanted to argue. Hell, he wanted to drop to his knees and beg and plead for her to forgive him. Unfortunately, he's been asking for her forgiveness a lot lately. Maybe going to therapy with her would turn out to be good for them.

"I'll see you at home," he said mildly. When Eve said nothing, he sighed. This did *not* turn out the way he had hoped. He was sure that a repeat from last night was not going to happen either. *Fuck.*

"If you came in here to apologize, please don't," Eve said as soon as Lainey walked in her office.

Lainey opened her mouth, then closed it again. That was precisely what she had come in here to do. She couldn't help but feel guilty about what went down with Adam.

"Nothing that happened was your fault," Eve continued through Lainey's silence. "Adam's attitude was unacceptable. Especially for something so innocent."

"I'm sure it can't be easy for him to see me with you," Lainey said as she sat down in the visitor's chair.

"Well, it's something he should be used to," Eve said distractedly. She was looking at schedules. Hers, Lainey's, and Adam's. The quicker she got these sessions over with, the better.

"Do you think he told Jack?" Lainey asked suddenly.

Eve looked up with surprise. "Why do you think that?"

Lainey shrugged. "Things haven't been the easiest lately. I keep wondering where I went wrong. What happened to make him go back to the way he was. Only this time, a little worse."

"Has he hurt you?" Eve asked seriously.

"No."

"Lainey, you promised to tell me."

"I promised to tell you if I thought I couldn't handle him, Eve. I intend to keep that promise. He hasn't gotten physical past that day you came in, and he had a hold of my arm."

Eve believed her. The one thing Lainey was horrible at was lying to Eve. Her face always told the real story.

"To answer your question, no, I don't think Adam has said anything to Jack. I don't see Jack as the type of person to let that go. He would confront you with it."

Lainey snorted. "That's true."

"How's he with Kevin?"

"Standoffish. More so than usual." Lainey shook her head. "Kevin says he's cool with it, but I'm not sure."

"Kevin is pretty outspoken about how he feels," Eve said smoothly. "If he was bothered by it, I think you'd know. Besides, he's definitely your son. He wears his emotions all over his face."

Lainey rolled her eyes. "I'm working on that."

"I can tell." Eve winked at her playfully. She laughed genuinely when Lainey made a rude gesture.

"Eve? Would it help you and Adam if I didn't go with you to see Dr. Woodrow?"

"No. When it comes to therapy, Lainey, I can't worry about other people's feelings. I know that sounds cold, but . . ."

"It doesn't," Lainey said softly. "It sounds right. This isn't about us. It's about you. All I want to do is what's right for you."

"Then come to a session with me, Lainey. I don't know if it'll solve anything or even if it's right. But it's what I need."

Lainey stood up and leaned over Eve's desk. She took Eve's hand in hers. "Then I'm there."

Chapter Eighteen
Therapy

Sharing is caring.

"Hello, Eve."

Dr. Woodrow greeted Eve with a friendly smile as the younger woman sat down in front of her. She noticed Eve look around, and Willamena had a moment to hope her office was calming. She had chosen a muted mint color and understated, yet impeccable furnishings that she hoped would appeal to all her patients.

Unbeknownst to the doctor, Eve was trying to capture that relaxed feeling she usually had there in that office. And with Dr. Woodrow. But she was feeling agitated today. She didn't want to be here. She didn't want to talk about her past. She was tired of feeling vulnerable.

"Doctor."

Dr. Woodrow studied Eve long enough to make her fidget. Eve hated it when she did that. She didn't want the doctor to see into her soul. There were too many secrets there. Secrets she tried to hide even from herself.

"Are you having a bad day?" Willamena asked gently.

"Not really," Eve lied. It *had* been a tough day. Was it really just hours earlier that she had asked Lainey to come in for a session? She sighed inwardly as the memory of Lainey and Adam's reactions filled her brain.

"Can you tell me what the sigh was for?"

Eve looked up sharply not having realized she had sighed out loud.

"Today I asked Lainey if she would be willing to come in for a session," she explained.

"I see. How did that go?"

Another sigh. "It was fine. She was hesitant at first but asked if it would help me if she did." She looked at the doctor. "I honestly don't know if it will, but since you suggested it, I said yes."

"I think it will," Dr. Woodrow stated, then waited for Eve to continue.

"She agreed. I thanked her by hugging her. I didn't think about it. It was just natural for me."

"Eve. Lainey is your best friend. Why wouldn't you feel natural hugging her?"

"Because of everything that has happened between us." Eve had thought about nothing else since Adam's outburst. Was it truly impossible to have a friendship given the feelings they once shared? *Still share.*

"I don't think you should withhold all affection because of that. In fact, I think that would be harmful to you both. It would put an even bigger strain on your relationship."

"The strain my affection for Lainey puts on Adam is killing me," Eve muttered. Even though it was a version of the truth, Eve acknowledged the fact that she wasn't entirely forthcoming.

Willamena frowned. "Did something else happen between you and Lainey?" She was alarmed by the sight of tears in Eve's eyes.

Eve felt those tears and blinked rapidly to keep them at bay. She knew for sure she didn't fool the keen doctor when she started writing in her notebook.

Patient is overly protective of her emotions today. More so than usual. I can't help but feel there will be parts missing from today's session. Parts, perhaps, the patient is not willing to deal with, yet.

"Eve?"

"I almost kissed her." Eve spewed her confession so rapidly that it nearly sounded like a five-syllable word. Another small fib, but Eve didn't see a big difference between the act and *wanting* the act.

"I see."

"What does that mean? What do you see?" Eve asked irritably. "Please tell me, because I *don't* see! I'm *in love* with my husband! What is it that draws me to Lainey? *Please. Help me.*" Eve's plea sounded pathetic to her own ears. Not to mention, a desperate attempt at convincing herself that she meant every word of it. There was probably zero chance that the doctor couldn't tell something was *off*.

"Eve, what you felt for Lainey is not going to just go away. It doesn't just stop. She was the first person you trusted completely. Lainey is the one that helped you begin to break down the walls you built around you."

Eve shook her head. "I am married, doc. I love my husband with every fiber of my being." *Liar.* Eve swallowed the invading thought, ignoring it as she always did. "Lainey is married. What we feel is wrong." *It's right.*

Willamena did something she rarely allowed herself to do. She showed her emotions. Her eyes flashed with annoyance as her fingers clenched her pen.

"Eve." She took a deep breath. If she didn't calm herself, she was going to say something she regretted. Perhaps something Eve wasn't ready or willing to hear. But her need to be honest won over in the end. "You have this notion in your head that life and relationships are black and white. You are letting this guilt about having feelings for Lainey consume you. We will not be able to move forward until you can forgive yourself for being human."

"Adam walked in when I was hugging Lainey," Eve confessed softly. "The look on his face shattered me. He tried to hide it, even tried smiling at both of us, but I saw it. I saw the distrust and sadness. How do I forgive myself for that?"

There it was again. Yes, she had seen the distrust and sadness. But why didn't Eve tell the doctor about his outburst? Why didn't she want Dr. Woodrow to see what it was really like with Adam these days? Why did she continue to make herself look like the bad guy while Adam was the saint?

"Did you explain to him why you were hugging Lainey?" Willamena asked, interrupting Eve's thoughts.

"Of course. But I think it only made things worse."

"Why is that?"

"Because I asked Lainey before asking him." Eve leaned forward, putting her elbows on her knees and burying her face in her hands.

"Why do you think you did that?" Dr. Woodrow asked while writing down notes. **Patient is exhibiting signs of deceit. As good of a poker face as the client has, there are tells. However, the more I push on a subject the patient is not open about, the more the patient shuts down. I will have to test how far the patient can be pushed.** When Eve shrugged, the doctor continued with a risky move. "You do know. Don't come up with an answer that you think will satisfy me. Tell me the truth."

Eve thought about using the excuse she told Adam. It was true enough. Yet, the more she thought about why she asked Lainey first, there was another plausible answer.

"Because I hate when Adam sees me vulnerable," Eve confided, finally being completely honest. "I know he asked me to come here and talk to you. But knowing that and actually having him here to see me . . . like this . . ." Her voice trailed off as that thought made her extremely uncomfortable.

"How do you think it makes Adam feel when you shut him out like that?" Another risky question, but one Willamena thought was essential to have answered especially if she wanted any chance of figuring out the dynamic between Adam and Eve.

Eve knew the doctor's question wasn't meant to be mean, but it still felt as though she had just been slugged in the gut. "This isn't who he fell in love with," she murmured.

"I beg to differ, Eve. You are exactly who he fell in love with. Flaws and all. You are also the one he stood beside during everything that happened. Even after learning of your feelings for Lainey." When Eve failed to respond, Dr. Woodrow sighed and wrote another note. **Baiting the patient resulted in no response. I will have to explore that avenue more thoroughly.** She looked up at Eve again. "Did you ask Adam if he's willing to sit in on a session?"

"Yes."

"What did he say?"

"He readily agreed." Eve raised her head and looked at the doctor solemnly. "He deserves so much more. He would be better off with someone who can give him all he deserves without all the damn problems." *That*, Eve thought to herself with disdain, *was the most honest you have been tonight.*

"Eve, you just told me that you love Adam with every fiber of your being." Something, due to the small tells Eve had, Willamena had trouble believing was the whole truth. She would explore *that* later, as well. "You are not whole at the moment, for many different, very legitimate reasons. I think Adam realizes that. You both deserve to live and love without the past hindering you. But I don't think Adam would be better off without you." She reached over and placed a comforting hand on Eve's forearm. It was a slippery slope giving advice and opinions when you weren't sure you had all the facts. There was an excellent chance her opinions would change with more perspective. She would have a better understanding once she sat down with the couple. "He would not be happy without you, Eve. I've seen you two together outside of the office enough to know that. You need to give *both* of you a chance. I would like to see you and Adam next time. Are you ready for that?"

Willamena accepted the fact that she had merely observed the two in social situations where the "perfect couple" scenario was amplified. Truth be told, if even just to herself, she felt the same way when she saw Eve and Lainey together — *not* surrounded by people. She would continue to play Eve's game of "Adam is the one" until Eve's thought process began to change. She had little doubt it would.

"Adam first?" Eve asked hesitantly. Eve wanted to work this out.

She wanted Adam to know that she loved him completely. Right? Wasn't that the right thing to do? Still, allowing her vulnerable side to show, especially to him, was appalling.

"Yes. I think Adam needs this as much as you do, Eve. I believe that one of the reasons you still feel so drawn to Lainey is because you're still closing a part of yourself off to Adam. A part that you still feel safe only showing Lainey."

Eve considered that. She nodded only to acknowledge that Adam should be first but silently questioned if what the doctor suggested was correct. Maybe Woodrow's opinion on why Eve was still drawn to Lainey was valid in the doctor's perspective. She could only surmise by what she's been told, and Eve hadn't been as candid as she should have been. Wasn't that what these sessions were for? *Shit.* Was Eve ready for this?

"I will ask if he will join me next time."

Dr. Woodrow smiled brightly. *A small breakthrough,* she thought to herself. Having Adam here will give her a clearer picture of their relationship. Whatever the case, Willamena hoped it would bring some clarity to Eve. The conflicting feelings, plus not being able to paint had to be wearing thin.

"Very good. I look forward to speaking with you both next session." Willamena stood, as did Eve. "It will be okay, Eve. Remember you're safe here. Adam wants to be there for you. I think you know that."

Eve nodded. She did know that. But was it for purely selfish reasons for him? Or could a positive change between them be as simple as just letting him in?

"Thank you, doctor. Have a good night."

"Goodnight, Eve."

Chapter Nineteen

"Hey, kiddo. What are you working on?" Lainey kissed Darren on top of the head as she walked by him. He was sitting at the kitchen table, papers strewn everywhere, with a severe look on his face. Her youngest boy wasn't as carefree as he used to be, and Lainey often wondered what was going on in that head of his. Unfortunately, he also wasn't as talkative as his big brother.

"Stuff."

"Oh, well, that explains everything," Lainey muttered. "Do you want some hot cocoa?"

"'Kay."

"Marshmallows or whipped cream?" This was turning out to be the perfect time to get Darren to talk to her. She hoped. Kevin was out with friends and Jack — thankfully — had already turned in for the night. She wondered how much she was going to suffer by bribing him with a ton of sugar so close to bedtime.

Darren looked up at his mom as though she had lost her mind. "Both, mom."

Lainey could practically hear the "duh." "Right, of course. How could I be so silly?" She went about making the cocoa — with milk, not water — trying to think of a way to get through to her young son. She hoped it was merely growing pains to blame for his change in attitude and nothing more serious. She put the mug in front of him, trying to sneak a peek at what he was doing. But he covered it up before she could get a good look.

"Five marshmallows, whipped cream, and a dash of cinnamon sugar." She put another marshmallow on a napkin next to his cup. "Bonus marshmallow."

A small smile formed on Darren's face. "Thanks."

"You're welcome. Mind if I sit with you?" Darren shrugged. "You don't want to tell me what you're up to?"

Darren looked up at her through his long lashes and shrugged again.

"Come on. I gave you a bonus marshmallow. That counts for something, doesn't it?" Lainey opened her eyes wide and stuck her tongue out at him. It warmed her heart to hear him giggle in return. She wished it lasted longer than a few seconds.

"It's nothing."

"If you're doing it, it's something. Please?"

Darren thought about it, drank his hot cocoa, wiped the whipped cream off his lip with the back of his hand, and thought about it some more. He wished Kevin was there. What would his big brother do? He took a deep breath and pushed the papers toward his mom.

Lainey felt as though she had won the lottery, only better. She took the papers with care and looked them over. Astonishment was the first feeling that overwhelmed her. Pride was a close second, for in her hand she held the beginnings of a comic book. Characters were drawn with care and determination. The facial expressions on each were meticulous. No words were needed to know how each character felt, yet a story existed — a story of a young man just learning of the superpowers he possessed. From what Lainey could tell, the powers weren't readily accepted.

"You did this, Darren?" The young boy nodded silently. "They're incredible! How haven't I seen these before?" Darren shrugged again, and Lainey began to see the gesture for what it was. He wasn't being sullen as she once thought, but insecure. "Oh, sweetie, these are so good! And the story, too? Did you write that?"

"Yeah. Kevin is helping me a little," he said timidly.

Lainey noticed then that the young man in the comics resembled Darren's big brother. Oh, how she loved their closeness.

"This really is terrific, sweetie. Is this the first one you've done?"

Darren shook his head, emboldened now by his mom's enthusiasm. "Nope. I have, like, ten of them. They follow Captain Good on all his adventures."

"Captain Good? I love it! Why haven't you shown me these before? You know I love art. I work at a gallery!"

Darren's smile faltered. "Dad says they're a waste of time. That I need to focus on football or something because art will get me nowhere."

Lainey made a valiant attempt to keep her temper in check. How dare Jack stifle their son's creativity? She knew Darren was telling the truth, too, because she could hear those exact words coming out of Jack's mouth.

"Sweetie, your father is being ridiculous. Eve is an artist; did you know that?"

Darren shook his head. When he was younger, he knew Eve took photos and worked in a gallery. But he never equated that to what he did. He supposed it was a different kind of art.

"She's quite amazing. You've been to the gallery before, but you've mostly stayed in my office. How about, tomorrow I take you into work with me, and I'll show you some of her work, as well as other great artists?"

Darren perked up. He had always pretended that the gallery and art were "boring." But now that his mom knew he liked to draw, the gallery could be cool. "What about school?" He asked the question only because he knew his dad would be upset if he missed school.

"Well, I'll go and talk to your principal in the morning and tell her where you'll be. We'll make it like a field trip of sorts."

Darren grinned widely. "'Kay! Will Eve be there?"

"You bet she will. Now, why don't you go upstairs and get ready for bed? We have an early day tomorrow."

Darren drained the rest of his hot cocoa and scooted his chair back. He was about to run upstairs before he remembered his manners. After taking his mug to the sink and filling it with water, he returned to his mom's side and kissed her on the cheek.

"Thanks, mom."

Lainey smiled. "Thank you for trusting me with this. May I see the rest?"

Darren nodded and took off like a shot. Not even three minutes later, he was back. "Here ya go. Don't tell dad, 'kay?"

Lainey crossed her heart with a finger. "I promise. Is it alright if I show Eve?"

Darren nodded. "Yeah, that's cool."

"Cool," Lainey repeated with a chuckle. "Off you go!" She swatted him lightly on the tush receiving a happy squeal in return. "I love you!" she called after him.

"Love you, too!" he yelled back.

Eve was curled up in her favorite oversized chair. She had a cozy blanket, a good book, and a hot cup of tea. Quiet nights like this felt like a lifetime ago. She couldn't even remember the last book she read. The one she picked for tonight was for pure pleasure. A sweet, little romance with a tidy happily ever after that she could lose herself in. She was close to finishing chapter one when the doorbell rang.

She pouted for a selfish moment before setting her book aside and throwing the blanket off her bare legs. Though she thought it was still early at nine o'clock, it was late enough for her to be concerned about who could be visiting. Eve peeked through the peephole, then quickly opened the door.

"Lainey? Is everything okay?"

It took a moment for Lainey to find her voice. She hadn't been prepared for Eve opening the door in what looked like nothing but an oversized sweatshirt. Surely, she had something on underneath.

Lainey cleared her throat. "Am I only allowed to come here when I have a problem?" she asked curiously.

"No, of course not!" Eve stepped back, waving Lainey in. "I'm sorry, I wasn't expecting company. Come in."

"Am I interrupting anything?"

"Not at all. Bella is in bed, Adam is in the shower, and I was reading." Eve pointed to her chair as though she were offering Lainey proof.

"Reading?" Oh, how Lainey wanted to walk over to the end table and see what kind of book Eve Sumptor would read. But she refrained. Barely. *Only* because she knew she would be inquiring about it later. Right now, she was on a mission. "I caught you at the right time, then."

Eve lifted a brow. She was impressed by Lainey's restraint. The woman was inherently curious. "For?"

"Will you take a look at these?" Lainey held out the papers she had in her hand. As soon as she had read them all, she couldn't wait to have Eve see them. As the owner of many prestigious galleries, Eve's opinions were valuable. As Lainey's best friend, they were cherished.

Eve took the papers and led the way to the kitchen. She hit the light on her way to the counter, then spread the sheets out in front of her using most of the massive space. With the critical eye of an artist, Eve began her review.

"These are quite fantastic, Lainey." She looked up at her friend. "Did Kevin do these?"

Lainey shook her head. "Darren."

Eve's brows shot up. "Darren! These drawings are from an eight-year-old?" Lainey nodded with a proud smile. Eve picked a sheet up, bringing it close for examination. "The details are phenomenal. Not just the central characters, but the background, as well. Look," she turned the page for Lainey to see. "These facial expressions are spot-on. Even without the text, I would know how the character was feeling."

"Darren says Kevin has been helping him with the story."

"Does Kevin realize he's the inspiration for," Eve searched the page, "Captain Good?"

Lainey laughed. "I haven't talked to him, yet. He's still out with friends, but I imagine he can tell."

"Why haven't you shown me these before?" Eve sat down on one of the bar stools, motioning for Lainey to join her.

"I literally just found out myself right before coming over here." Lainey sighed. "Apparently, Jack has been telling him that art is a waste of time. Which, understandably, made Darren afraid to tell me what he was working on. Seriously, it took a mug full of hot cocoa, six marshmallows, whipped cream, and cinnamon sugar to win him over."

"Sounds like Jack," Eve muttered. She then apologized. "That was brave of you, by the way. Filling the kid up on sugar this late just to get him to talk."

Lainey shrugged with a smile. "It worked. I, um, told him he could come to the gallery with me in the morning. Is that okay?"

"Absolutely. You know, these give me an idea."

"Having a pop culture section in the gallery?" Lainey guessed. She had thought the same thing when she saw Darren's work.

"Exactly. Superhero movies are big. So are comic books. Perhaps we can open art up to a whole new generation by combining fine art with pop culture."

Lainey grinned. "I bet Darren would love to help out."

"He has a job. Though, he may have a fight on his hands with Mikey. Either that or they'll bond over their love of graphic novels."

"I can hear it now," Lainey laughed. "We may *never* get Darren to leave!"

Their laughter was interrupted by the sound of Adam clearing his throat. Lainey looked over her shoulder, turning back around quickly when she saw Adam only had on pajama pants.

"Hello, Adam," she said amicably if not a little uncomfortably.

"What are you doing here, Lainey?"

Eve turned around with a frown. It deepened when she saw her husband was half undressed. "Lainey is welcome here anytime, Adam."

He ran a hand through his wet hair. "Right, of course. I just meant it's late. Is everything alright?"

"Yes, everything is fine." Lainey began gathering Darren's work. "I wanted to show Eve something Darren had done."

"It couldn't have waited until the morning?"

"Adam." The warning in Eve's tone was unmistakable.

"No, he's right. I could have waited." Lainey glanced at Eve with a small smile. "I'll see myself out."

"No, I'll walk you to the door." Eve glared at Adam as they passed him. "I'm sorry, Lainey."

"Don't be. I don't think he'll ever forgive me for what happened between you and me. I don't want to make it worse for you."

"You're not. Please. Please don't shut me out because of Adam's insecurities."

Lainey sighed softly. "I need to stop by Darren's school in the morning. So, how about we meet at the gallery?"

Instead of riding in together like we usually do, Eve thought with sadness. "Sure. Whatever you want."

"Eve, I'm not shutting you out," Lainey said quietly. "I'm not even stepping back. I'm trying to respect Adam and his needs."

"Why? He's not respecting you."

Oh, she's angry, Lainey thought. *I almost feel sorry for Adam.* She laid a hand on Eve's arm. "He feels threatened by me. Maybe things will get better once you two have your session with Dr. Woodrow."

"Maybe. Thank you for coming over and showing me these." Eve tapped the papers in Lainey's hand. "Darren will grow into his talent and perhaps get better at naming superheroes," she chuckled. "If you want me to help him, I'm here."

"I do, Eve. I want you to show him that art is not a waste of time. I don't want him to feel like he needs to hide this or be embarrassed."

"Then that's what *we* will do." Eve knew Adam was waiting. He could wait a little longer. "I want you to remember something, okay?" Lainey nodded. "You are *always* welcome in my life, in my home. No matter what time of the day or night, I'm here. Do you understand?"

"Yes." She gave Eve's arm a little squeeze before letting her go. "Goodnight, Eve."

Eve watched Lainey until she made it safely back inside her own house before closing the door. She felt Adam behind her but gave herself a full twenty seconds before she turned to him.

"Eve . . ."

"You embarrassed me," she said coldly.

"That wasn't my intention. Baby, I heard voices and thought I'd come down to see who was here so late."

"Half naked? What was this about, Adam?" she asked, gesturing to his bare chest. "You know what? Forget it. I don't care. What I do care about is that Lainey came over to show me some artwork that Darren had done, and you made her feel awful for it."

She pushed past him to get to her chair and book again. The tea was probably a lost cause, but she could always make more.

"Eve, wait. I'm sorry."

"You say that a lot, Adam," she said without turning back. "There comes the point when the words lose their meaning."

"Eve!" Darren ran to the elegant woman, throwing his arms around her waist. At eight-years-old, showing affection like this could be embarrassing, but he never felt that way with Eve. He felt cool that they were friends. Some of his friends at school knew of her, or their parents talked about her. But he *knew* her.

"Hey, kiddo!" Eve knelt to his level. "I'm glad you're here," she whispered conspiratorially. "I need your help."

Darren's eyes widened. "You do?"

"Absolutely! I told Mikey we were going to add a spot for superheroes and he's gone insane! He wants to turn the entire section green!"

"For the Hulk or Green Lantern?" Darren asked seriously.

"Well, I don't know. That's what I need you for. He's been muttering all morning about things I don't understand."

Darren nodded solemnly. "I got this." He looked around until he spotted Mikey, then took off after him.

"Hey!" Eve called out. "I want to talk about *your* work when you're done."

Darren gave her a big, toothy grin. "'Kay!"

"You're so good with him." Lainey stood beside Eve and watched her son talk animatedly with Mikey across the room. She couldn't hear what they were saying but didn't think she would understand it even if she could.

"I've told you before, your kids make it easy."

Lainey shook her head. "You're good with Bella, too, Eve. You're a natural at this mothering stuff. Sometimes I feel like I'm still trying to figure it all out."

Eve glanced over at Lainey. "We all have those days," she confessed. "But your boys are proof that you're doing a fantastic job." *Especially with someone like Jack trying to undermine you at every step.* Of course, Eve didn't say that out loud. She didn't think it was the time or place to get into that discussion.

When Lainey opened her mouth to respond, she was interrupted by her phone buzzing. A quick check of the screen had her rolling her eyes.

"Jack. I'm guessing he figured out I kept Darren out of school today. No doubt he's calling to bitch about it."

"Want me to answer?" Eve asked mischievously.

Lainey chuckled. "I would say yes if I didn't have to go home later and face the firing squad."

The humor fled Eve's eyes. She wondered briefly if things were much worse than Lainey let on. Though, if she kept asking and not trusting that Lainey would tell her as promised, she was no better than Adam and his empty apologies.

"Are you going to get it?" she asked instead.

"Nope." Lainey hit the button on her phone to end the call, sending it to voicemail. "Today is all about Darren. I won't let Jack ruin that."

Eve didn't put it past Jack to show up here and make a scene. She took out her phone and sent a quick message down to her garage attendant. Jack Stanton was not allowed upstairs until further notice.

"Did you just do what I think you did," Lainey asked, eyeing Eve suspiciously.

"I have no clue what you're talking about," Eve responded with innocence. "Come on, let's go crash the nerd party."

"Eve, don't try to change the subject. Wait. Did you just call my son a nerd?"

Eve laughed. "Yes. It was a compliment. Nerds are cool these days."

Lainey watched as Eve sauntered off towards Darren and Mikey. She hadn't been fooled. She knew Eve did something to keep Jack away for the time being. Lainey wished Eve would have owned up to it so that Lainey could have thanked her.

"I know a sculptor who specializes in superheroes," Eve told an excited Darren. "I've already seen his Spiderman, which if I'm not mistaken, is your favorite."

Darren nodded. "He is! But I like them all."

"Yeah? So, if you were to design this room here as a comic book room, what would you do?"

"Hmm." Darren tapped his chin with his finger, reminding Eve of Lainey. "I like pictures, but statues are cool, too. Can there be both?"

"Absolutely. This is a gallery. That means art in every type and genre is welcome. Including yours."

Darren stopped in his tracks. "Mine?" he squeaked. "But . . ." He looked up at his mom, then at Eve again. "I'm not that good."

His voice was so little and insecure that it broke Eve's heart. She knelt beside him, not caring if her expensive slacks got dirty.

"You, young man, are incredibly talented. You're doing things at eight-years-old that takes some artists years to accomplish. You should be proud of that."

"Dad says . . ."

"Sweetie," Lainey interrupted. "Your father doesn't understand. He sits behind his desk all day looking at facts and figures. He doesn't get to see the beauty of all this," she gestured around them, "every day as we do. And he can't even draw a stick figure."

"Ah," Eve cut in. "He's jealous!"

Darren giggled. "He's terrible at drawing! I took after mom."

Eve glanced up and caught Lainey blushing. She fleetingly wondered if there were more to Lainey's artistic abilities than merely arranging displays. Which she was exceptional at. By the look of her friend, Eve would venture to guess there was. Why would Lainey keep that from her?

"Well, I think you took after the right parent." Eve tickled Darren's tummy. "So? May I use some of your work here in the pop culture room?"

"Pop culture?"

Eve chuckled. "The comic book room."

"Oh! Um." He looked at his mom again who gave him a slight nod. "'Kay. Do you need my notebook?"

Eve shook her head. "Originals are too valuable. We'll make prints of them. How's that?"

Darren nodded and asked if he could help. He wanted to pick the best ones for Eve and the gallery. Wait until he told Kevin what just happened! He wasn't going to believe it! The brothers had always thought Eve was cool, but this was totally awesome! The thing that wasn't awesome, though, was thinking about sharing the news with his dad. This was exciting for Darren, and he didn't want his dad to ruin it. Maybe his mom wouldn't make him. At least not right away.

As he thought of ways to get his mom to agree to keep this from his dad, he took her hand. Then he took Eve's, and they walked like that through the rest of the gallery. He listened carefully as Eve and his mom told him stories about each piece of art that was there. He had listened to his dad before. Believing him when he said going to the gallery with mom would be boring. But now he knew better. Who knew what the future would hold for him and his art? All he knew was he was having fun right now.

Chapter Twenty
Therapy

Facing the façade.

"Adam, it's so nice to see you, again." Dr. Woodrow took Adam's hand as he leaned in to kiss her gently on the cheek.

"It's good to see you, Dr. Woodrow."

His deep voice reverberated through Eve, even in its softness. She had always loved her husband's voice. It used to be one of the things she found soothing and sexy. That was still there — most of the time.

"Hello, Eve."

She gave the doctor a small smile. It was all she could muster up at the moment, and she didn't trust her voice. Nerves were always a factor when she came here. Having Adam with her now intensified that. Especially with all the problems they'd been having. She hadn't exactly been forthcoming with *that* part of their relationship with Dr. Woodrow. She wondered if Adam sensed that when he sat next to her, immediately grasping her hand.

The silence was uncomfortable. Eve waited for Dr. Woodrow to begin because she honestly didn't know what to say. There was a written rule somewhere, she was sure, that she was not allowed to be the first to spill her guts. Not in front of Adam. It didn't help matters at all when she noticed the doctor watching her and then scribbling something in that damned notebook of hers. *Great.*

Patient is displaying an unusual amount of discomfort today. It could be that the spouse is here as well. Or there is something more, deep down, that I am not privy to, yet.

Willamena kept her pen poised and looked up at Adam. "Do you know why I asked you to come here, Adam?"

"Eve didn't say much about it, just that you wanted to see both me and Lainey."

Eve knew the way Lainey's name came out of his mouth wasn't her imagination. It was no secret he had issues with her best friend. She just hoped they could get past them here.

"I had no idea what to say," Eve defended herself, irritably. "I told you that she wanted to speak with us together because that's what she said."

"I didn't mean anything by that, beautiful. I was just answering the question honestly." He squeezed her hand gently before turning back to the doctor. "I'm willing to discuss anything you think would help."

Eve took a brief moment to regret her outburst. He was trying to help. He was here because she asked. The least she could do was drop the bitch act.

"Eve?" *Crap.* "Would you like to tell Adam why you asked Lainey about these sessions first?"

Was she serious? Wasn't there some rule or something about what is said in here? "Can't you?"

It was childish and pissed Eve off more than she already was. This wasn't who she was! After everything she had been through in life, she had learned to be strong. She did *not* want to feel vulnerable with Adam here. Perhaps in a solo session, she and the doctor could figure out why it scared her so much to have him see her that way.

Dr. Woodrow stared at Eve for a long moment then wrote more. **Patient's defenses are up. Despite the other occupant being a spouse, the patient is wary of showing emotions. It will be interesting to see how the patient moves forward.**

"I saw a lot of emotions on your face just then, Eve. Why don't you say what you just felt out loud?"

Eve clenched her jaw. Despite knowing the truth of the situation, she couldn't help but feel the doctor was trying to destroy her.

"I don't like feeling vulnerable," Eve whispered low enough that Adam had to lean closer to hear.

"Eve. You're safe here. No one in this room wants to hurt you," Dr. Woodrow said softly. "Adam wants to help. Look at him and tell him how you feel."

Eve considered giving the good doctor a death stare but decided against it since Willamena was in no way intimidated by Eve. Hell, if Eve met the "Eve" in here, she wouldn't be intimidated either. So, she turned to her husband, seeing nothing but compassion and love in his eyes. Where was *this* Adam when she needed him the most? Did she know, deep down, that he would be this way once in front of Dr. Woodrow? Could that have contributed to her need not to be completely honest? Unfortunately, she couldn't think of that now. She had to think about how she felt.

"This isn't who you fell in love with. This shell of a woman that can't paint, who isn't strong, and is scared all the time. I didn't want you to come here because I didn't want you to see me this way. I'm afraid." Well, look at that. She was finally honest about something when it came to Adam. Of course, there was more to it than that, but this was a start.

"Afraid of what, beautiful?"

Adam's eyes glimmered with unshed tears. It reminded Eve of the last time she saw him cry when he had found out Eve had betrayed him. That old familiar feeling of guilt spread through her. There were times, when she was angry with him, that she forgot what a good man he was.

"*Afraid that you won't love this person*," Eve barely whispered. Another truth.

Adam dropped to his knees in front of her. "Eve, do you think my love for you is that superficial?"

He paused long enough for her to answer, so she shook her

head. A fib. She *did* think it was superficial. Sex was their go-to form of communication. Adam calling her "Beautiful" felt more like an adjective than an endearment. She wished to hell she didn't have those negative feelings towards her husband. Lately, however, his actions spoke louder than his sweet words.

"When we got married, and I said my vows, I meant every one of them. For better or worse. I love you unconditionally, beautiful. When you're strong, I'll stand beside you. If you need help, I'll be there to hold you. Let me in, Eve. Please?"

A tear slid down Eve's cheek, and he lovingly brushed it away with his thumb. If only it were that simple. If only she could have loved him the way he deserved.

"I'm so sorry." Eve's voice broke, and she fought to control the sob she knew wanted loose. Therapy was either magnifying her problems or creating more. She didn't know which one, yet. "I don't mean to shut you out, I just . . ."

"You just find it easier to be open with Lainey?"

To Eve's surprise, she didn't hear accusation or resentment in his voice. *That's a first.* Since she couldn't deny it, she shrugged.

"And is that why you . . . had the affair?"

There was the hurt Eve had become accustomed to hearing. It still tore her apart to know she caused him pain. Eve focused on his question, hoping against hope that this session would somehow get easier. But how did she explain to her husband why she was inexplicably drawn to someone else when she didn't understand it herself?

"I don't know," she answered honestly.

Adam studied Eve for a minute, then nodded. "I can't say that I enjoy seeing how close you still are with Lainey, beautiful. It makes me feel like an outsider sometimes. And I'll admit that I sometimes feel insecure and untrusting."

Sometimes? At least he was finally admitting it. "I haven't slept with her! I swear!" She said hastily, not knowing if it were for his sake or Dr. Woodrow's who was quietly watching the exchange.

"But you still think about her that way," he countered sadly. "I can see it. I'm trying to understand, Eve."

"May I say something," Dr. Woodrow interjected. When Adam sat back in his chair to face her, she continued. "From what I've been able to determine, Eve is as confused with her feelings as you are, Adam. She knows she loves you, and that she doesn't want to hurt you. However, if I may, she feels a certain kind of protection from Lainey." She quickly raised her hand when Adam began to speak. "I'm not saying she doesn't feel safe with you. I'm saying that she is able to let down these barriers with Lainey because Eve feels in control in that relationship."

Eve's brow furrowed as she listened to the doctor. Did she feel control with Lainey? Eve *was* the one who pursued Lainey — a married woman. Adam pursued Eve. Lainey was the inexperienced one. Adam taught Eve what making love was and all the different ways to do it. As much sense as it made, there were holes. However, Eve was open to exploring this avenue if the doctor felt it worthy enough to bring up.

"Because she's a woman?" Adam asked.

"No," Eve answered herself. "I've been hurt by a woman." She thought of how Madame Bussiere used to treat her. Use her. Beat her. "It's because of who Lainey is and our dynamic together. With you and me, you're more dominant."

"So, I shouldn't be that way?"

"No, that's not what I'm saying. Look," Eve sighed and ran her hand through her blonde hair. *Give him something. Embellish on Dr. Woodrow's opinions. If she sees it, it has to be a reason.* "I'm not clear on all of this, yet. It's just, something clicked with me when Dr. Woodrow said what she said. I think I need more time to figure it all out."

Adam looked at the doctor. "I would like to come back to discuss this further. Can I do that?"

Wow. That stung. These were Eve's sessions, and yet he didn't ask *her* how she felt about him coming to more of them. Perhaps that control thing really does have some relevance.

"You should ask Eve that question," Dr. Woodrow admonished gently. The look on Eve's face told her they had the same concerns.

Adam looked downright contrite as he turned to Eve again.

"Damn. I should have asked you. I'm so sorry, beautiful. Forgive me?"

She nodded silently and wondered if forgiveness was infinite.

"May I come back, Eve? I really would like to explore this further. And if I'm doing something that makes you shut me out, I would like to change that. Please, baby?"

"I think that would be good," She answered softly. Maybe he would show his true self. Eve nearly snorted at the hypocrisy. They both needed to work on it.

He grinned. "I love you so much. Thank you. And, if you need Lainey to come in before that, I don't mind. Or if you need us both here . . ."

He nearly sounded sincere which scared Eve to her core.

"No! I'm not ready for that!"

Of course, he could hear the fear in her voice. If he missed that, all he had to do was look in her eyes. He placed his hand on Eve's thigh and rubbed it gently.

"Okay. You tell me what you need when you need it. I'll accommodate you. Deal?"

Haven't I been doing that? The thought went through her head, but she didn't say it aloud. One day she would figure out why they both felt the need to keep the façade up for Dr. Woodrow. And herself. "Deal."

"I think that's a good place to end tonight," Dr. Woodrow announced as she glanced at her watch. "I don't want to give you homework, but if you do decide to keep talking, make sure you listen completely to each other without judgment. Honestly, I think you should go home and hold each other."

"That's homework I can do," Adam told her with a smile.

"Sounds good to me," Eve agreed. "I'll see you next time, Doc."

Dr. Woodrow smiled at them both. "Goodnight you two."

Chapter Twenty-One

"Eve?"

Eve looked up from her computer, and her jawed dropped. Lainey stood at her office door in all her beautiful, naked glory. Even with Eve's photographic memory, she had forgotten just how exquisite Lainey's body was. Full breasts fell naturally, drawing Eve's eyes down to a toned belly. Eve tried her best not to go down any further, but it was a losing battle.

"Lainey . . ."

"I don't want to think anymore, Eve. I don't want to talk. All I want to do is feel."

Eve stood and walked towards Lainey. She could feel her own skin heating up the closer she got. Of course, she had questions. Very important questions. None of them came to mind. Her hands itched to touch Lainey. Over two years of denying herself — denying her true feelings — caused Eve to hesitate.

"It's not wrong," Lainey whispered. "It can't be. Being with you has always felt right. Tell me you don't feel that, too."

"I do," Eve confessed softly. "I don't understand it."

"We don't have to. Not right now. All we need to do is feel. Touch me."

Eve didn't hesitate this time. She reached out a slightly trembling hand and brushed her fingertips from Lainey's neck to slightly below her navel. She replaced her fingertips with her lips and tongue. God how she missed the taste of Lainey. She knew it only got better the lower she went. Eve had never experienced anything so intoxicating before Lainey. Or after.

"You're making my legs shake." Lainey caught Eve's face in her hands and tugged lightly. Once Eve was face to face with her, Lainey leaned in and kissed her. It was the kiss she had wanted to give Eve every single time she saw her. Full of passion and emotion. Full of everything Lainey fought to hide. Full of the love that was inside her, struggling to be set free.

"Now my legs are shaking," Eve panted. "Come with me."

"I hope to," Lainey replied with a sexy grin.

She allowed Eve to pull her towards the large, white sofa. White, Lainey thought. Always white. Eve wasn't pure, but that's not what Lainey thought of when she saw the color. What she saw was white, hot power. The kind of power Lainey desired. She sat when Eve nudged her, but held a hand out, stopping Eve from joining her.

"I want to watch you take your clothes off."

Eve raised an eyebrow. She loved when Lainey was bold. The first few times they made love, Lainey had been shy. Understandable since it was a first for them both. Eve couldn't help but wonder how the dynamic would have changed for them had they made different decisions. She smiled. Well, she thought, I'm here now. Let's see what happens.

Eve began unbuttoning her shirt. Though it killed her to go slow, she forced herself to take her time. If Lainey wanted to enjoy the show, Eve would oblige. She slipped the shirt from her shoulders, then unbuttoned her slacks and slid out of her shoes. The way Lainey watched her created a fire in Eve's belly. She moaned in response when Lainey began touching herself. Her mouth watered. Her fingers tingled, aching to replace Lainey's fingers.

"Let me do that." Eve's voice was hoarse with want.

"Finish undressing," Lainey demanded. Her breath was coming quicker. The need was building. If Eve didn't hurry, Lainey would finish this on her own soon. She smiled secretly. Eve can always make me come again, she thought.

"You're driving me crazy."

Lainey ogled Eve in her white lingerie. The lace of her bra did nothing to hide her rosy, taut nipples. When her eyes traveled south to where white lace covered a most prized possession, she wondered if Eve was as hot and wet as she was. And then there were the garter belt and thigh high stockings. Lainey could have come right then.

"Tit for tat," Lainey breathed. "Since when do you wear all that?"

"Well, if I had known you'd show up in my office completely naked, I wouldn't have bothered with all this." Eve unhooked the garter belt straps from the stockings. "But this could be fun, too."

Eve propped her foot up on the couch next to Lainey. She leaned in, looking Lainey in the eye.

"Come on, baby. You want me naked? Get me naked."

Lainey's nostrils flared as they were filled with the scent of Eve's desire. This wasn't how this was supposed to go. But Lainey could work with this. Most definitely. She ran her hand up Eve's leg, starting from the inside of her ankle and ending where the stocking began. Lainey tickled the inside of Eve's thigh before hooking her thumb in the top.

"Uh-uh. Use your teeth."

Lainey looked up at Eve with a smirk. "Must you always be in control?"

Eve smiled. "Not always. In fact, when you get me the way you want me, you can *have* me any way you want me."

Lainey breathed in deeply. "Hmm. Tempting."

Eve wiggled her toes. "Any. Way," she reiterated with passion.

Lainey bent forward. If Eve wanted to play, Lainey could play. Instead of using her teeth on the stockings, Lainey placed her hot, wet tongue on Eve's panties. She knew she hit the right spot when Eve's knees buckled.

"Lainey," Eve warned.

"You said I could have you any way I wanted," Lainey reminded her. "Do you think you can keep standing while I use my tongue on you?"

"Is that a challenge?"

"No, a serious inquiry," Lainey winked. She pulled Eve's panties aside, exposing her velvety, wet sex. Before Eve could protest, Lainey flattened her tongue over Eve's clit. They moaned in unison. Eve due to the feeling of having Lainey's tongue on her. Lainey due to once again tasting Eve's sweet nectar.

Eve's hips moved with Lainey's tongue. She tried to get Lainey to go deeper by thrusting forward, nearly toppling over in the process.

"You win, baby. I need to lay down. I need your tongue inside me."

Lainey helped Eve out of her remaining clothes before pushing her down on the couch. She laid down on top of Eve, savoring the feel of their naked bodies coming together again.

"I don't want to lose you again," Lainey whispered.

Eve stroked Lainey's beautiful face. "You could never lose me, Lainey. My heart belongs to you."

Lainey's heart was beating so fast it woke her up. Tears stained the pillow beneath her, and her body was so turned on; she ached from head to toe. Oh, how she longed to go back to sleep and stay in her dream forever. Her reality snored beside her, causing more tears to fall. Unable to stay in that bed for one more minute, Lainey got up as quietly as she could. Jack was never much of a light sleeper. Lately, however, he had been waking up any time Lainey left the bed. That started when Lainey had begun sleeping in the guest bedroom. She would blame it on his snoring and not being able to sleep through it. But the truth was becoming more apparent each day.

She locked herself in the guest bedroom. This had become her sanctuary. No boys allowed, much to Darren's chagrin and Kevin's amusement. Jack had been indifferent the way he was with most of the things Lainey did. Except, of course, her job. As she settled into the bed, she took the book she had been reading out of the nightstand. This was not a psychology book. Oh no. In her sanctuary, Lainey read for pleasure.

Logically, Lainey could attribute her dream to what she was reading. It *was*, after all, a book about two best friends, women, falling in love under extraordinary circumstances. Before she had gone to bed, she had read a particularly racy scene. It was weak logic, but Lainey was determined to hang on to it as she settled in to read.

"Why are you angry, Eve?"

"I'm not angry, Adam." She tried to move around him to get to the bathroom, but he moved with her, blocking her. It didn't matter that he was naked; she didn't appreciate being "kept" in place by her husband. "Please, let me by."

Though her tone was soft, Adam could tell she was losing her patience. He didn't understand her. They had just made love, and it was phenomenal. He took her slowly, allowing her to guide him at times. He had been trying to give her what she sought from Lainey. If he could do that, she wouldn't need Lainey anymore.

"Beautiful, what we just did . . ."

"Was great." Eve tried to smile. "Can I get by now?"

"Did I do something wrong?"

Eve sighed. Ever since their session together, Adam had been different. He wasn't being *him* in bed. His attitude outside of the bedroom, however, hadn't changed. She wondered if *she* demanded he go to his own therapist if he would agree as she did. Obviously, he was holding on to things concerning her and Lainey. She wouldn't be surprised if there were more he was holding onto as well. "No, you didn't do anything wrong."

"Usually making love relaxes you. You seem more agitated."

"I'm sorry. I'm stressed." It wasn't a total lie. The LA gallery was behind schedule, H. Agosti's manager was trying to bully her way into the deal, an important shipment was delayed, and worst of all, Bella was coming down with a bug or something. She didn't even want to think about the thoughts she had during their lovemaking. *That* wouldn't help either one of them. "It's not you. I'm tired, and I want to wash up and check on Bella."

"I'm sure she's fine, Eve."

"She has a temperature. I want to keep an eye on her."

Adam clenched his jaw. "Even after what we shared tonight, you're going to sleep in there?"

What we shared? It was sex. Nice, safe, good sex. It wasn't anything *like what Lainey and I have. Had.* Eve ignored her thoughts by throwing the blame back at Adam. She wondered if he realized what he had been doing. Twisting her words from their session, overcompensating for what he thought drove her towards Lainey. *If only it were that simple.* "Yes."

"What do you want from me, Eve?" Adam called after her as she stepped into the bathroom.

She turned back to face him. "I could ask the same of you, Adam. Have you changed your mind about me having Lainey in my life?"

Adam hesitated. He knew deep down there was only one answer to this question that would be acceptable. *No.* But he had. He couldn't get over what happened between Lainey and his wife. Why didn't Eve see that? Why didn't the woman who stepped in front of a gun for him recognize that, in this scenario, Lainey was the gun? Adam's stomach dropped when he remembered that day. He tried not to think about it often. But how does one forget the worst day of his life?

"No," he said finally. "I would like to go to another session with you."

Eve nearly asked him why. The only thing to come out of the last session was Adam thinking changing the way they had sex would fix everything. She could only hope that Dr. Woodrow would have better luck with getting him to understand it was more profound than that.

"Okay. We'll see how Bella is feeling later this week. I won't be going if she's still sick."

"No, you should go. I can stay home with Bella. These sessions are important." What he didn't say was they were vital to him, too. The faster she got this shit with Lainey cleared up, the faster he and Eve could move on with their lives. Intellectually, he understood he was creating his own problems. The two women hadn't had any indiscretions since he had married Eve. He just wished he could be confident that wouldn't change.

Eve nodded. At this point, she would agree to almost anything if he would just let her clean up and check on her daughter. "That sounds good. Hopefully, she'll be feeling better, and you can go with me. If not, you can come to the following session."

Adam agreed and leaned in to kiss his wife's cheek. "I guess I'll see you in the morning, then. If her cough worsens, come and get me?"

"Sure."

Talk me off the ledge.

Lainey jumped slightly when her phone buzzed beside her. Reluctantly, she put her book aside — even though she was at a particularly good part — and read the text. It was from Eve. Lainey's first response was to panic. In her experience, when Eve Sumptor had a problem, it was usually life and death. Eve had assured her, however, that there were no more threats. So, Lainey took a breath and texted back instead of calling.

What ledge are we on?

In Bella's bedroom, Eve smiled at the response. Lainey had no clue what Eve was talking about, but she didn't hesitate to put herself right next to her. Of course, the ledge was more like a molehill, but Lainey didn't know that.

Bella is nearly three years old. When does this worry end?

Lainey let out a relieved chuckle. Eve was the most confident woman Lainey knew. Except when it came to being a parent. As wonderful of a mother as Eve was, she always felt a little out of control. Out of sorts. Lainey knew how hard that was for her. She would keep reassuring Eve as long as it was needed. However, she would *always* be honest.

Never.

Eve rolled her eyes. She should have known that Lainey wouldn't pull punches with her.

Thanks. I'm jumping now.

Lainey laughed. Since Eve was texting, she was obviously awake. And likely alone. Lainey took the chance and pressed the call button.

"Calling to talk me out of it?"

Eve's sultry voice never failed to give Lainey the chills.

"Of course. Why don't you tell me what the problem is before you leap?"

"Bella is sick."

Lainey frowned. "I thought it was just a low-grade fever and occasional cough."

"Try telling that to my heart." Eve sighed. "This happens every time. To me, a low-grade fever and occasional cough are equivalent to raging fever and whooping cough."

"Oh, honey," Lainey chuckled. "That's normal, but it will get better as time goes on. When I first had Kevin, I was calling the doctor if he hiccupped. By the time I had Darren, I was an expert at every illness, cut, scrape, or bruise a young boy could get."

"Fine. I'll step off the ledge. I'm sorry if I woke you."

"You didn't." *Not in the way you think.* "I was reading."

"Oh? What are you reading? Please tell me it's not a psychology book."

Lainey blushed even as she laughed. "No, it's not a psychology book."

Eve waited a beat. "You're not going to tell me?"

"It's nothing. Just a silly, mindless book." Okay, so it wasn't silly. Nor was it mindless. But it *was* sensual, witty, and incredibly hot. She cleared her throat. "Are you in Bella's room now?" she asked, effectively changing the subject.

"Yes. I'm checking her temperature every five minutes. Needless to say, I'm not a very popular person in this house right now."

Lainey smiled. "Bella knows you're doing it because you love her so much. She may not understand that right now, but one day she will."

Eve thought of her mother. Had she been just as scared when Eve was a baby? With Tony in their lives, Eve couldn't imagine how difficult that must have been for her mother. Was she constantly worried? Eve's mother hid her. She took beatings for her. She made a future for her. She died for her. Eve would do the same for Bella. She took a moment to be grateful that Bella would never experience what Eve did.

"Eve?"

Eve blinked the tears from her eyes. "I'm sorry, Lainey. I was just . . ."

"Thinking about your mom?" Lainey guessed.

"How do you know these things?"

"I know you," Lainey answered softly. "I wish I could have

known your mother, Eve. But I believe you have the best of her in you. Trust in yourself."

"Easier said than done, Lainey," Eve responded just as quietly. "I'm not the best role model."

"Bullshit."

"Lainey Stanton!"

"Don't you chastise me while I'm chastising you. How dare you say you're not a good role model!" Lainey forced herself to lower her voice. The last thing she needed right now was an audience. "You are intelligent, successful, talented, kind, generous. Should I go on?"

It was Eve's turn to blush. Something she rarely did. "No. However, you made a mistake. The talent is gone."

"I would repeat bullshit, but . . . no. No, but. Bullshit. It's not gone, Eve. It's there, and you'll find it again."

"Can you be so sure?"

"Yes. If you don't believe in yourself, I will."

This is why you love her. Eve closed her eyes, letting that thought and Lainey's words roll through her mind.

"*Thank you.*" Eve cleared her throat. She had had enough emotions for the day. "So, you're really not going to tell me what you're reading?"

Lainey settled back, sinking into the pillows. "It's just a romance book, honey. Nothing groundbreaking."

"I've been reading my fair share of those myself." Eve curled up on the oversized chair. After the experience of trying to share Bella's toddler bed, Eve decided the room was in serious need of a more comfortable place for her to sleep.

Not like this one. Lainey was sure of that. "Maybe one day we'll start a book club," she joked.

Only if I want you to know what I've been reading. "Maybe. While I have you on the phone, I have to go to the auction house in the morning. Want to tag along?"

"Are we bidding on more stuff?"

"Not this time. They've failed to get the last lot to me. I'm going there to see what the holdup is."

"In that case, yes."

Eve smiled. "You don't like going to auctions?"

"Oh, I do. But I like watching you intimidate people more."

Eve snickered, covering her mouth when Bella stirred. "Sadist."

Lainey lifted a shoulder even though Eve couldn't see her. "I don't like seeing people hurt. It's just fun watching them think they have a hand up on the beautiful, young woman only to get put in their place." She was possibly saying more than she should, but it was innocent enough.

"On that note," Eve chuckled, "I should probably try to get some sleep. I do my best work when I'm well rested."

Lainey looked at her watch, her eyes widening. "It's midnight!"

"Mmhmm."

"Wow. I should probably go to sleep, too. Did I successfully talk you off the ledge?"

"Yes, dear. But I'm still sleeping in here with her."

Lainey smothered her laughter. And her inappropriate pleasure at that. "Not on her bed, I hope. You had such a pain in your neck the last time."

"No, ma'am. I have a very comfortable chair in here now."

Lainey's brows furrowed. How much time did Eve spend in Bella's room to warrant getting her own space? Though, she had no place to talk since she spent most of her time here in the guest bedroom.

"Well, good. I'll see you in the morning."

"Yes, you will. Bright and early. Sweet dreams, Lainey."

Already had those. "You, too, Eve. Goodnight."

"Ms. Sumptor. Mrs. Stanton. To what do we owe the pleasure? Are you here for the auction this morning? I don't recall having any items on the block that may interest you."

"Don." Eve shook the auctioneer's hand. She had worked with him several times before and never had a problem. She hoped there would be an acceptable explanation as to why there was one now.

The last time a shipment for the gallery had been botched a man was murdered in front of her. *Please let it be something simple.* "We're here about the last items Sumptor Gallery bought. We haven't received it, yet. I was expecting it for a showing this weekend."

Don Ferrill frowned. Sumptor Galleries was the auction house's best client. It would not do to have Eve Sumptor angry. "That's unacceptable. One moment, Ms. Sumptor. I will find out what happened."

Lainey snickered softly. "I half expected him to say heads were going to roll. I am surprised, though, that you were so cordial."

Eve bumped Lainey amicably. "I can be cordial. Besides, it's not his fault. I'm sure there's a perfectly good explanation."

Lainey sighed quietly. "I can't help but think of Mr. Branson," she said carefully. The last time a shipment for Sumptor Gallery was wrong, a man was murdered in front of Eve's eyes. Mr. Branson had been paid to steal Eve's valuable artwork as revenge by Laurence. When Eve found the paintings and questioned him, Mr. Branson paid with his life by one of Laurence's goons. Lainey still had nightmares of seeing Eve walk out of that building with blood all over her.

It pained Eve that Lainey had those memories. How much different would Lainey's life have been if Eve had stayed away? "I've brought so much pain into your life."

Lainey turned to Eve. "No, honey. I . . ."

"Ms. Sumptor?"

Eve turned to Don with reluctance. She too had thought of Branson the moment she found out the shipment was missing. She had to remind herself that everyone from her past was dead. They couldn't hurt her anymore. If there were a new threat, she would know about it. Wouldn't she? James constantly had his ear to the ground. There was no way he wouldn't know about a new enemy. *Please, let that be true. I'm enough of an enemy for myself.*

"Please accept my apologies. We have a new employee, and there was a mix up with the invoices. I will *personally* deliver your lot within the hour. I am truly sorry for the incompetence."

"Don, it's fine. As long as the items are there before Thursday, we're good." She was relieved. This time it was a simple mistake. "Thank you for correcting the situation."

"I cannot apologize enough."

Eve was sure Don would get on his knees and grovel at any moment.

"Don." Eve touched his shoulder lightly. "It was a mistake. I hope you'll treat it as such. I don't want anyone fired or reprimanded. I only want my paintings."

Don nodded. "Yes, ma'am. Within the hour. Thank you so much for your understanding."

Eve's hand involuntarily found its way to the small of Lainey's back as she guided her out of the auctioneer's office. She wished it would feel wrong. But it didn't.

Lainey's skin burned where Eve's hand laid. Deep down, she knew that Eve touched her without thinking about it. Did that make it better? Or worse? Lainey sighed silently. Did it even matter anymore?

"About what I said in there, bringing up Branson, I hope you know I didn't mean anything by it. You've brought much more to my life than I could ever express. I wouldn't change anything if it meant you wouldn't be in my life any longer."

Lainey blushed slightly and looked away when Eve peered at her.

"Thank you for saying that." Eve took a breath. "But what you've gone through because of me," she held her hand up when Lainey began to argue. "Please, Lainey. We both know you wouldn't have had a gun held to your head if it weren't for me."

"No, I don't know that. The world is crazy," Lainey argued defiantly. "You saved my life. What if you hadn't been there?"

They had this debate often enough that Eve decided to let this one go. She had learned these past few years that a happy Lainey was worth losing a few battles.

"Okay." She smiled. "Want to get something to eat?"

"Wait. You're giving up? You usually put up more of an argument."

Eve shrugged. "What can I say? You've given strong points."

"I give those points *all the time*." Lainey squinted suspiciously at Eve. "What's going on?"

Eve chuckled. "Nothing! I'm just hungry. And," she continued seriously. "I don't want to argue with you."

Lainey studied Eve for a moment. She didn't want to argue either. She did enough of that with Jack. "Diner?"

Eve smiled. "Greasy burger?"

"Onion rings."

"Ugh." Eve rubbed her tummy. "Let's go before my stomach starts arguing. Hey." She caught Lainey's arm before she walked away. "Are you still willing to go to therapy with me?"

Though it made her stomach flip, Lainey nodded. "Yeah, honey, I am."

"Thank you. I hope Bella will be better soon. I don't want to go when she's sick." Eve started walking again, sticking close to Lainey's side. She didn't miss the smirk on her beautiful friend's face. "What?"

"You're such a good mother."

"Did you mean neurotic?"

Lainey laughed. "No! Worrying about your child doesn't make you neurotic. If it does, I'm in big trouble."

Chapter Twenty-Two
Therapy

Breakthrough.

"Are you ready for this?"

Eve glanced at Lainey, her hand resting on the doorknob of Dr. Woodrow's office.

"As I'll ever be," she replied softly.

Eve saw the trepidation on Lainey's face and the slight tremble of her hand.

"Hey." Eve lifted Lainey's chin until they were eye to eye. "You don't have to do this, Lainey."

"I want to, Eve. For you." She took Eve's hand in hers, squeezing it slightly before releasing it. "For me, too."

Eve knew this was hurting her. If the quick release of her hand wasn't a good indication, the tension that was radiating from Lainey certainly was. They both still felt guilty about the feelings they had for each other. But Eve also had a theory that Lainey was scared that these sessions were going to change those feelings. It was a complicated situation, feeling guilty but not wanting to lose that closeness. As Lainey told Eve once before, it was akin to being bipolar. Eve gave her a small smile and opened the door.

"Good evening, Eve," Dr. Woodrow greeted. Her eyes widened

with surprise when she saw Lainey step in as well. "Lainey." The doctor stood and greeting Lainey by offering her hand. "It's so nice to have you joining us tonight."

"Dr. Woodrow, it's nice to meet you finally. Formally." Lainey smiled politely, shaking the doc's hand briefly.

Dr. Woodrow slanted Eve a look, shaking her head when the younger woman shrugged. She hadn't warned her that Lainey was coming along. After their last couple of sessions, including a second with Adam, Willamena wasn't sure Eve would invite anyone else. The woman hated feeling vulnerable. Willamena was curious to see how Eve would handle that in front of Lainey.

"Let's have a seat," Woodrow suggested. She noticed Lainey hesitate before settling in beside Eve. "Are you nervous about being here, Lainey?"

"A little."

It unnerved Eve to see Lainey so timid. It reminded her of how she was when they first met. Though Lainey often found the courage to let Eve know precisely what she thought, the reality was that she had been painfully modest. It was only after their affair that Lainey found her confidence. Unfortunately, she wasn't showing any of that confidence here in Dr. Woodrow's office.

"Lainey." Eve decided to give Lainey an out. It wasn't worth it to have her feeling so miserable here.

"Eve, wait." Lainey interrupted. "I want to be here. I told you that. It's just a little intimidating. Just give me a moment to get adjusted."

Well, she had found a little bit of that spirit. Eve was thankful for that and nodded. She noticed then that Dr. Woodrow was watching the exchange intently.

"I would like to start by making an observation while you 'adjust,'" Willamena said to Lainey, who nodded in return. "Just this small interaction has told me a lot about your relationship with each other."

Eve glanced at Lainey who blushed. Involuntarily Eve's mind noted how cute Lainey looked when she blushed, and she closed her eyes, chastising herself for that thought.

"Eve?"

"What did this interaction tell you," Eve asked quickly to avoid the question she knew the doctor had for her.

Dr. Woodrow watched Eve for a moment, then signaled her understanding. "Well, you had mentioned to me that you felt more control when you were with Lainey."

Lainey's head popped up at that, and she looked at Eve with a mixture of amusement and confusion.

"Control?"

"Um. Yeah, well . . ." *Good lord*! Why did she suddenly feel like a scolded child?

"Because of my inexperience?" Lainey asked, turning fully towards Eve with undivided interest.

"I'm not sure what it was. Perhaps it was that."

"But I pursued you."

Eve laughed softly. "You did not. I pursued you!"

"No . . ." she trailed off when she saw Eve's brow lift. "Fine, but I let you."

Maybe it was the defiant little lift of the head. Or perhaps it was the bold statement of 'letting' Eve pursue her. Whatever it was, it made Eve laugh. A loud, hearty laugh that she hadn't had in a while. Lainey frowned, and Dr. Woodrow looked at Eve curiously.

"You let your guard down so much with Lainey," Willamena said softly after Eve finished laughing. "But with Adam, you are constantly trying to be that woman everyone who meets you believes you are. Why?"

And there went any joy Eve just felt. "Isn't that what I'm here to figure out?" she asked irritably.

"Eve."

Eve turned her glare on Lainey, only to have it soften when she saw concern. *Protective*. Eve was protective of Lainey. But she didn't want to be protected. She wanted to know she could protect herself. Lainey wasn't fragile by any means, but she had a vulnerability about her. That brought out Eve's protective side. There was nothing like that with Adam. He was self-sufficient, self-confident, strong and he would fight for Eve until his dying breath. Was that what she didn't like?

"So much just went through your head. I can only help you if you tell me, Eve."

"I don't want to be protected," Eve said simply, as though it answered all questions. To her surprise, the doc nodded and scribbled a note in her notebook.

Patient is able to be more open with the best friend. The vulnerability that is normally hated is embraced. The dynamic between the patient and the best friend is completely different than with the spouse. I now believe I know one of the main reasons the patient's creativity has been blocked. The patient has cut off a very emotional part.

"And with Adam, you feel like the protected and not like the protector that you feel with Lainey?" Willamena asked once she finished her note.

Damn. Though it wasn't the full extent of what Eve felt for Lainey, it was a big part of it. There were moments when Adam's love felt more like obligation. He went through everything with her, and now he felt obliged to be her protector. While Lainey was protective in her own right, it was a natural caring. That nurturing side of Lainey caused Eve to feel protective of her.

"Yes."

"You feel like my protector?" Lainey asked warily. "Is that why you? Why we?"

Eve could tell Lainey was getting irritated. When she got to the point of not being able to articulate what she was feeling, it was time for Eve to try to smooth things over. With honesty.

"We had an affair because we felt . . . *feel* something for each other, Lainey," she reassured softly. "It wasn't because I wanted to conquer you, or whatever you thought when you heard the word protector. Yes, I feel that way. I want to shield you . . ."

"I don't need you to protect me, Eve."

"I know you don't, but I can't change how I feel. Obviously." Eve sighed. "I'm trying to figure out what's going on in my head, so this is all as new to me as it is to you."

Lainey's eyes softened, and she reached over to place her hand over Eve's. "I'm sorry."

Eve shook her head. "Don't be. We need to be able to express ourselves freely here, right?" Her question was directed at Dr. Woodrow who nodded. "I don't think there's *one* thing that attracted me to you. *Still* attracts me to you. And I know you feel just as guilty as I do about our feelings for each other."

Lainey nodded sadly. "It's not fair to Jack. Or Adam." It was getting harder and harder to care about that, especially with Jack. But Lainey wasn't ready to go down that road with Eve just yet. She turned to Dr. Woodrow. "Is that what's blocking Eve's creativity? Her feelings for me?"

Eve wondered briefly why Lainey didn't ask her. But if she knew Lainey — and, she liked to think she knew her very well — Lainey would think Eve would give her any answer that spared her any kind of responsibility for Eve's problems.

"Lainey, I believe there's a myriad of matters that are blocking Eve's creativity," Willamena answered carefully.

"That doesn't answer my question, does it?"

That's my Lainey. Eve waited for the guilt to hit her after that thought, but it didn't. Perhaps it was because it wasn't a sexual thought. Lainey was her best friend and would always be important to her.

"I suppose it doesn't," Dr. Woodrow admitted with a smile. "All of Eve's feelings are what is blocking her."

"So, yes."

"Lainey, honey, it's not you." Okay, honestly the endearment just slipped out. "It's not you, and it's not Adam. It's me." Eve slipped off her chair and knelt in front of Lainey. "I love you. I will always love you. I don't know how to stop that, or if I even want to." Her heart broke a little when a tear slid down Lainey's cheek. "You were the one who showed me that I was worth being loved. Could Adam have done that?" *No.* "Perhaps, if I had let him in enough. But I wasn't able to open myself up. Until you. So, for that, I will always be grateful. And I will always be protective of you, love you. I don't want to feel guilty for that, but it hurts Adam."

Eve refused to listen to the little voice in her head telling her that guilt was fading more and more every day.

"I know," Lainey whispered softly. "It must be harder for you because Adam knows. Jack doesn't know. He doesn't hurt from this. But you know I never want to hurt Adam. Knowing that I am, or that I'm part of the reason . . . knowing that you're hurting . . ." She paused to take a deep breath. "I love you, too, Eve. But I also understand how much you're in love with Adam. Do you hear me, Eve? I understand. And if you need me to step back . . ."

You don't understand! "No!" She gripped Lainey's hands. "I don't want you to step back. It was the possibility of losing you forever that started this chaos in my head." Eve stopped when she realized that was the first time she had come to that conclusion.

"Eve? Did you have a breakthrough?" Dr. Woodrow asked curiously.

"I guess I did."

"Would you like to talk about when that chaos started?"

Eve glanced at Lainey. She hadn't told her exactly what happened when Adam was taken. She didn't tell her how she had to stand in front of her bloodied and battered husband, his life on the line, and confess to what happened with Lainey. She hadn't told her about how Laurence had tried to force her to kill someone she loved.

"Maybe you should wait until next time when you have a one on one session," Lainey suggested knowingly.

Eve squeezed her hand in gratitude.

"I think you're right," Dr. Woodrow agreed. "We're close to our time, as it is. I would like to see the two of you again if you both agree."

Eve stood, taking a step back. "Yes, I think that would be good."

Lainey nodded. "I'll do whatever I can to help. If having me here does that, I'll be here."

"Good." Dr. Woodrow smiled at both ladies, standing to say her goodbyes. "I hope you both have a good night."

"I'm surprised, doc. No homework?" Eve teased.

She chuckled, as did Lainey. "My homework for both of you is to go home to your husbands. Try to forget all of this guilt nonsense." *And maybe each of you will realize something you're trying to suppress.* Willamena laughed again when Eve raised her eyebrow. "Yes, I think it's nonsense. We can't help how we feel, only how we react to it. You two have done nothing to be guilty about, have you?"

Lainey and Eve glanced at each other.

"No," they answer together. It's not that they hadn't thought about it. But Eve knew she'd never hurt Adam like that again. At least she hoped she wouldn't. The pull of Lainey, however, was intense.

"Then go home," Willamena continued. "Forget the guilt and try to relax. Eve, if you need homework, try to flesh out your breakthrough."

"Hmm. Perhaps I'll relax with my husband and daughter." Eve smiled, noting the twinge of guilt from talking about her husband in front of Lainey. *Damn it. This situation may very well be the death of me.* After everything she'd been through in life, it was *love* that broke her.

"Very well. Next time we'll also discuss what just went through your head."

The good doctor missed nothing. Eve merely nodded and told her goodnight. Once they were outside the office, Eve turned to Lainey.

"Thank you."

Lainey smiled, leaning in to hug Eve. "You're welcome."

She took a second — just a second — to enjoy Lainey's arms around her then took a step back.

"Goodnight," Eve whispered.

"Goodnight, Eve."

Chapter Twenty-Three

"Mommy!"

Eve smiled at her daughter's voice. Even loud it was cute. Perhaps that would change when Bella became a teenager and yelled at Eve for not letting her do stupid things. But for now, Eve enjoyed the sound of Bella's little girl voice calling out for her mommy.

"In here, bug!" she called back. Adam sat across from her, saying nothing. He had a look about him that she couldn't quite get a handle on. This wasn't the awkwardness that had become almost normal these days. He was watching her as though waiting for her to say something. Confess all her sins. *Keep waiting.*

"Hello, mommy!" Bella ran up to Eve and flung herself into Eve's waiting arms.

"Hello, my love. You're up awfully early this morning." Eve looked up just as Lexie entered the room, slightly panting. "And by the looks of it, already wearing Lexie out. Good morning, Lexie."

"Good morning, Mrs. —" The words died on Lexie's lips when Eve's eyebrow raised. "Eve. Mr. Riley asked me to come in early today."

Eve glanced at Adam. He hadn't told her that. Neither of them had early morning meetings that she knew of. "Of course." Eve looked at her daughter currently bouncing on her knee. Eve wondered if she ever had that much energy when she was younger. Did she ever bounce on her mother's knee? She had spent so much time thinking about the horrible things in her past that Eve wasn't sure she could remember anything good. "Did you drink coffee this morning, bug?"

Bella giggled. "No! Siwwy!"

"Mmhmm. So, Miss Bella, what do you have planned for the day?"

Bella stopped bouncing and let out a "hmm" while tapping her chin. At that moment, Eve didn't care if she couldn't remember the good from the past as long as she remembered these moments.

"Pway," Bella answered finally. "Tea pawty wif Lexie and my animals. And draw all day."

It was wrong to be jealous of your daughter, right? Eve smiled at Bella. "Sounds like heaven."

"Want to come to my pawty, momma?"

"I wish I could, baby girl. Unfortunately, I have boring meetings today." Eve rolled her eyes dramatically causing Bella to giggle hysterically. "Will you save me some tea? I'll have some tonight when I'm reading you a bedtime story."

"'Kay! I draw you sumpin'?"

"Please? You know I love your drawings." Eve took in every ray of light beaming from Bella's smile. "You be good for Lexie, okay?" Bella nodded enthusiastically. "If you want, you can come with me to the gallery tomorrow."

"Yea!" Bella wrapped her arms around Eve's neck and gave her a loud kiss on the cheek. "Wuv you, momma! Bye, daddy!" Bella waved at her dad before taking off.

"More meetings?" Adam said once they were alone.

Eve nearly forgot he was there. He had been silent the entire time she and Bella had their little conversation. Since he wasn't in the talkative mood, until now, she picked up her phone to catch up on her emails.

"Seems the thing to do these days," Eve answered. "Have meetings about work instead of actually doing work." She grinned at him and received a small one back. "What's on your agenda?"

"Meetings," he said with a bit of humor. "We have a new client coming in today."

Eve looked up from reading her emails. "That's great."

An uncomfortable silence followed, so Eve went back to the email she had received from Guillaume Cortet, Bussiere's lawyer. Apparently, she was going to have to stop putting this Paris trip off. She put that thought aside and began mentally preparing for the holidays. Thanksgiving was coming up. Does she invite Lainey, Jack, and the boys? Would Adam agree to that? Or did she have just a small family Thanksgiving with Adam and Bella?

"Are you going to talk to me about Paris?"

Eve frowned, switching gears once again. "What?" Did he know about her email?

"Paris. Have you made plans, yet?"

"No," Eve answered hesitantly. "Why?"

"Time is running out, isn't it?"

Eve studied Adam. "Are you reading my emails?"

Adam snorted in response. "No. Though I don't see a problem with a *husband* having access to their wife's passwords and vice versa, I don't have anything to hide. Do you?"

Eve's eyes narrowed. "I'm a business owner with sensitive material. Even when it comes to my *husband*."

Adam smirked. Probably not the wisest thing to do with a woman like Eve, but he was aggravated enough not to care. "You own galleries."

"I own many different companies, Adam. You of all people should know that." It was Adam's name on the building of his architect firm. It was Eve's name as the owner. She never threw that fact in his face before. It seemed he needed a little refresher. He also knew there was the restaurant, the club, and Sumptor, Inc. She didn't know what his endgame was here, but if he wanted to play, Eve could play.

Adam bowed his head in acknowledgment. "You're right. That was stupid to say. But if you can't trust me with your info, who can you trust?"

"Have you been reading my emails, Adam?"

He sighed. "No. That lawyer has been trying to contact you. Obviously, you haven't answered, so he came to me. Asked if I could get my wife to talk to him before this thing expires. Personally, I think you should forget about it. Let it rot."

"Do you?"

"Yeah. I said before she doesn't deserve redemption."

"I'm not doing it for her, Adam. I'm doing it for the young girls who don't have it easy. What part of that don't you understand?"

"I understand the sentiment, Eve. But why does it have to be you? Why can't you sell it and be done with it?"

"Because then she wins. I get to go in there and exorcize the demons. *My* demons. I get to exorcize *her*. Something I think you need to do with Laurence and Billy," she finished delicately.

"I'm fine." Adam was tight-lipped but forced himself to shrug with indifference. "They're dead. I don't have to worry about them anymore." *I have to worry about Lainey.*

Eve nodded. She didn't believe it for a second, but she let it go. There would possibly come a point in his life when he'd have to deal with it. But that would be up to him. She wouldn't force him the way she felt forced.

"I need to get to the gallery."

"Eve? If you want me to go to Paris with you, I will."

Eve shook her head. "You don't believe in what I'm doing there. Besides, if I'm going to one of the art capitals of the world, I can turn it into a business trip."

"Which means Lainey is going with you?"

"If she can, yes." Eve didn't hesitate. She didn't falter at his tone. She wasn't apologetic.

"What about an architect for the changes you want to make?" Once again, he stuck his hand in the fire and got burned. If only he could figure out how to avoid this fucking dread he felt himself hurtling towards.

Gray eyes met blue. "Paris has different laws concerning construction. I think it's more efficient to go with someone local."

Adam scoffed. "So, you'll take Lainey, but I get a pass. All because I suggested you get rid of the place?"

Eve drew a deep breath, letting it out slowly. She had to remember that Bella was upstairs. "One has nothing to do with the other. If I decide to do gallery work while in Paris, I will be taking Lainey because it's her job. You are a fantastic architect, Adam, but you have no experience with the laws in foreign countries. If it makes you feel better to think the way you do, so be it. Have a good day."

Adam watched his wife walk out on him. He couldn't help but think it wouldn't be the last time.

"I'm sorry I'm late." Eve touched Lainey briefly on the shoulder before taking the seat across from her.

"If I bought you a watch for Christmas, would you wear it?" Lainey asked, a small smirk playing on her lips.

Eve, who never wore a watch, smiled. "I would cherish anything you got me."

"That's not what I asked." Lainey glanced at Eve's delicate wrist. It would almost be a sin to cover it with a bulky watch.

Eve chuckled. "Yes, Lainey. I would wear it." Even though the exorbitantly expensive Tiffany watch Adam got her sat in a safety deposit box.

Lainey gave her a satisfied nod. She didn't quite believe her, but it was a nice feeling, nonetheless.

"How were your meetings?"

Eve rolled her eyes. "Boring. Sitting in a room discussing how to get things done instead of being out there actually getting stuff done." They shared a laugh. "How was your morning?"

Lainey sat up a bit straighter. "While you were sitting around talking about getting things done, I was *doing* things."

"The Herzlingers?" Perhaps she was a masochist, but Eve loved getting razzed by Lainey. It meant she was comfortable enough with Eve to let her playful side out.

"Mmhmm. They were on the fence, but I got them to come over to my side."

Eve felt that familiar pull. "You're good at that," she said suggestively.

Lainey blinked to break the mesmerizing eye contact Eve had with her and cleared her throat. "It's, um, been a while since we've been here." She picked up the menu, but none of the words made any sense. That's what Eve did to her. She thought about the first time they came here together. Lainey's life changed that day.

Eve caught the blush that came along with the change of subject. God, she hated this awkwardness with Lainey. It wasn't supposed to be this way. "I'm sorry if I made you feel uncomfortable."

Lainey looked up at Eve's sad face. "No! No, you didn't. I just . . . I . . ."

"We should order," Eve said, trying to let Lainey off the hook.

"Eve?"

"It's okay." Eve attempted to smile. She knew it she didn't quite succeed by the look on Lainey's face.

"No, Eve." Lainey took a breath. "I didn't feel uncomfortable. It was . . . you fluster me. Given our situation, I'm not sure how appropriate that is." *Even though I love it when you flirt with me.*

Eve couldn't argue. Oh, she wanted to, but she couldn't. She also couldn't refute that it gave her a good feeling knowing she could still fluster Lainey. Maybe it wasn't appropriate, but it was getting harder and harder to deny her feelings. So, she merely nodded.

"Are you ready to order?" This time when she smiled, she meant it. She wasn't giving in, but she had to walk a fine line.

Lainey watched Eve for a moment, noticing she never once picked up the menu. "You've brought me here a couple of times," she began. "Both times you ordered the same thing. Why?"

The skin between Eve's brows crinkled when she frowned. "Because I like it?"

Lainey tilted her head in response. Eve Sumptor wasn't usually hesitant, but her answer sounded more like a question. Lainey opened the menu, scanning it. "There are so many things on this menu that sound amazing. I want to try them all."

"I suppose I'm a creature of habit," Eve said carefully.

"Doesn't that get boring? Don't you ever want to try something new?"

The tables have turned since the first time they came here. It was Eve who was bold in the beginning, asking Lainey what she had on underneath her drab gray suit. That was the beginning of Lainey's personal transformation. Gone were the dreary clothes. In their place were trendy outfits that garnered a look or two from passersby. She used to believe those looks were directed at Eve until she started getting them when she was by herself.

While Lainey was thinking about transformations, Eve was mulling over what Lainey had said. *"Don't you ever want to try something new?" More than you know, Lainey. I just don't know how . . .*

"May I take your order?"

Eve looked up at the young waitress who smiled pleasantly at her. She referred to Lainey first.

Lainey pointed at the menu. "The chef's special, please? Dressing on the side."

"Yes, ma'am." The young woman turned to Eve once again. "And for you, ma'am?"

Eve saw the light of recognition in the waitress's eyes. Even when the restaurant hired new people, they seemed to know exactly who signed their paychecks. Eve decided to use that to her advantage.

"Have the chef make me something. Her choice."

"Yes, ma'am." The waitress bowed her head slightly before walking away.

"You're trying something new." Lainey smiled proudly at Eve.

"Mmhmm. Speaking of changes, may I run something by you?"

"Of course." Lainey took a sip of her iced tea. She could admit to herself that she was a bit antsy about what Eve may want to change. The hell if she would show it, though. Whatever Eve said, Lainey would support. Eve deserved that.

"I asked you here for a reason. I've been thinking about selling."

Lainey nearly choked on her tea. "Your restaurant?"

"Yes. And the club."

"Why? They're always packed. Business must be good."

"It is," Eve agreed. "Both places are like well-oiled machines. I owe that to Rebecca and the staff she chose."

Lainey's eyebrows shot up. "Rebecca?"

Eve nodded. "When I opened these places, owning restaurants and clubs were the trends. I had no idea how to do it, though. That's when I met Rebecca. It's because of her expertise that they flourished as they did."

Lainey had known that Eve and Rebecca met through business, but she hadn't put the pieces together until now. It all made sense. Rebecca owned an extremely profitable club. Even being off the grid and private didn't hurt the bottom line.

"I don't get it. If they're so profitable and self-sufficient, why would you want to sell?"

Eve shrugged. "They were a vanity project for me. As you said before, we haven't been here in a while. And I haven't been to the club since . . ." *Since you and I danced there together.* "At this point in my life, I'd rather focus on the galleries. I'll keep Sumptor, Inc., but these," she gestured around them, "are something I don't need anymore."

That was something Lainey could understand. Some decisions, after thought and time, needed to be reevaluated.

"Are you asking for my opinion?" Eve nodded. "Then, given the way you feel, I think it's a good idea to sell."

Eve smiled. "Perhaps you should hear my idea before saying that."

"Okay," Lainey drawled suspiciously.

"I want to sell them to the employees. The bulk of the restaurant would go to the chef, the club to the general manager. But each employee that has been here since the beginning will have a stake in the business."

Lainey, with her accountant's brain, did some numbers in her head. "That doesn't seem lucrative."

"It's not. And Rebecca will probably punish me for it. They deserve this, Lainey. Did you know that restaurants have an obscenely high failure rate? The Garden of Eve never even hit a snag. O was the hotspot since the doors opened. The employees did that, not me. I was purely the startup money."

Lainey's eyes softened. "You're such a good person, Eve."

Eve lowered her head. "I'm just trying to do the right thing, Lainey."

As you always do. Lainey reached over and took Eve's hand. "I don't just think it's a good idea, honey, I think it's sweet."

"Do you know how much you could make if you sold to investors?" Adam put a forkful of chicken parmesan in his mouth, then continued. "Selling it off to the employees is a terrible idea."

What had she been thinking, telling Adam her plans? Eve pushed her food around on her plate. She had been feeling good about her decision ever since lunch with Lainey. Even Rebecca, after a bit of coaxing, conceded that it was a good idea.

"I disagree," she said calmly.

Adam scoffed. "Look, beautiful, I get the gesture. But there's money to be made here — a lot of it. I'm working with a client who happens to be a restauranteur who's looking to expand. I'll talk with him."

"No, you won't. This isn't your decision, Adam."

"I'm your husband, Eve. Big decisions like this need to be discussed and agreed upon."

From the corner of her eye, Eve could see Bella watching them. If Adam weren't pissing her off, she would think it was cute the way Bella's head went back and forth as though she was watching a tennis match. The problem was, the little girl was smart. Eve would have to tread carefully here.

"My businesses, my say," Eve said sweetly. "Stick with your firm, Adam. I'll take care of what's mine."

Adam leaned in. "The firm is yours, too, sweetheart. Are you going to sell it for pennies on the dollar to me?"

He kept his tone light, but from the look in his eyes, Eve could tell he was pissed. *Join the club, buddy.*

Eve gave him a smile that could turn lava to ice. "Prove yourself as the others did and maybe I will." She pushed her plate away from her and turned her attention to Bella. "Did you draw me a picture today, bug?"

Bella eyed her father for a second, then gave Eve a big grin. "Yep! Four!"

"Four pictures?" Eve laid a hand over her heart. "That's amazing! I can't wait to see them. Did you also save me some tea?"

Bella nodded eagerly. "My dowwy can have some wif us!"

"Hang on. Are we talking Miss Moffit or Ju Ju?"

"Ju Ju!" Bella pumped her arms in the air jubilantly.

"Oh, good. Miss Moffit and I are not on speaking terms. *That* would have been awkward." Eve shivered dramatically.

"Momma!" Bella giggled. "You siwwy!"

Eve leaned down and rubbed Bella's nose with her own. "Are you done eating, bug?"

"Yes, momma."

"Wanna help momma wash the dishes?"

"'Kay!" Bella hopped up and grabbed her plastic plate off the table.

"No running!" Eve called out, immediately hearing Bella slow her steps.

"I suppose we're done with our conversation," Adam said coolly.

"Yes. Are you done eating?"

Adam pushed his plate towards her. "Does it always have to be your way, Eve?"

She paused in her motions. "No. However, when it comes to my businesses, I'm not asking for your advice, Adam. Just your support." She didn't want to think about why it was different with Lainey. "And just so we're clear, *you* came to me for help with the firm. The only one who seems to have a problem with that now is you. I don't interfere with your company. Don't interfere with mine."

Chapter Twenty-Four
Therapy

Feelings.

"You've been avoiding your sessions, Eve." Dr. Woodrow offered Eve a cup of hot tea as she sat down.

"Not avoiding," Eve began but was immediately silenced by Willamena's disbelieving look. "The holidays are a busy time," she tried again.

"They are," the doc agreed. "But I don't think that's why you haven't been in. Would you like to talk about the real reason?"

"You're not going to let me get away with the busy holiday time, huh?" Dr. Woodrow shook her head and smiled. Eve sighed. "I just wanted to get out of my head for a while."

"And you thought you could do that by skipping your sessions?"

"All I do here is stay inside my head. It's not always a great place to be, Doc."

"You're only delaying the inevitable, Eve." She took a sip of her tea, watching Eve over the rim. When Eve remained silent, she set her cup to the side and picked up her notebook. "You had a breakthrough in your last session with Lainey. Have you thought more about that?"

Eve closed her eyes for a moment. If she allowed herself to

think about her "breakthrough" she would have to admit that Lainey — or the thought of losing Lainey — was one of the major issues blocking her creativity. She would have to admit that her feelings for Lainey went deeper than she wanted to acknowledge.

"What were you just thinking, Eve?"

Eve sighed once again. "What is this hold Lainey has on my heart?" she asked quietly. "Why can't I let her go? At least *that* part?"

"Eve, I'm going to ask you something, and I don't want you to think about the answer. Thinking will make you consider other people's feelings. Just answer." Eve nodded. "Are you in love with Lainey?"

"*Yes*." The whispered answer shocked Eve as much as it scared the shit out of her. "How? How can I feel that for her *and* my husband? How do I stop?"

"I don't think it's something we have control over, Eve," Dr. Woodrow said softly.

"No. There *has* to be something we can do. Help me." She knew she sounded desperate. She was. She couldn't have these feelings for Lainey. It wasn't fair. To Lainey, to Adam. Hell, it wasn't fair to Eve.

"Alright, Eve. Let's say there is something I can do for you. That I can help you turn your feelings off for one of the two people you love. Which one would you like to stop loving?"

Eve opened her mouth to answer and not a damn word came out. *Shit.* Why wasn't Lainey her automatic answer? She should want to stop loving Lainey, right? She was married. *Eve* was married. That's what she should want. Why wasn't it?

"*I can't do this*," she whispered. "I don't want to do this anymore."

"Avoidance isn't the answer."

"It's the only answer I have!" Eve stood and began to pace. "Life was so much easier when I didn't have to worry about *feelings*."

"Easier or emptier?" Dr. Woodrow asked quietly. "Sit down, Eve. Let's see if we can talk through this."

"Talk through what?" Eve asked irritably. "You just said I

couldn't change the way I feel. So, what are these sessions good for?"

"You're fighting me, fighting your feelings. I can practically see you building your walls again. Reverting to the way you were will not help you."

"At least I was able to paint then," Eve muttered.

"Fine. Go back to the way you were. That way you risk losing *both* Adam and Lainey." Willamena was frustrated with Eve. It was completely unprofessional — something she allowed to happen too often with Eve. "I'm sorry. I shouldn't have said that."

"It's fine. Perhaps I need a kick in the ass." Eve sat back down with a sigh and ran a hand through her hair. "Okay. Let's talk about this."

Dr. Woodrow studied Eve for a moment, then made a note in her notebook. **Patient is desperate for answers yet fears them. The love the patient feels for the best friend has not gone away. Instead, it has grown exponentially. We need to explore that avenue if there is any hope of the patient getting past this block. However, I feel the patient is reluctant to acknowledge what is already apparent.** "Let's begin with the breakthrough. In our last session, you said that," she glanced at her notes again, "the possibility of losing Lainey is what started the chaos in your head. Can you tell me more about that?"

Although they had touched on the subject of what happened when Laurence took Adam, they had never really gotten into the details. Somehow, Eve talking about seeing her husband, bloodied and beaten, was harder to talk about than what happened to her all those years ago. *Because you feel guilty.*

She took a deep breath and let it out slowly. "I believe I've told you before that I let my guard down after I killed Tony."

"Can I just stop you right there for a moment?" Dr. Woodrow interrupted. "I don't like when you say you "killed" Tony."

Eve's brows furrowed. "But I did. I shot him."

"No. I've read the reports. I know there was a struggle, even though you haven't gone into details about that day. The way you say it, it's like you think you shot him in cold blood. You saved

Lainey's life. You protected your own life. If you're holding on to some kind of guilt for that, you need to let it go."

Guilt? For killing Tony? Eve didn't think she held guilt. But what the hell did she know? "Fine," she conceded. "After Tony died, I felt safe again. My feelings for Lainey were still there, but I was dealing with them. I *thought* I was dealing with them," she corrected before continuing. "But, when they took Adam, I wasn't prepared for the flood of emotions that took over. His disappearance, coupled with my fear of something happening to Bella and Lainey, maybe that's when the chaos started. But when I had to stand in front of my battered husband, seeing the pain in his eyes when . . ." she paused and stood up again, not able to keep still. "You know, I couldn't even say it."

"Say what, Eve?"

"I still didn't know who was behind it all, he used text messages to communicate," she began again, not yet answering the doctor's question. "When I walked in that warehouse, all I saw was Adam tied to that chair. I was told to confess. But I didn't know what I was supposed to confess to. Or maybe I did, but I didn't want Adam to find out. If I think that way, each time Adam was electrocuted because of my hesitance weighs on my conscience."

Patient holds incredible guilt for what happened to the spouse. This could be a big reason the patient chooses to stay instead of exploring different routes that may be what the patient truly wants.

"Continue."

Another sigh. "I still didn't say it," she repeated. "I didn't tell Adam about the affair. He was the strong one. He protected me once again and saved me from having to say the words. But that pain I saw in him after I confirmed it; that pain had nothing to do with his physical state. I hurt him. And I knew I would possibly have to give Lainey up if we made it out of there alive. A part of me died at that moment."

"Your guilt is overwhelming you, Eve." Willamena put her notebook to the side and stood up. "You're demonizing yourself for being human and having human emotions."

"I hurt him! I hurt Lainey!"

"Stop." Dr. Woodrow stood in front of Eve, placing her hands on Eve's shoulders in an attempt to either stop her from pacing or calm her. Perhaps both. "I get that loving two people can be confusing. I even get how it can cause guilt."

"Do you? Have you ever been in love with two people before?" God that was childish and Eve immediately felt shame for saying it.

"Yes, actually," she answered, surprising them both. "But this isn't about me."

"What do I do?"

"Let's continue talking." She guided Eve back to her seat. "After that situation, did Adam confront you?"

"Not like I thought he would. He never yelled at me, never got mad at me." She looked up at Dr. Woodrow. "He was more upset with Lainey."

"He loves you."

"That makes things much better," Eve mumbled.

"Would it have made it better if he left you? If he didn't love you? Lainey would still be married," she reminded Eve. When she didn't answer, Willamena nodded and picked up her notebook.

"What did you just write?" Eve asked.

"That you find it easier to believe someone should stop loving you for your faults, than love you more." Willamena paused, debating on whether she should tell Eve the rest. She decided she wanted to see what Eve's reaction would be. "I also wrote that you wonder if Lainey would still be married if you weren't with Adam."

Eve frowned at her. "I didn't say that."

"Your expression did. Let me ask you this. If you weren't with Adam, would you pursue Lainey?"

"Of course not! She's married."

"What if it were something she wanted?"

There was a definite hesitation. "I — I don't know."

"You're not being honest. Whether it's with yourself or just me, I don't know. Eve, would you want to be with Lainey if you both were free to do so?"

"Yes." God. How many times had she dreamt of that? As much

as she loved her husband, she still dreamt of someone else. That *had* to be wrong. She *knew* that was wrong.

"Does Lainey know this?"

"Hell no. Why would I do that to her?"

"Have you discussed your feelings with Adam?"

Eve blinked at her. Surely, she must've been joking. "And hurt him even more by telling him, 'hey, I love Lainey and still think about being with her'?" she said irritably.

"I understand your frustration, Eve, but we're here to talk about these things."

"I know. But all of this talking is doing nothing but confusing me more!"

"You said you were dealing with your feelings for Lainey. How?"

"What?"

"How were you dealing with them? By denying them?"

"What else could I do? We're both married. Denying them or hiding them just seemed like the right thing to do." Wow. Eve's frustration was running rampant tonight.

"You must realize from your past that covering it up doesn't mean it goes away, Eve."

"My past doesn't hurt other people. It only hurts me. My feelings for Lainey? Those feelings hurt others. Adam, Bella, Jack, Kevin, Darren. *Lainey*."

"And what about you, Eve? Are you willing to sacrifice yourself, your creativity to keep those around you from feeling the pain you're feeling yourself?"

"Yes."

"It'll only get worse," Willamena said softly. "Are you also willing to stop seeing Lainey if that happens?"

Eve's chest tightened with pain. She felt her eyes begin to fill with tears. "I can't. God help me, but I can't."

"You need to talk to Lainey about this, Eve."

"What good would that do?" Besides make Lainey feel worse about what's going on. She already felt guilty enough.

"You must realize that she feels the same way about you."

Eve's heart sped up at that thought. And then the guilt came. Or perhaps it was irritation. "She's in love with her husband."

"She's in love with you, too. Do you not think she's going through the same things you are? Perhaps talking about it would help you both. And, if you're afraid to have that conversation alone, have it here."

"She's not in love with me," Eve said defiantly. If she said it enough, maybe she would start believing it. That would be easier to handle. Eve wouldn't begin to hope for things that could never be.

"You can deny all you want. Her feelings, yours. That doesn't change the facts, Eve. So, if you want to actually move in some direction, you're going to have to face it."

"This is so fucking hard." Eve was seriously considering going back to her old, solitary life. But of course, that was impossible. She was a mother. Bella depended on her. If she couldn't get her shit together, she wasn't going to be of much use to her. What would it do to Bella if Eve left Adam? What would it do to her if Eve stayed? Her stomach lurched at the thought of leaving Adam. She couldn't imagine not having him in her life any more than she could imagine not having Lainey. *But in what capacity? As a husband or just a father to Bella? God, I'm such a fucking mess.*

"People typically come to see me when things are too difficult to handle on their own," Dr. Woodrow said with a small smile. Relief moved through her when Eve returned the smile. "Eve, I see no other way of you getting past this block. You need to be truthful about the way you feel."

"So, I don't paint anymore. There could be worse things." Like losing Lainey. Or my daughter if Adam is angry enough.

"Not for someone like you. Art is like breath to you." Dr. Woodrow closed her notebook and put it to the side again. "Your night terrors are back, and you don't laugh nearly as much as you should. These are things Adam and Lainey told me when they first contacted me. So, even if you're not worried about yourself, *they're* worried about you."

"Do you think Adam would want this if he knew that all it's doing is bringing my feelings for Lainey to the forefront again?"

"Is that what you think it's doing?" Eve shrugged, and Willamena continued. "For therapy to work, we must get to the root of the problem. Then it's like peeling an onion. Layers and layers of feelings that are most likely going to make you cry and feel worse."

"It's a wonder you don't use that in your advertising," Eve said acrimoniously, then smiled teasingly.

Willamena chuckled before becoming serious once again. "Eve, you are a very complicated woman. You have many reasons for that defense mechanism. We need to work our way through it. And you're going to need help with that."

"By talking to Lainey about my feelings?"

"That's one thing, yes."

"And you wondered why I was avoiding the sessions."

She laughed. "I thought you weren't avoiding them. That it was just the busy holiday time."

"Caught me," Eve smiled before sighing. "You'll be with me when I talk to Lainey?"

"Of course."

"And you'll put me back together when I lose everything?"

"Why do you think you'll lose everything?"

"Lainey isn't in love with me, Doc. She won't want to be around me anymore when she finds out how I feel. And the next thing you'll tell me to do is confess all to Adam. He'll leave me for sure and take Bella with him. This is what your suggestion is likely to do."

"Have you always been a pessimist?"

"I don't think that's pessimism. I think it's realism. It's possible."

"Alright. I'll concede that it's possible. And you know you don't have to do anything you feel uncomfortable with."

Eve laughed harshly. "I'm uncomfortable with *this*, but Adam and Lainey wanted me here." She paused. "I'll bring Lainey in next time. I can't promise I will do what you ask, but I can try."

"That's all I ask, Eve."

"I'm not ready to tell Adam anything, yet."

"Very well. We'll go at your pace. With Lainey and Adam both." She looked at her watch. "Would you like to stop here?"

"Yes." Eve's head was pounding, and she felt a little sick to her stomach. She couldn't imagine what she'd feel like during the next session. "I know I should thank you for tonight's session, but . . ."

"Eve, you don't have to thank me." She stood when Eve did. "In fact, there will be times you want to curse me. Like tonight, perhaps?" She laughed. "Just remember that we're here for your benefit."

Eve nodded. "Maybe one day I'll feel that way," she said truthfully. "Goodnight, Dr. Woodrow."

"Goodnight, Eve."

Chapter Twenty-Five

"Boys? Do you have a minute?"

Kevin and Darren glanced up from their phones and muttered something that sounded like a yes.

"Phones down, please."

"Aww, mom! I'm on a tough level!" Darren whined.

Kevin eyed his mom who was looking a bit nervous. She got like that these days when she had to go somewhere for work. The difference this time was she didn't tell them at dinner like she usually did. She waited until their dad was in bed. Kevin hated that she had to do that. He knew she was protecting them from the inevitable fight, but he'd rather be there when that fight occurred.

He whacked his brother on the shoulder. "Pause it, squirt. Mom has something to tell us."

Darren sighed heavily but did as he was told. "Fine. It's paused."

"Thank you." Lainey gave Kevin an appreciative smile. "Eve has asked me to go to Paris with her." She sat down on the couch between them. "Part of it is for work. The other part is a personal matter for Eve."

"Is that why you didn't tell us around dad?" Darren asked.

"Actually, I wanted to ask you both if you're okay with me going. It would be for a week, and I would leave in two days."

Kevin and Darren looked at each other. "It's okay with us, mom," Kevin answered for them both. "Maybe, uh, Darren and I could go visit grandma and grandpa? If you leave me the car, I can drive us . . ."

"Kevin, sweetie, you only have your permit. You can't drive without an adult." Lainey took a breath. "Though, spending time with your grandparents may be a good idea. You haven't seen them for a while. I'm sure they'll be happy to have you."

Kevin nodded knowingly. His mom didn't want them alone with their dad. Not that he would hurt them, he just didn't put in enough effort when it was the three of them. Dinners sucked. Bedtime was like two hours earlier. And they never got to watch anything cool on TV unless it was in their room with the volume so low, they had to turn on closed captioning.

"Grandpa likes getting out and about early. I'm sure he'll take us to school."

"Grandpa drives so slow!" Darren complained, causing Lainey to laugh.

Jack's parents were the only grandparents that were close enough to visit often. Lainey's parents lived the retired life in Florida. And while they loved the boys, they loved their freedom even more. It was selfish, but Lainey was used to it. They had never been the touchy-feely type.

They loved her in their own way. But when she met Jack, they encouraged her to accelerate the relationship any way she could. She was eighteen, and they thought that was a good time for her to be someone else's burden. Lainey managed to hold off getting married until she received her master's. She knew, even then, that Jack wanted kids immediately and didn't want Lainey to work while they were babies. Unfortunately, her time being a stay-at-home mom stretched on much longer than she anticipated. This was her chance to be the woman she had always intended on being, yet still be a mom to the two boys she loved dearly.

"Your grandpa," Lainey said, giving Darren a wide-eyed, silly look, "stops and buys you ice cream *all* the time. You can deal with the slow driving."

Darren grinned. "Oh, yeah. Stay in Paris as long as you want."

Lainey laughed heartily. "Thanks! Replaced by ice cream." She playfully pushed her young son over on the couch.

Kevin was laughing so hard he was crying. He wiped his eyes with the back of his hand. "Seriously, mom. Have fun in Paris and help Eve with whatever she needs you for. Don't worry about us."

"I'll always worry about you two. You're my boys." She put her arms around them and brought them close. "I love you both. Thank you for understanding my having to travel occasionally."

"We're keeping score, you know." Kevin looked at Darren and winked. "We expect to go everywhere you've been when school is out. On the private jet."

Lainey laughed again. "Is that right? Well, I guess I'll have to talk to Eve."

"Yes!" Darren pumped his fist in the air.

Lainey ruffled his hair. "I have a couple more trips to LA after Paris because of the opening of the gallery, but I promise I will take you guys somewhere over the summer. Deal?"

"Deal!" They yelled in unison.

It was going to be hell dealing with Jack. She still hadn't told him about Paris, yet. But if the boys were happy, she would put up with Jack's shit. Anything for her sons.

"Hey, bug!"

"Mommy!" Bella got up from her tiny desk and ran to Eve. She launched herself into Eve's waiting arms as though they hadn't seen each other for weeks instead of just this morning. Eve was home early for once, so it hadn't even been more than a few hours. Eve never minded, though. She lived for her daughter's love.

"Hello, Lexie." Eve smiled at Bella's nanny.

"Hi! You're home early." Lexie began cleaning Bella's play area.

"Yeah, I wanted to spend some quality time with bug here. You don't have to do that. We'll probably end up messing it up again."

Lexie put the toys down. She always felt a bit nervous around

Eve. The woman was nothing but nice to her, but she was incredibly intimidating. And someone Lexie totally wanted to be like.

"Would you like me to stay and fix you both something to eat? I was about to make Bella her afternoon snack."

"That would be awesome, right, bug?"

"Yeah!" Bella caught her mother's eye. "Thank you, Wexie."

"You're welcome." Lexie grinned at them both and skipped out of the room.

"Were you having fun with Lexie?"

"Yes, momma." She wiggled until Eve let her down, then ran over to her desk. "Look! I wrote my name!"

Eve took the paper from her daughter and studied it. It was clear that Lexie helped Bella write the letters, but Eve loved it, nonetheless. She hired Lexie because she had experience with teaching children at a young age and helping them develop at a faster pace. So far, she was impressed.

"That is amazing, bug! I'm so proud of you!"

Bella beamed at her mom. Eve wished she had her camera right then. The best she could do was pull out her phone and snap a quick picture. It wasn't the same as watching it develop under the red lights of her dark room, but it would do.

"Snacks!" Lexie announced.

The three of them feasted on apple slices, cheese, and milk. That, along with the lively account of Bella's day, was better than any expensive meal she ever had.

"Let's wash your hair, baby girl."

Bella tossed her bath toys to the side and held her head back for her mom. She closed her eyes tight as the warm water ran over her blonde hair.

"Feel good?" Eve asked as she massaged Bella's scalp with shampoo.

"Yeah, momma."

"Momma needs to tell you something, okay?"

When Bella nodded, bubbles began floating all over the place. She giggled and clapped her hands together to pop them. Eve let her play, even giving her a cute, bubbly hairdo.

"Are you listening, bug?"

"Yep!"

Eve smiled and shook her head. Bath time was probably the wrong place to have this conversation.

"Bella, momma has to go away for a couple of days."

Bella stopped playing and looked at her mom. Her little bottom lip trembled.

"Oh, baby, don't cry. It won't be for long, I promise."

"How many sweeps?" Bella asked with a shaky voice.

Eve knew she told Lainey a week, but she didn't know if she could leave Bella for that long. Looking at that cute little face all sad after being so happy broke Eve's heart.

"No more than four sleeps," she said resolutely. Lainey would understand.

"Why?"

"Mommy has something important to do, sweetie." She took Bella's face in her hands, wishing she could explain this in a way a two-year-old would understand. "Come on, let's finish up in here and mommy will tell you a story, okay?"

Bella nodded silently and let her mom finish washing her. She no longer wanted to play with her toys. All she wanted to do now was spend time with her mommy.

"Comfy?"

"Yes, mommy."

"Ready for a story?" Bella nodded and Eve settled in next to her daughter and began.

"Once upon a time, a princess lived in a faraway place called Paris. Her mommy and daddy were gone, and she had to stay with this mean old lady who locked her in a tiny room. Every night, the princess sat in her room and painted, sometimes until the sun came up. She loved to paint. It was the only thing that made her happy. But the mean old lady wouldn't allow the princess to have supplies unless she did . . . her chores. So, the princess did everything she was asked to do, but it was never enough. Things got worse, and the princess vowed to get away from there and never look back. One night, the mean old lady forgot to lock the door to the princess's room."

"She wan away!" Bella yelled enthusiastically.

"She did!" Eve confirmed. "She ran and ran until she made it back to where she came from. It took her a long time to get over being in that tiny room, but she did it. The princess took her rightful place at the throne and ruled with an iron fist, yet soft heart. She was happy. And then, she got news that the mean old lady had gone away, too. Like her parents."

"Was she sad?" Bella asked quietly.

Eve thought about the question and answered as honestly as she could. "She was relieved. If the mean old lady was gone, no one else had to be locked in that tiny room. However, the mean old lady did something the princess never expected. She gave the place where that tiny room was to the princess."

Bella gasped.

"Exactly," Eve said with a nod. "The princess struggled with what to do with that place. She never wanted to see that tiny room ever again. More importantly, she never wanted anyone else to see that room ever again. After many nights of thinking about it, the princess had a plan. So, she made the journey back to Paris."

"What the pwincess do wif woom, momma?"

"She tore down the room and built other rooms in its place. Rooms where little girls like she once was — like you are — could learn. Where they could eat good food, sleep in warm beds, be happy and healthy, and be safe."

Bella clapped and cheered. Then she eyed her mom suspiciously. "Where you go, momma?"

The kid was way too smart. Sometimes it felt as though Eve were talking to an old, knowing soul in a tiny body.

"Paris, bug."

"You the pwincess?"

"Yes, baby girl. I'm going to turn that scary old place into something good."

"Four sweeps?"

"Four sleeps."

"You come back?"

"Always, baby girl. You know I can't stay away from you. You're momma's little bug! I love you more than anything, Bella."

Bella relaxed against Eve's side. "I wuv you, pwincess momma."

Eve smiled against Bella's soft hair. She would do anything for this little girl in her arms. Anything.

"I don't think I'll ever get used to this." Lainey practically sank into the plush leather seats of Eve's private jet.

"You're certainly getting used to flying," Eve remarked with a smirk. "You no longer need any distractions."

Lainey blushed thinking about how Eve distracted her the first time they had flown together. This time when she squirmed in her seat, it was for a different reason.

"We've, ahem, flown so frequently lately that . . ."

"Lainey, I was teasing you. I'm sorry if it was inappropriate." Eve sighed silently. It was these awkward moments between them that caused her the most pain. *And the fact that you can't get your head out of your ass.*

Lainey touched Eve's hand. "Flustered," she reminded Eve.

Eve gave her a small smile. Flustered was better than uncomfortable. Right? Eve sighed.

"Does it ever get easier leaving your children?" she asked softly. That afternoon, Bella cried when she and Eve said their goodbyes. It broke her heart and nearly got her to scrap the trip altogether.

Lainey squeezed Eve's hand. She hadn't even realized she was still holding it. Since this seemed to be an appropriate time to comfort Eve, she held on.

"Honestly? Not really. But my boys are older now and can understand better when I explain why I must go. Bella, however, only knows that her momma is leaving."

Eve leaned her head back on the seat and closed her eyes. "Her tears devastate me." She glanced over at Lainey. "I told her a story about a princess who used to live in a tiny room in Paris. A princess who had to go back to turn that tiny room into something positive."

A lump formed in Lainey's throat. "That's incredibly sweet. And heartbreaking."

Eve hummed her agreement. "It was the only way I knew how to tell her why I needed to go so that she would accept it." She laughed a little. "She is far beyond her two years, you know. After I finished the story, she asked me if I was the princess?"

Lainey chuckled. "That little girl is something else. You've seen her artwork. Darren is a great artist now, but when he was Bella's age, his pictures were scribbles. I think you're in for a world of trouble when she grows up."

"Yay me." Eve rolled her eyes for effect. But the reality was, she would be thrilled with every moment she had with Bella. "She has me wrapped around her finger."

"They do that."

"I hope you don't mind, but I've decided to shorten our trip. Bella asked me how many sleeps I would be away. I couldn't bear to go above four."

Lainey's heart swelled. She loved seeing Eve as a mother. "Of course, not. The boys will be disappointed, but too bad."

Eve's brow rose. "Disappointed to have you home? Somehow, I doubt that."

"No!" Lainey laughed. "Disappointed that their time with their grandparents will be cut short. Grandpa buys them ice cream every day after school. Grandma bakes the cookies."

How on earth did such sweet people have a son like Jack? Eve wondered to herself.

"I wondered that myself," Lainey said.

"What?" Surely, she hadn't said that out loud. Had she?

"You always tell me I'm an open book. But when it comes to Jack, you never hide your displeasure. I assume you were wondering how he came from such great parents?"

"Oh, honey, I'm so sorry. I didn't . . ."

"Eve, it's fine. I was glad the two of you were getting along for a while there. But he has given you many reasons to be stand-offish."

Or completely hostile, Lainey corrected silently. She honestly didn't blame Eve. Lately, whenever she's been around, Jack became, well, a jackass. It was going to be fascinating to see how things go when they're all together at the opening of Sumptor Galleries, LA. Jack was cordial with Adam and vice versa. Yet, with Adam's distrust of Lainey and Jack and Eve's dislike for each other, things could get interesting.

"Stand-offish. Okay, let's go with that," Eve joked. "Still, he's your husband, and I should be more respectful. However, your wondering that yourself brings up many questions. Did he do something?"

Lainey shook her head. "I don't want to talk about Jack."

His reaction had been exactly what she expected. A lot of male posturing, forbidding, and yelling. When she had told him that the boys were going to his parents while she was gone, he accused her of thinking he couldn't take care of his kids. If he hadn't also sounded relieved, she might have believed his ire. None of it meant anything, though. She was here with Eve, and the boys were being well taken care of. There was a part of Lainey, though, struggling to keep up the façade of a good marriage. At least for Eve's sake.

"That's fine, honey. Why don't you get some sleep? Since we're cutting the trip, we're going to be hitting the ground running once we get to Paris."

Lainey felt bad shutting Eve out the way she did. Talking about Jack just wasn't in anyone's best interest right now. And considering Lainey didn't get much sleep the night before because of Jack, a long nap sounded divine at the moment.

"What about you?"

"I'm going to send Bella a little video, and then I'll get some sleep as well."

"Eve? I'm sorry . . ."

"Don't be," Eve interrupted. The only reason she brought Jack up was to make sure Lainey was okay. Eve would never apologize for wanting to protect her best friend. But she also knew when to back off. "I know you'll come to me when you're ready. I can wait." She gave Lainey a wink before pulling out her phone.

Lainey, however, took a moment to compose herself. She knew what Eve meant, but her mind — and heart — went in the opposite direction. Yeah. She *really* needed a nap to turn off those thoughts. Dreaming was fine. After all, no one could control their dreams. Right?

"Are you sure you don't want to go to the hotel first, honey?"

They had been silently standing outside of Bussiere's café for more than ten minutes now. As soon as they got off the plane, they went to Cortet's office and Eve signed the necessary papers. The key was handed over, and now here they were. Lainey would, of course, stand here as long as Eve needed to. She just wished she knew the right things to say to make this better.

Eve looked over at Lainey. "We're not staying at a hotel. I, um, have an apartment here. I thought we could stay there. Unless that will be too uncomfortable for you?"

"No, not at all." Lainey smiled. "Now I'm even more excited to be done here."

Eve chuckled. "We're going to go in. I promise."

"I'm not rushing you, honey. I want to make sure you're ready for this."

"I'm not. But since I don't think anyone could ever be ready for something like this, let's get it over with."

Eve took a deep breath, steeling herself from the onslaught of emotions she was anticipating. She drew from the strength of

Lainey beside her and took the first step. The first step out of the past and into the future. She unlocked the door. Normally, she would let Lainey enter a door before her, but not this time. This was her fight.

Lainey followed Eve in. Her first thought was how innocuous the place could look to someone who didn't know what went on behind these doors. It was dirty and dingy, but Lainey had expected that from what Eve had told her. When she thought of what a café in Paris would be like, this wasn't it. It didn't carry the aroma of sweet Parisian pastries. Instead, it boasted the stench of cigarettes and cheap booze.

"The first thing we need to do is open all the windows," Lainey remarked.

"They're sealed shut down here," Eve answered distantly. "But I'll have the contractor fix that. What else?"

"Hmm? Oh! Eve, I was just thinking out loud. I wasn't being serious."

Eve turned to her. "You don't think we should open the windows?"

"No. I mean, yes, we should." She huffed. Eve had a habit of doing this to her. One of these times, Lainey would be ready for it. "Fine, I think we need to gut the place. I'm sure every bit of this café is soaked in grossness."

"Grossness?" Eve laughed. "I suppose you're right." She looked around. "This would be a good common room, you think? If I took the bar and tables out, it would be a good size."

"Is there a kitchen?"

"A small one. I bought the property next door and got the necessary permits to expand." Once Eve had decided to accept the deed to the café, she did her due diligence. She wasn't naïve to trust everything was on the up and up with Bussiere, so Eve made sure there would be no pitfalls to fall into by taking on this endeavor. That tenacity is what made Eve who she was today.

That was new information to Lainey. Eve hadn't said much about the café, Bussiere, or Paris until it was nearly time to leave.

Lainey understood the need for Eve to process things. It sounded like she was processing by researching everything that needed to be done. Lainey wouldn't even ask how Eve was able to obtain permits when the ink on the deed was most likely still wet.

"What does the other property add?"

"Besides a full kitchen? I want to see some ideas from architects, but I'm hoping to house at least thirty girls here once it's all said and done. A full-functioning home."

"With multiple bathrooms, I hope?"

Eve snorted with laughter. "Yes. We're creating housing for girls. If we don't want them turning on each other, we're going to have to have multiple bathrooms with stalls."

Lainey looked one way and saw a narrow hallway. The other way exposed a narrow staircase. That must have been where Eve's room was. She could practically feel the dark energy.

Eve followed Lainey's eyesight. Those stairs. She had gone up and down those stairs many times. Her spirit broke a little more with each step she took back then. It took all she had to remind herself that she had been building that spirit back up for years now. She was bigger than that tiny room's memories. She hoped.

"Come on," Eve said with a conviction she didn't quite feel.

Lainey followed Eve to the stairs. She struggled with wanting to be supportive and not wanting to realize the horrors that lie at the top of those stairs. In the end, being supportive would always win when it came to Eve. They passed a couple of run-down doors with peeling paint. Lainey knew Bussiere had made money off Eve. She certainly didn't put it back into this place.

Eve came to a stop in front of a door. It wasn't the same ugly green as the rest of them. This one was a grimy, dirty white. Seeing this door now as an adult, she couldn't help but wonder. Is this where it came from? Her love for pristine, clean, pure white surrounding her? Was it her way of cleansing the past? Perhaps one day she would ask Dr. Woodrow. First, she would have to come clean about everything she *hadn't* told her, yet.

"Is this it?" Lainey asked softly.

"Yes."

"Eve? Honey, we don't have to do this."

Eve looked over at Lainey. "I do. I understand if you don't want to go in there. I won't blame you, Lainey. But I have to."

"Then I'm going, too."

Eve nodded and opened the door. Her chest felt tight as she walked in. It was as though she walked through a time portal. Nothing had changed. The small, twin bed still had the stained sheets, still mussed. Eve couldn't determine if the stench in the air was real or her imagination. Why would Bussiere keep this room like this?

Lainey hesitated at the door. She ordered her feet to move, but it took a full ten seconds for them to obey. She saw the bed from the corner of her eye but couldn't bring herself to look directly at it. Instead, she followed the light. This time, her feet didn't hesitate at all. They walked her straight to — and out on — the balcony. She let out the breath she hadn't realized she had been holding and took in another full of clean air.

Eve came up beside Lainey. "It's beautiful out here, isn't it? It almost makes you forget what's in there," she said, gesturing behind them.

"Almost," Lainey answered quietly. "I can see why you stayed out here most of the time."

"Even when it was cold. I would bundle up as much as I could and sleep out here. Spring was always my favorite. The flowers would begin to bloom, and their scent would drift up to me. It smelled of hope and a different future. It kept me going as much as art did."

Eve gripped the railing so tight her knuckles whitened. The feel of Lainey's warm, soft hand relaxed her more than art or the aroma of new blooms ever could.

"You've faced your fears, Eve. Now it's time to go."

Eve knew that tone of voice very well. She wasn't about to argue. "Yeah, okay."

They held hands until Eve closed the door to her past.

"What are the rest of these rooms?" Lainey asked.

Eve shrugged. "That one is a bathroom. I don't know about the rest. I've never been in them, but I've always assumed they were storage."

"Do you care to find out?"

Eve thought about it for a minute, then shook her head. "No. I don't want to know if there were more like me back then. I'd rather focus on the ones I can help now."

"Good answer." Lainey winked at her. "Let's get out of here."

"There is one more room I need to go in," Eve said apologetically. She guided them back downstairs and across the main floor to the other small hallway.

"Where are we going?"

"Bussiere's office."

Lainey stopped in her tracks. "Why? Wasn't the room bad enough?"

Eve turned back to face a cranky Lainey. "I need to make sure there's nothing left in there. When I came here to confront her, she told me she was going to destroy everything. But she was a manipulative, greedy old woman. I don't trust she did as she said."

Lainey's expression softened, and she sighed. "Okay." She began walking again. "What are we looking for?"

Eve tugged Lainey's arm when she passed the office. "Here." She pushed open the door to Bussiere's office. "We're looking for things like files or photos. Anything that could be used against me if it fell into the wrong hands."

Lainey looked up, startled. "Blackmail?"

Eve shrugged a shoulder and nodded. "Why don't you start over there."

"*Never a dull moment*," Lainey muttered. Since she had her back to Eve, she missed the sad expression on Eve's face. "Where should I look?"

"Everywhere," Eve responded. She started in the corner where Bussiere's safe sat. It was open and empty, but Eve searched it anyway. "Under drawers, behind photos, in the pages of books."

"I thought this stuff only happened on TV." Lainey leafed through book after book. Thank goodness there weren't many. Apparently, Bussiere wasn't an avid reader.

Welcome to my life, Eve thought sadly. It was moments like this that convinced her she made the best decision for Lainey by letting her go. Eve's next stop was Bussiere's desk. She pulled out each drawer, checking every side.

"Something like this?" Lainey called out. She held up a small thumb drive.

"Toss it here." Eve caught the small drive when Lainey tossed it to her. "Maybe." She slipped it into her pocket and went back to her search.

"Are you going to see what's on it?" Lainey asked as she went through yet another file.

"I don't know."

"If you want, I can . . ."

"No!" Eve closed her eyes, cursing silently. "I'm sorry." She caught Lainey's green eyes. "If there is something of me on here, I don't want you to see it."

That was understandable. As much as she wanted to do what she could for Eve, Lainey didn't want to see evidence of the horrors Eve went through.

"Okay, well, I have been through every nook and cranny on this side. That flash drive is the only thing I found that's suspicious." She chuckled despite the seriousness of the situation. "I'm sorry, Eve. I just never thought I'd say anything like that."

Eve grinned at her. "No problem. We can either find the humor in the situation or continue to let it haunt us."

"Therapy seems to be helping you."

With some things, Eve thought. "I guess so," she said out loud. "I'm done here, as well. Let's get out of here."

"Gladly." Lainey resisted the urge to shake off all the bad aura from the café when they stepped outside. She watched silently as a man dressed in a dark suit walked up to Eve and waited.

"There's a computer in the office. Destroy it irreparably."

"Yes, ma'am."

"Any other equipment you find in there, destroy. I want everything gone before the contractors get in there."

"Yes, ma'am."

He whistled and two other men appeared, seemingly out of nowhere. Lainey watched them file into the place on a mission. She frowned. "If you had them, why did we have to search the office ourselves?"

Eve turned to face Lainey. "Loyalty and trust that is bought only run so deep. The price of that loyalty rises exponentially if they have something to bargain with. None of those men know what happened to me in there. I would like to keep it that way. So, if there was something in there, I wanted to get to it before they did."

"What if they go through the files on the computer and finds something on there?"

"Bussiere was old school. She hated computers. Didn't know how to use them. Still, I couldn't take the chance that one day she would. Or that she didn't have copies of the photos and videos already uploaded."

"You did something to the computer already, didn't you?"

Eve nodded. "As I said, trust only runs so deep."

It felt like she was in a movie. This wasn't how Lainey's life was before Eve. She never went to Paris. Or Italy. She never dealt with people who wanted to kill her. Or blackmail her. She never had to worry about someone coming out of the woodworks to hurt her in some way. How did Eve deal with it all? Was it Tony who brought this into Eve's life? Or was there something Lainey was missing? What exactly did Sumptor, Inc. deal in?

"Is that why you wanted me to give you the drive? Do you think I would do something to hurt you?"

"No, honey. I took the drive to protect you, not me. *If* something is on that drive, I don't want you to have to look at it." Eve wanted so badly to touch Lainey's cheek. She settled for briefly stroking her arm. "I trust you with my life, Lainey. You would never hurt me."

Lainey smiled at her. She knew then that it didn't matter what Sumptor, Inc. dealt in or that her life was now unpredictable. What mattered was Eve.

"Never."

They stood there for what seemed like an eternity — just looking at each other. *This doesn't help anything,* Eve thought. She cleared her throat. Unfortunately, it didn't clear her mind. Or her heart.

"Ready?" she asked.

"Hmm?" *It is so easy to get lost in your beautiful eyes.* "Oh. Yes. Let's go home."

Chapter Twenty-Six

Eve pushed open the door to her home in Paris. She had, of course, called ahead to make sure the heavy, velvet drapes were pulled back. The historic Avenue Foch through the window was like viewing a picturesque painting as they walked in.

"*Bienvenue,*" Eve said, giving a slight bow and a smile to her companion.

"My God. It's beautiful, Eve." Lainey stepped through the threshold and couldn't hold back the small gasp of delight. The loft-style duplex apartment, housed in the beautiful 1930s stone building, was exquisite. The entire wall opposite the entrance was comprised of arched windows and sliding glass doors that stepped out onto a splendid balcony. She tilted her head back to take in the high ceilings, as well as the mezzanine surrounding the second floor.

"Thank you. I'll take you for a tour if you want." Eve stood a respectable distance from Lainey, even though she wanted to be holding her in her arms.

"I'd love that. Maybe after I've freshened up?" When Eve nodded, Lainey smiled. "Do you have a studio here as well?" She immediately regretted her question when Eve's mood darkened. It only lasted a split second, but Lainey knew Eve. Very well.

"Do not apologize," Eve said before Lainey could speak again.

She knew Lainey. "It's a perfectly normal question to ask me. And, yes. I do."

"Eve, I should have been more sensitive . . ."

"Stop. Please, Lainey? I don't want to think about not being able to paint. I want to finish what we came here for, and then spend the rest of our time showing you around Paris. I promised you this trip a couple of years ago. We're going to make the best of it."

"You never told me how Adam reacted to me coming here with you." Lainey grimaced when Eve's eyes darkened again. *Shit*. On the flight here, she had shot down Eve's attempt to talk about how Jack felt about this trip. What made her think bringing up Adam would be okay?

"If you want to talk about these things, can we at least do it while I'm drinking wine?"

"I'm sorry. I know you don't want to hear that either," Lainey sighed. She was nervous. It was ridiculous really. She and Eve had been together — alone — many times since they stopped sleeping with each other. They were both married, and Lainey knew nothing would happen while they were here in Paris. They had done the same in Italy. So, why did Lainey feel apprehensive?

"What were you just thinking about?" Eve caught the slight blush on Lainey's cheeks. She had always thought it added to Lainey's beauty, even though saying so always added to Lainey's embarrassment.

"Nothing." She watched as Eve raised her eyebrow and wondered if she said things that irritated Eve just to see that. "Really, Eve. If we're going to talk about *that*, I'm going to need more than wine."

Both of Eve's eyebrows rose at that. Could Lainey be feeling even a fraction of what she was feeling? Probably not a good thing to think about. Or know. Especially after everything that had been discovered in Eve's last therapy session. Damn it! She didn't want to be thinking of therapy or not being able to paint or the café. If she were completely honest, all she wanted to focus on was being here with Lainey. Even if she had to play the part of a best friend instead of a lover. *I don't have to hold back in my dreams*, Eve thought.

"Come on. I'll show you to your room." Without thinking, she placed a hand on the small of Lainey's back. When she felt the slight tremble, she let her hand drop. "Sorry," she muttered.

Lainey stopped before climbing the stairs. She laid her palm on Eve's cheek and touched Eve's bottom lip lightly with her thumb. "No apologies, Eve." She turned then, leaving a stunned Eve stumbling to catch up with her.

They sat on the terrace, enjoying oysters and lobster, paired with an exquisite 2007 Bouchard Pere & Fils Chardonnay. Was it a wise choice? Probably not. Especially after Lainey floored her with whatever that 'no apologies' was before. Eve had spent the entire time in the shower — cold shower — trying to figure out if there were some hidden meaning behind it. This confusion thing was becoming all too familiar, and Eve wasn't happy about that.

"What time will we be going to the gallery tomorrow?" Lainey chose a succulent piece of lobster, drizzled in a light, buttery sauce and popped it into her mouth. She managed to hold back a moan of complete bliss, but just barely.

"We'll go early. That way we can have the rest of the day to explore." Eve knew she shouldn't do what she was about to do, but the urge was too difficult to resist. So, she reached over and brushed buttery sauce off the side of Lainey's mouth with her thumb. Bringing her thumb to her own lips, she licked it clean.

"Eve. What are we doing?"

"*I'm sorry.*"

"I don't want you to be sorry, honey. I just need to know what's happening." Lainey reluctantly pushed her food to the side. "Let's talk about this."

"Lainey. All I do anymore is talk." Eve took a sip of her wine, almost wishing it was brandy. "It hurts."

"What hurts? Talking?"

"Talking, feeling. Everything hurts."

Lainey's heart filled with compassion. She knew that therapy was going to be hard for Eve. She was a woman that wasn't used to being open. And, now, that's all she was asked to do. Regrettably, Lainey was about to ask her to be open with her.

"You've been a little different since your last session a couple of weeks ago. During our session together, you mentioned having a breakthrough. Is that what's been bothering you?"

Eve stood and walked to the railing of the balcony. "What is it with you and trying to get me to talk?"

Lainey walked up behind Eve, close, but not touching her. "Honey, talking is the only way we're going to figure anything out."

Eve closed her eyes. For once, she just wanted to *stop* talking. All these emotions inside her were getting to be too overwhelming. Guilt, love, desire, need. How much can one person hold before it becomes too much?

"Eve?"

Eve turned, not expecting Lainey to be as close as she was. Before she could think, before she could stop herself, she kissed Lainey. Hard. She let every emotion she was feeling out in that kiss. And, when Lainey's arms came around her neck, when she felt fingers fisting in her hair, all doubts left her mind. She wanted this. God help her, she *needed* this.

"*Lainey.*" Eve's voice was hoarse with need. She touched Lainey's cheek with her fingertips. She only said Lainey's name, but the plea was loud and clear.

"*Yes.*"

If she were able to think, Eve would have stopped this. She would have thought about Adam and Bella. She would have thought about Jack and the boys. But all she could think about was the woman she was leading up to her bedroom. Lainey. The woman that occupied her mind, her heart, even when she tried keeping her out.

Lainey willingly walked through the door of Eve's bedroom. She had a fleeting thought of Jack and Adam, an even longer thought of the boys and Bella. But in the end, Lainey knew what she wanted.

And, right at this moment, it was Eve. Hell, it had been Eve for a while, as much as she hated to admit it. Lainey wondered where the "oh shit, what am I doing" feeling was. Or, maybe that would happen later. For now, she was going to block everything out except what was happening right here, right now, with Eve. It would most likely end up being just a moment in Paris for Eve. But for Lainey, it was more.

"Are you okay?" Eve kept her voice quiet, not wanting to break the moment.

"Yes," Lainey answered, as much to answer Eve's question as to grant Eve permission once again to what she wanted. "Kiss me, Eve."

Eve moaned softly and complied. The kiss was softer this time, slower. Their lips brushed together, and the familiarity hit Eve with a force she wasn't prepared for. She had missed this so much, missed Lainey. Eve pulled back slightly, smiling when Lainey groaned in protest. It helped her confidence knowing Lainey wanted this as much as she did.

As she had done the first time they kissed, Eve licked Lainey's lips from the bottom to the top. The move elicited a deep moan from Lainey, making Eve want more. She slipped her tongue inside Lainey's mouth, reveling in the warmth of Lainey's tongue against hers. She held Lainey closer, their bodies molded together. Eve could feel Lainey's hardened nipples against her, even through their clothes. Clothes that *had* to go. And soon.

"Take this off," Lainey breathed, lifting the hem of Eve's t-shirt as though she had just read Eve's mind.

Eve leaned back and helped Lainey take the shirt off, chuckling slightly when Lainey tossed it over her shoulder.

"Now yours." She was thankful Lainey was wearing simple clothes consisting of a t-shirt and yoga pants. She brought the shirt up, discarding it and Lainey's bra in one swift motion.

"Well. That was convenient but unfair," Lainey smirked.

"I'm sorry. Let me remedy that." Eve reached behind her, unhooking her own bra, letting it slide off. Her eyes fluttered closed when Lainey brought her hands up to cup her breasts.

"I've missed you so much, Eve."

Eve placed her hands over Lainey's and squeezed. "I've missed you, too, baby." She lowered her head to Lainey's to kiss her again. She moved down, kissing Lainey's chin, then trailing her tongue down her neck. She loved how Lainey's skin tasted, how smooth it was against her wet tongue.

Eve's hands slipped down Lainey's sides until her thumbs were hooked into Lainey's pants. When Eve hesitated, Lainey touched her cheek. "Don't stop."

Eve sank to her knees, bringing Lainey's bottoms and panties down with her. She closed her eyes, drawing in a deep breath. Lainey's scent. God how she'd missed that. Eve wanted to bask in that scent, but the need to taste Lainey was quickly taking over.

"You're so beautiful." Lainey was smooth, pink and glistening with abundant wetness. Eve's mouth watered. She looked up into Lainey's eyes. "May I taste you?"

Lainey's legs almost buckled at Eve's question and the pure want in her eyes. "*Yes.*" She gripped Eve's shoulder for balance, or maybe to keep from falling completely when Eve's tongue touched her clit. "Jesus, Eve! I won't be able to stand much longer with you doing that."

Reluctantly, Eve stopped teasing long enough to guide Lainey to the bed. "Lay back and put your legs over my shoulders."

Lainey did as she was instructed, letting out another guttural moan when Eve's mouth found its way back to her. This was different, yet so familiar to Lainey. Eve used her talented mouth on her like she knew each and every secret erogenous spot Lainey had. It also felt as though Eve was searching, learning, and that feeling had Lainey dizzy with intense pleasure.

Eve sucked, licked and nibbled Lainey's clit until she was grinding against her mouth. The feel of Lainey's hands in her hair, pulling her closer only increased Eve's passion. She dipped her tongue inside Lainey, tasting her excitement fully.

"Mmm, so good," she said against Lainey.

"Inside, Eve. Please. I need more, baby."

Eve did what she was asked, slipping two fingers inside Lainey's velvety warmth. She almost came herself when Lainey contracted around her, gripping her fingers, and sucking them in even deeper. She pumped her fingers faster, bringing her mouth back to Lainey's clit. Eve could feel Lainey begin to throb against her tongue, and she sucked it in, bringing Lainey over the edge.

Lainey couldn't remember the last time she had come this hard. The intensity of the orgasm had her crying out Eve's name, loud and unapologetically, as she came in Eve's mouth. "God!"

Frantically, Eve stripped the rest of her clothes off. Naked, she crawled up onto the bed with Lainey. They both moaned when their bodies touched for the first time in what seemed like forever. "Lainey."

"Come here, baby." Lainey situated her leg between Eve's thighs, feeling the hot wetness coating her. "You're so wet."

"That's what you do to me." Eve began to move her body, grinding herself on Lainey. She needed to come, needed that release. But more than that, she needed Lainey. "Touch me."

Lainey slipped her hand between them, finding Eve's hardened clit. She began massaging her, circling her clit with two fingers, then pinching slightly. Eve jumped at the sensation and started moving faster.

"You've learned new moves," Eve panted.

"I've been thinking about you a lot," Lainey responded, slipping three fingers inside Eve. She smiled at the throaty groan that came from Eve. "And I've been experimenting. On myself."

"God!" The sensation of Lainey inside her, and thinking of Lainey masturbating, almost had Eve coming. But she controlled it long enough to get what she wanted. "Move your hand, baby."

"But . . ." Lainey looked at Eve, and took her hand away, albeit with some reluctance. Lainey brought her fingers to her mouth and sucked them.

"My God, Lainey. You're killing me. Spread your legs for me." When Lainey obeyed, Eve planted herself between Lainey's thighs. "Open yourself to me."

Lainey gasped, using the same hand coated with Eve's wetness to open herself up. She watched as Eve did the same, then lower herself until their clits were touching.

"Eve!"

"Move against me, baby. I want to come like this."

"Yes!" Lainey moved her body, grinding her sex to Eve's. Nothing came close to what this felt like. It was intimate, erotic and perfectly amazing. "I'm going to come again, Eve."

"Please, baby. Come with me!" She couldn't hold back anymore. "Lainey!"

"Eve!"

The force of the orgasm sapped the strength out of Eve, and she collapsed onto Lainey. Their bodies were hot and sweaty, yet neither of them made an effort to move.

"That was incredible," Eve murmured, her face buried in Lainey's hair.

"Beyond," Lainey agreed. She stroked Eve's back lovingly. It was her dreams coming to life. Deep down, she knew she should feel guilty about what they just did. But with Eve's naked body on hers, she couldn't dig that deep to find it.

Eve kissed Lainey's neck. She was purposefully blocking everything else out of her mind, determined to make the most of this time she had with Lainey. Tomorrow. She would deal with the backlash tomorrow. Tonight was hers and Lainey's.

Eve would keep that thought in her head as she and Lainey made love until the morning sun began to rise.

Lainey gently awoke to the scent and feel of Eve's naked body. Even though they spent most of the night making love, she had never felt more rested. Or satisfied. Her hand sleepily trailed over Eve's taut stomach, feeling the small tremors it caused. Lainey couldn't help but smile at the effect she had on this powerful woman. She brought her hand up and cupped Eve's breast, squeezing slightly. Her smile turned into a wicked grin when Eve moaned quietly.

"You're so incredibly soft. I love touching you," Lainey murmured.

Eve shivered. "I love it, too. When you touch me, I mean."

Lainey looked up at Eve with a smirk. "Are you okay?"

Eve raised a brow. "You know exactly what you're doing to me, don't you?"

"Maybe," Lainey drawled. She maneuvered herself until she was on top of Eve. When she looked down into those beautiful gray eyes, Lainey sighed softly. "Why doesn't this feel wrong?"

Eve tucked a stray strand of Lainey's dark blonde hair behind her ear. "Maybe because it isn't," she suggested.

Lainey briefly closed her eyes. She wanted so much for that to be true. She didn't know if it could be. There were so many obstacles in their way.

"Let's pretend it isn't wrong," she said finally. "While we're here, let's pretend nothing is standing between us."

"As you wish." Eve flipped them so she was on top. "There's certainly nothing between us right now," she grinned.

"I feel that. If you would just move your leg to the left a tiny bit, I'd feel *that*, too."

Eve laughed and positioned her thigh in just the right spot. "How's that?"

"Much," Lainey gulped when Eve moved again, "much better."

Eve rotated her hips, opening herself to Lainey's thigh. *She's been working out*, Eve thought with lust. Lainey's body had always been perfect to Eve. The extra bit of hardness in Lainey's quads only served to enhance that perfection. Of course, she could be thinking with her clit that was currently being massaged by said quad.

Lainey ran her hands down Eve's back, over her tight ass. She gripped Eve's cheeks with authority. They couldn't get any closer than they were, but that didn't stop Lainey from trying.

"How is it that you can make me come over and over again?" she panted.

"We're just that good together," Eve answered breathlessly. "I'm coming, Lainey."

"God, yes!"

It didn't take Lainey long to catch up. Soon they were both gasping for air, wishing this moment could last forever.

"What would you like to do after we've finished our business at the gallery?"

Eve passed Lainey a jar of homemade jam. The woman who took care of the apartment always made sure Eve had enough for her visit and to take home. It was something Eve appreciated very much since the raspberry jam was to die for.

"Anything shamelessly touristy." Lainey took a bite of what Eve called *Tartine*. Lainey called it French bread with a healthy slather of butter and unbelievably fantastic jam. No matter what it was called, it hit the spot after the morning they just shared.

"So, the Eiffel Tower, the Louvre, the Arc de Triomphe, while we eat pastries and drink wine?"

Lainey sipped her café au lait, peering at Eve over the rim. "You say that jokingly, but it all sounds good to me."

Eve let out a hearty laugh. "I wasn't joking. If that's what you want to do, I'll be happy to be your guide."

"Will it be boring for you? Haven't you seen those things many, many times before?"

"Not with you," Eve said, effectively answering both questions. She reached across the table and took Lainey's hand. "Seeing Paris through your eyes helps me forget how ugly it can be. I've been blessed to be able to travel and experience the things I have. That's something I would like to give to Bella when she gets older and can appreciate it. And something I love sharing with you."

Lainey laced her fingers with Eve's and smiled. "I love it, too. I think Bella will enjoy going places with you. The boys told me they were keeping score on everywhere I was traveling with you." She chuckled. "I promised I would take them somewhere when school was over."

"Where will you take them?"

Lainey shrugged. "I don't know, yet. Jack hates to travel, so I'm hoping he won't give me hell for promising them that."

"Well, Bella and I would be happy to go with the three of you." Eve winked at her. "Adam's not a big traveler either. Especially now with the firm. I'm surprised he agreed to the opening of the gallery in LA."

Relieved that Eve didn't release her hand, Lainey smiled. "Same with Jack. I'm sure if he hadn't already requested the days off on one of his more supportive days, he would stay home."

While neither of them wanted to be talking about the men they were married to, it was inevitable. *If* Eve and Lainey miraculously found a way to be together without creating an apocalyptic disaster, Jack and Adam would continue to be a constant in their lives because of the kids.

"Whatever you decide to do," Eve said. "The jet is yours. Take the boys anywhere they'd like to go. My treat."

Oh, you're going, Lainey thought with conviction. It was too bad she didn't have the courage to say it out loud.

"You know, I think the Eiffel Tower and some pastries are good for today. After that, I just want to come home and be alone with you."

"Are you sure?" *Please say yes!* All Eve wanted to do since she got another taste of Lainey was barricade them in the bedroom and never leave again. It was a dream. She knew that. But here in Paris, that dream could be a reality. If only for the few days they were there together.

Lainey squeezed Eve's hand. "Absolutely."

Chapter Twenty-Seven
Therapy

A moment in Paris.

"Thank you for seeing me on such short notice." Lainey stood awkwardly at the door of Dr. Willamena Woodrow's office.

Dr. Woodrow smiled pleasantly. "Of course, Lainey. Please, come in and have a seat."

She gestured to one of the comfortable chairs in her office, and Lainey sat immediately. Her legs shook, her heart raced, and she felt sick to her stomach. It made her wonder if this was how Eve felt every time she was here. Though Lainey was here without Eve's knowledge and that made her feel worse.

"Would you like some tea?" Willamena asked, interrupting Lainey's thoughts.

"Yes, thank you." Dr. Woodrow's voice was calming, yet it did not affect Lainey's frayed nerves.

"I must say, I was surprised to hear from you," Willamena said as she poured steaming tea from a charming teapot into a delicate cup. She couldn't help but wonder if Lainey could use a bit of liquid courage the way Eve did at times.

Lainey, however, had other things on her mind. As in, if the doctor's everyday life was this peaceful, she's either the luckiest woman in the world or just extremely good at categorizing what's in her brain. Lately, that had been something that Lainey hadn't been very successful at, which was why she was here.

"I was surprised I called you," Lainey admitted. "This is confidential, right? Even from Eve?"

"Of course, it is."

Dr. Woodrow handed Lainey the tea with steady hands. Unfortunately, Lainey's were not as steady, and the tea sloshed slightly onto the saucer as she took it.

"I take doctor-patient confidentiality very seriously, Lainey. I would never disclose anything you say in a session. Just as I would never reveal anything Eve has said."

Lainey nodded, sipping the hot tea cautiously. She had to confess, even if just to herself, that she would've given anything to know what Eve had said in these closed sessions. Reading someone as complicated as Eve Sumptor was impossible. *Riley, Lainey*, she reminded herself with a dash of self-disgust. Eve was married. Hell, *she* was married. They both had kids. There were so many reasons she should remember Eve's married name.

"Lainey?"

Lainey looked up, startled to see the doctor sitting in the chair in front of her with a notebook resting on her lap.

"Would you like to tell me where you just were?" Dr. Woodrow asked when Lainey didn't respond.

"I guess we're starting now." Lainey offered a tremulous smile.

"We could sit here and drink tea if that's what you prefer. It would be an expensive cup of tea."

The doctor's smile was contagious, and Lainey felt the laughter bubbling up. It was most likely hysterical laughter, but she doubted there was anything the good doctor hadn't seen before.

"To answer your question," Lainey began after she finished laughing. "I was thinking if what I'm feeling right now is how Eve feels when she's here."

"And how is that?"

"Scared shitless."

The doctor smiled again and made a note in her notebook. **Best** *friend called for a visit. Something has happened, and the guilt is almost palpable.*

Lainey remembered something Eve had told her once that made perfect sense now. She had said that whenever Dr. Woodrow wrote in her notebook, Eve felt as though she had said something wrong. That's exactly how it felt to Lainey.

"Remind me not to ask you or Eve for references," Dr. Woodrow chuckled.

"Perhaps we *should* be the ones to do that for you," Lainey countered with amusement. "It means you're very good at getting to the core of things. I'm just not sure I'm ready for that."

Dr. Woodrow nodded. "I'm sure you're aware that I haven't seen Eve for a couple of weeks. May I ask how she is before we get too far into this session?"

"She's . . . complicated. Honestly, I don't know, Dr. Woodrow. Maybe that's why I'm here. We've been spending a lot of time together lately with the opening of her new gallery in L.A." She paused, gathering her courage. "We even went to Paris together for work."

"Alone, I'm assuming?"

A nod.

"I sense there is more you need to say, Lainey."

"I don't know how fair it is for me to be here without Eve knowing. Or without her permission."

"Does she make you feel you need her permission?"

"No! Of course, not." Lainey sighed with frustration. "I feel as though Adam and I forced her into doing this, and I don't know if she would appreciate me interfering."

"Is that what you're here for? To interfere with Eve's therapy?"

"No." Lainey carefully placed her tea on the table beside her and sat back. "I'm not explaining any of this right. I guess I feel as though I'm intruding on something that was supposed to be for Eve. I want her to paint again and hopefully relieve herself of the night terrors. Be happy. It was never supposed to be about me. Yet, here I am."

"Oh, Lainey, surely you know that you are very much an

important part of Eve's life. That's not revealing any secrets, simply stating the truth. I feel Eve would encourage you to be here if you feel it's needed. Of course, you know Eve would probably want to fix everything for you."

She laughed softly, and Lainey joined in. She was absolutely correct. Eve was a fixer when it came to someone she cared about.

"As true as that is, the reason I'm here is very personal. I should have talked to her first." Lainey was now questioning her impulsive decision to make this call. Perhaps her very first call should have been to Eve. That would have been the decent thing to do.

"If you're that concerned, we could call Eve and have her meet us here."

Even that innocent suggestion had Lainey's heart beating even faster than before. Whether it was the prospect of seeing Eve or her knowing what Lainey was here for, she wasn't sure.

"I — I'm not sure if that's a good idea."

"It's okay. It was only a suggestion, Lainey," Dr. Woodrow soothed.

"I know, but even if I think it's a bad idea, I also think it might be the right thing to do."

"Do you always do the right thing, Lainey?"

Lainey released a sharp laugh. "Obviously not. I cheated on my husband with another woman. And, as much as I wish I could, I can't stop thinking about her. Or wanting her."

"Is that true? That you wish you could stop?" Dr. Woodrow asked carefully.

"Honestly? I'm not sure." Lainey pressed a hand to her stomach, hoping she could keep the contents in place. "I should stop. My husband deserves better than a wife who has feelings for someone else." *That's a lie. Why are you lying?* The voice in her head nearly had her looking around to see where it came from. She had been lying about her marriage for months now. To Eve. To herself. Hell, even to her sons. *What makes this any different?*

"For the sake of this session, let's keep others out of the equation," the doctor suggested.

"That's impossible!" Lainey argued heatedly. "They *are* in the equation! If they weren't, Eve and I would happily be together." Astonished, she slapped a hand over her mouth. She hadn't meant that. Had she?

"Is that what you want, Lainey?"

"I think we need to call Eve." Came the quiet response.

Eve knocked quietly, squeezing her hand into a fist in hopes it would stop the shaking. She had been beyond shocked when she received the call from Dr. Woodrow to meet at her office. Even more so when she found out Lainey was there.

She should have predicted this. After what happened between them in Paris, things had changed. It was much harder now to ignore what they felt. Perhaps they made matters worse, but Eve couldn't regret what happened. Even if that was the reason Lainey was here. *Oh, God. What if she's here because she can't handle what happened? Or if she can't handle the guilt? Guilt that I should feel, too. Do I?*

The door opened to Dr. Woodrow's pleasant face, and Eve was confident she was about to learn the answer to her questions soon.

"Eve, thank you for joining us."

She stepped back and gestured for Eve to come in. As usual, Eve's eyes immediately found Lainey's. When she saw fear in those lovely green eyes, her heart dropped.

"Lainey," she murmured.

"I'm sorry," Lainey whispered.

"You never have to apologize to me. For anything." Somehow, Eve resisted taking her hand. She glanced over to see the good doctor watching them intently. "Okay, I'm here."

"You seem a little defensive," Dr. Woodrow observed.

"Sorry." It was a defense mechanism. She didn't know what she was there for. What she was up against. She didn't know if her heart was about to be shattered into a million pieces by the woman sitting next to her. And she didn't know why, when she was married, it was so important that she kept Lainey in her life in the intimate way they've become accustomed to. With that many unknowns, how could Eve *not* be on the defensive?

She felt Lainey's hand cover hers and she involuntarily shivered. Lainey was the only one that had that effect on her. Even the man she was married to, as much as she loved him, didn't cause her this much turmoil inside. Eve blew out a breath and tried to relax.

"I asked Dr. Woodrow to call you, Eve. There are things we need to talk about, and I think it would be helpful to be here for some support. Or advice."

"All right. Is this about Paris?" Eve asked warily.

Lainey's eyes shifted to Dr. Woodrow before returning to Eve. "Yes."

"I've tried many times asking how you felt, Lainey." Eve tried desperately to keep her tone even. She wasn't upset with Lainey, just disappointed in the fact that she didn't feel comfortable enough to talk to her about this. Alone.

"If I may," Dr. Woodrow interrupted softly. "For me to be able to understand and help fully, I would need to know what happened in Paris. Do either of you feel comfortable telling me?"

"We made love," Eve told her matter-of-factly, and winced when she heard a small gasp come from beside her. "I apologize for my frankness, but I've learned that beating around the bush doesn't work here with the nice doc."

Dr. Woodrow smirked. "This is true. Besides, I've been in this business for — well, more years than I care to disclose. There isn't much that can shock me." She turned her kind gaze to Lainey. "If it helps, I pretty much discerned that for myself in the first few minutes you were here."

"Is it written all over my face?" Lainey asked as she slumped back in her chair.

"No," Dr. Woodrow chuckled. "But again, I've been doing this for a long time."

"What Eve said is true," Lainey said softly. "We let our emotions get the best of us while we were in Paris."

Eve turned to Lainey, hurt coursing deep in her soul. "Get the best of us? Is that how you feel, Lainey?"

Tears pooled in Lainey's eyes. The last thing she *ever* wanted to do was hurt Eve. But the fear that it hadn't meant as much to Eve as it had to Lainey was too much to bear. She had defense mechanisms, also. "That's not how I meant it. I wanted to be with you, Eve. I *want* to be with you. Every second of every minute of every day. Do you realize how that makes me feel when I'm with my family?"

"Yes! I do! I feel the same way when I'm with mine!" Frustrated, Eve ran a hand through her hair.

"Ladies?"

They both stopped staring at each other and turned to the doctor.

"What you're both feeling is normal." She held up a hand, effectively cutting off the retort she knew was brewing inside Eve. "Yes, normal. I know you both feel guilty and a bit crazy — as much as I despise that word — but I assure you, it *is* natural. You fell in love with each other in a time when you both needed something more in your lives. That isn't something that goes away. You didn't stop loving each other when you made your choices to be with Jack and Adam."

"But we *did* make those choices," Lainey reiterated. "Doing what we did, no matter how much I wanted it — *want* it — is not fair to our husbands. Or children."

"I would argue that ignoring how you feel for each other is not good for you. Or anyone else," the doctor countered.

Eve had to acknowledge that the good doctor was scoring major points with her right now.

"I don't regret it." Eve's voice was quiet, and for a moment she wondered if she spoke out loud.

"Oh, honey, I don't regret it either." Lainey's fingers threaded through Eve's and squeezed. "I don't think the guilt I feel is equivalent to regret. Is it?" she asked Dr. Woodrow.

"No. I believe they are separate emotions."

Willamena sat back, well aware of Eve eyeing her notebook, and watched. She was willing to remain quiet and let the two women hash it out themselves.

"I know I should feel terrible for what I'm about to say, but that moment in Paris with you is something I want to relive over and over. Even though we haven't repeated that moment since, when we're alone, when we go to L.A. together, whenever it's just the two of us, I feel free. I *want* to repeat that moment every chance we get, but I'm afraid."

"Afraid of what?" Lainey whispered. She couldn't control the tears or the shaking. Eve just said everything she wanted to hear, and it was amazing. Up until she said she was afraid.

"That you'll say no. That you'll tell me you don't want me anymore. That I'll touch you one day, and you'll pull away from me."

Lainey was full on crying now and Eve's heart broke.

"Don't you know, Eve, that that would never happen? Don't you realize that I hurt this much *because* I can't let you go? We're *married* to other people and, yet, my heart belongs to you. I don't know how to handle that. There's no scenario where someone doesn't get hurt. Including our children."

"Do you want me to walk away, Lainey?"

"No!"

"Do you *need* me to walk away?" she asked sadly and was devastated when Lainey hesitated.

"I — I *need* you, Eve. And I don't know how to have you without destroying multiple lives."

It was true. There was not a naïve bone in Eve's body. She knew everything wouldn't be full of unicorns and rainbows if she and Lainey decided to be together. But the thought of *not* being with Lainey was something Eve couldn't fathom, either. Especially after Paris.

"Eve?"

She heard Dr. Woodrow's voice penetrate her thoughts and turned her attention to her. All the while, she was still holding Lainey's hand and refused to give it up.

"Can you respond to Lainey's fears?"

"She's right. If we give in to our desires fully, we destroy the lives of our families. I love my husband." Eve held onto Lainey's hand tightly when she tried to pull away. "I love my daughter. And I know that Lainey loves Jack and her sons. It's an impossible situation."

"But?" Dr. Woodrow prompted.

"But," Eve turned to Lainey and gazed into her eyes, "it doesn't stop me from loving you. It doesn't stop me from wanting you. It doesn't stop me from wanting Paris all over again."

"How do we do that, Eve? How do we justify what we're doing?"

"You stop trying to justify it," Dr. Woodrow answered. "Neither of you are going to have the ability to rationalize what you're feeling. The only thing you *can* do is make decisions. And you need to realize that it's not just others who can be hurt."

"What can we do?"

Eve nearly laughed at the thought that Lainey was desperate enough to ask the therapist for step-by-step instructions on how to navigate through this dilemma. It wasn't a laughing matter, but it was either that or go a little (more) insane.

"That's something I can't tell you," Dr. Woodrow answered apologetically and then looked at Eve. "Do you object to me revealing something you've said in here?"

Eve shook her head. There wasn't anything that she wanted or needed to keep from Lainey. It should've been telling that she wouldn't have agreed had it been Adam in here with her.

Dr. Woodrow flipped back a couple of pages in her notebook. "In our last session, we delved a little deeper into your creative block." She saw Eve practically stop breathing and knew she was having second thoughts. But Willamena was confident that if Eve wanted her to stop, she would say so. "You explained to me that the possibility of losing Lainey is what caused this block."

Another small gasp beside Eve had her lowering her head. "It's not her fault."

"Of course, it isn't. I'm merely repeating what was said. I also recall telling you that you needed to discuss your feelings with Lainey." She smiled softly. "I must say, you took it a little further than I imagined and I'm not sure how much talking was done, but it's a good start."

Eve smiled back. She couldn't help it. Just thinking of being with Lainey made her happy. If she could stop loving her, life would be easier. Hell, if she could stop loving Adam, life would be easier. Though now she was wondering if it was the love or the fear of losing Bella that kept her with Adam.

"Do *you* need me to walk away, Eve?"

Lainey's voice was small and insecure. Very close to how she used to sound when she and Eve first met. Eve got down on her knees in front of Lainey and spoke from the heart. It was all she knew how to do with Lainey. The moment Lainey walked into her life, Eve changed. Lainey exposed the deepest part of Eve, and that was the part *only she* could claim. Maybe that was why Eve couldn't give her up. Perhaps that was why, despite loving her husband, Lainey would always be a part of Eve.

"I didn't want to do this, Lainey," Eve began, gesturing around her. "Therapy scares the hell out of me. I knew I was going to have to open every little box I have carefully closed in here." She tapped her head. "I already know I'm fucked up. I don't need to spend $150 an hour to hear someone else tell me that." She held up her hand to stop the protests from both of the women in the room with her. "You can't go through what I've gone through and not be a little fucked up. But the sanest part of me knows that if you walked away from me, I would never be the same."

She shrugged self-consciously — something else she'd never been accustomed to before Lainey.

"Maybe it's unfair of me to say these things to you," she continued. "Maybe I shouldn't tell you that the reason I can't paint is that I'm using so much energy trying to bury my feelings for you. Maybe I shouldn't tell you that I feel less and less guilt and more resentment towards Adam. That alone should make me feel terrible as none of this is his fault. It's mine. I pursued you even though you were married. I let you go even though I knew I still loved you. I got married and had a child even though I knew I couldn't get you out of my head or heart. I wanted it all. I was selfish. Perhaps not being able to paint is my punishment. I still can't let you go. Forgive me, but I can't."

Lainey slid off the chair into Eve's arms and hugged her fiercely, sobbing. After a moment, she pulled back and stared at Eve intently.

"You're blaming yourself," she said finally. "But it wasn't only you. You didn't do anything to me that I didn't allow. Or want. You weren't the only one who let go despite the love I still felt. And you're not the only one who feels resentment that we aren't together." She touched Eve's cheek gently. "God, Eve, you must know that the *only* thing holding me back is the children. I hate what I'm doing to Jack. I love him. He's Kevin and Darren's father. But if it were only between you and him, I would choose you."

Exhausted, Eve plopped back on the floor, still holding Lainey close, and looked at the doctor. Of course, she was watching everything with the eagle eye of a therapist, scribbling in that God-forsaken notebook. One day, Eve was going to rip that thing out of her hands and set it on fire. After she read it, naturally.

"There's your talk, doc. It doesn't fix anything, does it?"

"On the contrary, I believe both of you feel a sense of relief now that it's out in the open."

Well, hot damn, the woman is right. A pressure — slight as it was — had lifted. At least for Eve. She couldn't speak for the woman huddled in her arms.

"But Eve is right," Lainey sniffled. "It doesn't fix anything. All we've done is expose our feelings to each other. Where does that leave us? Where does it leave our families?"

"Well, as far as the two of you are concerned, it leaves you with validated feelings towards each other. I don't see why that can't help you in your decision-making." Dr. Woodrow set her notebook aside, and to the surprise of both women, slid off her chair to sit next to them on the floor. "This is a delicate situation, and I cannot tell you what to do. Those decisions must come from you. From your heart."

"No magic pills?" Eve asked flippantly, absently caressing Lainey's arm.

Both Dr. Woodrow and Lainey chuckled.

"No magic pills," the doctor responded. "However, I do have some homework for you both."

Eve and Lainey both groaned at the prospect of having to do

more after this draining session. Still, they dutifully nodded their heads and listened.

"Spend the night alone. No husbands, no children, not each other. Just you. Think about what was revealed here. Let your heart speak to you, not your mind. I understand that both will need to be present when you're ready to make decisions, but for this exercise, listen to your heart. Can you do that?"

Lainey and Eve looked at each other and then nodded. It would most likely be an easier task for Lainey. Eve wasn't used to listening to her heart. But, for some reason, she knew the only way to get through this, and possibly paint again, was to do what was being asked of her by the doc *or* Lainey.

"Good." Dr. Woodrow stood, waiting for the women to follow. "I think this is a good place to finish. You both must be weary. If you need me, I am always here."

"Thank you," Lainey said softly, receiving a smile from the doctor.

"Yes, thank you," Eve echoed. "For calling me and . . . everything."

"My pleasure. Please, try and have a peaceful night. I expect you back for regular sessions. That goes for both of you if need be."

"Yes, ma'am," Eve saluted. "Goodnight."

With her hand at the small of Lainey's back, she guided her out. She stopped in the empty hallway before getting to the reception area and turned Lainey towards her.

"Are you okay?"

She nodded, but Eve saw the truth in Lainey's eyes. Knowing how tired she must be, Eve let it go for now.

"Will you be all right getting home?" It was a silly question given that they lived next door to each other. She would be following Lainey on their way home. The only problem was, they would be going into separate homes.

"Yes. I just wish . . ." Lainey's voice trailed off. What good did it do to wish for the impossible? Then again, Eve was very good at pulling off the impossible. Would having a modicum of hope make this any harder than it already was? She felt a sliver of that hope when Eve took her in her arms and hugged her tightly. It made her want to tell Eve everything that had been going on with Jack lately. *After the gallery opening*, she vowed.

"It'll be okay. We'll work things out," Eve murmured close to Lainey's ear.

"Will we?" *I hope so.*

Lainey leaned back slightly and looked up at Eve through her long lashes. It was a look that always killed Eve. Without much thought to the consequences — which seemed to be par for the course these days with her — Eve caressed Lainey's face and leaned in.

"*Eve.*"

The kiss was meant to be quick and reassuring. When their tongues met, it became a battle for dominance. Something that surprised Eve a bit. She had noticed during their time in Paris that Lainey had become more aggressive. Which, coincidentally, was incredibly arousing. Just as it was now, only, she had chalked it up as pent-up frustration from being apart for so long. Perhaps this new Lainey that was emerging was more than just pent-up frustration. God, how Eve would love to explore that right now.

Lainey's hands moved up Eve's back, feathering her neck, then curled into her hair. She sighed against Eve's lips before pushing her back gently.

"I shouldn't . . . this . . . I have to go," she stuttered, agitated.

"Wait!" Eve grasped Lainey's arm and pulled her back to her. "You made that negative. I can't let you leave with a kiss like that being negative in your mind."

"Not negative, honey. Just more confusing."

Lainey caught the sadness in Eve's eyes and sighed again. She moved in until her body was brushing against Eve's. With her hands on Eve's face, she brought Eve's head closer.

"Tell me again this will all work out," she begged.

"It will all work out," Eve answered decisively. How? Hell if she knew, but she would promise Lainey the world when she looked at her like that. And when Lainey kissed her again, it was tender, yet full of heated desire.

"We should go," Lainey whispered against Eve's lips. "Before I can't let you go."

Eve was tempted to kiss her again and make her fulfill that need she knew they both had. But she found some idiotic inner strength and nodded.

"Goodnight, Eve."

"Goodnight, Lainey." She watched Lainey walk away, taking in the casual jeans and a white t-shirt. "*I love you.*"

Lainey turned back just then and smiled. "*I love you, too,*" she mouthed before motioning for Eve to follow her as she turned the corner.

"Eve?"

Startled, Eve looked over to see Dr. Woodrow leaning against the doorframe of her office. *How much did she see?*

"Is everything all right?"

"It will be," Eve answered as she took off after Lainey. Somehow, someway, it would be. One day.

Chapter Twenty-Eight

"I trust your judgment, Ellie. Everything you've made has been amazing, so if you feel finger-foods are the way to go, do it." Eve tapped her pen on her desk. The last time she had been in LA, Ellie surprised her with a huge tray of food to taste for the opening. Eve didn't lie. Everything she ate was incredible. She was sure about handing her trust over to Ellie.

Eve had been finalizing many of the preparations for the opening via phone this morning. The food was set. Blaise, who Eve was also confident in giving her trust to, was taking care of the flower arrangements. After speaking with Rebecca, Eve knew Cass was ready for her gallery debut. Everything was finally beginning to fall into place which gave her a little bit of peace.

"Knock, knock."

Eve looked up to see a shock of red hair poking around her door.

"Come in."

Eve smiled and stood to greet her lawyer. She hired the brilliant mind of Reghan Brannigan a little more than a year ago after everything happened with Laurence and Agent Donovan. She knew there was no avoiding being questioned by the police and FBI, and while Eve had a lawyer for business, she felt she needed someone more versed in criminal law to handle that situation. Enter Reghan.

With Reghan's knowledge in several different areas of the law and her no-nonsense Irish attitude, Eve decided to use her for her personal legal needs as well.

"Thank you for coming."

Reghan grinned. "When the person who pays you a ridiculous retainer calls for a meeting, you show up."

"Good to know. Please, sit."

Reghan made herself comfortable in the visitor's chair, swinging her briefcase up into her lap.

"I took care of everything," she began, bringing out a stack of legal papers. "You'll find all the information here."

Eve took the papers and began to leaf through them. "Thank you."

"Again, retainer. Plus, I like you." Reghan's blue eyes sparkled with mischief. "I do need a few signatures from you. I've marked them all. The property in LA is secured." She hesitated. Something she rarely did. "About the other issue?"

"A non-issue at the moment," Eve answered. "I have to get through the opening in LA before I go down that road."

"But you still want me to get the papers ready?"

Even Reghan's Irish lilt couldn't dull the sharp edges of Eve's reality. Getting all her affairs in order was a result of her last impromptu therapy session. She had promised Lainey things would work out. She still didn't know how, but this was her way of at least putting the ball in motion.

"Yes. But I have to talk with someone before we do anything more."

Auburn eyebrows shot up. "The great Eve Sumptor defers to someone else?"

Eve raised her brow. "How much do you like that retainer of yours?"

Reghan laughed. "Too much to keep teasing you. I'll get the papers ready, but I won't file them until I hear from you."

"Perfect. Will we see you at the opening?"

Reghan flashed her perfect, white teeth. "Wouldn't miss it. I meant to thank you for the invitation." She leaned forward and lowered her voice conspiratorially. "Think it will be a good place to meet someone?"

Eve chuckled. "I didn't realize you were looking."

"I'm forty-three, Eve. If I don't start looking now, it'll be too late."

"It's LA, Reghan. Anything is possible."

Lainey waved at Eve's lawyer as the elevator doors closed. "Should I be worried?" she asked as Eve sidled up beside her.

"Why would you be?"

"Your attorney was here. That's usually not a good sign. Especially a criminal attorney like Reghan."

Eve laughed. "She's also my personal attorney, Lainey. She brought me some paperwork for Bella that I needed to sign." There was no reason to bring up anything else now. Eve would tell Lainey everything she had been up to when the time was right.

"Oh, good. So, I can ignore the little flutter in my tummy?"

"Not if it's because we're standing so close," Eve flirted. She was relieved when Lainey chuckled.

"It could be that. Is everything set for the opening?"

"Mmhmm. I just talked to Ellie, Blaise, and Rebecca. The food is taken care of, as are the flowers, and Cass is working feverishly on her canvases. I can't wait to see them."

"Me, too," Lainey said with feeling. "If they're anything close to what her murals are, we're in for a treat. Not to mention Ellie's food." She hummed with pleasure.

Oh my. Eve cleared her throat. "Yes, um, the only hiccup we have now is Agosti."

Lainey smiled knowingly. She had broken Eve's concentration there for a brief moment and took immeasurable pride in that. *I am so going to hell.*

"Even if Agosti doesn't sign with us before the opening, we have enough for a full house. I've been working with Lauren on the central display via FaceTime. She's doing very well."

"How could she not with you as a mentor."

Lainey blushed. "Well, I learned from the best." She bumped Eve's hip.

"Your talent is all you, honey." She smiled at her best friend. Since their session together the air around them kept changing. She never asked Lainey if she did the homework Dr. Woodrow had given them. But Eve had much to Adam's dismay. She had been distant, she knew. She couldn't help that. Something inside Eve had shifted. Unfortunately, even listening to her heart hadn't given her a clear answer as to what to do about it.

"Eve?" Lainey touched Eve's arm gently.

"Hmm? I'm sorry. I guess I zoned out there for a minute."

"Are you okay?"

"Yes." She patted Lainey's hand. "There's so much going on that sometimes I lose focus." Eve shrugged as though it was no big deal. "Could you do me a favor?"

"Anything."

"Could you get another call out to Agosti? I'm having a difficult time getting a read on where she's at. Maybe you'll have better luck."

"Sure, I'll get right on that. You know, I think she's just scared."

"Of?"

Lainey shrugged. "Being alone? Dealing with the outside world herself? She's relied on Camilla for so long perhaps she thinks she can't do it on her own."

"Do you think you can convince her she can? Let her know that we'll give her all the support she needs, but we can't do that with Camilla around."

"I can try."

"Hey, you got me to open up when I didn't want to. Made me believe things about myself that I thought was impossible."

"I — it was different with you."

"Why?"

"Because I care deeply for you." *I love you.* "I did back then, and I still do. I can try my best with Henley, but it definitely won't be for the same reasons."

Eve turned to Lainey, barely resisting touching her face. "Your best is better than most. I have faith in you."

Lainey smiled shyly at Eve. How was it possible to feel such emotions from a simple compliment? It didn't take hours of listening to her heart to determine what she truly wanted in her life. However, wanting something and the power to have it didn't often go hand in hand.

"I'll go make that call. Lunch later?"

"You're on." Eve winked.

"Are we flying commercial for this thing in LA?"

Lainey looked up from her book. Jack was staring at her, so he was obviously talking to her. It was the first time since she had been back from Italy that he spoke to her without an attitude.

"We'll most likely go on the jet with Eve and Adam," she answered. "I wasn't sure you still wanted to go."

"I've already asked for time off work."

Of course. It wasn't to support her. It was merely his unusual need to keep the schedule as precise as he could. It didn't matter that they weren't getting along. He would play the part for as long as he could tolerate it. She could imagine him leaving in the middle of the opening like he did for the New York gallery.

"Right. Well, Eve is bringing Bella and Lexie, so I think we should let the boys come." *It'll save me from being in the room alone with you.* "They've wanted to do some traveling."

It was as good a time as any to slip that into a conversation and get a feel of his position on it.

"You put that in their heads," he grumbled. "All this damn traveling you're doing is not good for them."

"Why?"

"Because, Lainey, they need to focus on education not lofty dreams of traveling the world or drawing ridiculous pictures."

Here we go. This was how the same argument began every day. He would find one small thing to hook his traditional beliefs into, and it would take off from there. *"You're a terrible mother. You're never here for your sons. How could you encourage Darren's childish hobby? Why do you coddle the boys?"* It never took much to get the argument started. However, it took a migraine and Lainey leaving to sleep in a different room to finish it. At least for that night. *Rinse and repeat.*

"I can't do this tonight, Jack."

"Fine."

That was too easy. First, he asked about a job-related event. And now he was relenting on an argument.

"Thank you." Lainey wasn't about to push her luck. She settled back into her pillow and opened her book again only to be startled when it was taken away from her.

"I want to spend some time with you."

Oh, shit. "Jack, I — I can't."

"You're my wife. Why can't you?"

"Because I'm on my period," she lied. She didn't have an ounce of regret for that lie when she saw his face twist with disgust.

"If you're going to read, could you do it in the other room? The light bothers me."

Lainey sighed with relief and exasperation. "Sure, Jack." She gathered her things and headed out of the master bedroom and towards the guest bedroom.

"Mom?"

Lainey dropped everything she had in her hands. "Kevin! Why do you insist on scaring me?"

Kevin snickered at his mom as he helped her pick up her things. He pretended he didn't notice how she hid the book's cover when she snatched it from his hands.

"I didn't mean to scare you. We came out of our rooms at the same time." He nodded at her belongings. "Another fight?"

"No." She rolled her eyes when he looked at her with skepticism. "I'm telling the truth. No fight. He said the light bothers him when I read and asked that I go to the other room."

"And you happily obliged?" Kevin grinned.

"We are not talking about this," she responded as she opened the door to the guest bedroom.

"We could. You know, if you needed to."

His kindness never ceased to soothe her weary soul. "I know, sweetie. Why are you up?"

Kevin knew avoidance when he heard it. One day he hoped his mom would talk to him. About everything. "Hungry."

"How could you possibly be hungry? We had dinner less than two hours ago."

Kevin jerked his shoulder. "I don't know. You made me. Maybe you gave me an extra stomach."

Lainey laughed. "You're blaming me for you being a bottomless pit?"

"Yep. It's always the parents' fault, isn't it?" he said cheekily. "Hey."

"Uh oh."

"What?"

"Every time you start a sentence with "hey" it means you have an idea that won't be popular with everyone in the house."

Kevin snorted with laughter. "I don't give a crap what dad thinks."

"Kevin. He's still your father. You should respect that."

"Why? He doesn't respect anything I do."

Well, she couldn't argue with that. Kevin was right. Jack fought him and Darren about everything that wasn't Jack's idea. Hell, he had been doing that to Lainey since they met. *And, yet, you still married him.*

"You got me there. What is your idea?"

"I was thinking about what you said before you went to Paris. About taking us anywhere we wanted to go?"

"Oh. Okay. Have you and Darren decided on a place?"

"Kinda. We wanted to go back to Disney. Exactly the way we did it the last time."

"With Eve?"

"Yep. She still has the house there, right?"

"Um, I'm pretty sure she does. What about your dad?"

"Mom, we want it *exactly* the way it was last time."

She couldn't explain why, but Lainey felt there was an

underlying message there. There couldn't possibly be, right? She was merely projecting her emotions for Eve onto the situation.

"I'll talk to her. Though, I'm sure she'll want to bring Bella."

"We're okay with Bella. But just moms and kids. Okay?"

Lainey pursed her lips in thought. "Okay. Do you still want to go to LA for the opening?"

"Yeah, we do. We want to eat at Ellie's since you rave about it all the time."

"Great. I'm going to have to ask Eve for a raise."

Kevin scrunched his nose. "Why?"

"Because one taste of Ellie's food and you're never going to leave that place! I'll have to buy you a permanent booth!"

Chapter Twenty-Nine
Therapy

Unscheduled.

"Eve?"

Eve stood up straight, pushing away from her Lexus. "Hello, Doc. I'm sorry for ambushing you like this."

She had been waiting for the doctor in the parking lot of her office building for the past thirty minutes. It wasn't the most orthodox way of getting a session in, but . . .

"It's all right." Dr. Woodrow pointed back from where she just came from. It was late, and she was surprised to see Eve waiting for her. However, she had a feeling that things were coming to a head with Eve and her situation. As much as this impromptu visit surprised her, she couldn't say Eve's need for a session wasn't expected. "Would you like to go inside?"

"No." Eve's voice was harder than she had intended. "Sorry, I've been feeling a bit closed in lately. Would you mind talking to me out here?" She lifted her face to the star-filled sky. It was a chilly night, but not unbearably so.

Dr. Woodrow checked her watch. She didn't have anything pressing to get to and Eve, as unprofessional as it was, had become important to her.

"Of course. There's a bench right around the corner. We can sit there if you want?" She led the way and sat, waiting patiently for Eve to do the same.

"I'm sorry . . ." Eve began again, but Dr. Woodrow stopped her.

"Eve, whatever it is that's on your mind must be important for you to be here at all. I'm available anytime for you. You know that."

After that statement, Willamena stayed quiet, waiting for Eve to get to the reason she was there at her own pace. Fleetingly, Eve wondered what the doctor would do without her trusty notebook. How would Eve know if what she was saying was bothersome to her?

"I'm going crazy." Dr. Woodrow raised her eyebrow at Eve's choice of words, and Eve smiled apologetically. "Poor choice of words even if I *do* feel exactly that way."

"Why do you feel you're going crazy?" Willamena reached into her purse and pulled out a notebook.

You have got to be kidding me. "Do you always walk around with one of those things?"

"I find they come in handy. You know, just in case a patient is waiting for me in the parking lot and refuses to come inside." She smiled warmly at Eve.

Eve knew she was teasing her, but being called a patient made her cringe, nonetheless. Intellectually, she knew there was nothing wrong with needing help. Unfortunately, Eve wasn't very intellectual at the moment. Her heart was winning over everything else. Including logic. Which was what brought her to where she was now.

"I need to talk about my last session," Eve blurted out unceremoniously.

"I'm surprised it took you this long."

Eve was sure one of the reasons she liked Dr. Woodrow so much was because she was unconventional. Eve could pretend that they were old friends sitting out here having a normal conversation.

"Yeah, well, I had homework to do."

"The being alone and thinking," Woodrow nodded. "I had a feeling that would be difficult for you."

"For years, I thought I didn't have a heart, Dr. Woodrow. Those men who hurt me stole that from me. Then, I meet Adam, and I start to feel *something*. I didn't allow myself to give in because no matter how nice he was to me, I just never felt I could completely be myself with him. He has this image of me, as most people do, and I strive to be that person for him."

She took a deep breath and let it out slowly, collecting her thoughts before continuing.

"Then, I meet Lainey. God, it was so easy with her. She never expected anything of me. And, maybe that's because she knew how it felt, being a wife and mother who *everyone* expected things from. I don't know. I just know there wasn't a moment when I felt I couldn't be me. Oh, I wanted to resist getting close to her. I couldn't. I knew that what I was feeling was more than just friendship. Seeing the way she looked at me, I knew she could feel it, too. It suddenly became a *need* to be close to her."

"Do you think Lainey being a woman has anything to do with the way you feel?" Willamena asked carefully.

"You mean because it was men who hurt me?"

"Precisely."

"That was one of the things I thought about. With my heart, I might add. I have been pulling at every little thread trying to figure out why I'm hurting Adam."

"And?" Dr. Woodrow prompted when Eve paused.

"No, I honestly don't think that's it. I don't see Adam as someone who can hurt me. Not like they did."

"May I ask you a few questions?"

"Isn't that your job?" Eve smirked, and the doctor smiled back.

"Part of it. Is Lainey the only woman you've been attracted to?"

"Yes."

With the question of whether the best friend was the only same-sex attraction, the answer was yes. I have to wonder if that was because the patient deliberately closed off her feelings. Feelings that are now becoming abundantly clear. Woodrow wrote in her notebook, then looked over at Eve.

"Do you love Adam?"

"Yes."

"Are you *in* love with Adam?"

Eve's answer wasn't as quick this time, and Woodrow noted that in her notebook.

"Should I take your non-answer as an answer?" she asked kindly.

"I don't know," Eve answered honestly. "I thought I was. I thought that by letting Lainey go — in that way — I was doing the right thing. For both of us. What if I was wrong?"

"Well, I can't say you were wrong in your decision that you made then."

"What can you say?"

"I can say that when I asked you a few sessions back if you were in love with Lainey, you said yes," she answered matter-of-factly.

"So, I should divorce my husband, leave my daughter, and whisk Lainey away from her family? What are you writing?" Eve asked as the doctor scribbled something in her notebook.

"What about this notebook bothers you so much?"

"Every time I say something wrong, you write."

"What makes you think what you said is wrong?"

Eve stood abruptly and started pacing. All of this shrink back and forth was frustrating her.

"I can't do what I just said! *That's* what makes it wrong! Cheating is wrong! Being in love with someone who belongs to someone else is wrong!" Eve stopped and looked at her therapist pleadingly. She was breathing heavily, and her entire body was shaking. "I'm not a bad person, Doc. I just fell in love with the right person at the wrong time."

"I know you're not a bad person, Eve. Nor is Lainey." Willamena stood as well and took a step towards Eve. "The thing about love is it's never predictable. Both you and Lainey have circumstances that may be factors in what has transpired between you two."

"You still think this has to do with men hurting me."

"No. What I mean is, from what I've learned from Lainey, Jack is her first, and only, before you. They met when she was young, and she's been with him ever since."

"So, she's sowing her oats with me?"

"Eve."

Eve winced inwardly at Dr. Woodrow's tone. Her mom used to say her name like that when Eve was being a brat. She felt the same way back then that she did now. Like a chastised little girl.

"She's not 'sowing her oats.' But perhaps, when she met you, she discovered there was someone else out there who could capture her heart. That doesn't make her a bad person. It makes her human. As for you," Woodrow continued. "You grew up so fast, and yet, in a way, you remained a child."

Eve frowned. "I don't understand."

"The things that happened to you should *never* happen to anyone at any age. Having gone through it at such a youthful age, you were forced to grow up. But you never went through the normal phases of a relationship. Adam was nice to you, and you weren't used to that. So, you held on to that. Now, I'm not saying that what you feel or felt for him isn't real. It undoubtedly is. But you weren't able to explore your feelings more in-depth as a woman."

"So, Lainey and I are exploring?"

Dr. Woodrow sighed. "You can be extremely hard-headed sometimes. You continually want to hear what makes you look bad. What I'm saying is that each of you found someone in each other that you're completely comfortable being yourselves with. In doing that, you both found something you might have been missing in your lives."

"Then why did we make the decision we made to stay apart?" That was the question that was always in Eve's head. If she loved Lainey so much, why did she marry Adam? Why did she have Bella? Had she known deep down that Lainey would never leave Jack because of her sons? Was it that she wanted what Lainey had, only since Eve couldn't have it with her, she chose the next best thing? If that was true, what kind of person did that make Eve? And how in the hell was she supposed to right her wrong? The thought of hurting Adam, of breaking up her daughter's home, killed her. The problem was, the idea of never being with Lainey again had the same effect.

"I can only assume, Eve."

"Assume, please."

"It's what you both know. Lainey has been with Jack for more than twenty years. They have two sons. How daunting it must be to change your entire life after so long. And you are as selfless as you are self-deprecating. You're willing to give up what you truly want if you think it will make those you care about happy."

"Are we talking about Lainey or Adam?"

"Both."

Eve sat back down, not trusting her legs to keep her upright anymore. "Am I a lesbian?"

"I don't think we need a label, Eve. Love is love."

Eve chuckled. "Spoken like a true advocate."

Willamena smiled at Eve. "As you know, my niece Rebecca is a lesbian. That's what she has always identified as. I have no problem with labels, Eve. I don't think we need one in your case. But if it helps you, I'd say either bisexual or pansexual."

As worldly as Eve was, *this* was all entirely new for her. "Hmm. I guess I have more homework to do."

"I can give you pamphlets."

It was the sparkle in Dr. Woodrow's eyes that gave her away. "I wouldn't have been surprised if you *did* have pamphlets," Eve laughed. It hit her then that she had laughed more in the past thirty minutes than she had all weekend. "What am I going to do?"

Willamena sighed and sat next to Eve. If this were Rebecca, she would have no problem telling her exactly what she should do. But Eve wasn't Rebecca. Willamena's training told her that the *only* one who could tell Eve what to do about this situation was Eve herself. "What did your heart tell you?"

"That I'm in trouble." Eve shook her head. "They deserve so much better," she murmured.

"What about you? What do you deserve, Eve?"

"I don't think you want me to answer that right now." Restless, she stood again. "I've scratched and clawed my way out of hell, doc.

I've been beaten, raped, shot. I'm still here. Against all the odds, I've become a very successful woman. I have galleries all over the world, businesses that flourish, more money than I will probably ever need, and a beautiful family. The one thing that brings me to my knees is love. Fucking love. I've fought my demons and won. But how in the hell do I fight something I can't see, change, or control?"

"Perhaps you shouldn't be fighting it."

"Right," Eve scoffed. "Just keep on like we are. More of Paris. Marriages be damned."

"Eve, I'm not advocating cheating. In fact, I would normally say cheaters are selfish and cruel. But your situation is different."

Ouch. "Why? Because we're women?"

"No. Because you're not purposefully trying to hurt others. You're fighting so hard *not* to hurt others that you're hurting yourselves."

"That doesn't make it right."

"No, it doesn't. And that's something the two of you will have to come to terms with. My point is, you're so focused on that aspect of it that you're ignoring everything else. I won't deny that this is a severely complicated situation. But it is my job as your therapist to get you to think about yourself and what makes you happy."

"I'm in this mess because I only thought about myself."

"Do you really believe that?"

"I don't know what to believe anymore," Eve confessed softly. "Why couldn't I leave her alone?"

"Vilifying yourself won't help. And you can't keep taking away Lainey's accountability for her actions. I realize many may see you as irresistible, but you didn't force her to be with you. She *chose* that." Willamena reached out and took Eve's hand. A move that she could tell still surprised Eve despite Willamena's occasional lack of professionalism. "You're scared, and I get that. You're not used to putting yourself out there. I think you're feeling extra pressure now because I've tasked both you and Lainey to think about what your hearts want. As much as you know she loves you, you can't be sure her heart will choose you."

Eve's eyes fluttered shut as she felt her stomach drop. "Guess I should stop referring to you as a quack," she joked lamely. Suddenly uncomfortable, she pulled her hand away. "And if that's what happens?"

"Fear is never an effective way to live life, Eve."

Eve shook her head. "Such a psychiatrist response."

"As much as I would like to help you, I can't make your decisions for you." She held her hand up before Eve could speak. "There are no negotiations on that, Eve. But I can be here for you — for both of you — no matter what those decisions are."

Eve thought of her mother just then. If she were still alive, Eve had no doubt she would be like Dr. Willamena Woodrow. Caring, yet firm. Always there when needed. The thought saddened Eve even more, and she realized how tired she was. There was an exhaustion that no amount of sleep would help. She was so tired of always fighting to be happy. There were times, more frequently now than ever, when she wondered just how far her strength would stretch.

"I need to go. You can bill me for this," Eve said suddenly. She saw a flash of disappointment in the doctor's eyes, and she softened her tone. "Thank you for talking to me out here. I apologize for disrupting your night."

"No need to apologize. The good thing about bubble baths and wine is they're always there no matter what time I need them."

Eve gave Willamena a genuine smile. "That sounds like heaven right about now."

"It does, doesn't it? Should I give it to you as homework?"

"Don't ruin it!" Eve chuckled. "I think I need to spend some time with my daughter. She brings light to my world in the times when I need it most."

"I think that sounds perfect." Willamena took her keys out of her purse. "I want you to remember that I'm available *anytime*."

"I will, thank you."

"Eve? One more thing. I know you probably can't imagine this right now, but perhaps it would be a good thing for you to talk to Adam about this."

Eve's eyebrows shot upwards. "Are you crazy?"

"Wouldn't that be something?" she laughed. "But I'm pretty sure there's a clause somewhere in some legal mumbo jumbo that says therapists can't be crazy."

"Perhaps you've found a loophole," Eve countered jokingly.

"Perhaps," she shrugged with a smirk. "But, in this case, I believe it might help you."

"Because he'll divorce me and take my daughter away which leaves me completely available to ruin Laincy's life?"

The doc shook her head. "You're not a villain, Eve. I will keep telling you that until you get it through your head."

"You may want to save your voice by recording it," Eve suggested. "Listen, I'm capable of many things, Doc, but talking to Adam about this isn't one of those things."

"You must be aware that your feelings are changing for him. I can only imagine he's aware of it as well. No matter what decisions you make, he needs to know how you feel."

"I'm not ready for that."

Willamena nodded. She knew the suggestion would be met with resistance. "All right. At least keep it in mind?"

"If I can find the room for it up there, I will do just that." *No promises*, Eve added silently. "I get it, okay? I'm not being fair to him, and that kills me. But I'm in no hurry to devastate him even more than I already have."

"As I said earlier, Eve, it is my job to help you think of yourself in these situations. With that said, I'm not here to pressure you into doing something you're uncomfortable with."

Eve laughed. "That's *all* you've done by making me talk, Doc." She preempted the therapist's response with a shrug. "Work in progress, Dr. Woodrow."

"As long as you remember to progress, Eve."

"Such a shrink."

"That's what it says on my doorplate," she winked. "Go home and hug that beautiful daughter of yours." Willamena thought about prolonging the spontaneous session by asking more about Bella and her role in keeping Eve where she is. However, she sensed

Eve had had all she could handle for the night. "I expect you back here regularly."

"I'm doing my best. Goodnight, Doctor. Enjoy your night of relaxation."

"Goodnight, Eve."

Chapter Thirty

"Are you coming to bed?"

Eve looked up from her computer. Adam was in his usual attire for bed and, once again, Eve didn't feel what she was supposed to feel.

"I have some things I need to finish up here." Things that could easily be done in the morning.

"For the opening?" Adam asked evenly.

"Mmhmm. It's coming up and time seems to be flying by."

Adam nodded. "That's why you've been spending a lot of time in here, I suppose. Will that change once the opening is over?"

God, I can't keep doing this to him. Or to myself. "Things will change, yes," she answered. How? She hadn't figured that out, yet.

"Do you still want me to go with you to LA?"

Eve frowned. "Of course, I do. You worked hard on the gallery, Adam. You deserve to celebrate that."

"Right." He started to walk away, then turned back against his better judgment. "Am I going there as your employee or your husband?"

Eve sighed. "Adam." She wished she could be confident about her answer. "We're going as a family. Bella is pretty excited."

He nodded again. "Lexie is going, too?"

"Yes. As are Jack and the boys. It'll be fun." *It'll be miserable.*

"Fun? You'll be busy working, and I'll be stuck with Jack," Adam said with a hint of mirth.

"I thought you liked Jack."

"I tolerate him. The man is a chauvinist, Eve. But at least Kevin and Darren will be there. Hopefully, they'll be able to save my brain."

Eve smiled at him. "Jack is usually on his best behavior when he's in a social situation."

Adam shrugged a shoulder. "I don't know. He was an ass and left in the middle of the last opening, remember?"

Oh, Eve remembered that night very well. Though Jack Stanton never played a role in her memories.

"Yes, well." Eve cleared her throat, but the visions remained. "If Jack wants to leave this time, he'll have to Uber back to the hotel."

Adam's lips twitched. "I'll, um, let you get back to work. Try not to fall asleep in here again, yeah?"

Don't count on it. "I'll do my best. Goodnight."

Adam left without returning the sentiment. She didn't blame him. Since she'd gotten back from Paris, Eve was finding every excuse she could *not* to be in the same bed with Adam if he was awake. She would be naïve if she thought Adam didn't sense the difference in her. And the one thing Eve wasn't was naïve.

She jumped slightly when her phone chimed. Picking it up, she smiled when a text from Lainey popped up.

I'm craving an éclair.

Eve laughed. While in Paris, the éclair was Lainey's go-to dessert. She even brought a few back claiming they were for the boys.

Did you eat the ones you smuggled in? Eve texted back with a knowing smirk.

Excuse me, but those were for my sons.

Eve laughed out loud. **Did they enjoy the bite they got?**

You are not nice. ;) Do you think Ellie makes eclairs?

It's possible. It's also possible that they're better than the ones in Paris.

OMG. I almost hope they're not. But knowing Ellie, they probably are. I'm going to get fat.

Eve snickered as she rolled her eyes. **You're not going to get fat. You have great genes.** And jeans. *God, now I'm thinking of Lainey in jeans.*

I miss eclairs.

Eve's eyes fluttered shut. A tear inexplicably rolled down her cheek. They were talking about desserts. But she knew, deep down, there was more to Lainey's words beyond the surface. She missed Paris, too. She missed Lainey. She couldn't determine whether knowing Lainey felt the same way was better or worse for her heart.

I do, too. She responded simply. It didn't matter that Eve didn't have eclairs while in Paris. She stuck with chouquettes. She also knew Lainey knew that. The text was read, but Lainey hadn't responded yet. Had Eve gone too far?

We'll have to go back. Lainey finally replied. It was simple and short, but the sentiment hit deep.

Anytime.

Goodnight, Eve.

Goodnight, Lainey.

Eve sat back in her chair. Whatever she was working on had been forgotten. It no longer held her interest. Her hands itched to pick up a paintbrush and paint who owned her heart. Unfortunately, she had had this feeling before. Excited by the influx of inspiration, she went to her studio. As ready and willing as she was to paint, her mind simply couldn't push through the block. It had been as humiliating as it was heartbreaking. She couldn't do that again. Even if this time it felt a little different.

Lainey tapped her pencil on her desk, staring intently at the photo that she kept there. It was the photo of her, Eve, and the boys at Disney. That trip had been unbelievable for Lainey. It was the first time Eve had let Lainey touch her. To make love to her. She had been so nervous, but Eve was patient. And responsive. God, she had been so receptive to Lainey's touch. Lainey had never felt so powerful and sexy before.

Many things happened during that trip. It was the first time she learned of Eve's father. She had also learned that Eve had been taking anti-depressants and about the cigarettes. The trip was enlightening, incredible, scary, and one of the best times of her life. Finding out that Eve wasn't perfect only strengthened Lainey's bond with her. Sadly, that trip was also the beginning of the end for them. Things happened so fast after that. It made Lainey's head spin. Perhaps if Lainey had spent more time thinking about the decision to stay with Jack . . .

"May I come in?"

Lainey looked up. *God, she's beautiful.* "Of course." Lainey gestured for Eve to sit in the visitor's chair. "What's this?"

Eve placed a white sack on Lainey's desk. "Something to tide you over."

Lainey reached over and picked it up. The aroma of chocolate hit her almost immediately. She unfolded the top of the sack and opened it. "You got me an éclair?" she asked, deeply breathing in the scent of the pastry.

Eve nodded. "Apparently, they're the best in New York City. It's not Paris, or Ellie's, but . . ."

"Thank you," Lainey interrupted quietly. "No matter where they're from, they're perfect." *Just like you.* "This is where you were this morning?"

Eve nodded. "Do you have any idea how many bakeries there are in the city? All claiming to have "the best" everything."

Lainey chuckled. "I can't believe you did this. You said you had a meeting."

"I did! With bakers."

"How did you end up with this one?" Lainey carefully took the éclair out of the bag as though it was a valuable prize. To her, it was. She didn't know why she was surprised by Eve's actions. That was who Eve was. Selfless and generous. Always wanting to do things that made Lainey happy. The total opposite of Lainey's goddamn husband.

"I, um, called in a favor."

"Ellie?"

Eve laughed. "Yes. It turns out she went to school with the baker who made that," she said, pointing at the éclair. "The woman was second in their class."

"Let me guess. Ellie was first?"

Eve tapped her nose. "Ding, ding! Good news is, Ellie gave her pointers so that that thing could have a little bit of Ellie magic."

Lainey took a healthy bite. She didn't care one iota that it was messy or that she most likely had chocolate all over her mouth.

"Verdict?" Eve asked as she stared at Lainey's mouth. It seriously took all her strength *not* to lean over that desk and lick that chocolate clean.

Lainey held up her finger. She made a show of the tasting, smacking her lips with gusto.

"Verdict is," she began after she swallowed. "I don't think anyone can touch Ellie's magic, but this is definitely a close second."

"I did good?"

Lainey held Eve's gaze. "Very good."

"Mrs. Riley?"

Eve stopped at the sound of her name. She turned to face a young, brunette. "Hello, Claudia."

The woman blinked as if she couldn't believe Eve knew her name. "To what do we owe this pleasure?" she asked cheerfully.

"I'm here to see Adam."

"Oh, um, he's in a meeting. Is there something I could help you with?"

Eve tilted her head, scrutinizing the woman Adam used to fuck. "I'll wait."

"Right. Yes, of course. It's just that he may be a while. If there's something I can do . . ."

"There isn't."

She watched Claudia visibly gulp and shift uncomfortably. Eve nearly felt sorry for her behavior, but it quickly passed when Adam appeared around the corner. Apparently, "a while" meant something different to her than it did to Claudia.

"Eve? What are you doing here?"

Eve kept her gaze on Claudia long enough to make her shift again, then smiled thinly.

"I need to speak to you about the expansion for Sumptor Gallery, NY."

Adam's surprised smile faltered. "Oh. I've been swamped recently, and I handed that project over to Claudia. I'm sure she has time to go over everything you need."

Eve remained quiet. Instead of making a scene, she walked past him, directly to his office. She saw Adam say something under his breath to Claudia, who turned on her heel and scurried away. After that, it didn't take Adam long to join her.

"That was unlike you," he began. "You're typically not rude to those around you."

"Would you like me to apologize to her, or did you do that for me?" Eve asked. She continued without waiting for an answer. "My irritation was not with your old girlfriend, Adam. It's with you. Sumptor, Inc. is your biggest client. I hired *you*, not a junior architect with enough experience to fill a thimble."

"Claudia is good, Eve."

"Maybe she is. I want great. I want you."

"It's been a while since I've heard that," Adam joked cynically, heart-broken when Eve rolled her eyes.

"I funded this company because I believed in your work, Adam. These are my galleries we're talking about. I do not trust them to just anyone."

"It's a simple room expansion, Eve."

Her brows knitted together as she studied him. Eve readily admitted that she had changed after Paris. Hell, she had begun to change way before then. However, if Adam denied that he was changing as well, he was either oblivious or a liar.

"Sumptor, Inc. and Sumptor Galleries will be finding a new architect," she stated with authority.

"Eve, wait." Adam sighed. "I have the plans here." He walked over to his blueprint cabinet and opened the top drawer.

She narrowed her eyes at him. "If you had this, why the hand-off?"

"Because!" That's as far as Adam's outburst went before he took a breath and counted to ten. "I'm trying to build my client list, Eve. Yes, Sumptor everything is our biggest account, but I don't want that to be the case. How do you think it looks when my *wife* is the one keeping the company afloat?"

"Sumptor, Inc. and Sumptor Galleries are *not* your wife, Adam. They are prestigious, highly successful businesses. If I didn't feel you were qualified, I wouldn't have hired your firm. Hence, the reason I didn't hire you for the project in Paris."

"Yeah, thanks for that," he said sullenly.

"You can't have it both ways, Adam." She fully understood the irony of that. Isn't that what she was doing right now? Having it both ways? She was married to Adam, and in love with Lainey. That last thought sent a myriad of emotions through Eve. *I am in so much trouble*, she thought sadly.

"I'll do the expansion," Adam said quietly. "However, I believe you should give the others here a chance. You had them vetted. You must know they're good."

"Perhaps you're right. But not with my galleries." She gestured towards the blueprints. "May I?"

"Yeah." Adam unrolled them onto his drafting table. "It's pretty simple, but since it was a fun, pop culture room, I added this here." He pointed at an opening in the far wall on the design. "I thought we could use bricks around the entrance here. Make it a not-so-secret secret entrance. You could use that for the more popular superhero displays."

Eve visualized Adam's ideas. It was good. Very good.

"I like it. When can you get started?"

"After the opening in LA?" Adam suggested. "I figure you have enough to deal with now without the stress of more renovations."

Eve nodded. "That sounds good. Thank you."

"You could have asked me about this at home, you know."

She brought her gaze to his. "I could have. However, business should be separate from our home life. Isn't that what you wanted?"

"Yeah."

"One question before I go."

"Sure."

"This design. Was it your idea? Or one of your employees?"

Adam frowned. "Mine. You said you wanted mine, Eve."

"I did. Do you have any of their designs in here?"

"Um, no. I got a few submissions, but . . ."

"But you asked them to go back to the drawing board?"

Adam chuckled. "Literally."

Eve smiled. "I'll see you at home."

"Hold on. Did you want to see the other designs?"

"No. I wanted you to understand why I was so adamant that you were the one who worked on the galleries."

She kissed him on the cheek before leaving. It broke her heart that the feelings she once thought she had were fading. Or maybe they were never what she believed them to be. Was it possible that she exaggerated her emotions for Adam? Did the guilt and fear she felt because of Lainey or her past hurting him somehow manifest themselves into love?

"*Jesus, I'm in trouble,*" she muttered to herself. She needed another session which pissed her off. Eve Sumptor didn't like to rely on anyone but herself. She was a fighter. Someone who could fend off any opponent that dared to challenge her. Hadn't she proven that with Tony? With Laurence and Billy? With Madame Bussiere? Who was left standing? Eve. What happens when she becomes her own opponent? Who wins in that situation?

Chapter Thirty-One
Therapy

Decisions made.

"I'm so sorry I'm late!"

Willamena rushed into the office, tossing her briefcase to the side. Eve couldn't remember ever seeing the doctor this flustered before. It was nice to know she was human as Eve was.

"Not a problem. I just got here myself." Fifteen minutes ago, but Eve felt there was no need to make Woodrow feel worse. Whatever it was that was bothering her was enough. "Everything all right?"

"Oh!" Willamena waved a hand in the air as though she could fan away all the bad vibes. "Yes, yes. My flight was a bit delayed, then my car service . . . and, we're not here for me."

"Please, doc. It makes me feel a little better that your life isn't perfect."

Dr. Woodrow let out a bark of laughter. "Perfect! Child, I wish. I made an impromptu visit to my niece in L.A. for the first time in a while. I had forgotten how terrible traveling could be when you don't have a private jet." She winked at Eve to soften her slight jab.

"All you have to do is ask, Willamena." Eve had never used the doctor's first name before. But if she was going to offer her plane,

Eve figured it was more appropriate. "You tell Lainey and Adam I'm all cured and I'll *buy* you a plane of your own."

"You don't have a disease, Eve."

"Are you sure about that?"

"Quite positive."

"Hmm. How is Rebecca, by the way?" Yep, she was stalling. Seemed to be her M.O. these days.

Dr. Woodrow handed Eve a cup of tea and parked herself in her usual seat. She set her tea on the small table next to her and laid her notebook on her lap, noticing Eve's small wince.

"She's fine. Actually, she's more than fine. She's happy."

Eve smiled genuinely. After everything Rebecca had been through, Eve was glad she could now be happy. She made a mental note to send Cass a nice gift basket for her part in Rebecca's happiness. Or, maybe she would buy a Cass Giles original painting. The woman was amazingly talented. And Eve was trying her best not to be jealous that Cass did it so effortlessly.

"Eve?"

"Hmm?"

"Where were you just then?"

Eve nearly rolled her eyes. She sometimes wished she could see the look on her face when her mind started to wander. Was it that obvious, or was Dr. Woodrow just that good at what she did?

"I was thinking about how happy I am for Rebecca and Cass. They're truly great for each other."

Dr. Woodrow opened her notebook and poised her pen. "And which part of that bothers you more? That they are happy, seemingly without problems? Or that Cass is doing what you want to do the most?"

The urge to get up and walk out was nearly too great to ignore. Eve hated that Dr. Woodrow asked the damn question. She hated even more that she wasn't sure which bothered her more. And that, of course, made Eve feel like a terrible person.

"It's normal to feel a bit of jealousy when your life seems to be in shambles," Willamena suggested gently when Eve didn't answer.

"Get out of my head, doc."

Dr. Woodrow chuckled. "I'm a head shrink. It's in the rule book that I get in there."

"I don't like it." And now Eve sounded like a petulant child. "Sorry. The truth is, I don't know how to answer your questions."

Patient feels painting is as important in her life as love. I believe they could be interconnected for the patient. Without one, could there be the other at this point?

"Give it a try," Woodrow said after finishing her note.

Eve cleared her throat, took a sip of her tea, and cleared her throat again. "Fine. I'm happy for Rebecca. She deserves someone good like Cass. I'm happy for Cass. She deserves to have the world know about her talent. And I wonder what the hell I ever did that was so wrong . . . no." Eve shook her head. She had been thinking of this for weeks. She wasn't pleased with her conclusions, but life wasn't all rainbows and unicorns, was it?

"Eve?"

"I'm incredibly lucky," Eve said quickly. "I'm loved by a great man. I have a beautiful, smart daughter. I'm rich, successful, and respected. What the fuck do I have to complain about?"

"Your mother was killed by your father who also tried to kill you. You were sold to the highest bidder when you were a mere child. You fell in love with someone you feel you can't be with." Willamena flipped through her notebook with deliberate movements. "Did I miss anything?"

"That is the past."

"Things that happen in the past tend to linger, Eve. What happened to you is bound to stay with you forever. It affects you. You may be a powerful woman in the business world, but you're not immune to human emotions."

"Obviously," Eve muttered.

"Have you talked to Lainey lately?"

There was that familiar flip of Eve's stomach. That little extra beat of her heart. *Damn it.*

"Every day. She's my partner." Unfortunately, not in the way Eve would like her to be.

"I think you know what I mean, Eve."

Eve sighed. "Doc, we don't spend every moment talking about how we can't be together." Just *some* moments. "I try to avoid it for her sake."

Dr. Woodrow clicked her tongue and wrote a note. **Patient is still thinking of others' feelings before the patient's own feelings. There is so much need for things to be discussed. However, there is too much fear. Perhaps the real fear is being rejected.** "I'll address that in a later session. First, have you talked to Adam?"

"Every day. He's my husband."

"You're particularly stubborn today, Eve. If this is how you want to conduct the session, it's a waste of time for both of us. I came here straight from the airport after a very long flight. If you'd rather not be here, let's call it a night and go our separate ways."

Well, Willamena Woodrow was not playing games today. She must've been just as tired and irritable as Eve was.

"I apologize. And, while I never really wish to be here, I made a promise."

"There's one of your biggest mistakes." Dr. Woodrow closed her notebook. "This will not work if you're doing it for someone else. Whether that's Lainey, Adam, *Bella*, it's not enough. You must do it for *you*, Eve. No one else. The others, they may feel the residual effects of your time here, but only if you allow you to be here for *yourself*."

Damn it. "For me."

"Right. What do you want for you, Eve? Let's take everyone else's feelings out of it. Take all the consequences away. Say what you would do the moment you walk out of here when everything is right in your world. Don't think, just say what's in your heart."

Eve closed her eyes and let her heart show her the future she desired the most.

"I go home, and Lainey is waiting for me. The boys are still up, playing with Bella. Lainey looks up at me and smiles, welcoming me home with open arms and a light kiss. There's an easel in the corner of the living room because I can't bear the thought of being away from my family for too long. So, I paint right there while they play or while Lainey reads."

"And how do you feel in this scenario?" Dr. Woodrow asked softly.

"*Happy*," Eve whispered.

"What else?"

"Just happy." She opened her eyes. "Is that even possible?"

"For you to feel happiness?"

"Without guilt," Eve amended.

Dr. Woodrow leaned forward. "I believe that the one thing we forget as we get caught up in our lives is that we're all adults. We may get hurt or hurt the people we care about, but we're resilient. We move on. Unless you refuse to let yourself live, you move on."

"You're saying I'm blocking myself."

"It's a genuine possibility, Eve. You're stuck in limbo. You are paralyzed by your love and desire to be with Lainey, and your obligation to Adam and Bella. You're not moving forward. You're not even in the moment, Eve, because you're afraid that by living, you'll be hindering someone else from living their life."

"Won't I?"

"People survive heartbreak, Eve. I believe that with enough discussion, anything can be worked out."

"Do you think I could survive the loss of my daughter, Dr. Woodrow?"

"You're a good mother, Eve. Adam knows that. But he couldn't keep her away from you just because you don't want to be with him if that was your choice."

"I cheated."

"While some would see that as a moral indiscretion, it is not illegal. Nor does it play a role in determining who gets custody of a child. Unless you have a prenup?" she asked.

"No prenup."

She nodded. "My best advice for you will always be to talk to Adam. People are more intuitive than you realize."

"I've been thinking about it. Even if I don't end up with Lainey, it's not fair to Adam to keep stringing him along. I love him. I truly do. But it's hard for me to be with him now."

"Is sex off the table with Adam?"

Eve averted her eyes. As much as Adam had tried to be with Eve, she couldn't. Of course, that made her feel like shit. He was a desirable man and very good at sex. But . . . "I haven't been able to be with him since I was with Lainey in Paris."

"I see. Is that because you've realized Lainey is the one you truly want to be with?"

"I . . ." She had no idea how to answer that. *Was* it the only reason? Or was there something more?

"May I ask you something personal?" The doc asked into the silence.

Eve let out a very unladylike snort. "What in the hell have you been doing since the moment I first walked into your office?"

Dr. Woodrow smiled devilishly. Sometimes Eve wondered what she was like outside of the office. According to Dr. Woodrow's niece Rebecca, she was a hoot. Eve would take Rebecca's word for it. Not that she didn't like the doc. It was just hard to look at her and not think about all of the shit she was going through.

"Has sex with Adam changed for you? Do you no longer enjoy it?"

"It's not that I don't enjoy it . . . him. How can I be with him, give him hope, when I honestly don't know if I can stay?"

"What is it like at home between you and Adam?"

"Awkward at times. Comfortable at others. He's incredibly sensitive and attentive. Then, things change, and he's distant and irritable. I can't blame him because I've been distant. I make it a point to have Bella with us at all times."

"And when it's bedtime?"

"I stay awake until he falls asleep. Reading, doing nonsense stuff on the computer, researching artists. There's always something I can do to keep myself busy. I know he knows what I'm doing, but he never says anything."

"Is that a problem? Do you wish he would say something? That he would fight you? Or perhaps that he would leave you, so you don't have to be the bad guy?"

"I'm already the bad guy, Dr. Woodrow. With that being said, maybe I do wish that. I've seen him agitated a few times, and each time has been because of me. When I broke up with him the first time, when I was shot, and when I was almost killed again. But when he found out about Lainey, he shut down. There was no yelling, no anger. I don't know why that makes me feel worse."

"He asked you to stay away from her," Dr. Woodrow reminded Eve.

Eve didn't need a reminder of that. She felt her heart tear in two that day.

"Only to change his mind when I went crazy. And I've slept with her since then," Eve reminded her in return.

"I'm going to put a jar here on the table, and each time a patient says they're crazy, I'm going to make them add five dollars." She raised an eyebrow at Eve. "Except you. You will have to put five hundred bucks in."

It just so happened that Eve was taking a sip of tea the moment Willamena flung that at her. She somehow managed not to spit the liquid in the good doctor's face. As tempting as that was. "How is that fair?"

"You can afford it. Five dollars is nothing to you. Maybe if I make a dent in your deep pockets, you'll get the hint," she said defiantly.

"I get it. You don't like the word crazy."

"I don't like that you think you're crazy, Eve. Though I will admit that sometimes love does make us a little . . ."

"Crazy?"

"Ah, ah." She waggled her finger at Eve. "I was going to say bonkers."

Eve laughed out loud. "I take it that's the medical terminology?"

"The extremely clinical term, yes."

She said it with such a straight face that it made Eve laugh harder. She had the honest thought that this right here was the reason she kept coming back to therapy. It drained her. Left her completely raw. Yet, these moments of levity by the good doc healed bits and pieces of Eve. She felt a moment of normalcy in her chaotic life. Even her time with Lainey was strained these days because there was so much tension there. They just tried to ignore what kind of tension it was until they figured out what to do about it.

"So, I can say I'm bonkers without having to pay the fee?"

Dr. Woodrow tapped her lips with a fingertip. "Hmm. Since it is the clinical term, I may allow it in the right circumstance."

"Thanks," Eve smiled slightly before it faded. "I have to talk to him."

"I agree."

"I'm working my way up to it. But I think I have to talk to Lainey first."

"Working your way up to that one, too?" The doc asked gently.

"Yes. I see the way she looks at me. I know she wants me as much as I want her. But I'm also intelligent enough to know that she would never choose me over her kids. And I would never want her to."

Dr. Woodrow nodded. "Believe it or not, you're making progress." She chuckled. "When you roll your eyes, I'm reminded of how young you are. It's not always apparent when someone meets you. Of course, you *look* young, but you have an old soul. I like the moments I get to see what's underneath the sophistication."

"Underneath the sophistication. My childish side?"

"I wouldn't say childish. I'd say unguarded. There aren't many of those moments with you. Have you ever had one with Adam?"

Eve shook her head. "That's not who he wants. He fell in love with a confident, strong woman."

"So, you've hidden your vulnerable side to him. And Lainey?"

"She sought out my vulnerability," Eve confessed. "She wasn't fooled by the façade. I don't think I ever had a choice than to be exposed with her."

"My professional response to that is, the woman you portray to the world, Eve, is not a façade. You *are* that woman, through and through. However, you're also the sweet, sensitive woman underneath."

Eve resisted rolling her eyes again for fear she'd look even more childish. "It was much easier being the one without a heart."

"You've always had, and always *will* have, a heart, Eve. I've heard quite a bit about your generosity through my niece." She sighed. "I know I've told you that I can't make the decision for you and that remains true. I will say, though, I think deep down you know you've made your decision."

"If I take *everyone* out of the equation, being completely selfish, then yes. I've made my decision. Now, I have to find the strength to do something about it."

"You have it in you."

"Yeah, well. As you pointed out, I also have a scared little weakling in me, too."

"That's not exactly what I said, Eve."

"Close." Eve held her hand up when Dr. Woodrow got that *look* on her face. The one that told Eve the doc was not happy with her. "I apologize. I'm getting tired and cranky."

Dr. Woodrow laughed softly. "Perhaps you should go have a nap."

Eve embraced her inner child and stuck her tongue out at her. "I would argue with you just out of spite, but I could absolutely use a nap. All of us will be leaving for L.A. in the morning."

"Will you use this opportunity to talk to them?"

Eve shrugged. "I promise I will try. Is that good enough?"

"It's all anyone can ask."

"Is that my homework?" Eve asked cheekily. Okay, so stress, lack of sleep, and pure, unadulterated lust for someone she couldn't fully have were taking their toll on her. She was adult enough to admit that.

"Your homework is to accept your decision and forgive yourself."

Eve scoffed. "You could have asked me to take over the world. That would have been easier to accomplish. But, again, I'll try."

"It's all anyone can ask," Dr. Woodrow repeated.

"Right. So that you know, that's never been my experience in life. Trying was not good enough." Eve stood abruptly. She could not get sucked into another conversation about her shortcomings. "With the opening of the new gallery, I'll be gone for a couple of weeks. You do know you are invited, yes?"

Dr. Woodrow stood as well. "I do, thank you. I wish I could. But with this impromptu trip I just took to LA, I can't spare the time. I already moved appointments around. I can't do that to my patients again. I promise to stop by the next time I'm in town. You know how to contact me if need be."

Eve completely understood Dr. Woodrow's dedication to her patients. Including her. "I do. Thank you, Doc. Goodnight."

"Goodnight, Eve."

Chapter Thirty-Two

"Will there be a superhero section here, too?" Darren licked his ice cream cone as he looked around the new gallery.

"In time," Eve answered, smiling down at Darren. "Are you going to allow us to show your work here when we do?"

"Yeah! When?"

Lainey chuckled at her young son's enthusiasm. "We have to see how well it does in New York before we change things here," Lainey explained. "But *I* think it'll be a hit and we'll be placing a superhero section in *all* our galleries."

"*Our galleries?*" Eve mouthed with a sly smile. She winked at Lainey when she blushed. The truth of the matter was, Eve loved hearing Lainey talk about the galleries as though they were hers as well. In Eve's heart, they were. In the short amount of time she had been with Sumptor Galleries, Lainey had made an incredible impact. Not just on the owner, but on everyone she ever came in contact with. That's who Lainey Stanton was.

Darren seemed to be satisfied with that answer and ran off to find his brother.

"They like it here," Lainey said offhandedly.

"The gallery?"

She looked up at Eve. "Los Angeles. They said the sun feels sunnier here."

"Sunnier?" Eve laughed softly. "I suppose they're right. There's just something about this place." She looked out the gallery window. Here, they were street level. When people walked by, Eve could see their expressions. They still ran the gambit of emotions, but it wasn't so distant. Eve loved New York City. It would always be her home. However, she could see herself living here. In the right circumstances, of course.

"I usually feel that way," Lainey said quietly. "It's not the same this time."

"Because Jack is here?"

She shrugged. "Maybe. I love that the boys are here. And they're having a blast with little Bella. They love her so much. But it's strained. Kevin and Jack are still at odds. Darren picks up on that, not to mention Jack's opinions on Darren's love for art."

"If he hates this, why is he here?" Eve asked with a tinge of frustration. She would never understand how someone like Jack Stanton got such an amazing woman like Lainey. He didn't even appreciate her for chrissake. Nor did he support his sons.

Lainey shrugged again. "Because he already asked for the time off and made the commitment."

"Hmm." Eve held her tongue. The last thing she wanted to do was upset Lainey. "Want some lunch?"

Lainey smiled. "Only if it's Ellie's."

"Grab the boys, and I'll get Bella." Eve paused. "Adam is doing some work at the hotel. Do you want to ask Jack to lunch?"

Lainey laughed. "No."

"Can I have another piece of pie, mom?"

Lainey rolled her eyes at Kevin. "You had a huge burger, a ton of fries, a milkshake, onion rings, and a big slice of pie. How in the hell are you still hungry?"

"Ooo, you said a dirty word!" Darren giggled.

"Heck. I said heck."

"Nope, I heard you. So did Bella, Kevin, and Eve!"

Lainey looked to Eve for help, but the beautiful woman was busy laughing her ass off. "*Anyway*," she said dramatically, looking at Kevin. "Back to my original question. How are you still hungry?"

"You ask me that all the time, mom." He jerked his shoulder and grinned at her. "I take after you. I like to eat."

Eve pursed her lips. "He's got you there," she said brazenly.

Lainey scoffed. "You could eat me under the table!" As soon as the words left her mouth, Lainey could hear exactly how they sounded. She was surprised her face didn't explode with how fiery it became.

Eve bit her lip. Hard. Part of her wanted to laugh at Lainey's reaction to her own words. Part of her wanted . . . well, part of her wanted things she couldn't have. Especially with the kids around. Thankfully, she saw Ellie walking by and signaled her.

"Hey, guys!" Ellie leaned down and kissed Bella on top of her head. "Hey there, cutie. Did you like your pie?"

Bella's eyes lit up, and she threw her hands in the air, nearly smacking Ellie in the face. "Yes! More!"

Ellie's eyebrows rose. "More?" She looked at Eve.

"Apparently, we all have tummy reserves for your pie. Could we get another round?"

Ellie laughed. "Of course. Coffee, as well?"

"Two. And milk for the boys."

"And what about you, cutie? Do you want coffee or milk?" Ellie asked a giggling Bella.

"Coffee!"

Eve snorted with laughter. "I don't think so, young lady. You may have juice or milk. Which would you like?"

Bella furrowed her little brows in thought. She looked at Kevin and Darren who were mouthing milk to her. "Milk!" she yelled out with enthusiasm.

Ellie smiled brightly at the little girl. "Milk it is!" she yelled just as loudly.

"What's all this hubbub about milk?"

Eve watched Ellie's face illuminate at the sound of Hunter Vale's soft timbre. She knew Hunter via Rebecca. According to

Rebecca's gossip, the brilliant trauma surgeon was utterly smitten with the diner owner. She saw now that the feelings were mutual between the women.

"Oh, um. Hi," Ellie smiled up at Hunter. "We were just, ahem, excited to get some more pie and milk," she explained as though she were part of the family.

"As you should be!" Hunter said with eagerness. "Best ever!"

Ellie smiled coyly. "Hunter, this is Eve, Lainey, Kevin, and Darren. And this cutie here is Bella."

Hunter shook Eve's hand. "We've met, haven't we?"

"Briefly. It's good to see you again." Eve looked at Lainey. "Hunter was Rebecca's surgeon."

"Oh! It's nice to meet you." Lainey shook Hunter's hand as well.

"Likewise." Hunter smiled at Lainey and nodded at the boys, then turned to Bella. "So, little lady, what kind of pie are you getting?"

Bella tilted her head all the way back. She had to to take in the very tall woman. "'Nana," she answered as she stared into Hunter's blue eyes.

"Mmm! Banana is one of my favorites, too. Good choice!" Hunter held up her hand hoping Bella wouldn't leave her hanging. She gave the little girl a lopsided grin when Bella slapped her tiny palm to Hunter's bigger one in a high-five. "All right! I'll let you all get back to your lunch."

"You're coming to the opening, right?" Eve asked.

Hunter glanced at Ellie. "Wouldn't miss it."

Kevin watched the tall woman walk with Ellie to the counter. Her head was bent close to the diner owner's, their proximity close. "Are they together?" he asked.

Lainey's eyes met Eve's before she addressed Kevin's question. "I think so."

"According to my intel," Eve said, lowering her voice conspiratorially. "They just started dating."

She hoped she was doing the right thing by telling them the truth. Bella wouldn't understand, but Kevin and Darren were old enough to recognize what she was telling them. It was her way of gauging how they felt about two women being together. She probably should have let Lainey handle this, but a glance in her companion's direction told Eve Lainey was just as curious about their reactions.

"Cool. They look good together," Kevin stated matter-of-factly.

Darren squinted in Ellie and Hunter's direction. "That lady is tall. How do they kiss?"

Lainey slid down in her booth. "Oh, lord. I'll explain the mechanics later if you promise not to ask either of them."

Darren grinned. "'Kay."

Once again, Lainey's eyes sought Eve's. She knew what Eve was trying to accomplish by revealing Ellie and Hunter's relationship. She just wished their own future was more definite.

Lainey tried desperately to stay focused on the conversation going on around her. Unfortunately, it wasn't working. It was opening night, and she should be happy and excited. She felt the opposite. Eve had been occupied most of the night. And mostly by Adam. He was making it extremely clear that *he* was there with Eve. It didn't bode well for him later that his possessiveness perturbed Eve.

Jack, on the other hand, was the opposite. Lainey had to remind him to stop looking so bored and angry constantly. She was used to it, but this was an important night for Eve. For both of them, actually. She almost wished Jack would pull his disappearing act like he did the last time. Lainey took a healthy sip of her champagne and decided to give up on the conversation, and people watch instead. Besides, whatever was going on with Ellie and Hunter was way more interesting than these uptight men vying for Eve's attention.

Lainey caught Eve's eye and gave her a small smile before walking away from the small crowd. She knew deep in her heart that Eve wanted to follow. She knew Eve was wondering what was going on in Lainey's head. And Lainey knew that each time Adam embraced Eve, she saw guilt in those beautiful gray eyes. Since it broke her heart, Lainey was grateful for the distraction Ellie's apparent distress was giving her. *You're terrible*, she thought to herself as she made her way to the young diner owner.

"Girl troubles?" Lainey asked, nearly taking a step back following the look she received from Ellie. It only lasted a split second, but the young woman was definitely upset about something.

"You could say that," Ellie responded sadly. "I'm sorry. I know this is a big night for you and Eve."

Lainey waved off the apology. Would it really be a Sumptor Gallery opening if there wasn't drama? Lainey wondered if all of Eve's galleries went through something like this. Or was Lainey the common denominator?

"Please," she said aloud to Ellie. "We're no strangers to opening night drama. The night we re-opened the gallery in New York, my husband and I had a huge fight, and he walked out on me." Lainey hesitated. Since it was what was really on her mind, Lainey was candid. "That was also the night that Eve and I first made love."

She patted Ellie's back gently when Ellie choked on her champagne. Lainey hadn't thought she was revealing anything Ellie didn't already know. At least, according to Eve. Had Eve read Ellie wrong? Lainey highly doubted it. The woman was rarely wrong.

"Eve told me you knew about us," she explained softly. "The reason I'm telling you this is because I see something between you and Hunter that reminds me of us. A belonging. A fear. A need. A want."

"Why aren't you together?"

The question was asked with such gentleness, Lainey couldn't be annoyed by it. But she also couldn't answer it. As the days went by, the reasons for not being with Eve became less and less clear.

"It's complicated," Lainey answered finally with a hint of sadness. "Besides, this is about you and Hunter. Don't let fear stand in your way. Hers or yours. All of the best things in life are worth fighting for, Ellie. Don't live with regret." *Like I do every day.*

Lainey could practically feel Eve's eyes on her. When she looked up, sure enough, Eve was watching her discreetly.

"Nothing is standing in your way but you," Lainey continued, her eyes still locked with Eve's. "Nothing holding you back. Seize the opportunity to be happy."

With those last words to Ellie, Lainey patted the young woman's arm and, because of Eve's pleading look, made her way back towards the group she just escaped. Unluckily for her, Jack had hit his champagne limit and was getting handsy. *Perfect.*

Eve spotted Lainey studying one of Cass's paintings. It was one Eve knew well. She had studied it herself quite often in the days leading up to the opening. As with the painting that led her to H. Agosti, this one moved her as well. It was so full of passion, confusion, love, sadness, and anger that it touched every inch of Eve's soul.

Now that she finally pried herself away from Adam, she was free to seek out the one woman who had eluded her for most of the night. Not that Eve blamed Lainey. Adam was being particularly demanding of Eve's time. If Adam wasn't occupying Eve's space, Lainey was dealing with Jack's increasing inebriation.

"Rebecca told me that Cass painted this during the time Rebecca left for those two months."

Lainey looked over at Eve. The only reason she hadn't been startled by Eve's sudden appearance was the fact she had sensed the woman before she spoke.

"That explains a lot," Lainey responded delicately, then turned back to the painting. "There's so much sadness here."

"Is that the first thing you see?" Eve asked.

"You're asking about the anger," Lainey stated. Eve constantly challenged Lainey's perception of art. Not in a bad way, however. She wanted Lainey's full impression, making her think, study, and mull over the art with her brain, heart, and soul. Lainey felt it made her a better curator. She also loved these quiet moments with her best friend.

"I'm asking about everything," Eve corrected.

Lainey nodded. "Yes, the anger is there, but that's not the overwhelming emotion. Sadness isn't either. It's love." She glanced at Eve. "If one hadn't experienced these emotions before, all at once, I don't think they'd understand this piece. I think they'd find chaos. But isn't that what love is sometimes? Chaos?"

Eve breathed in deeply. "It can be." She nodded towards Rebecca and Cass. "But it can also be peace." She gave Lainey her full attention then. "Lainey . . ."

"Eve."

Eve looked up at the sound of her name. Adam stood nearby, a stern look on his face. Once again, she breathed in. This time, it was to reign in her anger.

"I'll be right there," she clipped.

"People are waiting to talk to you," Adam said.

"I said I'd be right there."

Though Eve kept her voice low, there was no mistaking the warning in her tone. Adam was brave enough to scowl at her but said nothing more. He also didn't go very far when he left them alone again.

"He's been especially attentive tonight," Lainey remarked. She tried keeping the bite out of the statement, but Eve's smirk told her she failed.

"Possessive is more accurate," Eve said. "And it's pissing me off."

"Do you think he knows what happened between us after the last opening?"

Eve shook her head. "I was never specific. And even if he did, that doesn't give him the right to be this way."

Lainey didn't want to disagree with Eve. But her conscience got to her. "Can you blame him for not wanting you around me?"

Eve sighed. "I know I have faults, Lainey."

"*We.*"

Eve chose not to acknowledge Lainey's self-inclusion. None involved were naïve. Nor were any of them innocent. Adam included.

"Whatever my faults, I cannot allow anyone to treat me as a possession. Not even my husband." Eve lowered her voice. "I went through all that before, Lainey. I won't do it again."

"And you shouldn't. I hate being the reason Adam is treating you this way."

"You're not." Eve raised a brow when Lainey began to argue. "Adam makes his own decisions. So do I. So do you. He realizes what he's doing, how he's treating me. He's doing it on purpose. That doesn't sit well with me no matter what excuse he's creating in his head to do it."

"Decisions are a strange thing," Lainey said as she looked back at the painting. "What you think is the right decision at the moment could turn out to be the worst decision you've ever made."

Eve felt Lainey's words in her entire body. She wondered before this night if more decisions needed to be made. Now she knew for sure. She had no clue what her future held or what Lainey's role in it would be. But Eve could eliminate at least one obstacle.

"Mrs. Sumptor-Riley?"

Eve looked over her shoulder and smiled at her new curator Lauren. Eve was extremely pleased with Lauren's work so far at the gallery. Not surprising since Lauren was vetted and recommended by Rebecca. "Yes?"

"There's a crowd gathering waiting to hear from the featured artist and the owner of the gallery."

Eve nodded. "Duty calls. Care to join me?"

"Are you trying to get under Adam's skin even more?"

"No, I'm trying to do my job with my assistant. And seeing that Jack is keeping our bartenders busy, I suspect you wouldn't mind being otherwise engaged."

Lainey smiled. "Lead the way."

Chapter Thirty-Three

Eve should have been in a good mood. The LA opening was an overwhelming success. Cass's work was a thunderous triumph much to Rebecca's delight. Cass herself, however, couldn't quite wrap her mind around people clamoring to own her work or meet the artist. What Eve loved most about the woman was her humbleness. Cass Giles was happy just being Cass Giles. As long as Rebecca was by her side, she had everything she wanted. It had been a long time since Eve had felt that way.

However, they had been back for one day, and things with Adam were even more strained. He had been pissed that Eve never returned to him when he had summoned her. And when she stymied his advances back at the hotel, he walked out, returning right before they were to leave for the airport. Eve never called him, never texted. She didn't have the energy to deal with his tantrum. Especially not when Bella was having a tantrum of her own. Eve was convinced that her young daughter felt the tension between her parents. That was another reason why she couldn't let this continue. When their problems began affecting Bella, it was time to remedy the situation. Now if she could find the courage.

"Eve?"

Eve closed her eyes and took a breath before turning to Adam.

He was sitting at the table in the breakfast nook looking as angry as ever.

"I don't want to fight, Adam. I just want to see Bella."

"She's not here."

Eve's nostrils flared. "Where is my daughter?"

"Sit down."

"Where is my daughter, Adam?"

He scoffed. "Does it always have to be your way, Eve? Everyone is so used to taking orders from you, but you take orders from no one?"

"Something like that. Bella?"

Adam sighed. "She's with Lexie. I asked her to take Bella for ice cream while we talked." He gestured to the chair across from him. "Please."

Reluctantly, she sat. Eve supposed she owed him that much. "You got me to sit. Congratulations. What now?"

Adam shook his head. This wasn't how his marriage to Eve was supposed to go. But here they were. He had given her space. He had given her time. And, yeah, he had given her a hard time in LA. Nothing worked. So, now he was giving her an ultimatum. And he was scared to death of her choice. He reached in his briefcase and took out a manila envelope and slid it over to her.

Eve laughed mirthlessly. "I really hate these things. Yet, people insist on giving them to me. What is it?" Adam remained silent. She picked up the envelope and opened it. Eve had no idea what to expect. But when she saw the contents, her blood boiled.

"You had me followed?" she asked angrily.

Adam rubbed his tired eyes irritably. "That's all you have to say? You're cheating on me, yet I'm the bad guy?"

Eve looked at the photos of her and Lainey, flipping through them one by one, recalling when and where they were. The diner by the gallery when she had taken Lainey's hand to offer comfort. Ellie's Diner laughing with Bella. Italy in the small village where they learned to make olive oil. And Paris. Up until then, the photos had been insignificant. Exposing nothing of the passion she felt for Lainey. But somehow, Adam had managed to get a picture of them kissing on the balcony of her Paris home. One that showed them partially naked the morning after they made love as they sat close and ate breakfast. And another that gave no doubt that Eve and Lainey were lovers.

"What do you want?" she asked coldly. "You obviously went through a lot of trouble to get these. Go ahead, Adam. I'm used to this. What do you want from me?"

"I want our marriage back," he stated, ignoring the pang of guilt her words inflicted on him. She was wrong to cheat, yes. But he was about to blackmail the woman he loved to keep her in his life. "We move away from here. Go back to the city. Lainey never comes near you again. She's poisoning you against me, Eve. If she wasn't in your life . . ."

"I'd be miserable," Eve finished for him. "I can't do what you ask. I'm sorry." And she genuinely was. It didn't matter how he was handling the situation. What mattered was that she had hurt him. Again. And would continue doing so until she let him go.

"Did you ever love me?" he asked dejectedly. He had been hoping that she would agree to his demands. Hadn't she been willing to stop seeing Lainey before? *Yeah, and look what happened then,* he reminded himself. No more painting and in therapy. Where was the woman he married?

"Yes. I still do."

"But not like Lainey?"

Eve stared at him for a long while. She wanted to be sure of her answer. It was a life-changing one.

"No."

"Mom?"

Lainey wiped the tears from her cheeks and smiled up at Kevin. "Thank you for not scaring the bejesus out of me."

Kevin gave her a grin that quickly went away when he noticed the tears. "Mom," he sighed. "When are you going to leave him?"

Jack had been in a mood when Lainey got home late from work.

Dinner wasn't ready, there were dishes (his) in the sink, and something Kevin really didn't need to know, they hadn't had sex in months. Though, as much as the thought of his parents doing it grossed him out, he was proud of his mom for not giving in to his dad pressuring her.

"It's not that easy."

"Bullshit!"

"Kevin!"

"I'm sorry, mom, but that's bull." He thought better of repeating the curse word. His mom could be tolerant, but he'd already been warned. Besides, he wanted to help her feel better not piss her off. "You go find a lawyer, file, and voila."

"That easy, huh?" Lainey asked with a mixture of hilarity and annoyance.

"Well, Darren and I are old enough to decide who we want to be with. I doubt dad would want to take care of us by himself anyway. Work up a custody agreement, do whatever with your possessions, and go."

Lainey's brows furrowed. "Have you been reading up on this?"

"Maybe. But it sounds like you have, too."

Lainey took a breath. Her gaze involuntarily moved to Eve's house. *If* she had the courage to do this, what would Eve do? What would happen between them? Would it even matter? Lainey shook her head. *No*, she thought. *If* she had the courage to do this, it would be for herself and her sons. Not for Eve. Even Eve herself would tell her to do that. But this wasn't a conversation she should be having with her fifteen-year-old son.

"Did you get enough to eat?"

Kevin scoffed. "It's like that? You're just going to change the subject?"

"Kevin . . ."

"I want to know what's holding you back, mom. He's an ass." He held up his hands. "Sorry, but it's true. The way he treats you isn't right. The way he belittles Darren's hobby, no, passion is wrong. And . . ."

"And what, Kevin?" Lainey asked seriously. She knew Jack and

Kevin had issues. She knew Jack wasn't easy on his sons. She also knew that everything Kevin was saying was indisputable. But there was something more behind Kevin's insistence that she leave Jack.

"Let me ask you this, mom." Kevin stood up and began to pace. "How do you think dear old dad is going to treat me when . . ." he took a deep breath. "When he finds out I'm gay."

You could hear a pin drop around them. It seemed even the evening crickets stopped chirping. Lainey was stunned. So much ran through her head at once that she couldn't hang on to just *one* of those thoughts and say *something* to her child who just revealed something so personal to her.

Kevin shook his head. "Somehow I thought you would understand. Guess I was wrong." He turned to go back inside, his heart hurting because of his mother's nonresponse.

"How do you know?"

He stopped. It wasn't the question, but the sheer emotion in his mother's voice that grabbed his attention.

"What?" he asked softly.

Lainey looked up at him. "How do you know?"

The vulnerability in her eyes told him everything he suspected was true. He came back and sat in front of her.

"I just do," he whispered. "Like you did when we were in Florida with Eve. Maybe even before that."

Lainey's eyes popped open with surprise and mortification. "What?"

Kevin chuckled. "Don't look so surprised, mom. I may be young, but we have the internet. And, you know, times are different."

"Are you calling me old?"

Kevin laughed. If she was joking with him, perhaps his news didn't disappoint her as he thought it did. "No, I'm saying the world is evolving. Maybe not fast enough, but it's better than it was. Am I wrong about you and Eve?"

Lainey opened her mouth, but nothing came out. She couldn't believe she was having this conversation with her son. Her *gay* son. Kevin was gay. That's what was running through her head now. And for some reason, it made things a little easier for her. It was utterly selfish to feel that way, but she couldn't help it. Her teenage son just became her ally.

"Okay, well, I didn't know for sure," he started again into the silence. "But in Florida, I know you didn't stay in your room."

"Oh, God!" Lainey buried her head in her hands and began to cry. "You needed me, and I wasn't there. I was . . ."

"No, mom, hey." Kevin took her hands in his, forcing her to look at him. "I didn't need anything. I just went in there to see if I was right."

"You were twelve!"

"And I knew who *I* was. It helped me knowing that you could be like me. Do you understand? I wanted you and Eve to be together so bad that I thought I was just making things up in my head. So, I waited until Darren was asleep and I snuck out. I went to your room hoping you wouldn't be there."

Lainey stood up. "This is a lot to process, Kevin. You. *Me*. You knowing about me!"

"It's a good thing!" He sprang up and stepped in front of his mom. "I don't know why you stayed with dad. Or why she married Adam. But if it was because you were afraid of how we'd feel, I can tell you I'm so okay with it. Darren doesn't know. At least I don't think he does. But he loves Eve, mom."

"She's married, Kevin. She has Bella. Even if I leave your father . . ."

"When."

Lainey sighed. "Leaving your father doesn't mean Eve and I will end up together, Kevin. We made choices . . ."

"Dumb choices! Sorry. I'm sorry. But tell me this, okay? Have you *ever* loved dad the way you love Eve?"

Lainey's eyes once again traveled towards Eve's house. The one she shared with her husband and daughter.

"No."

"Were you ever *in* love with me, Eve? You said the words, but did you ever feel them?"

She wanted to say yes. She told herself every day since that fateful night she got shot that that was how she felt. It was right. It was good. It was . . . not true.

"I tried."

Adam sat back heavily and sniffed. "Tried."

"I'm sorry, Adam. I wanted . . ."

"Lainey!" he yelled. "You wanted Lainey, but she's already married, not that that stopped you. You knew she wasn't going to leave her husband and kids for you, so I'm the consolation prize!"

Eve bit her lip and counted to ten. He had every right to be upset, but he wasn't exactly innocent in all this.

"You knew," she said finally. "You knew how I felt about Lainey. You knew we had been together before you asked me to marry you. You *knew* those feelings were still there. Why did you marry me?"

"Because I love you!"

"You love the *thought* of me, Adam! You love the side of me that's strong and successful. But the moment you saw the flaws, you sent me to therapy. Did you think it would "cure" my feelings for Lainey? That I would learn it was just because I was "mad at men" and therefore I slept with a woman? Once I learned that I'd figure out that you were the love of my life all along?"

Eve could tell by the look on his face that that was precisely what Adam had hoped for and shook her head.

"I should have known," he said. "Woodrow's niece is a lesbian, right? Is she one, too? Did she talk you into all this?"

Eve's jaws clenched as she ground her teeth. "I won't even dignify that with an answer," she said dangerously low.

Adam hung his head. "That . . . I didn't mean that. I'm just frustrated. You were the one, Eve! The woman I've always dreamt of. Different than all the others."

"But I'm not. You're romanticizing this relationship, Adam. I kept you at arm's length for most of the time we were dating. I never let you stay with me. You were constantly upset with me because I wasn't open enough with you." She looked him in the eye. "Then I was. And my past came up and bit us both in the ass. You may pretend you don't blame me for that, but you do. I turned out to be different than the woman you thought I was. A woman with a past. With issues. With emotional baggage. A woman that wasn't always strong. It's in *those* moments I see you look at me as though I'm a stranger."

"That's not fair."

"You're right. It's not. I can't pretend to be who you need me to be, Adam. I tried. I can't even paint because I've been trying so hard to cut off the emotions inside of me that make me different than who you want me to be."

"You've survived without painting, Eve. You can survive without Lainey." He leaned his elbows on the table and looked at her pleadingly. "You were going to do it before. You said you would stop seeing her if that's what I wanted. Well, I'm telling you now that's what I want. We could be so good together. All we need is some space. Away from here. Away from Lainey. We could find our way back."

"You don't get it, do you, Adam? There isn't a "back" to find. We were never there. I tried until I realized it shouldn't be that hard. It should be effortless. It never was. Not with you."

Adam stared at her. She basically just told him their entire marriage was a sham. He clenched his hands into fists, trying to keep a hold of his temper. "Where does that leave us?" he asked through clenched teeth.

"You tell me. You have the photos, Adam." Eve tilted her head, narrowing her eyes. "Are you going to give them to Jack?"

He scoffed. "You'd like that, wouldn't you? He finds out she's cheating, with a woman no less, and he divorces her leaving her free to be with you. You think I'm going to help you along with that?"

"Then what is it you want, Adam?"

"I told you what I wanted, Eve. I want you. I want our marriage. I want to raise our daughter together. But you want to give that up."

Eve's spine went rigid. "I'm not giving my daughter up, Adam. It's not fair to either of us to stay in this marriage, but if you think I won't fight for Bella, you don't know me well at all."

"You cheated, Eve. What makes you think you have the right to dictate the terms of what happens between us?"

"So righteous," Eve said snidely. "Have you ever known me not to be prepared for whatever life throws at me, Adam? I may be temporarily dazed, but in the end, I will always win. Do you know why?"

"Because you throw your money at it?" Adam answered hotly.

"No. Because I never let my guard down. You see, everyone wants something from me, Adam. And it usually comes down to two things. Sex or money. Sometimes both." *Everyone except Lainey,* she thought silently. Perhaps that's why Eve fell for her in the first place. She was the only one that ever wanted Eve for herself. Flaws and all. Especially the flaws.

"You think I wanted something from you?"

"You did. Sex was our thing. After what happened to you and the truth about Lainey and me came out, I felt the shift in our relationship. Then came the need for money from you. You wanted your own firm. I believed in your work, so I had no problem helping you. But I didn't do it blindly out of love, Adam."

"Of course you didn't. Why in the hell would Eve Sumptor do anything out of love?"

"Oh, I have." Eve thought of the Buddha she got for Lainey. It wasn't expected. It wasn't even wanted. But she bought it for Lainey because Eve loved her. "But business is business. I am neither naïve nor stupid. You wanted me as a silent partner, but that doesn't mean I don't know everything that goes on in that building. *Everything.*"

Adam's eyes snapped up. He shook his head slowly. "What does that mean?"

"That means I know about you and Claudia, Adam."

Adam stood abruptly. "Whatever it is you *think* you know." He stopped, changing tactics in his head. "I told you, Eve, Claudia and I ended way before you and I got together."

Eve nodded. "I know. Until about three weeks ago, right?"

"That was nothing. A one-time thing, Eve. You were in Paris and I — I just heard about . . ." He scrubbed his face. "You were with Lainey!"

"Tit for tit?" she asked, purposefully making a play on the words. "This is your M.O., Adam. You hired Claudia knowing full well I would vet everyone. You wanted me to be jealous. More so, you wanted someone around you that could feed your ego. She's still into you. You liked that."

"I wanted *you*, Eve. I *want* you."

"You wanted me to be the one that fed that ego. The woman on your arm that other men would envy." She was perilously close to sounding conceited. But she had been in this game long enough to know how things worked. "The woman who has no limits in bed."

"Obviously," he sneered. "How did you know?"

"You should be smarter than to have your rendezvous in a building that is owned by me. So, now we're back to; what do you want, Adam?"

"What if he wants to keep you boys away from me?"

Lainey was pacing. She and Kevin were still out on the back porch discussing the pros and cons of Lainey divorcing Jack. Well, Kevin was discussing the pros. Lainey was still worried about the consequences.

"Mom, he's not going to want us. Especially me."

Lainey shook her head. The last thing she wanted to do was badmouth Jack to his sons. She didn't know how to make Kevin understand the risks.

"Sweetie, your father loves you. But he also knows that the way to hurt me most is by taking you and Darren away from me."

"I won't let that happen, mom. Darren and I will tell anyone who will listen that we don't want to stay with him."

"What if he finds out about Eve?"

Kevin looked at Eve's house over his shoulder then back at his mom. "Honestly, I think dad would be scared to go up against Eve. Who wouldn't be?" He leaned in close and whispered dramatically. "*I think she's mafia.*"

Lainey laughed. "What?"

Kevin shrugged. "I'm kidding. Kinda. I mean, the woman has connections, ma. And if you want things done, all you have to do is ask Eve. It's just weird. Cool, but weird."

Lainey's belief that Eve wasn't in the mafia faltered. Her eyes slid towards the house again. Hadn't she wondered the same thing before? Could it be? *Nah,* Lainey thought definitively. She would know something like that, wouldn't she? Who cared that the evidence was strong? It was all circumstantial. *Great. Now I have it in my head that the woman I love is a mobster.*

"Did I freak you out?" Kevin grinned.

"No." Lainey rolled her eyes. "Maybe. Anyway, we were talking about you and Darren."

"We were talking about you leaving dad. Listen, do us all a favor and talk to a lawyer. I'm sure Eve has one who's, like, the best of the best."

Lainey shook her head again. "I can't tell Eve about this. Not until I make some kind of decision."

Kevin sighed. "For what it's worth, ma, I think that's a bad idea."

Good lord, when did he get so grown up? If it hadn't been apparent before, it certainly was tonight. Besides the occasional "teenage speak" Kevin had been articulate, knowledgeable, and supportive. All the things she could *not* attribute to Jack.

"You do, huh? May I ask why?"

"Because she loves you just as much as you love her. Don't you think she'd want to help you through this?"

Lainey blushed. "Part of me wishes you didn't know that. But that's exactly the reason I shouldn't say anything to her. She has so much going on right now. Plus, there's Adam and Bella. It wouldn't be fair of me to put this on her shoulders as well."

Kevin scratched his nose thoughtfully. "Well, I guess ultimately that's up to you."

"You still don't agree."

"Nope," Kevin answered even though it wasn't a question. "This world is, like, full of fear and stuff, ya know? The LGBTQ community lives every day in fear of loving who they love. My friend Mia? The one that was getting bullied? She's a lesbian. Wyatt and Landon mess with her all the time. That's why I walk her to classes. They say stupid things to her about just needing a real man to realize she's not into girls. I hate it. And dad's no better. I hear his comments when he sees a gay person on TV."

He walked up to his mom and took her hands, looking her dead in the eye.

"I don't want to hide who I am anymore. And I don't think you should either. The happiest I've ever seen you are those moments you're with Eve. What's the point of holding back? All you're doing is wasting the time you should be living happily and together. Let Eve help you. Who knows what could happen?"

Chapter Thirty-Four

Eve sat at her desk staring at the legal papers she held, but not seeing them. There was a part of her that couldn't believe this was happening. And then there was a part of her that was relieved. When she had promised Dr. Woodrow she would discuss her feelings with Adam this wasn't the way she had anticipated doing that.

Obviously, she would rather have come to terms with Adam without Lainey being in the crosshairs so to speak. However, Adam had finally shown his true colors, which made this surprisingly easier for Eve. Their conversation lasted way beyond the time Lexie brought Bella home. The only break was when Eve insisted on spending time with her young daughter and tucking her in. Unfortunately, she couldn't hide out in her little girl's room all night.

Instead, she spent hours listening to Adam run the gamut of pleading, anger, bargaining, and being downright nasty. Eve allowed most of it because of her role in the collapse of their relationship. When they finally got to the root of Adam's demands, a piece of Eve's cynical heart refused to be shocked. The problem was, the piece that loved Adam, shattered.

"Eve?"

Eve tucked the papers into her desk drawer and looked up at Lainey with a smile.

"Hey, come in. I missed riding into work with you this morning."

Lainey had texted Eve early that she would be driving into the city by herself that morning. Something about a meeting, but Lainey had been somewhat vague. All Eve knew was that it wasn't a work meeting.

"I'm sorry. I had a couple of things to take care of." Lainey discreetly took a deep breath. If she were lucky, Eve wouldn't notice how nervous she was.

Eve watched Lainey closely as she sat in the guest chair. Something was definitely off. "Is everything okay?"

"Yeah!" Lainey cleared her throat. That had been a little too enthusiastic which meant she just tipped her hand. "We need to talk."

Eve wondered if her heart actually stopped or if it just felt like it. "Alright."

Lainey nodded her head once. Decision made. "This talk needs to be completely honest. No worrying about anyone's feelings."

Well, shit. Now Eve's heart was beating furiously. This did not sound good at all. She stood and walked around her desk, leaning back on it once she was in front of Lainey.

"Don't stand there," Lainey said quickly. "Not like that. That's how you were when you told me I was just an experiment for you."

Eve pushed away from her desk as though it were on fire. "Lainey," she dropped to her knees in front of Lainey and grasped her hands. "You know I didn't mean that."

Lainey gave her a weak smile. "I know. That doesn't mean it doesn't hurt still when I think about it."

"I'm so sorry."

Lainey waved away the apology. "That's not what I'm here to talk about Eve. Could we go over to the couch? And maybe tell Mikey that we'll be unavailable for a while?"

Oh, boy. After last night's epic showdown with Adam, Eve wasn't sure she was up for a fight. Not with Lainey. The fact that Lainey was most likely the only one that could defeat Eve was not lost on her. However, as she always would, Eve complied and sent down a message to Mikey telling him they were not available until further notice. Once that was done, she joined Lainey on the small couch.

"All yours," she said softly.

I wish. I hope, Lainey thought with longing. She hoped to hell she was doing the right thing. If this goes wrong, Kevin was so grounded.

"Okay. First, I must ask you a question. No judgment, but I need to know the truth."

Eve nodded. She was wracking her brain thinking of questions Lainey may ask her. Was it about her past? Was it about Adam? Would she ask her again how much money she had? Eve nearly shook her head at that thought. Lainey had been curious when they first met, but money wasn't important enough for a conversation like this.

"Are you a mobster?"

Eve froze for a split second before she burst into laughter. "What?" she managed while wiping tears from her eyes.

Lainey squinted. "Come on. It's a legitimate question. One, I might add, you haven't answered."

"No!" Eve said, still laughing. "Why would you think that?"

"You are rich," Lainey began, ticking off points on her fingers as she went through them. "You are friends with powerful people who do favors for you. There have been people trying to kill you. Blackmail is always a concern."

"Okay, okay." Although Lainey was presenting a good argument, Eve couldn't stop chuckling. "You know where the money came from. I took what my mom gave me and turned it into successful ventures. Art is a very lucrative business that attracts the elite. By catering to these people and making generous donations, I've earned a few small favors here and there. We won't get into the people trying to kill me. I'm hoping that's over for good now. And blackmail is always possible when your finances aren't completely private. Where is this coming from?"

Lainey shrugged with a hint of embarrassment. "Kevin mentioned something last night and it kind of stuck with me. It made sense. A little."

Eve smiled. Kevin was a teenager with an active imagination. He also loved a good mystery. Of course, Lainey would never have told him the intricate details of Eve's life. But Eve had his principal fired within mere minutes. She could see that imagination going off by that alone.

"I assure you, honey, my businesses are legitimate. I'm not paying anyone off or extorting anyone. No tax fraud, no money laundering. There is nothing illegal going on."

"What about some of the paintings and how they were acquired?" Lainey reminded her. When Eve had made a trip to Paris a couple of years ago, she came back the proud owner of multi-million-dollar paintings. Ones that were previously owned by the same man that brutalized Eve at a young age. Eve had said they were "payment for services rendered." Lainey had hated that explanation then as much as she did now. "And what about holding Katherine at some abandoned warehouse?"

Oh, yeah. Eve had forgotten she had confessed the warehouse thing to Lainey. "I explained the paintings, Lainey. That had nothing to do with being a mobster and everything to do with revenge on those who hurt me. Same with the subsequent consequences that occurred after that meeting."

There would always be a pang of guilt for the loss of life that resulted, no matter who the men were. She looked at Lainey intently. If she had said yes to being a mobster, would that have caused her regret?

"I also explained what happened with Katherine. I took her there because Tony didn't know about it. I was protecting her."

"I know." Lainey sighed. "I'm just trying to understand, Eve. Things like this don't happen to normal people."

Eve laughed again. "I said I wasn't a mobster. I *didn't* say I was normal." She laid a hand on Lainey's knee. "You wanted this to be an honest conversation. I agreed to that. No lying."

Lainey took a deep breath and nodded. "I believe you. I mean, I didn't actually believe that you *were*, I just had to hear it from you."

"What would you have done if I had said yes?"

Lainey's mouth worked, but no words came out. "I don't know," she said finally. "Nothing, I guess. It wouldn't have changed anything." To Lainey's surprise, she meant that. If Eve had said yes, Lainey would still be leaving Jack. She would always love Eve whether Eve stayed with Adam or not. And she would still be Eve's best friend if that was all she was allowed to be.

"Okay, well, now that that's cleared up — I hope — was there something else you need to get off your chest?"

"Yes. This is where it gets difficult. And if you think having Dr. Woodrow with us would be better, we can schedule a session if you like."

"Would that make you more comfortable?" Eve asked causing Lainey to chuckle.

"You're starting to sound like Woodrow." She thought about it. Weighed the pros and cons. What appealed to her most was staying right here. Just her and Eve laying the cards on the table once and for all with no interference. "I'd rather it just be us."

Eve nodded. "What do you need to know, Lainey?"

"Why did you choose Adam? Why didn't you fight for me?"

The question hit Eve in the gut like a punch from a heavyweight champion. Hadn't she been asking herself the same question? If Lainey wanted a truthful answer, Eve would have to speak from her heart. This time without fear.

"I thought it was the right thing to do."

"Because you loved Adam more?"

Eve let out a short, mirthless laugh. "No. Because you were married. You had just told me that you wanted to be with your husband. That you were in love with him. And you being in my life nearly got you killed. I didn't think I was good for you."

She closed her eyes, unable to face Lainey. *So much for the no fear.* "I loved Adam very much. But I was *in* love with you, Lainey. You were the dream. You were the one I wanted to be with. But, because of fear, just like I did when I stood over there and told you that you were an experiment, I lied." She opened her eyes. "I looked you in the eye, and I lied to you when I told you I understood everything you said to me. You were telling me how you were in love with Jack and wanted to be with him. I *had* to tell you I understood. Someone was still out there after me. I thought I was doing the right thing by letting you go back to your safe life. No matter how much I wanted it to be you I was going home with."

Tears cascaded down Lainey's cheeks. Eve just told her everything she had dreamt of for more than two years. Now it was her turn to be honest with Eve. *God, let this be the right thing to do.* Lainey had no idea how Eve would take what she was about to say. Especially since she and Adam were still married. But Eve did just tell her that *she* was the one she was in love with and not Adam. Lainey held on to that to boost her courage.

"I lied, too," Lainey confessed quietly. She shook her head when she thought about the decision she made back then. It was easy to think "what if" and feel sorry for the time they lost together. "I was so scared, Eve. Before I met you, my life was boring." She stopped. That sounded terrible for a mother to say. "I love my boys very much. But I had lost myself, you know that. Then you came along, and my life changed completely. Soon I was in this world where I didn't belong. It was as terrifying as it was exciting. You were flying me around in a private jet, buying me $65,000 Buddhas, taking my kids on a VIP trip to Disney, and people wanted to talk to me about my work with your gallery."

Lainey scooted closer to Eve and took her hand before continuing. This was going to be the hard part.

"Then came the threats. People were getting hurt or killed, some right in front of you. My God, Eve, their blood was splattered on you, you were so close. Security followed me everywhere I went. They followed my boys. And then came that night. When Tony held me at gunpoint, I wondered what happened to my boring life. Instead of watching TV with my sons, I was watching you do and say unthinkable things all to keep me safe." Lainey shivered at the memory. If there were a way to get the image of Eve unbuttoning her shirt for her father or hearing him call her a whore out of her head, she would do it in an instant. "I was so afraid. I was afraid of your life and what mine had become. I was afraid *for* your life. I was afraid of never seeing my boys again and the danger I had put them in. And most of all, I was afraid of losing you."

Eve wiped a tear from her cheek. "So, you let me go?"

"Oh, honey. I think I knew it didn't end with Tony. I could see it in your eyes that there was something more about to happen. You were so cruel to me in order to get me out of your life the first time. I didn't know if I could survive that again. Even after the threat was over, I always had the fear that you would believe you weren't good for me. I was scared that the next time you said goodbye to me, you would stay away." She took another breath before she asked the next question. Lainey knew the agony Eve went through when Adam was kidnapped and tortured. She hated to bring it up. But if they were going to clear the air, Lainey needed to know it all. "If it had been me and not Adam that Laurence took, what would you have done?"

Died. Adam being taken by Laurence was devastating. If it had been Lainey, it would have been debilitating.

"I would have found you like I did Adam. I would have died for you."

"Exactly." Lainey squeezed Eve's hands. "That's what scares me so much, Eve. You took a bullet for me already. Do you ever stop to think what it would do to me if you *did* die for me? So, out of fear, I told you I was in love with Jack. It made it a little easier when Jack came to the hospital worried about me. I thought maybe the prospect of losing me had made him see what he had in me. It didn't last, though. By the time I realized he was the same old Jack, I was afraid he'd keep the boys from me if I tried to leave him. All he had to do was say that being with me put them in danger."

"And it would have been true because of me," Eve stated sadly.

Lainey sighed. She wished she could ease Eve's mind. But it was the truth. But it was a truth that no longer mattered anymore.

"Do you remember when I told you I felt bipolar when I was with you?" Lainey asked. Eve nodded silently. "It was because I realized I made the wrong choice and didn't know how to fix it."

"But you didn't. You were right, Lainey. Being with me caused Adam a lot of pain."

Lainey shook her head. "You would have had me out of the country at the first sign of trouble. Hidden away on some private island and made it impossible to get to me, the boys, or Bella. As you did. I should have known that then. I know that now. So no, I wasn't right, Eve. What made me feel so mercurial was the fact that I knew I wasn't in love with Jack. Based on the way I feel about you; I was never in love with him. But I kept up the façade because I knew you were happy with Adam. Seeing you with him, though, made me realize how wrong my decision was and it's killing me inside. I'm jealous. I know how wrong that is to tell you, but . . ."

Eve stood and walked to her desk leaving behind a confused, and slightly hurt, Lainey. She took the papers she had been looking at earlier out of her desk. Once she settled back down next to the woman she loved, she handed them over.

Lainey unfolded the papers and read them. She considered herself an intelligent woman. However, for some reason, she wasn't comprehending what she was seeing. "I don't understand."

"I'm divorcing Adam."

"What?"

"I've been contemplating this for a while now, but things came to a head last night."

"Last night?" Lainey swore at herself silently. She sounded like a goddamn idiot. But she had been caught completely off guard by Eve's announcement. Her emotions and thoughts were jumbled chaos.

Eve kicked herself for not easing into this news with Lainey. It was out there now, and Eve had to tell Lainey about the photos. God, she didn't want to tell her about the images. *Honesty.*

"Yes, last night. There was a reason he's been insufferable lately."

The fog cleared from Lainey's mind slightly. She didn't like the tone of Eve's voice. And if divorce was the answer to Adam's reason, it couldn't be good.

"What happened?"

Here's to losing Lainey before I have her. "He's been having me followed," Eve divulged. "Lainey, he has photos. Most of them are innocent. Except for the ones from Paris."

Lainey's hand clenched around the papers. "Jesus. He knows about us in Paris?" Eve nodded, and Lainey searched the papers for information she couldn't seem to find. "Oh, Eve. Is he using the photos against you? Is he going to take Bella away from you?"

Eve's eyebrows rose. "You're not concerned that he'll give the photos to Jack?"

"I couldn't care less if he gives them to Jack. I've already begun the process of filing for divorce. Eve, is he threatening to take Bella?"

It took Eve a full ten seconds to comprehend what Lainey just said. "Did you say . . . Lainey, did you just say you're divorcing Jack?"

"Hmm?" Lainey looked up from the papers and caught Eve's flabbergasted look. "Oh. Um, yes. That's where I was this morning."

"Why didn't you tell me?"

"Honey, I'm telling you now. As weirdly coincidental as it sounds, I made the decision last night."

"Last night?"

Lainey couldn't help but laugh. It was as though they were taking turns being stunned into stupidity.

"Let's focus on one thing at a time, okay?" Lainey suggested. "First, could you answer if Adam is threatening you with these photos? Are you in danger of losing Bella?"

"He tried," Eve answered honestly. "But no, I'm not losing Bella. Adam realized that separating me from Bella was not what was best for anyone."

"On his own?" Lainey asked carefully.

Eve chuckled. "Are we back to the mobster thing again? Do you think I pulled his fingernails off one by one until he agreed with me?"

"No?"

A full belly laugh escaped from Eve before she could stop it. This wasn't the best time to be laughing, but the look on Lainey's face was hilarious. Uncertainty with a little "he would deserve it" mixed in.

"There was something more he wanted from me," Eve finally got out. She cleared her throat and wiped her tears. This next part wasn't funny at all. "He tried to get me to stay with him and move back to the city."

"And let me guess, never talk to me again?"

"Good guess. When I told him I couldn't do that, he did bring up Bella. I let him know that I would use every ounce of power and money I have into fighting him for her. He said he deserved something for what I've put him through."

Lainey scoffed, then apologized for interrupting. "What does he think he *deserves*?"

"His company free and clear of me. And enough money to keep it going without Sumptor, Inc. or Sumptor Galleries as a client."

"Money? That's what he wanted? He wouldn't fight for Bella, but he'd fight for your money?"

Eve shrugged. "Bella is worth everything to me. If he signs over full custody to me for a few bucks, I'm okay with that."

"You're okay with that?" Lainey repeated, not believing a word of it. "How long did it take him to bring up money? Is that why he had you followed? So he could hopefully get something to blackmail you with?"

Lainey was angry. Eve didn't blame her. She had felt the same way when Adam finally revealed what he wanted. Ultimately, he had nothing to hurt Eve with. He could have if he hadn't cheated himself. But his ego was bigger than his brain this time. Of course, Eve had yet to tell Lainey that bit of information. *That* should be a fun conversation.

"I've become used to it. As I told Adam, most people want something from me. Mostly it's sex or money. If he can't have one, he'll take the other."

"Do you think that's what I want from you, Eve?"

Eve smiled at her. "You're the only one that's ever looked beyond the money and beyond my body. You're the only one that's gotten to the core of who I am. So, no."

"Good." Lainey blew out a breath.

"Now, about you divorcing Jack."

"Hang on, I'm not done with being pissed off at Adam. I know we were wrong doing what we did, but if he can use this to hurt you or take Bella away from you . . ."

"But he did it, too," Eve revealed.

Lainey frowned. "Did what?"

"He cheated."

Again, Lainey found it difficult to comprehend the words coming out of Eve's mouth. Eve Sumptor was the ultimate woman. An incredible lover. Why on earth would anyone cheat on her?

"He cheated on *you*? Is he insane?"

Eve chuckled. "I can't blame him. I did the same. It doesn't make either of us right. It is what it is."

"How can you be so blasé about this, Eve?"

She shrugged. "I'm not blasé. I'm accepting my fate. I had Reghan draw those papers up a couple of weeks ago." Eve sighed softly. "Honey, this was inevitable. I don't love Adam the way I should. It isn't fair to him or me. Or to you," she added quietly.

Lainey felt that small admission in her soul. She may not have been the main reason Eve was divorcing Adam, but Eve's apparent love for her was a factor. Lainey wanted to reach out and touch Eve, but she supposed it was her turn to talk. Though, since Eve brought it up . . .

"Do you think Adam will use the photos against me? He and Jack aren't exactly friends, but if it means hurting me in the process, could he give Jack ammunition against me?"

"He said he wasn't interested in helping me *get you* — his words. Besides, I have my own ammunition that assures Adam stays quiet. Not bullets!" she said quickly when Lainey gave her a look. "I have video of his little rendezvous. If he wants his money, those photos of you and me are to be destroyed."

"I still can't believe this is happening."

"I can't believe you're divorcing Jack." *I had hoped.* "How? What?" Eve paused and blew out a frustrated breath. It wasn't often that she was at a loss for words. Lainey seemed to be the only one that brought that out of her. "What happened?"

God, she's beautiful. Even when bewildered. "It's not getting any better with him, Eve. When my boys notice and beg me to leave their father, it's time to listen."

"Why didn't you tell me it was bad, Lainey?"

Lainey lifted a shoulder. "I didn't know how. I thought it was my punishment for not trusting in you or our love when I had the chance."

"Honey, you had your boys to think about. I understood that then. I understand it now."

"Well, now those boys are old enough to choose who they want to be with. As for me, I've come to see Jack for who he is. He doesn't want me, Eve. He wants a submissive wife who will bend to his will. I've been around you too long to be that woman anymore."

"Don't give me credit for your accomplishments, Lainey. You were a strong woman before me. *If* I had anything to do with it, it was merely to remind you of who you are." She gave Lainey one of her signature winks. "So, Kevin and Darren would choose to be with you?" Lainey nodded. "Would that change if I was in the picture?" Eve asked carefully.

Being in Lainey's life the way Eve wanted to be was not guaranteed. She knew that Lainey's boys would always come first, as they should. If being with Eve would cause problems, Eve would bow out.

"No," Lainey answered, interrupting Eve's internal musings. "Kevin is encouraging us to be together." She smiled secretly as she waited for what she had just said to click in Eve's mind.

Eve nodded thoughtfully. Then . . .

"Wait, what?"

Lainey chuckled. "I think I had a little more of a shocked reaction. Kevin knows about us."

"What?" Eve repeated in complete shock. "How?"

Lainey was enjoying seeing Eve rattled a little too much. "Apparently, he's known since Disney."

"Disney!? He was twelve! How? Were we careless? God, Lainey, I'm so sorry."

Lainey grabbed Eve's agitated hand. As intriguing as it was to see someone like Eve Sumptor off—balance, Lainey couldn't let Eve take responsibility for this.

"Hey, don't apologize. We were careful. You told me once that kids were more perceptive than we wanted to believe. Kevin proved that to me last night. But I think there's a good reason for his perceptiveness."

Lainey filled Eve in on her entire conversation with Kevin. Of course, she had asked for Kevin's permission to do so. He readily agreed if it meant his mom would be seeking Eve's help.

"Kevin is gay," Eve recapped. "He hoped we were together and that we'll get together again. And he wanted you to come to me for help. Did I get all that?"

"Yes."

"Does he really think I'm mafia?"

Lainey shrugged with a grin. "Probably. But that's a good thing. It'll keep him in line."

Eve shook her head, smiling. Honestly, after her marathon argument with Adam, she wasn't sure she would smile again for a while. The news that Lainey was divorcing Jack, however, made her want to skip around New York with joy. She was most likely going to go to hell for that. She'd been to hell before. At least this time, it was her choice.

"Why didn't you come to me for help with a lawyer?" she asked mildly. "I would have paid anything to make sure you get everything you want."

"Because I needed to do this for myself, Eve. I could tell you that I'm leaving Jack for you or Kevin and Darren. But the truth is, I'm leaving Jack because I honestly never wanted to be married to him. So many of my decisions have been made out of fear. Of being alone. Of not being loved. Of not being *enough*."

Lainey stood up and walked to the window. "Jack never once made me feel like I was enough. Or loved. Or even a part of a loving relationship. My parents never wanted kids. They did their best, but as soon as I was of age, they were pushing me to get married. I was desperate enough to agree to marry Jack because I couldn't take their indifference anymore. All I asked in return was that they paid for my education. Once I graduated, I got married. You know how Jack is. Utilizing my degree wasn't part of the agreement. He wanted a housewife. A mother for his children that he wanted right away. He allowed me to go to school and that was enough."

Eve came up behind Lainey and laid her hands on Lainey's shoulders. "Why have you never told me about your parents before?"

"Because it didn't matter. I may not talk to them much, but they're still here. It felt wrong complaining about disinterested parents after what you've been through."

"Honey." Eve turned Lainey to her. "We're not in a competition. Things that have happened to us in our past affects us. No matter what it is. I don't want you to keep things from me because you think it's insignificant. *Everything* about you is significant to me."

"I wasn't trying to keep anything from you, Eve. Truly, it just wasn't important until now." Lainey leaned into Eve, asking for and receiving just a small amount of Eve's strength. "I went to see Reghan this morning. For reasons that now make sense to me, she gave me a referral. What do you think about that?"

Eve wrapped her arms around Lainey protectively. "I think Reghan is a shark and will send you to another shark," she chuckled. "I trust her to send you to the best."

Lainey looked up at Eve. "Reghan thinks she's the best."

Eve laughed. "True. But she knows and cares about you. She'll do right by you. Did you meet with whomever she referred you to?"

Lainey nodded. "I liked her. She seemed knowledgeable and fierce enough to give Reghan a run for her money. She doesn't think we'll have any problems getting me custody of the boys due to their preferences."

"But?" Eve asked hearing the doubt in Lainey's voice.

"But a judge doesn't always listen to kids. What if Jack is given custody? What if my relationship with you is revealed? I can't lose you, but I won't allow my sons to stay with Jack alone. Particularly Kevin."

"Do you think he would be in danger?"

"I think you know how Jack is, Eve. He has never made it a secret how he feels about things that don't conform to his view of the world. I will not subject Kevin to that scrutiny. Especially now. Jack's temper has been getting consistently worse. My defying him makes it worse."

"Has he been threatening you? Hurting you?"

"Not yet."

Eve tensed. She could practically feel herself vibrating with anger. "What does not yet mean?" she asked tightly.

"It means there's the normal emotional shit he puts me through almost every day. But it's getting more volatile. He's grabbed me a few times, as you've seen." Lainey, too, felt the anger exuding from Eve's rigid body. "But it feels like he's ready to explode. It has come to the point where Kevin rarely leaves me alone with him anymore."

"Lainey, why haven't you told me this?" Eve stopped and took a breath. This was not the time to be scolding Lainey. "I would have been there for you."

"I know you would have, honey. You've been going through so much lately." Lainey touched a fingertip to Eve's lips before she could argue. "I'm asking for your help now. Don't let him get my sons."

Eve kissed Lainey's fingertip. "I won't," she vowed. "I'm guessing Jack doesn't know, yet?"

"No," Lainey confirmed.

"Do you want me there when you tell him?"

Lainey smiled nervously. "I would, but I'm afraid he's already going to blame you. I don't know what he will do if you're there."

"You don't think I can handle him?" Eve asked with a raised brow.

"I don't want you to have to."

"It's your choice, Lainey, but I'd rather not have you do this alone. You can have him served at work, or I can be with you. James can be outside in case Jack causes problems. You and the boys can pack a few things and come home with me once it's done."

Lainey pursed her lips. She had to admit that telling Jack by herself was daunting. But going next door to the home Eve shared with Adam wasn't exactly appealing.

"You think going next door is a good idea?" she asked.

"Bella and I are moving back to my apartment here in the city," Eve explained. "Adam is moving out of the house, and we'll most likely sell it."

"You're not wasting any time," Lainey remarked with surprise.

"I see no reason to. I've wasted enough time with all this."

"Do you think Bella is going to understand why she and mommy are not living with her daddy anymore?"

Eve considered Lainey's question carefully. "I think she'll be confused for a while. All I can do is love her and answer any questions she may have truthfully."

Even if those questions involve me, Lainey wondered silently. *Will I be involved?*

"Where do we go from here?" she asked aloud. "I mean, I'm not going to lie anymore about wanting to be with you. But is there some sort of grace period? Do you even want . . ."

"Yes," Eve answered before Lainey could finish the question. "I want to be with you. I've wanted it the moment I met you. I don't know about any "grace period" or whatever. All I know is I want to be free to love you in public the way I love you in my heart."

Lainey sighed happily. "One step at a time?" she asked. This would be new territory for them both. And Lainey imagined they would have obstacles to overcome. However, they could be happy as long as they conquered those obstacles together.

"One step at a time," Eve agreed. "Big, gigantic steps. Towards each other. Because, honestly, I'm tired of not being with you."

Lainey laughed. "What do you think Dr. Woodrow would say about all this?"

"Is that your way of telling me I need to schedule an appointment?"

"No!" Lainey pushed Eve playfully. "Though, it couldn't hurt to have another opinion on what's going on."

"I'll call," Eve smiled.

Chapter Thirty-Five
Therapy

The beginning.

"Thank you for taking the time to see us," Eve said as they walked into Dr. Woodrow's office. It was the middle of the afternoon, and oddly enough, the atmosphere felt different. Perhaps that was because Eve felt lighter than she had in years. They hadn't broken the news to Jack, yet. First things first.

"My pleasure. I'm glad I had an opening this afternoon." Willamena gestured towards the two chairs. "Lainey, it's always nice to see you." She didn't miss the fact that the ladies were standing very close but not touching.

"Despite why we come here, it's nice to see you as well." Lainey smiled genuinely at the doctor.

"There's an aura of change around you two," Willamena stated. "Has something happened?"

Eve glanced at Lainey, then looked at Dr. Woodrow. "I see your degree isn't just for show," she teased.

"It's very hard finding those in the Cracker Jack boxes. I was one of the lucky ones," Willamena grinned. She laid her notebook on her lap and picked up her pen. Afternoons were usually busy for her, but she'd had a late cancellation. She had planned to catch up on paperwork when Eve had called. "So?"

"I'm divorcing Adam," Eve revealed with little emotion. She noted that the pen Dr. Woodrow was fidgeting with stopped.

"I think you shocked the poor doctor," Lainey chuckled. "I don't mean to add on to that, but I'm divorcing Jack."

"Oh my." Willamena couldn't even bring herself to open her notebook. Instead, she reached for her cup of tea. After taking a long, thoughtful sip, she focused on the couple in front of her. "You've made your decisions. Does that include being together?"

"Yes," they answered together.

"However," Eve continued. "Our decisions were made independently and for additional reasons than just us wanting to be together."

"Would you like to discuss those reasons?" Dr. Woodrow asked.

"You're such a shrink," Eve muttered humorously.

"That's what they told me when they handed me that piece of paper up there," Willamena winked.

Lainey touched Eve's arm lightly. It was a sign to Eve that it was time to take this seriously.

"Adam has been having me followed. He knows about Paris. Last night, he decided to confront me."

"Followed? Does that mean there's evidence of what transpired between you two?" she asked, addressing both women.

"Yes, but it's not a factor."

"Oh?"

"He had his own indiscretion. We've come to an agreement on the divorce."

"I take it that includes custody?"

"Yes."

"Convenient, don't you think?" Skepticism wasn't always a part of Dr. Woodrow's job. However, she had been in the business long enough to know that things that seem too good to be true usually were.

"I do," Eve agreed. "Believe me, doc, I have my eyes open. I understand who Adam is now." Thankfully, Eve had told Lainey of her suspicions on the way here, so this was not new to her. "He could have confronted me when I returned from Paris. But he waited."

"Why do you think he did that?"

"I know why," Eve responded. "He was waiting until after the opening of the gallery in LA. He handed out business cards the entire night while he paraded around with me on his arm. He rarely left my side."

"*Ain't that the truth*," Lainey muttered earning a smile from Eve. When Eve told her about her theory, Lainey was pissed. Well, more pissed than before. "All he wanted from Eve was her goddamn money."

"You have a protector," Dr. Woodrow commented to Eve.

"Eve doesn't need a protector, doctor," Lainey responded. "What she needs is someone to love her for *her* and not what she can give them. Adam gave up his *daughter* for money. What kind of person does that?"

"I imagine it's the kind of person who feels he doesn't get or deserve the love he craves," Willamena answered carefully.

"You're defending him?"

"Lainey, I understand your anger. I'm not defending Adam's actions. However, I'm a psychiatrist. It always has been and always will be my job to get to the root of why people do the things they do." Willamena purposefully blocked out her own niece's abuser. She could reason that it was the drugs that caused Samantha to be evil. But there was more. She shook her herself mentally to keep on track.

"He's a greedy bastard," Lainey offered.

Eve took Lainey's hand. "I don't think he was after my money in the beginning, honey. He loved me. Unfortunately, he figured out I didn't feel the way I pretended I did."

"I happen to agree with your assessment," Dr. Woodrow inserted. "Are you sure you don't want my job?"

"Ha! I'm sure."

Willamena smiled. "Alright. Lainey? Would you like to tell me your story?"

"We're done with Eve?" Lainey asked nervously. Eve she could talk about. When it came to her own issues, that was harder.

"I believe Eve has a good grasp on why she's leaving Adam. There's really nothing more I can offer on that front. You, on the other hand, seem a bit more nervous. Are you second-guessing your choice?"

"No, absolutely not. Jack isn't much different than Adam, though it was never money he wanted from me. It was my submission. My obedience. The more successful I become, the angrier he gets."

Willamena sat up in her chair. "Is he abusive?"

"Not physically."

"Yet," Eve interjected. "I know his type. It's only a matter of time before he feels disrespected enough to use force."

"Eve, you can't know that."

"You said he gets angry," Dr. Woodrow said before Eve could respond. "Has he scared you? Lunged for you? Raised a hand, yet never struck?"

"Y—yes."

"That's not exactly true," Eve added. "He's grabbed her before. I've been a witness to that a couple of times." *Please, forgive me for betraying that confidence,* Eve pleaded silently.

But Lainey wasn't upset. She merely nodded her confirmation.

"Then I must, again, agree with Eve's assessment that he is likely to become more physical as time goes on. This is becoming a habit," she said to Eve before turning her attention back to Lainey. "Did Eve's situation have anything to do with your decision to divorce Jack?"

"No, I didn't know about that when I began the process this morning. My son, Kevin, is a big reason. And Darren, my youngest. They're supportive of this divorce."

"Kevin convinced her to do it," Eve said and received a look from Lainey. "Well, he did!"

"Is that true?" Woodrow asked.

"He talked to me last night. Jack was in a particularly bad mood, and Kevin thought it was time to get out. When Kevin came out to me, and ultimately, I to him, I agreed."

Willamena crossed her legs. This was a breakthrough for Lainey, but she kept her focus on Kevin. "Do you fear for his safety with Jack?"

"Yes. Jack is a bigot, Dr. Woodrow. I don't even want to think about what he could do to Kevin once he finds out he's gay. Kevin needs to be away from Jack for the same reasons I do. I can't let him get custody."

"I told you I wouldn't let that happen, Lainey," Eve said softly.

"What if even you don't have that kind of power, Eve?"

"If I may?" Willamena said. "Assuming Kevin and Darren are willing, I would love to speak with them. To get their side of why they want to live with you and not Jack. Not to toot my own horn, but I'm a highly respected psychiatrist with a good reputation with the courts in this city. If you agree, I would be willing to testify on your behalf with my findings."

"You don't think I can stop it from getting that far, doc?" Eve raised a brow at Lainey's snickering.

"I don't doubt your abilities, Eve. I'm merely offering a different solution. One that doesn't include threats."

Eve sat back and sighed with a half-smile. "Does *everyone* think I'm the damn mafia?"

Willamena's eyebrows shot up. "Mafia?"

Lainey shrugged. "It's plausible."

Willamena studied Eve. With everything she knew about the young woman, she could see Lainey's point. "I suppose it is."

"Oh, come on! I am not . . ." Eve stopped abruptly when Dr. Woodrow and Lainey burst out in laughter. "Funny."

Lainey composed herself the best she could. She had been so stressed out since yesterday, or for the past three-plus years, that her laughter almost felt hysterical.

"How long do we have to wait to be together?" she asked Dr. Woodrow.

"That's entirely up to you."

"Please give me a real answer," Lainey begged.

Willamena gave Lainey a kind smile. "I say it's entirely up to you because you must evaluate your true feelings. For Jack, for Eve. For yourself. What do you want? How long has your marriage been over? Can you leave this marriage free of regret? You and you alone can answer these questions without letting the opinions of others skew your emotions. That goes for both of you," she said looking at Eve. "Divorce, no matter how easy it may seem to you now, is a big change. Whether you've been together for two years or twenty, your lives have been altered. I know you love each other, that's clear. Make sure that you're entering a relationship with each other without any doubts. Otherwise, I'm afraid you'll end up in the same place you are now."

"I had doubts when I married Adam," Eve said evenly. She looked at Lainey. "I have none with you."

"I have none with you, either," Lainey responded with a smile. She looked back at Dr. Woodrow. "I never wanted to marry Jack," she confessed. "I'm tired of letting fear control my life. I'm ready to live and be happy."

Willamena smiled. "There's your answer. Social etiquette plays no part in your personal life."

Lainey took a deep, cleansing breath. "Now I just have to break the news to Jack."

Chapter Thirty-Six

Eve pulled her Jaguar into Lainey's driveway and cut the engine. The scene was reminiscent of the day Eve whisked Lainey and the boys away to Disney. Eve had been uneasy that day, unable to predict what would happen when Jack found out Lainey was taking the boys on vacation without him. This time, Lainey would be leaving for good. Endless scenarios played in Eve's head, none of them good.

Lainey thought of that day as well. She had been nervous, yet determined then. Now, all she wanted to do was get this over with and move on with life. She glanced at Eve.

"Are you ready for this?"

Eve grinned. "Absolutely."

They walked towards the house with purpose. It was quiet, though they knew Jack was home since his car was in the driveway. Kevin and Darren should be home from school as well. Lainey had wondered if she should do this without the boys present, but they were as involved with this decision as she was. As much as she wanted to shield them, she thought it was essential to treat them with the respect they deserve.

"I miss Rufus," Eve mentioned absently.

Lainey stopped and looked back at Eve. "Aww. I miss that goofy dog, too. When he passed, I thought about getting the boys another dog, but Jack forbid it."

"I think Bella would like a dog."

Lainey smiled. "I think she would, too." She caught sight of a familiar car parked at the curb. "Did you ask James to be here?"

"I told you I would. He's for emergencies only, Lainey. I don't think Jack would be stupid enough to try anything, but I love you too much to take that gamble."

"Thank you." Lainey closed her eyes for a moment. When they opened back up, they were filled with bravery. "Let's do this."

She unlocked the door and pushed it open. Though her step stuttered, Lainey held her head high as she walked into the house.

"It's about time!" Jack yelled from the other room. "What have I told you about being this late? Dinner isn't ready. What kind of mother lets her sons suffer . . ." He stopped abruptly when he saw Eve standing next to Lainey. "Haven't you taken up enough of Lainey's time today?"

Out of respect for Lainey, Eve remained quiet. This was Lainey's show, and Eve would follow her lead. That is unless Jack became violent.

"Where are the boys?" Lainey asked.

"I don't know. Most likely in their rooms. Hungry."

"You have hands, Jack. So do they. If they were really hungry, they'd make something. Kevin does it all the time." Lainey walked past him to the stairs and called for them to come down.

"It's not my job, Lainey. I work hard all day. I expect to come home to a hot meal."

Eve bit her lip, hard, and reminded herself to stay out of it.

Lainey rolled her eyes at her soon—to—be ex-husband. "You sit in a cubicle all day, Jack. It's not like you're doing hard labor."

Jack snarled and Eve took a step in Lainey's direction ready to defend if needed. Luckily, the boys came bounding down the steps at that time.

"Hey, mom! Hey, Eve!" Kevin greeted. He couldn't contain the shit—eating grin. If Eve was here, that meant his mom took his advice and asked her for help.

"Hey, Kevin." Eve tilted her head and peered around him. Darren was much more reserved. Obviously, he knew what was happening as well, but was a bit more apprehensive about it. "Darren."

Darren gave her a tumultuous smile. "Hey."

Lainey smiled at her sons. "Do you remember what we discussed this morning?" They both nodded. Kevin gave her a particularly intense look until she nodded back. The grin she received in return bolstered her resolve.

"What is this all about, Lainey?" Jack asked irritably.

"Jack, before I say this, there's something you should know. My security detail is right outside." Okay, so it was just James, but against Jack, that was enough.

"*She's* the reason you even need a security detail." Jack glared at Eve.

"That's not true. There are no threats to me because of Eve. The only threat here is you."

"You're being ridiculous and dramatic, Lainey. Typical of you." He turned to Eve. "I don't know what she's been prattling on about, but everything is fine. However, if you want to *help*, let her be home with her family more often."

Lainey sighed. "Jack, I filed for divorce this morning."

One, two, three . . . Eve counted how long it took for Jack to understand what Lainey had just said. When she got to five, and Jack made his move, she did, too.

"No," she growled, stepping between him and Lainey. It didn't surprise her that Kevin and Darren moved as well, surrounding their mother in a protective cocoon.

"Stay out of this, bitch! This is all your fault!"

Eve smiled coldly. "As much as I would like to take credit for Lainey leaving you, Jack, this is all you."

"If you think I'm going to allow this, you're sorely mistaken." Jack glowered past Eve at Lainey. "I'm not letting you do this. I forbid it."

"Kevin, Darren, go pack a bag," Lainey said steadily. At least her voice sounded stronger than she felt.

"The hell they will! You are not taking my sons from me! They need a man in their lives."

Kevin scoffed. "Not one like you," he sneered.

"Kevin," Lainey warned quietly.

"What, mom? It's true. Let's ask him how he plans to treat me. Answer this, dad. Do you still want me to be here with you even though I'm gay?"

Jack stared at him, then turned his ire onto Lainey. "Do you see what you did? You coddled him, let him quit football, and turned him into some pansy ass faggot!"

Lainey's hand snaked out from behind Eve and slapped Jack. "Don't you dare talk about my son that way! You are ignorant and prejudiced. I will not have my children exposed to your way of thinking any longer! And *I* will not tolerate the way you treat me anymore."

"You are my *wife*! I will treat you how I see fit." He pointed a shaking finger at Kevin. "As for this . . ."

"Careful, Jack," Eve warned, already tired of his bullshit.

"You are *nothing* to me! I don't give a fuck who you think you are, cunt, but this has nothing to do with you! You came into our lives and changed my wife! Whatever the hell this sissy is thinking was probably your influence as well!"

Eve stood her ground as Lainey lunged at him again. The last thing Lainey needed was assault charges brought against her from this asshole.

"Jack, it's sweet that you want to give me so much power. The truth is, Lainey is leaving you because of who you're portraying yourself to be right now."

"Fuck you! Darren, get over here. Get away from him!"

Kevin scoffed. "What? Do you think I'm going to do something to him? That because I'm gay I'm some evil molester or something, *dad*?"

Jack didn't answer Kevin. He didn't even look at him. But no answer was the equivalent of a yes. "Darren, now!"

"No!" Darren ducked behind Eve after his outburst. "I don't want to!"

Jack's face twisted with fury. He pointed at Lainey. "You get this *filth* out of my house! I won't have *my* son, my *only* son around this depravity! And take the bitch with you!"

"I won't leave Darren with you, Jack."

"You have no choice. He is mine."

"Jack . . ."

"I'm gay, too!" Darren yelled.

Lainey's eyes widened. She glanced at a stunned Eve, then turned to Darren and gave him an encouraging smile.

"What the fuck have you done to my family?" Jack roared.

Eve couldn't tell if he was talking to her or Lainey. At that point, it didn't matter. She started backing up towards the door, Lainey and the boys still behind her.

"Make this easy on everyone Jack and let them go. Sign the papers when you get them," Eve said.

"I want full custody of our sons," Lainey interjected hotly. "They want to live with me. If it's a fight you want, I'll give you one, Jack. One I intend to win."

Jack's face was a picture of disgust. "I have no sons. You've destroyed everything, Lainey. All you ever needed to do was be a wife and a mother. You couldn't do either one right. You've failed. Now get out of my house."

Any other time, his words would have devastated her. But she had read enough psychiatry books to recognize that *he* was the problem. Not her. She was a damn good mother. She may have been a shit wife to him lately, but Lainey could probably get away with giving him partial credit for that as well.

"We'll come back when you're gone to gather our things."

"The locks will be changed by then," Jack warned. "I won't have any of you defiling this house any longer."

Eve took a step towards him. "They will be back tomorrow with a moving company. I suggest you put sticky notes on anything you want to keep. If anything is missing, broken, or trashed, it will be included in the child support."

"I'm not giving them anything! I work hard for my money. I'm certainly not going to *donate* it to some homosexual charity cases."

"Then you will be served with papers to give up your parental rights," Lainey announced. She took Kevin and Darren's hands, squeezing them. It pissed her off that Jack was treating them like this and saying the things he was saying. *I should have done this alone.*

"Fine. I never wanted weak girls anyway. Now get out."

Eve ushered the three of them out the door. James stood nearby, alert and ready to intervene if necessary. She made eye contact and gave him a slight nod.

"Remember what I said about their belongings, Jack. James here will stick around to give you a hand. My treat." She barely resisted giving Jack a condescending pat on the arm.

"I don't —"

Whatever Jack was about to say was cut off by James's intimidating presence.

"I don't mind helping." James's low voice was as terrifying as his muscular physique. "How about you put on a pot of coffee?" James gave Eve a wink as he closed the front door.

Lainey snickered. "I don't think I've ever seen Jack that confused or scared."

"I don't think I've ever seen a man that hot before." Kevin gave his mom and Eve an innocent grin when they both looked at him. "What?"

"Mom?" Darren said softly.

"Yes, sweetie?"

"Where are we going to go? All my stuff is in there. My drawings, my iPad, my bed. He wouldn't even let us pack."

Lainey hugged Darren to her. "We'll get everything tomorrow, I promise. As for tonight, we'll be staying with Eve in her apartment in the city."

"You're going with us?" Kevin asked Eve.

"Yes. We'll talk about everything later, but right now let's go pick up my daughter and go home."

"Wait," Lainey called out. "I have one question. Darren? Did you mean what you said? Are you gay?"

Darren gave her a toothy grin. "Nope. But I sure as heck wasn't staying here by myself! Ooo! The Jag!" He took off with the resilience of a young boy.

"Well. Did you tell him to say that?" she asked Kevin.

Kevin laughed. "No. But I did tell him about me. I didn't want him to be surprised by that news when he was going to have enough to deal with."

Lainey accepted his answer with a nod. "Do you think he'll be okay?"

"Yeah. Look, ma, I've been talking to him a lot about how dad treats you is wrong, but he already knew. When he thought you and dad were getting a divorce a couple of years ago, it scared him. Now, he was hoping for it. He was nervous because he didn't know how dad would react."

Lainey nodded again. "And you? Are you okay? Those things your father said were . . ."

"Were the same things people like me hear all the time. I expected that from him. He can't hurt me, mom. The only ones I care about are you, Darren, Bella, and Eve. So, as long as you all love me for who I am, I'm good."

Lainey hugged him tightly. "I do love you, Kevin. Always. And I'm trusting you to come to me if you need to. About anything."

"I will. I promise." He moved back some, shuffling his feet. He looked sheepishly at Eve. "Hey, that therapist lady you see? Do you think she'll talk to my friend Mia?"

"I think we can arrange that," Eve said, unsurprised that he knew about Dr. Woodrow.

"And maybe me if I need it?"

Eve sought out Lainey's approval before answering that one. When Lainey nodded, Eve placed a hand on Kevin's arm. "Absolutely. May I give you a piece of advice?"

"Sure."

"Don't wait until it's needed. In my experience, thinking you're strong enough to handle whatever comes your way, isn't always the smart thing to do. Accepting that you're human and need help every now and then will aid in your growth."

"Yes, ma'am." He gave Eve a quick hug and ran to the car.

"Thank you," Lainey said tenderly. "I wish I could give you a hug."

"You're welcome to do that and more later," Eve winked. "Come on, let's go home."

"Hey."

Lainey blinked seeing the ghost of the flames she was watching every time her eyes closed. She scooted over to give Eve room on the oversized chair she was sprawled out in.

"Hi."

"The boys are settled in. Bella is snoring. All is quiet in the land."

"I've heard Bella's snores. They're anything but quiet," Lainey teased.

"True. She did *not* get that from me."

Lainey chuckled. "No, she didn't." She glanced towards the stairs. "Did I do the right thing having them there?"

"The better question would be, would Kevin have forgiven you if you tried that by yourself?"

"Hmm. I guess you're right." Lainey settled in, allowing herself to relax as Eve wrapped her arms around her. "I should have known he'd be that cruel."

"You know what we're not going to do anymore?" Eve asked as she pulled Lainey even closer. "We're not going to take responsibility for other people's shortcomings."

Lainey tilted her head and looked up at Eve. "You're right." She threaded her fingers in Eve's hair, bringing her closer for a kiss. She sighed dreamily against Eve's lips. "So that's what that feels like."

"Hmm?" Because she couldn't resist, she kissed Lainey again.

"Kissing you without guilt," Lainey explained once her lips were free again. She felt rather than saw Eve smile.

"No more of that either," Eve declared.

"Kissing?"

Eve laughed. "No more feeling guilty. We're free, honey."

"Technically —"

"Ah, ah, ah. I don't want to think of technicalities. Let me have this, Lainey. Just for tonight. Tomorrow, we'll worry about the technicalities."

"Okay. But can we talk about one thing before we shut it down for the night?"

"Do I get more kisses if I say yes?"

Lainey smiled. "Yes."

"Then go for it."

"I appreciate you letting us stay here with you."

"But?" Eve's heart began to race. She had hoped that Lainey would want to be with her now. Perhaps it was wishful thinking that Lainey would get out of one relationship and jump into another. Eve was ready, but if Lainey needed time, she'd respect that. She'd hate it but respect it.

"I can't believe I'm saying this about such a beautiful apartment, but it's not big enough. The boys need their own rooms. So does Princess Bella. I think we're going to have to find a bigger place."

Eve shifted until they were face to face. "Are you saying what I think you're saying? You want to live with me?"

"I thought that's what you wanted, too? But if you think it's too soon."

"No! I mean, yes, I want it!" Eve kissed Lainey enthusiastically. "I thought you were going to tell me you needed to be on your own for a while."

Lainey shook her head. "I feel like I've been on my own all my life, Eve. I'm ready to be with someone who actually loves me."

"I do, you know. I love you."

"I know. I feel it. I love you, too." Lainey gave Eve a quick peck. If she allowed more, they would forget about their current discussion. "So? Do you think we could look for a bigger place?"

"Before I answer that, may I run something by you?"

"Of course."

"I, um, sort of bought a house."

"What? Where? Why?"

"Would you like to ask the how and when as well?" Eve joked. Probably not a good idea since Lainey didn't look amused.

"Sure. How and when?"

"Okay, will you hear me out?" Lainey nodded. "You and I have been going to Los Angeles quite often lately. I thought that if I'm going to be there so much, it would be cost effective to buy a house." Eve pulled out her phone. "But that was my guilt talking. Look."

Lainey studied each of the photos that Eve scrolled through. She had to admit, the house was an architectural paradise. The secluded residence boasted a gated drive, soaring ceiling heights with a modern, open floor plan.

"Six bedrooms," Eve said. "Six full baths and two half-baths. The outdoor living space is perfect for the kids. The beauty of the infinity pool is perfect for us. This," she scrolled to one particular photo, "is the master suite. Walls of glass, Lainey. Can you imagine the light that flows into that space? And, see? There's an office, a sitting area, as well as an outdoor lounge all right there. Like our own little retreat. I could see myself painting there. I could turn the office into a studio."

Lainey put her hand over Eve's phone to get her attention. "You can see yourself painting?" she asked seriously.

Eve hadn't hesitated when she said those words. She could envision them being happy there. That feeling alone sparked her creative desire.

"Yes," she answered softly.

"You want to move to LA?"

"I want *us* to move there. I chose this place with Bella, you, and the boys in mind. I want this to be our home."

"What about New York?"

Eve breathed in deep, letting it out slowly. "I love New York. It will always be home to me. In fact, I want to keep this apartment. But I think this could be good for us. We can start over there."

"And be around friends who understand us?" Lainey guessed. "Who've been rooting for us?"

"It's a plus, that's for sure. Honey, there's nothing left for us here. We've conquered New York. It tried to kick our asses, but in the end, we came out on top. I'm ready to conquer LA. With you by my side this time."

Lainey picked up Eve's phone and looked at the house again. It was a dream home. A forever home. She could feel that simply by looking at the pictures. Los Angeles would be a huge change. And that's what appealed to Lainey the most. She and Eve would be making this change together.

"I would have to talk to Kevin and Darren," Lainey said thoughtfully. "They'd be leaving their school. Their friends. Though I think one look at this place, and they'll be throwing peace signs and telling everyone they'll send postcards."

Eve chuckled. "I want us all to be happy, Lainey. Whether that's in LA or here, I don't care. If you're with me, I'm happy. So, if the boys aren't ready to move, we can look for something here."

"I love you." Lainey laid her head on Eve's shoulder. This is what she had always wanted. Someone who loved her. Someone who asked for her opinions. Someone who talked to her as though she mattered. Someone who would hold her in a way that it didn't matter where they were. As long as they were together, they were home. She lifted her head again. "Wait, what about my job? And the gallery here?"

"Mikey is ready to take over here. I wouldn't be surprised if he threw us a going away party with a banner that read "It's about time you left." As for you, you'll be promoted. Lauren is doing a fantastic job as curator in LA. She'll be even better with you as her mentor and boss."

"Are you giving me special treatment?" Lainey grinned.

"Ha! No. I'm giving you everything you deserve, Lainey."

Lainey's heart beat a little harder. She could kick herself for wasting two-plus years of their lives together. Or, she could start making up for that right now.

"I'm ready to go to bed, honey."

"Oh! Okay. Um, I want you to take the bedroom. If you want me to sleep down here, I understand."

Lainey stood up and held her hand out. "I want you in bed with me, Eve. Tonight and every night after this."

Chapter Thirty-Seven
Therapy

The end.

"I must admit, I didn't think I'd see you again, Eve." Dr. Woodrow handed Eve a cup of tea before settling in her favorite chair.

"Now, doc, do you think I'd leave without a proper goodbye?" Eve gave her a brilliant smile before sipping her tea.

Willamena enjoyed seeing this side of Eve. "Considering how you feel about therapy, yes."

"Therapy aside, I've taken a liking to you. Besides, Rebecca scares me. Lord help me if I did something to upset her favorite aunt."

Willamena laughed heartily. "I'm her *only* aunt! But thank you. The feeling is mutual." She studied Eve for a moment with a psychiatrist's eye. "There's something different about you."

"I'm happy."

Dr. Woodrow smiled. "That I can see from the radiance emanating from you. I have concerns."

"Of course you do," Eve laughed. "You're a shrink. You'd be remiss if you didn't question every emotion."

Willamena considered picking up her notebook and writing in it just to get under Eve's skin. She realized then that her feelings for

Eve had crossed the line from doctor and patient into friendship. Obviously, that was the opposite of what they taught you in med school, but there were bound to be exceptions. Besides, Willamena wasn't one to always conform to rules. She was counseling her own niece for goodness sake.

"Perhaps it's more of a query," Willamena said, deciding to ignore Eve's little quip. "You seem awfully happy and carefree considering you're going through a divorce. Everything must be going well on that front."

Eve grinned. "I've never known you to beat around the bush, doc. Normally, you'd ask the hard-hitting questions, sit back with your notebook, and watch me squirm." Willamena said nothing. "Ah, there you go. Now, I'm squirming."

"So, things are *not* going well?" Willamena asked in the silence.

"Things are as expected," Eve answered vaguely. She sighed when Willamena raised a brow. "It hasn't been a bed of roses, Dr. Woodrow, but we're handling it. My divorce has been expedited and should be finalized any day now."

Willamena tapped her teacup with her fingernail. "It pays to be well connected, I'm guessing."

"I have a friend, a judge, who owed me a favor," Eve shrugged. "Adam had to agree to an expedited divorce, however. That took a little more convincing."

"Why the rush?"

Eve tilted her head. "Because I have a life to get on with, doc."

"Does Adam know you're going to be with Lainey?"

Eve sat back in her chair and let out a moody snort. "He knows. It's something he wasn't betting on, and he's certainly not happy about it."

"He didn't think Lainey would leave Jack?"

"No. He was banking of the idea that I would be left alone."

"And you would return to him once you got tired of waiting for someone who clearly didn't want you," Willamena guessed.

Eve touched her finger to her nose. "Right on, doc. When he found out Lainey was divorcing Jack, he threatened to contest the divorce."

"I get the feeling he changed his mind."

"You're on a roll. He has no bargaining chip. Perhaps if he hadn't cheated, he would have been able to threaten me to give up more money or even my daughter."

"Instead?" Willamena was beginning to put more thought into this mafia thing Lainey had brought up. She knew it wasn't true, but Eve Sumptor seemed to be able to get the impossible done and somehow come out in a better position.

"Instead, he gets nothing more from me. The payment I gave him for the business is it. That includes no alimony from me, nor will I ask him for child support."

"And the expedited divorce," Willamena said and Eve nodded. "All this in addition to full custody?"

"Yes. He loves Bella, doc, and I will never deny him time with her. He's her father. I want him in her life. However, I won't tolerate him making choices for her based on his dislike for me. We agreed that I would have sole custody of Bella and be responsible for her well-being. Adam is welcome to use the jet anytime he would like to visit."

"Jet? Are you leaving New York?"

Eve nodded. "Lainey and I have decided we need a fresh start. All of us. The boys, Lainey, me, and Bella are moving to LA."

"I must ask, aside from the fresh start, do you think you and Lainey will be more accepted there? I assume you'll be moving close to Rebecca and her circle of friends."

Eve took a moment to consider Willamena's question. "Accepted," she repeated at length. "I don't think either of us cares if we're accepted here in New York. We've been through way too much to let something as ignorant as homophobia stop us from being together. On that same note, New York has been the backdrop of those problems. We don't want or need the ghosts of the past standing in our way."

"Ghosts tend to travel, Eve. Whether you're in New York or LA, they will be there unless you exorcize them."

"I know. I also know that's easier to do when you're not running into them at every corner. I know you don't think I listen to you, Dr.

Woodrow, but I do. Very carefully." Eve took a breath. "I went to visit my mom recently. I forgave her. I didn't say the words, but I felt it in my heart. I forgave myself. And though I may not forgive those from my past, I can let go of them. Because, truly, they're *all* ghosts now."

"All?" Willamena asked. She had been moved by Eve's words. There were those rare cases that got under Willamena's skin. The ones where she wasn't sure she had enough of the right words to pull her patient out of whatever was holding them hostage. This had been one of those cases. Having Eve sit in front of her now, telling her that she forgave herself, was a true win.

Eve chastised herself silently for forgetting one piece of relevant information. "All," she repeated. "Everyone who hurt me in my past is now dead. Including Bussiere."

Willamena's eyebrows rose in surprise. "That's a development." She itched to bring out her notebook, but she was sure she would remember this. "When did this happen?"

Oh boy. "Um, a few months ago."

"Months! Eve, while it's not mandatory to tell me everything, you must admit this is huge. May I ask why you neglected to reveal this information?"

"When it happened, I was given papers and a check," Eve divulged. "The papers were the deed to the club. The check was what she made off my body. I didn't know how to feel, so I decided to take the time to explore that on my own. By the time I came to terms with that, other things happened. Namely, making love to Lainey and realizing that *she* was the one. Honestly, it had become unimportant to me."

Willamena studied Eve for a long moment. As a therapist, you hope to give your patients the knowledge, ability, and encouragement to handle anything that comes their way. She couldn't fault Eve for wanting to figure this out herself.

"Out of sheer curiosity, what did you do with your so-called inheritance?"

Eve told Willamena all about the girls' home and giving the money to charities chosen by Lainey's sons.

"That's fantastic! Speaking as your friend, Eve, I'm proud of you."

"Thank you. That means a lot." And Eve meant it. Willamena Woodrow reminded Eve more and more of Eve's mother. Or how Eve imagined her mother would be had she lived past her thirties.

A light knock at the door had both women jumping slightly.

"That should be Lainey," Eve said.

Sure enough, when Willamena opened the door, a frazzled looking Lainey walked in.

"Sorry, I'm late." She gave Eve a sweet peck on the lips before sitting down.

"Are you okay?" Eve asked, immediately concerned.

"Yeah, yeah. I'm fine. Honey, I'm fine," she repeated when Eve gave her a look. "I've been at my lawyer's office," Lainey explained to Dr. Woodrow. "Jack isn't making any of this easy."

Willamena slanted a look at Eve.

"Don't look at me like that. I offered to help."

"You offered to pull out his eyelashes, honey," Lainey chuckled. "I don't think that's even legal."

"What?" Eve shrugged. "It's just eyelashes."

Lainey rolled her eyes. After the day she's had, it was nice to be next to Eve and smiling.

"Is there anything I can do to help?" Dr. Woodrow asked once she stopped laughing. It was probably wrong of her to laugh about violence of any kind, but as Eve said, it was just eyelashes.

"Can you declare Jack insane?" Eve asked for Lainey.

Again, Lainey rolled her eyes. "*I* could declare Jack insane." She turned her attention to the doctor. "He's suing me."

"For what?" Willamena asked with a bit too much emotion.

"Restitution. He's arguing that I misrepresented myself causing him suffering. He wants me to pay him for the years of his life I wasted."

Willamena scoffed. "Perhaps he is a bit crazy."

"Ah ha! Where's your jar? You owe that jar five bucks." Eve winked at Lainey. "She said crazy. We're not supposed to say that word."

"My apologies," Willamena laughed. "I meant bonkers. What does your lawyer say?"

"That he's bonkers," Lainey deadpanned, then smiled. "It's kind of true. She says she could hear him "ranting and raving" in the background. Complaining that I turned his sons gay and that I broke my vow to obey him."

Willamena's brows furrowed. "You had that in your vows?"

"Unfortunately. Jack is very old-school. He wanted those vows because he believes that's a woman's role. To obey her husband. My attorney did warn me that adultery is a misdemeanor here in New York. If Jack were to be privy of my relationship with Eve before the divorce, he could use that against me."

Willamena nodded. "It's a rarely enforced, antiquated law. One I find to be as ridiculous as Jack's lawsuit. Surely, you could allow Eve to get involved in helping settle this. *Without* pulling out eyelashes, Eve."

"I don't want Eve's money," Lainey said hotly.

"Honey, I don't think that's what the doc meant." Eve turned in her chair to face Lainey. "I know you don't want my money. I also know that dragging this out with Jack isn't what you or the boys need. If money is all it will take to make him sign the damn papers and leave you alone, I'll pay any amount."

Lainey sighed. She took her phone out and cued up a video. "Emotional abuse is a crime, isn't it, doctor?" She handed the phone to Dr. Woodrow. The video depicted Jack's tirade when Lainey revealed she was divorcing him. It also showed the way he treated Kevin and Darren when he heard them say they were gay. "I have tons of video of him berating either my sons or me. *That's* why I don't want to give him money! Especially Eve's."

Eve reached over and took the phone unapologetically. "Why didn't you tell me you had this?"

"Because I didn't want to resort to this, Eve. I wanted to get a quiet, clean divorce and move on with my life. Jack's parents are already worried that I'm going to keep the kids from them. I didn't want to put them through this, too." Lainey took a calming breath.

"Besides, I thought you knew. Your company set up the cameras in my house when Tony was threatening me."

How could Eve have stupidly forgotten that she had had security installed everywhere when Tony was alive? The cameras were well hidden, and no one knew in the house except Lainey. That was Lainey's one condition before agreeing to the cameras. She had wanted Kevin and Darren to live a carefree life, not worrying about the threats surrounding their mother. And Jack, well, she didn't want to open that conversation with him. Hell, Lainey even made Eve swear that none of the footage would be watched unless it was absolutely necessary. Now Eve understood why.

"We don't have to go public with this, Lainey," Eve said softly. "Just having it gives you the edge. We let him know it exists and he'll stop the lawsuit."

Lainey scoffed. "Have you met Jack? He thinks how he treats me and his sons is right. Do you think he's going to care that you have video of him disciplining his wife for not doing what she's told?"

"He will care," Eve promised.

"Are we back to the eyelashes?" Lainey asked only half joking.

Eve grinned. "Not yet. However, Captain Harris could make Jack aware of his crimes."

"I thought Charlie retired from the force and works for James now."

"He did, and he does. But he still has his shield. And, no offense, but Jack obviously isn't that bright. Look at the woman he had in his life for years. She's incredible, and he had no clue how to treat her right."

Eve's words caused a small smile to form on Lainey's lips. "It's no wonder I love you." She blew out a breath. "Promise me that no one else gets hurt, Eve."

"I promise, honey. That includes Jack if that's what you want. As for George and Rosemary," Eve said of Jack's parents. "I saw how devastated they were to learn of Jack's behavior towards you and the boys. They are welcome to use the jet anytime to come and visit us in LA. They can even stay with us for as long as they want."

Lainey laughed. "Let's not go overboard. I agree with the jet, but a weekend is sufficient. I love them dearly, but I want to be comfortable in our home. Having my ex-in-laws around for long periods of time doesn't sound appealing."

"Deal," Eve grinned.

"Well," Willamena clapped her hands together. "It looks like my work here is done," she said, taking credit for the resolutions that had just taken place. "I hate to be unprofessional . . ."

"Since when?" Eve joked.

Willamena nearly threw her pen at Eve. "As I was saying, I will miss both of you. I wish you nothing but success and love in LA."

"You know, you should think about moving there yourself. Rebecca is there. Hell, most of your clients are there."

Willamena laughed at Eve's suggestion. "Maybe I will. I'll make sure to bring my notebook."

Eve groaned. "Forget I said anything," she said with mirth.

"Too late. You've planted the seed." Willamena looked at Lainey. "If Eve's plan of intimidating Jack with the videos doesn't work, come see me. I'm still willing to testify on your behalf."

"I will, thank you." Lainey stood, followed by the others. She thought about shaking Dr. Woodrow's hand but opted to go for a hug instead. "I can't tell you how much I appreciate all you've done for us."

"I just listened," Willamena replied humbly, returning the hug with sincerity. "You two did all the heavy lifting."

"Take credit where credit is due, doc," Eve said as she stepped forward. She wasn't necessarily a hugger, but she owed this woman a considerable debt. With that in mind, she held her arms open.

Surprise helped propel Willamena forward into Eve's embrace. It felt the same as it did every time she hugged her niece. Her family.

"As long as you both realize how strong you are," Willamena said as she stepped back. "I'm happy that you found your way back to each other."

Eve's eyebrow quirked. "You were rooting for us?"

Willamena smiled as she reached for her notebook. "You hated this thing. So, I'm giving it to you to do as you please. You can burn it if you like."

Eve took the notebook with two fingers as though it would bite her at any moment. Since she started therapy, she had wanted to know what was in the damned thing. Now that it was in her hands, she wasn't so sure.

"You don't need it?" she asked.

"No." What Willamena neglected to say was that she had already recorded all her notes on an encrypted hard drive. "It's all yours."

Eve slowly opened the notebook, read a little, flipped the page, and read more. Her eyes found Willamena's. "You knew."

"Knew what?" Lainey asked, craning her head to read what Eve was reading.

"She knew I was going to choose you. From the beginning," Eve said almost accusatorily.

"Now, wait," Willamena soothed. "That notebook is full of my *opinions*, Eve. Not fact."

"Why didn't you tell me?" Eve wasn't ready to accept the good doctor's explanation.

Willamena placed her hands on her hips and gave Eve a very stern — very motherly — look. "Eve, if I had told you that Lainey was the one for you, you would question it every day. You would wonder if I was the one who put it in your head or if it is truly what you feel in your heart."

"She's right, honey. I wanted Dr. Woodrow to tell me what to do just as much as you did. But I think we both needed to come to this outcome ourselves." Lainey closed the notebook in Eve's hands. "This is our decision and no one else's."

Eve breathed in through her nose, slowly letting it out through her mouth. Then she nodded. "You're right," she said finally, addressing them both. "I apologize."

"No need," Willamena said with a kind smile.

"Well, I have something for you, too." Eve looked at Lainey who nodded slightly before walking to the door. Lainey returned with a large, covered object and handed it to Eve. "Little more than three years ago if you asked me what was important to me, I would have given you one answer. Painting. While that list has grown exponentially in these short years, I thought painting was lost to me forever. You and Lainey have helped me find it again. I will never be able to repay that. But I can give you a token of my gratitude."

Willamena accepted the gift with awe. "You're painting again?"

"Open it."

The doctor did just that. What greeted her took her breath away. It was a portrait of her in her office. The likeness was so incredible, Willamena was sure if she touched the steam coming from the teacup, she would feel the heat. Or if she touched the notebook on her painted lap, she would feel the leather.

"This is . . . I have no words, Eve. I've seen your photographs in your gallery, but I've never had the pleasure of seeing your paintings. I now understand why it means so much to you. This is extraordinary. You somehow make paint seemingly come alive on the canvas."

If she were the type to blush, Eve would be red now. "That's a lot of words, doc," she said uncomfortably. "But thank you."

"No, thank you. I shouldn't accept this. It's an Eve Sumptor original and most likely worth more than my apartment here in the city. But the hell if I'm going to turn down your generous offer."

Lainey chuckled. "Wise choice."

She kept her composure on the outside. On the inside, Lainey was weeping with joy that Eve had found her creativity again. A week before, she had awakened from a deep, peaceful sleep to find herself alone in bed. It took her a moment to realize that wasn't normal anymore. She and Eve had slept together every night since they confessed their true feelings for each other. When Eve wasn't there, Lainey went looking for her.

It hadn't taken long since Eve sweetly left the secret door that led to her studio open. Half asleep, Lainey wasn't prepared for what she'd find when she walked in. Eve stood there with her hair up in a messy bun, a white button-up shirt (unbuttoned just enough to show cleavage), one paintbrush in her teeth, and one paintbrush in her hand. Lainey had thought it would be impossible for Eve to be any sexier than she was right then. That thought shattered when Eve looked up at Lainey — eyes shining bright with joy, paint smeared on her beautiful face — and smiled. Lainey wouldn't exactly call what they did that night making love. It was too hot, too animalistic, too raw for that. It also ended with both of them being covered in paint. The next morning, Eve carefully folded the drop cloth they rolled around on. When Lainey asked what she was doing, Eve had told her she was preserving their artwork.

"Lainey?" Eve wondered what exactly her beautiful partner was thinking about that was putting that peculiar look on her face. Then Eve remembered the night in her studio.

Lainey cleared her throat, but that didn't help the images in her mind. "Hmm?"

"Are you ready to go?"

"Yes!" *Too enthusiastic!* "No offense, Dr. Woodrow."

Willamena gave her a knowing wink. It didn't take a head shrink to determine what Lainey had been thinking about.

"Go. If either of you needs anything, you know where to find me." Willamena hugged them both again, then shooed them out the door. In her experience, it was uncommon for people who faced trauma together to last. As evidenced by Eve and Adam. However, Willamena had never seen a bond quite like Eve and Lainey's. Theirs was a relationship she could have faith in.

Epilogue

Eve pulled into the driveway and switched off the engine of her new Porsche Cayenne Hybrid. She tapped her fingertips on the steering wheel with a smile. The Porsche matched Lainey's. The only differences were the colors. Eve's, of course, was white while Lainey chose black. The perfect yin to Eve's yang. The new cars had been Lainey's idea, with the exception that she could pick them and help pay for them. "New city, new eco-friendly cars," she had said. Eve was so happy that Lainey and the boys had agreed to move in with her, she would have driven the Flintstone's car if Lainey had wanted her to.

She looked up at their house. *Their* house. Eve had insisted on putting Lainey's name on the deed. It wasn't something Lainey had needed, but the sparkle in her eye when Eve gave her a copy said it all. Eve needed Lainey to know without a doubt that she would never be a guest in this house. It was hers. *Theirs*. And, with that same thought running around in Eve's brain, she wondered why the hell she wasn't inside instead of out here looking in wistfully.

Grabbing her stuff, Eve made her way to the front door. She and Lainey were usually together, coming home from the gallery. Today, however, Eve had several things to take care of outside of the art world. Lainey had been gracious enough to offer to come home early for Bella. They were going through a transition period with the move and not having Lexie around. Thankfully, Bella's young nanny decided to transfer from NYU to UCLA to finish her studies. Eve knew Lexie loved Bella, but her practical side also knew it had a lot to do with the significant raise she offered Lexie. Not to mention the paid tuition.

Eve shook her head. The things she would do for her daughter. In her defense, though, it *was* Lainey's idea to extend the offer to Lexie. She felt the nanny's familiarity would help Bella cope with all the changes going on in her life. When Eve heard Bella's squeal of laughter coming from inside the house, she felt her baby girl was well on her way to getting adjusted.

She pushed the door open with her hip and followed the gleeful sounds. Eve found her family sitting in the living room. Lainey looked as though she was having a ball watching the boys who were sprawled out on the floor playing with Bella. Each time Kevin or Darren would make a funny sound, Bella would laugh hysterically. It was music to Eve's ears. Her eyes left the beautiful scene momentarily and moved to the far corner of the room. There sat one of Eve's many easels. She was painting again. Her muse, she was learning, was serenity. The work she had been doing since the move was vastly different from the past. The colors were lighter, loftier. There was no mistaking the happiness that radiated from Eve's art. While she still loved doing portraits, modern art had become her preferred style. When she would paint down here near her family, she mainly focused on simple landscape paintings. Ones that she didn't mind if Bella or the boys "helped" out on.

Lainey looked up, her smile widening when she saw Eve. It began to fade, however, when she saw a tear rolling down Eve's cheek. She was about to address her partner — god, it felt good to say that finally — when a little girl zoomed past her.

"Momma!" Bella ran to Eve as fast as her little legs would carry her.

"Hi, bug! I missed you!"

"Miss you, momma!" Bella raised her little hand and touched Eve's tear with her fingertip. "Cwy?"

Kevin had noticed his mom staring at Eve, and Bella's question cued him in on why. When Eve didn't respond right away, he thought it best to take control of the situation.

"Hey, Bells. I bet if we raided the fridge, we'd find some ice cream!"

"Ice cweam!" Bella clapped her hands together furiously. She didn't hesitate in leaving her mom's arms — tears forgotten — when Kevin reached for her. "'Mon, Dawwen!" she yelled as they zipped by him.

Once they were alone, Lainey stepped up to Eve and placed a soft hand on her cheek.

"Honey?" Since her brain was preoccupied with why Eve would be crying, Lainey was grateful for her son's swift thinking. Eve was getting better at showing her emotions more, but if this was related to Eve's past, Lainey thought she'd want some privacy.

Eve bent her head and kissed Lainey softly on the lips. "*They're happy tears, baby,*" she whispered. She pulled Lainey into her arms and hugged her fiercely. With her mouth close to Lainey's ear, she explained. "Dr. Woodrow once asked me what I wanted for myself. She told me to listen to my heart." Eve pulled back a little. "This was it. My heart gave me this scenario: this exact one, Lainey. I walk in and see you with the kids. The boys were playing with Bella; there's laughter, happiness, and peace." She held Lainey's hands and brought them up to her lips, kissing them. The ring finger on each of their left hands was unadorned. Eve hoped to amend that when the time was right for all involved. "*I'm home.*"

Now tears were flowing from Lainey. She had dreamt of this day. All she ever wanted was for Eve to be happy. Lainey thanked all that was good in the world that Eve's happiness included her and her sons. Moving to LA was turning out to be the best decision either of them could ever have made. There were no words Lainey could say that would convey her emotions. So, she showed them by kissing Eve deeply.

"Uh, mom?"

Even with Kevin's interruption, Lainey let the kiss come to its natural end. She and Eve had agreed not to hide the way they felt about each other from their children. They may have been more discreet in front of Bella and Darren, but with Kevin, they were a little more comfortable being "caught" in a kiss.

"Yes?"

"Sorry to interrupt, but Bella just remembered we hadn't had dinner yet. She's insisting we do that before ice cream. Your kid has priorities." He grinned at Eve.

Eve shrugged with a chuckle. "What can I say? She loves her food."

"*That* she gets from you," Lainey teased. She poked Eve lightly on her toned tummy. "Why don't you go and change. I'll get dinner started."

"Good idea," Eve winked. She gave Lainey a quick peck on the cheek. "I'll be right down to help."

"Eve?" Kevin had waited until his mom walked away before calling after Eve. When she stopped and turned back towards him, Kevin nearly lost his nerve to say what he had to say. It was odd. When it came to his mom, he had no problem speaking his mind. Though, when he was standing in front of Eve, he felt a bit more intimidated. She never did anything to make him feel that way. She was literally one of the nicest people he'd ever met. There was just something about Eve that brought that out in him.

"What's up?"

"I, uh." He cleared his throat and tried again. "I just wanted to, um, thank you."

Eve's brows furrowed. "For?"

Kevin had to laugh. Had she not seen the dope digs she put them up in? He spread his arms wide. "For this. For opening a section of your gallery for kids like Darren. But mostly for making mom happy. I've never seen her like this before. So carefree and . . . alive."

"Your mom does that for me. I'm merely returning the favor. As for this place, I should be thanking you and Darren for agreeing to come here with your mom. She wouldn't have moved if you two weren't ready. And Darren earned a spot in my gallery. His work is remarkable, especially for someone his age. There's nothing you need to thank me for, Kevin. I'm glad you're here."

"I'm glad to be here," Kevin smiled. "Darren and I didn't hesitate, Eve. I wanted you to know that. We wanted mom to be with you. *We* wanted to be with you."

Her heart swelled with emotion. However, there was more Kevin wasn't saying. "I hear a but in there."

"No," Kevin shook his head. "No but . . . but," he sighed.

"You're worried about Mia," Eve guessed. The teen was always on his phone texting the young woman he had helped before. Eve knew the amount of time he spent on the phone would have been a problem for Lainey if she hadn't known he was worried about his friend.

"Yeah. I mean, she's the only reason I may have been a little apprehensive about moving. She doesn't have anyone to protect her now. She's defenseless."

Eve laid a hand on his shoulder. "The first thing you should know about girls, Kevin, is they are *never* defenseless. We have to fight harder, but we're not helpless. The second thing you should know is your mom told me of your concerns. So, I went to see Mia and her parents before we left."

"You did?"

"Mmhmm. I extended them an offer, and they readily accepted."

"Wow." Kevin shuffled his feet and rubbed the back of his neck. "Um, am I allowed to ask what the offer was?"

Eve had been ready to tell him, but she was having fun watching him squirm. "Sure you are."

Kevin waited, but Eve said nothing else. "Eve!"

"I thought you were going to ask," Eve teased. "Okay, okay," she laughed when he groaned. "Mia is going to go to Paris for a while."

"Your home for girls?" Kevin assumed, wondering why Mia didn't say anything to him about it.

"You know about it?"

"Yeah, mom told me a little about it, but I'd love to know more. What about school? I don't like the way they treated her there, but will she be able to finish school in Paris?"

"Sumptor House provides education, Kevin. More than just

teaching you what's on tests. When Mia is ready to leave Paris, she will do so with the knowledge and confidence she needs to become the most successful woman she desires to be."

"Like you."

Eve shook her head. "I would hope not. No one should strive to be someone else. Only the best version of themselves. Even in their flaws, there is perfection."

"I wish dad felt that way. All he ever sees are my flaws."

"Kevin, being gay is not a flaw. Being a good, caring person is not a flaw. If Jack sees it that way, that's *his* flaw, not yours."

"Thanks." Kevin smiled shyly at her. "I, uh, guess I should get in there and help mom with dinner."

"And I should go get changed before she thinks I abandoned her," Eve joked.

Kevin snickered. "I think you're afraid of my mom."

"I am." Eve winked at him before turning away.

"Oh, hey." Kevin grinned sheepishly when she turned back once again. "Sorry. Do you think we could visit Mia sometime when she goes to Paris?"

Eve grinned back. "Your mom and I have already talked about it. We want to sit down with you and Darren and come up with a travel plan for summer. Perhaps we could start at Disney."

Kevin beamed and pumped his fist in the air. "Yes! Can I tell Darren?"

"Sure. But I get to tell him he'll be my featured artist when we open the Pop Culture section at the gallery."

Kevin's eyes got as round as saucers. "Whoa! Are you serious? Oh, man! That's . . . ." He didn't know what to say. So, he did something impulsive and hugged Eve. He thought he'd made a mistake when she went rigid for a split second. Then he felt her arms come around him and hug him back tightly. Since she had already told him he didn't need to thank her, he thought it'd be a good idea to let the hug speak for him. Afterward, he took off in a trot to the kitchen.

Eve pulled her shirt off as she closed her bedroom door behind her. She was in a hurry to get back to her family. A smile formed on her lips at that thought. Even when she was married to Adam, she hadn't felt this level of tranquility. Maybe it was because she had been harboring feelings for Lainey the entire time. Or, perhaps this had something to do with everyone from her horrible past being dead and buried. Whatever it was, Eve was grateful. She had Bella, Lainey, and the boys and it felt as though the pieces of her life were finally falling into place.

She wished her mom could see her now. To see the woman she'd become. But, more importantly, to see how happy she was. The only hard part of leaving New York for Eve had been leaving her mom behind. Lainey had been sympathetic, telling Eve that no matter where she was, her mom would always be with her. She hoped that was true.

As she shimmied out of her jeans, she noticed a gift box on the bed. Nearly naked, she walked over and picked it up. There was a card with her name written by Lainey's hand. For some reason, it made Eve's heart rate jump. Eve Sumptor was not used to getting gifts. She was the giver. That's what made her comfortable. But she had to admit, seeing this gift from Lainey — without even knowing what it was — made her feel special.

It was light and she brought it up to her ear giving it a little shake. The muffled sound that came from within gave nothing away. Eve pulled on one end of the ribbon, releasing it from the tidy bow it had been tied into. She didn't know why she was being so careful with it. What Eve wanted to do was rip into it and get to whatever Lainey thought to get her. Still, she took her time taking off the top of the box. When she lifted the tissue, she wasn't sure if she wanted to laugh or moan.

Eve let the box fall as she held up the lingerie that was inside. Lainey didn't miss anything. White lace bra, panties, garter, and thigh high stockings. Eve definitely appreciated Lainey's newfound boldness. She couldn't imagine the meek woman who applied for the accounting position at Sumptor, Inc. buying something like this. This Lainey, though, apparently had no qualms about gifting Eve with sexy lingerie. If Lainey wanted Eve in this attire, that's exactly what Lainey would get.

Lainey sighed and leaned against the closed door of the bedroom. "I forgot how much work a toddler was," she said tiredly.

"Bella is a handful," Eve called out from the bathroom.

Lainey pushed away from the door and trudged to the bed. She needed to brush her teeth and wash her face, but right now she needed to lay down on the plush bed even more. Dinnertime had been wonderful. Lainey had made a quick, healthy meal which all the kids — and Eve — gobbled up. During, they spoke of their summer plans. Florida, Paris, and Italy were a must. After that, spontaneity would take over. Darren had suggested that they throw darts at a map while on the plane. Eve had to explain flight plans to him, as well as how dangerous it would be to throw darts inside the aircraft.

They settled on each of them giving a dream destination. If they were unable to reach every destination during the summer, those missed would be the first on the list on their next traveling adventure. The hardest part was choosing who's journey they would pick first. Ever the pragmatic, Eve suggested rock, paper, scissors. Lainey, however, took control and proposed a better solution. Bella would choose. Since the little one had no destination — since she didn't even know what that word meant — Lainey thought it only fair for Bella to pick the first place they went.

Of course, there were rules, not for Bella, but for the adults and older kids. The first rule was no bribing the judge with ice cream. Lainey had to quickly initiate that rule when Eve tried doing just that. The second, and final, rule was no one could "sell" their destination to the judge. *That* one Lainey implemented when Kevin began telling Bella all about the unicorns at his vacation choice. In the end, Darren came out on top. To everyone's surprise, it wasn't an adventure park or Legoland he wanted to go to. It was camping. Lainey and Eve had their work cut out for them. Neither had been camping before. It was going to be interesting sleeping in a sleeping bag. Lainey wondered if they had tandem sleeping bags.

"Thank you, by the way."

"Hmm?" Lainey vaguely registered the deeper octave of Eve's voice. She had been in that half-awake, half-asleep state where her brain was just beginning to shut off.

"I said, thank you."

Lainey turned her head towards the sound of Eve's voice and slowly began to open her eyes. "Thank me for wha . . . *oh!*"

How could she have forgotten about her gift for Eve? The sleepiness she felt just seconds ago evaporated. In its wake was an intense desire that she felt deep in her bones. Eve stood in front of her wearing the white lace lingerie. Lord help her, but the reality was one million times better than fantasy.

"Are you too tired?" Eve teased.

"Second wind," Lainey gulped. "You look . . ." She searched for the right word, but nothing seemed to be enough. "Good enough to eat," she said finally.

Eve groaned. "The things you do to me," she said, her voice throaty with need. She spread her arms, giving Lainey the full effect of her gift. "Now that you have me like this, where do you want me?"

Lainey sat up and crooked her finger, beckoning her lover. "I had a fantasy about you." She spread her legs and pulled Eve close. This was a bit of a different dynamic for them. Eve was usually the aggressor. Lainey had her moments of being assertive, but this time she wanted to call *all* the shots. Whether it stayed like that remained to be seen.

"Just one?"

Lainey smacked Eve's backside playfully. "I've had many, *many* fantasies about you. However, this one stuck with me."

"Oh yeah? Why's that?" Eve purred. She was enjoying the way Lainey was feathering her soft hands up and down the backs of Eve's thighs. Every time she brought them up to that point right under her ass, Eve would get goosebumps all over her body.

"Because I was in charge." Lainey kissed Eve's firm stomach.

"You tried in the beginning, telling me to use my teeth to take your stockings off." She smiled secretly when Eve groaned again. "But I took over. I even issued you a challenge."

Eve's brows shot up. "A challenge?"

"Mmhmm. I wanted to know how long you could keep standing."

Though Eve was sure she knew exactly where this was going, she played along mostly because it was turning her on like crazy. "And what were you doing to me?"

Lainey looked up at Eve through her lashes. "Do you want me to tell you or show you?"

"Show," Eve said quickly. "Definitely show. I'm a big fan of show. Showing is good. Showing is *great*!"

Lainey chuckled. "So, show?" *Mmm.* She wondered if Eve knew how sexy it was when she put her hands on her hips and gave Lainey that fierce look. "Before we get into that, I have one more thing for you."

Eve narrowed her eyes. "You haven't been getting pointers from Rebecca, have you?"

Lainey raised a brow and gave Eve a saucy grin. "Maybe I have. But that's for later." She moved to the nightstand and took out some papers. "Right now, it's just this. I know you hate envelopes, so I'm handing these directly to you."

Papers weren't what Eve was expecting to come out of the nightstand. That's usually where they kept the . . . other things. Things they had bought one night when they stayed up late, after the kids went to bed, and did a ton of research on. Eve had no idea it could be so much fun buying sex toys online with your partner. It certainly made for a fun time afterward.

She took the papers, feeling oddly underdressed to be reading unless it was a sexy book. Then she read them and looked over at Lainey. "It's final?"

Lainey nodded. "My marriage to Jack is officially over." She took the papers and tossed them aside. With a fingertip, she nudged Eve towards the bed. "Your marriage to Adam is over." The back of Eve's knees hit the bed, and she fell back. "We are free, honey. Nothing will stand between us ever again. I won't allow it."

Eve moved back so she could rest her feet on the bed. With her knees bent, she opened herself up to Lainey, grateful she didn't have to stand anymore. She didn't think she could. Assertive Lainey was fucking *hot*!

"You said something about using your teeth," Eve rasped.

Lainey smiled. "I did." She pulled her t-shirt over her head, then purposefully removed everything else very slowly. She could see Eve's legs visibly trembling and that power coursed through her. "Take the bra and panties off," she ordered. "leave the garters and stockings."

"*Lainey*." Eve took half a second to compose herself. Then she did as she was told. "I'm yours, baby. Wholly, eternally."

"Are you?" Lainey crawled up onto the bed and hovered over Eve. Her nipples hung tantalizingly close to Eve's. All she had to do was lower herself an inch, and they would be touching.

"You know I am. My heart has never fully belonged to anyone but you."

"And I never knew true love until you," Lainey responded softly. She lowered herself until their bodies merged. "I want to marry you, Eve," she whispered. "I want you to be a parent to my sons. I want to be a parent to Bella. I want our family to be happy and healthy. And most of all, I want to show our children what love and marriage should be. Warm and caring. Equal." Lainey reached under the pillow and brought out a small box, placing it on Eve's naked chest.

Eve's heart pounded. There was no fear. No regret. No guilt. No pain. There was only joy. She had planned to ask Lainey to marry her in the coming weeks — maybe even before that since it had been torture waiting for the divorces to be final. But to have Lainey be the one to ask her, to give *her* a ring and say the words she had longed to hear, *that* was the best gift she could have ever received.

"Eve? Will you marry me?"

Eve's eyes had been fixated on the ring. It was simple and elegant, exquisite. The size or the purity of the ring didn't matter;

that was all the technical stuff. What meant most to Eve was the emotion behind it. The tears in Lainey's eyes. The anticipation she could feel in Lainey's rapidly beating heart. The hope on her face.

"Yes."

. . . A new beginning

Acknowledgments

This is my TENTH book! I finally made it to double digits. As I said at the beginning of the book, I heard you. You are *passionate* about Eve and Lainey and weren't afraid to let me know you weren't happy with the endings of the other books. I didn't know if I would ever write another full-length novel for Eve and Lainey. I had to wait until they were ready to speak to me. The therapy sessions online helped Eve (and me) find her direction. After so many emails, comments, messages, etc., I got the hint. It was time. Though Lainey was the first character I came up with, Eve Sumptor is very important to me. She is a part of me. Fun fact: Eve was originally going to be named Jules. She was having none of that.

    I know that this book took a long time for me to finish. I apologize for that. It's been a difficult time in my personal life. My mom's Alzheimer's has progressed, and we made the difficult decision to place her in a home. I believe the transition was harder on those of us who love her so very much. The day I had to leave her to come home to Texas, I cried harder than I can ever remember. I tried so hard to keep it together in front of her. But she saw the tears, held me tight, and told me not to cry. Which, of course, made me cry even more. Then she started crying. And when I touched her cheek, she leaned into my hand and asked me to "please come back." Mourning someone who is still alive is difficult on your soul. But I will take having her with us still over the alternative.

When I was able to clear my mind and sit down to write, it came easy. Eve and Lainey were ready to finish their story. Probably as much as you all were. It's a little unconventional incorporating the online therapy sessions, but I wanted to give you a glimpse of the turmoil inside Eve's head. There were a few changes here and there. Most notably, it's not first person and we get to see more of Dr. Woodrow's thoughts. And yes, I've also heard you about Dr. Willamena Woodrow. *If* she wants to tell me her story, I will write it. We'll just have to wait and see.

Now — who shall I thank?

Mom — I love you. I know you can no longer read my books, but I will forever feel your support and love. Even as I fade from your mind, I remember how you always encouraged me to do what I love to do. #endalz

Dad – I can focus on other things because I know you are there for mom. I also know you'll never read this, lol. But others will, and they will know how much I love and appreciate all that you do.

Daisy – It's done! Sometimes it is great having a non-reader around to bounce ideas off of. If you tell me something is too wordy, I listen. Avid readers will read wordy, but I want to appeal to occasional readers as well. So, thank you for not being scared to give me your honest opinions. Also, I love that your face will tell me the truth before your words do.

Karen – Dude! I know life has been difficult for you, yet you still took the time to read and tell me your opinions. You're so animated about these characters. You get mad at them, love them, hate them. I love it! Thank you, beastie, for being a great beta reader!

Janice – This is our first time working together. I'm pretty sure it won't be our last. Your attention to detail was incredibly helpful. You've probably read this book more times than I have, and I wrote it! Thank you for your understanding, help, and points of view. It's been nice working with someone who was always ready to give help when I needed it.

Jeyzel and Vanessa – I decided to choose another beta reader for this book because I wanted an "outsider's" opinion. I chose two because both of you are as passionate about Eve and Lainey as I am. It turned out to be one of my best decisions. The detail and care that went into your responses to the book were incredibly constructive. I loved hearing your thoughts and enthusiasm for this book. It made it even easier for me to keep going when I wasn't sure I would ever finish. Thank you!

To my readers – Here you go! I truly hope that I did this book justice. I LOVE hearing from you (even if you're cursing me out for the decisions my characters make). I appreciate the excitement you have for this book and Eve and Lainey. I thank you all so much for joining me on JoKels and keeping me going with all the love. Thank you for cheering me on!

Here's to another book! When I write, I don't think about what will sell. I think about what I feel. I want to write something that will touch others. Would I love a best-seller? Absolutely. Will I change my writing to do that? Absolutely not. It's too personal, and I have to write from the heart, not my wallet. So, we're back to; if I can inspire *one* person with my writing, it truly is worth it. "Just one more chapter!" Peace, love, and light!

About the Author

I reside in the Houston area where I live in a bit of a zoo. With five dogs, three cats, an axolotl, a bearded dragon, and ten aquariums with various other creatures, every day is certainly an experience. Needless to say, I'm an animal lover.

I'm an introvert who loves adventure. However, I love spending quiet evenings at home on the couch just as much. I tend to write at night when the rest of the world is sleeping. That's usually when my mind lets go of everything else except the lives of the characters that live within.

What's next? A bit of a break. There are a few directions I could go with what's in my head. I will figure out who's story needs to be told when I'm ready to write again. It won't be a long break since writing keeps me sane. I know that I will be continuing the LA Lovers series. As most of you know, each LA Lovers book is a stand-alone, HEA. As always, look for all my characters to show up here and there. I truly hope you enjoyed this book and are happy with the outcome. I've enjoyed hearing from you about these characters!

Where you can find cameo characters

REBECCA CUINN

Fifty Shades of Pink
Becoming
Coming Out

ELLIE MONTGOMERY

Coming Out
Coming Home
Becoming

HUNTER VALE

Coming Out
Becoming

BLAISE KNIGHT

Coming Home
Coming Out
Flawed Perfection
Destined to Love

Connect with Jourdyn Kelly Online

- My Website: (http://www.jourdynkelly.com/)
- Twitter: (https://twitter.com/JourdynK)
- Goodreads: (http://www.goodreads.com/author/show/2980644.Jourdyn_Kelly)
- Facebook: (https://www.facebook.com/AuthorJourdynKelly)
- Secret Society: (https://www.facebook.com/groups/JoKels/)
- Instagram: (https://www.instagram.com/jourdynk/)
- Amazon Author's Page: (http://www.amazon.com/-/e/B005O24HK8)

Printed in Great Britain
by Amazon